THE OWL'S NEST.
TRANSLATED
FROM THE GERMAN

Published @ 2017 Trieste Publishing Pty Ltd

ISBN 9780649666492

The Owl's Nest. Translated from the German by E. Marlett & Hettie E. Miller

Edited by Trieste Publishing Pty Ltd.
Cover @ 2017

www.triestepublishing.com

E. MARLETT & HETTIE E. MILLER

THE OWL'S NEST. TRANSLATED FROM THE GERMAN

Trieste

THE OWL'S NEST

BY

E. MARLETT

AUTHOR OF " OLD MA'M'SELLE'S SECRET " ; " THE SECOND WIFE," ETC., ETC.

TRANSLATED FROM THE GERMAN BY

HETTIE E. MILLER

CHICAGO
E. A. WEEKS AND COMPANY
521–531 WABASH AVENUE

THE OWL'S NEST.

THE hawthorn and syringa bushes in the corners of the Gerold Manor courtyard were covered with blossoms; the water from the fountain, sparkling in the bright May sunlight, splashed in the stone basin, while the sparrows twittered upon the roofs of the stables and barns. It seemed as if on this day all bloomed, sparkled, and twittered more than ever in the Gerold court with a feeling of true home comfort, for the bushes, the fountain, the sparrows in their old nests, were going to remain; they would not be driven out, like the startled spiders and moths behind old cupboards and chests at the manor. Yes, it looked truly miserable there, almost as in time of war : the walls were so bare, and there was dire confusion upon the floor of the dining-room! There was nothing of all that frugal housewives had collected in the way of linen and of bedroom furniture, and their husbands' collection of silver and household effects, as well as hunting paraphernalia, which was not put into that room in order to be exposed to the cold, scrutinizing gaze of strangers, and later on to be scattered in various directions, to wander through the world sundered from all familiar associations.

How insolently the auctioneer's voice with its monotonous "No. 1—No. 2!" rang through the open windows of the room, a voice which seemed to be permeated with the thick dust of furniture and books. It was almost surprising that one of the veterans did not rise from his sleep of centuries in the subterranean vault of the chapel near by, protesting against this voice with its "by rights" accent! There moldered below many a fist which had once with vigorous blows bravely defended the possessi₄ as gained or perhaps only usurped. But the present owner of Geroldcourt, from before whose eyes everything that was not clinched and riveted was now being borne away, had gentler blood in his veins. He was a noble, handsome man with dreamy eyes, with a brow which thought and study had furrowed and at the same time exalted.

At this moment he was sitting in his quiet back room, in the corner where the syringas reached far above the windows. At every breath of wind, the white and blue blossoms tapped upon the windows which, fastened tightly, shut out with tolerable success the noise of the auction in the dining-hall, whence occasionally only came a faint sound.

Herr von Gerold was writing at a pine table which had been generously left him out of the bankrupt estate. He evidently cared not that his manuscript now lay upon the scoured surface of a kitchen table ; his mind, turned from the outer world, was deep in problems, while his hand traced small running characters upon the paper ; he only seemed to awaken to a consciousness of things external and an expression, like that of delight on a child's face, flitted across his own, when the syringas without nodded to him.

There was some one beside him, however, in the room ; a tiny, plump, fair-haired girl, who had crept into one of the window-corners. There was something as dear to the heart of the little one, as his manuscript was to the man writing there—it was her playthings. She had collected in the corner all that belonged to her alone,—yes, to her alone ! The pretty, decorated set of china the kind Princess had sent her, and all her dolls, those in trains as well as the crying babies, which had arrived on birthdays and Christmases in long boxes, upon the lids of which Aunt Claudine had herself written each time : "To little Elizabeth von Gerold." Papa had always read it to her.

Little Elizabeth sat in the midst of her treasures, as in a nest, her youngest baby in her arms and her large, blue eyes fixed timidly and anxiously upon the door through which, a short while before, the "naughty men" had gone with the last pictures and the pretty clock.

She patted her doll in a softly caressing manner, otherwise she was as quiet as a mouse ; for papa looked so annoyed if she disturbed him at his writing. Nor did a sound escape her lips, when the dreaded door opened noiselessly, but the doll glided from her lap to the floor, the plump form rose from the willow chair, toddled through the room as quickly as the tiny limbs could carry her, and, with a face radiant with delight, held up her arms to the lady who entered.

Ah, she had come, Aunt Claudine, her pretty aunt, whom the child loved a thousand times more than Fräulein Duval, her governess, who always said to the other servants :

" *Fi donc,* what a *pauvre* house ! It is nothing for Claire Duval !—I shall leave ! "—And she left, and was not at all polite to papa, and the child had cleansed her cheek from Fräulein Duval's cold, unpleasant kiss. . . . Yes, it was certainly quite different, when two, soft hands lifted her and a sweet mouth kissed her tenderly.

Then the young lady crossed the floor as noiselessly as she had entered—only her dark silk dress rustled somewhat—and laid her hand upon the shoulder of the writer.

" Joachim ! " she said in a gentle voice, leaning forward to look into his face.

He started up.

" Ah, Claudine ! " he cried in evident terror. " Little sister, dear child, you should not have come here ! . . . You see, I take it lightly, I am already over it ; but you will be deeply grieved at the sweeping away to the four winds of all you hold dear. Poor, poor child ! How your tear-swollen eyes pain me ! "

" But a few tears, Joachim," said she with smiling lips, though in her voice there was still a trace of sadness.

" The black horse is to blame for that, our old mail-carrier, who fetched the mail-bag daily. Only think, he recognized me at once, the faithful beast, as he was led past me—— "

" Yes, and Peter is gone, aunt," said little Elizabeth. "Good Peter will not come any more ; and the carriage is gone too, and papa will have to walk, to the Owl's Nest."

" He need not walk, dear heart ; I brought a carriage," comforted Aunt Claudine. " I will not lay aside my wraps, Joachim—— "

"I cannot ask you to in this house. I cannot even offer you any refreshment. The cook served our last potato-soup and then left, for she had to go to her new place. . . . You see, these are bitter pangs which you are experiencing, and which you might have spared yourself. You will have to struggle with yourself a long time, in order after your return to court to dissipate the disagreeable phantom of these memories."

She shook her lovely head slowly.

"I shall not return to court. I shall remain with you," she declared resolutely.

He drew back.

"How—with me? Would you share my—my beggar's livelihood? Never, Claudine, never!" He extended his hand as if to ward her off. "Our beautiful swan, the apple of our eyes, the delight of so many, is to pine in the Owl's Nest! What do you think me, that you attribute such selfishness to me? . . . I willingly, yes, with a light heart, retire to the old house, to *your* house and inheritance, which you have generously placed at my disposal,—it will be cosy and homelike to me, for I have my work which glorifies everything, which sweetens my frugal fare and gilds the old walks; but you—you?"

"I anticipated this protest, and therefore acted independently," said she firmly, looking affectionately in his face with her gentle, long-lashed eyes. "I know very well that you do not need me, you self-sufficient, silent hermit; but what will become of your little Elizabeth?"

With a startled glance he turned towards the child, who was trying to put on a small, cotton circular, such as is worn by the Thuringen peasants, preparatory to setting out.

"Fräulein Lindenmeyer is there," said he, with hesitation.

"Fräulein Lindenmeyer was grandmamma's faithful waiting-woman, and has all her life been as true as gold; but now she is old and gray; we cannot possibly entrust her with the care of the child. And what do you think would be the dear, old, sentimental soul's instruction?" she continued eagerly, while a mournful smile flitted across her features. "No, let me alone for my wrongdoings! I should not have gone to the old Princess; I should have refused the position of lady-in-waiting, to remain with you, to help support the backward-rolling wheel. Matters have looked bad at Geroldcourt for some time before——"

"Before your brother foolishly brought home from Spain a spoiled wife, who, for years, suffered in the German climate, until the angel of deliverance freed her from her torture, is it not so, Claudine?" he completed with an access of bitterness. "In addition to that he was a miserable agriculturist, a good-for-nothing, who studied field flowers and grasses under the microscope, and praised their beauty, and forgot that they were detrimental to good pasturage. Yes, it is true! The, at this time, rather neglected estate could not have fallen into worse hands than mine; but am I alone responsible? Am I to blame that there is within me no drop of peasant's blood, which was always tolerated in the blue-blooded veins of our ancestors? The plow and the breeding of cattle earned the greater part of the Gerold wealth, now scattered to the four winds, and I am forced to blush in the presence of the meanest day-laborer in the village, who by industry and toil seeks to improve his potato-patch. I take nothing with me but my pen and a handful of ready money, which is to provide myself and my child with bread until my manuscript is completed and disposed of. Therefore do I write with 'throbbing pulses'——"

He paused. With a bitter smile he advanced to the young lady and laid both hands upon her shoulders.

"Yes, do you see, child, darling sister? we two, the two last, are swimming birds which the honest old domestic fowl, the old Gerold genus, hatched at the close of its long earthly career! As children we instinctively took a particular channel, I, the dreamer, the hypercritic, the star-gazer, and you the nightingale with the sweet voice, the graceful and elegant form. And now you come to the wood-gatherer and bookworm, such as I am, and wish to go with him to the Owl's Nest"—he shook his head energetically—"you shall not go even to the threshold of the old house, Claudine. Drive home again in your carriage! My legs have become stiff from sitting still in this corner, whither I fled from the bustle; the walk to the Owl's Nest will do them good, and Friedrich, our faithful Friedrich, will carry the child if she gets tired. And now a brief farewell, Claudine!"

He opened his arms to clasp his sister in a last embrace, but she drew back.

"Who has told you I *can* return ?" she asked, seriously. "I asked for my dismissal and it was granted me. My dear old Princess understood me, and without a question on her part, she knew exactly how matters lay. And now, do you be sens: le, to^, Joachim,"—a deep, dark blush suffused her cheeks suddenly,—"and in silence accept the fact that there was another reason for my return besides the desire to be with you. Take me as I come to you, with sealed lips, but with a heart filled with true sisterly love—will you ?"

He drew her silently to him and kissed her brow.

She breathed a deep sigh of relief.

"We shall surely have frugal fare," continued she, "but it is no beggar's livelil ^od," said she, with a gentle, merry smile. "Her Highness would hear of nothing but that I should receive my salary as usual, and grandmamma's legacy yields a nice little sum annually. Consequently, we shall not starve, and you shall not write with 'throbbing pulse' in the future. I will not permit it ! You shall complete your excellent work undisturbed, at your own pleasure. Now, we will get ready."

Her eyes roved about the bare room and rested on a small trunk.

"This is all I can rightfully take with me," said Herr von Gerold, following her glance. "Not much more than the last descendant of the Gerolds unwittingly laid claim to on his entrance into life,—the most absolutely necessary clothing for the body. But no,—what atrocious ingratitude !" He put his hand to his brow and his eyes gleamed. "Listen, Claudine, is this not odd? Think ! do you know of a friend, one who without hesitation would take two thousand dollars from his pocket with his right hand without his left hand knowing it ? I know of no one, no matter how I rac! my brains, no one in God's world !... And yet, yesterday a few boxes were placed for me in the adjoining room, *by legal authority*, for ɪ am supposed to have bought them back at the auction through some one commissioned to do so. I, the beggar ! I laughed in the porter's face. But they went along and did not take with them my books, my valuable, little library, for which my eyes were filled with tears when profane hands threw book after book into waste-baskets, in order to carry them to the auction—my beloved books and faithful companions of my solitude! Whosoever saved them for me from the wreck, must know that he has with them given me the breath of life and a firm staff with which to wander in the wilderness, and for it may he be thrice blessed, the noble unknown with the heart of gold ! . . . You, too, think in vain, do you not, Claudine ? Give it up ; neither of us can solve the problem ! "

He put his manuscript into the portfolio beside him, and Claudine packed little Elizabeth's effects in a hamper, at which task the child's chubby hands assisted.

Ten minutes later this last refuge was likewise deserted, and Herr von Gerold, his child's hand in his and his sister leaning on his arm, passed through the corridor.

A more beautiful couple could scarcely be imagined, than these two, who, with averted eyes, for the last time passed through their ancestral halls ; the domestic nest, which for centuries the Gerolds had added to and improved, and in which now strange birds were to enter, birds with gilded plumage, for the property had been bought in by a stranger at a very high price.

On the staircase they came upon a lady who was on her way from the side-wing in which the sale was taking place. She was just raising the hem of her brown dress carefully, at the same time muttering irritably to herself, for upon the stairs lay a thick dust, which, during the entire time of the confusion, had not been swept away. A flush of sudden surprise suffused her cheeks, as on looking up she saw the brother and sister before her.

"Ah, pardon ! " said she in a deep, inflexible voice, stepping back. " I am barring the way ! "

For an instant Herr von Gerold looked as if he had these words upon his lips : " Must I drain *this* cup too ? " But he restrained them and replied with a courteous inclination :

"The way from this house is all too widely open to us ; a moment's delay would be pleasant."

"These stairs are horribly dirty,—it is really vexing ! " blustered the lady, as if she had not heard his reply, again shaking her skirts. " For that reason I never go to an

auction,—principally because one has to inhale so much
dust! But Lothar gave me no peace ; he wrote me twice
urgently, and so, well or ill, I had to drive over to buy
in the plate. He will be surprised—I was raised to an
enormous sum."

These words were uttered with changing color, and
without the speaker once raising her eyes from the hem
of her skirt.

"For grandmamma's sake, I am grateful to your brother
for the purchase, Beate,—she thought a great deal of the
old heirlooms," said Claudine.

"Well, how could he do otherwise? We have the other
half and cannot allow our arms to appear at some pawn-
broker's," replied the lady, shrugging her shoulders. "But
was it not your first right to save the plate, Claudine, for
your grandmamma's sake? If I am not mistaken, she
willed you several thousand dollars."

"Yes, *for a rainy day*, as it says in the will. My practical grandmamma would be the first to censure me,
were I to squander my inheritance, and to have silver, but
no bread in the cupboard."

"No bread? You, Claudine, you—the haughty, spoiled
lady-in-waiting?"

"Was I ever haughty?" She shook her head with a
charming smile. "And spoiled? Well, I can believe
that!—At court one learns to do no work."

"You did not know how to work before, Claudine,"
blurted out the lady. "That is——" She hastily sought
to correct herself, but could find no words.

"Speak on, you are right," said Claudine calmly.
"The kind of work which you mean, one does not learn
at school either. But from now on, I shall try. I shall
become a housewife in my old Owl's Nest——"

"You do not say——"

"That I shall remain with Joachim? I shall assur-
edly. Moreover, is he not in need of redoubled love and
sisterly affection?" She clung more closely to her brother
and looked up at him tenderly.

Again a wave of color rushed into the lady's cheeks.
She quickly bent over little Elizabeth and attempted to
fondle her, but the child frowned and drew back. "Go
away!" she cried, evading the caress with a pout.

Herr von Gerold started angrily.

"Ah! Let the little thing alone! I am accustomed to having children dislike me," said the lady with a harsh, embarrassed laugh, extending her hand protectingly over the fair head. "What was I about to say." She turned again to Claudine. "It will at first cost you a large apprentice's fee; one need only to look at your hands, and then this court *chic!* Many an elegant gown will be spoiled before you learn to stand at the fire and prepare a palatable meal, that is "—she again attempted to correct herself, while she timidly glanced at the pretty maid-of-honor's downcast eyes—"Pardon, child, I mean no harm; I simply wished to offer you the use of one of my maids for a while. My servants are well-schooled——"

"That is an established fact. Your fame as a housewife has gone far beyond the precincts of Geroldcourt," interpolated Herr von Gerold, not without sarcasm. "But we are obliged. You must know that we can no longer keep any domestics. Howsoever my sister may set about her difficult task, I shall be satisfied and unutterably grateful. She is and will remain my guardian angel, even though at first she does not prepare a 'palatable meal.'"

He raised his hat courteously, and with his sister and child descended the stairs; the lady followed in silence, for her carriage too stood at the door of the manor.

Meantime, Friedrich, the former coachman, had carried down the trunk, and now passed those descending the stairs with the hamper of toys in his arms. The little girl listened anxiously to the clatter of the porcelain and other sounds within the basket, and stood on tiptoe to obtain a glimpse at her possessions; there, indeed, was one of her favorite dolls on the point of falling over the edge of the hamper. Fräulein Beate seized the doll over the child's head.

"Don't touch my Lenchen with your big hands!" cried Elizabeth, at the same time clutching the lady's skirt.

"Ah, poor, little creature! have you been taught so soon?" laughed Fräulein Beate abruptly, as Claudine in affright laid her hand upon the child's lips. "Why should she not speak the truth? My hands are large, and compliments will not make them smaller. Their awkwardness in all delicate matters one can see at a glance. The little thing protests against them, like all our schoolmates,

—you must remember it, Claudine! I am not attractive
to mankind."

With an awkward bow she descended the last steps
toward the door and called her carriage. Her form, as
she stood in the doorway, was handsome and well-devel-
oped, but she had ugly, angular movements, and her sun-
burned face with the hair brushed smoothly back from the
brow was not improved.

Herr von Gerold shyly retreated, as he stepped out of
the door. He would have preferred to have fled to the
darkest corner of the court; confusion was distasteful to
him, and upon the lawn in front of the house was a confusion such as is to be seen at an annual fair. There the
plush drawing-room furniture was heaped upon a lumber-
wagon; there women dragged away whole loads of
feather beds; cooking utensils clattered in the packing,
while once more the prices paid passed from mouth to
mouth, amid laughter and oaths, even after they were
bought.

Fortunately the hired carriage, in which Claudine had
come, stood near the door. They entered it hastily;
Friedrich placed the hamper with the toys on the front
seat; with a mournful, farewell glance, he closed the
door, and away rolled the carriage, past all their former
possessions upon which now the free, blue spring sky
looked down; past the empty coach-houses and stables,
past blooming flower-beds and gushing fountains and the
green grass of the orchards upon which still lay the white
rime of fallen blossoms. Then the main road stretched
before them, to the right and left, still lined with the fields
of the manor, until the woods cast their shadow over it;
thence a broad drive branched off to the left, and upon it,
gleaming in the sun and dazzling the eyes, rolled the
elegant equipage in which Fräulein Beate von Gerold was
driving home.

"Had *she*, too, to cross your path of suffering?" said
Herr von Gerold to his sister, with a displeased glance in
the direction of the carriage.

"She did not wound me, Joachim, I know her better—
and have not the prejudices against her like most other
people," replied Claudine. She had taken little Elizabeth
on her lap and buried her face in the child's thick, waving,
fair hair; so she was spared the last painful sight of

what was left behind. "Beate is abrupt and apparently careless of the feelings of others only out of—embarrassment."

"Nonsense, child! She will not help you. This Beate is not good; she has neither heart nor the spirit which I admire in a woman, the ideal elevation of thought, the charm of soul, which my poor Dolores unconsciously possessed, and with which you again to-day surrounded me, the culprit, the poverty-stricken Job, not a breath of all this exists in this—barbarous woman."

The gay parasol of the "barbarous woman" once more loomed up between the mountain ash-trees of the road; then it disappeared behind the beeches, the vanguard of the narrow strip of wood which terminated the boundary of Geroldcourt.

On the other side of this wealth of foliage, far away on the mountain, lay another manor, a simple building of more modern style, with white walls and white shades. No fountains played there, nor were many flowers to be seen; but, instead, the estate had a wealth of trees almost unequaled. Veritably gigantic old lindens waved about the walls and courts, a pleasant green net-work; only the front of the house was without shade, and around the pretty dove-cote in the center of the spacious lawn before the house the May breezes and the golden sunbeams played undisturbed. This possession was, too, a Geroldcourt, the manor of the lords of Gerold-Neuhaus.

In olden times the lands of the broad Paulinenthal, and the forests which from that point wooded the hillsides, had been under one rule. The Gerolds of Altenstein had held sole sway over the life and death of every creature, who for miles around moved and had his being, over the peasants behind their plows, the game in the forests, the scaly creatures in river and pond. Later on, more than two hundred years ago, Herr Benno von Gerold, returning in safety from a long, bloody struggle, found a second son had come to bless his declining years, and divided the estate of Altenstein between him and his first-born.— So had arisen the line of Gerold-Neuhaus.—For years they remained the less well-endowed with worldly goods and position; then several times rich heiresses had married into the family, and several bearers of the name had distinguished themselves in war. Then descendants, building upon the merits of their brave predecessors, step by step obtained the highest positions at Court, and, finally, crowned this rise by a union of their youngest and handsomest member with a princess of the reigning-house.

Fräulein Beate von Gerold had consequently a right to drive home so calmly and confidently in her beautiful equipage; for she was the only sister of the "youngest and handsomest member," and, young as she was, ruled in his absence as authorized mistress of the old estate. The management she understood for the same reason that all her antecedents had understood it. To move hand and foot independently, to rise early and with clear, keen eyes to look into the darkest corner of the house: this had been in all times the maxim of the housewife's room at Neuhaus. The people in the village said it was not so long since the old spinning-wheel with its worn treadle had, day after day, whizzed at the window, while in the summer-time the homespun linen lay on the bleaching-ground in front of the house. This industry, together with the strict regimen in the store-room and dairy, were said to have principally amassed the wealth; the villagers were firmly convinced of it, and the spinning-wheel story was not so utterly infallible.

The Altensteins, of whom, just at this moment, the last were leaving the inheritance of his fathers forever in a hired vehicle, could too look back upon a long, unbroken line of good, industrious housewives—at Altenstein at all times care had been exercised and work done.

But the property lay lower than Neuhaus, and in the last ten years Fate had ordained that destructive storms should break over the Paulinenthal. Within a few minutes the falling masses of water and the overflowing river had flooded the lower-lying ground; the prospects for crops were destroyed and the land spoiled for years—with that, in spite of all industry, the fatal "backward" course began.

These buffets of Fate occurred in the time of a man who united within him all the virtues of his ancient race, the ability of the husbandman, martial courage, fidelity, and self-sacrifice for the inherited manor; Colonel von Gerold was a true son of his race. Only in one way, which all his forefathers had studiously avoided, had he gone astray—the passion for gaming had a terrible power over

him. He played whole nights through and lost enormous
sums, and when the storm broke and damaged his estates,
then vice penetrated rapaciously the old family-chest in
which for centuries valuable papers and documents had
been locked. This ruinous career was suddenly terminated by the pistol-shot of a comrade whom the Colonel, in
consequence of a dispute at the gaming table, challenged;
like an extinguished flame the life went out and left this
sphere—"just in the nick of time," the people said, but
they were mistaken, there was no longer much to lose.

The tearful eyes of the pretty lady-in-waiting glanced
at the face of her brother sitting beside her, a face pale
from study and close confinement,—over which, by degrees, with every revolution of the wheels, a gleam of
secret delight spread. Yes, this "visionary and star-
gazer," as he reproachfully called himself, was summoned
hastily home from his sojourn in Spain after the terrible
catastrophe, to save what it was possible to save. He
was unable to do so; so much the less so, as the young
wife at his side, the frail Andalusian, had turned her lovely
eyes with silent horror from the position of a German
housewife. He had finally only lived for her, the invalid,
and exhausted all his means, in order to maintain the
illusion of abundance, until "the angel of deliverance"
took her from her sufferings; then had he with resignation
allowed the ruins of his former prosperity to come upon
him.

At this moment Claudine heard a deep sigh of relief
escape his breast. She followed the direction of his
glance,—ah, yes, there rose the gray-black quadrangle of
the tower above the tree-tops! There lay the Owl's Nest,
the protecting roof which was to shelter them! How had
they ridiculed her at Court when she had given all her
savings to restore the old walls, to rebuild the inheritance
left her by her grandmother!

Now came the blessing.

She could go home from the heated, stifling atmosphere
of the Court to the coolness and quiet beneath the green
trees, and there she was at home. "At home!" how
soothing these words sounded after all the trials, the excitement of the past few months! He, who sat beside her,
need not to move into a hired house; he could remain
upon Gerold soil, if but in a corner of the forest, in the ex-

tremest point of the once extensive possession.   There had
once stood Cloister Walpurgiszella, near by the barrier
which separated the two Geroldcourts !

The cloister was built by a pious, sorely-tried ancestor,
but in the Peasant War was partly demolished ; then had
the Gerolds regained the ground given by them to the
foundress, and the smaller part, the piece of land with the
remains of the building, had fallen to the Neuhaus branch.
They had never paid any attention to the ruins, and time
and weather could wear away as much as they wished.
Only a side-building, the formerly so-called nuns' drawing-
room, had been damaged very little by fire, and had been
in a measure renovated for a forester's occupancy.   But,
on the whole, the remote, neglected possession was a burden to the owners, and they had therefore not hesitated
to sell the same later on to an Altenstein, the grandfather
of the last Gerold Altenstein, for a piece of land more con-
veniently situated.   An absurdly romantic whim, they
thought to themselves, as the Altenstein told them that his
wife desired the picturesque spot.   And he deeded it to
his beloved wife as her very own.   Thus had Claudine's
grandmother obtained the Owl's Nest.

Now the south door of the former cloister chapel came
in sight.   In the large aperture of the window was a stone
rosette whose frail pattern stood out against the background of foliage like a net-work.

Yes, grandmamma had expended all her savings in order
to protect her beloved " artistic spot of earth " from further
decay.   Of the church ruins not a stone had become
loosened for years, and the nuns' wing had with time become a very habitable place, the country-seat of the old
lady.   There she lived after her husband's death, and raised
the prettiest flowers on the once neglected mossy ground
beside the church, the graveyard of the nuns, the Walpurgis
cemetery, as the people called it.

Old Heinemann, the gardener of Geroldcourt for years,
was her factotum.   With great difficulty he had succeeded
in making the neglected piece of ground fruitful : a well-
bred child could not have pleased him more than this
fertile spot.   The old man therefore accompanied his mis-

tress when she withdrew to the Owl's Nest, and still occupied his room on the ground-floor, as a sort of *castellan*, required by the old lady in her will. And he watched every stone which became loosened, every weed-germ which the breeze from forest and meadow wafted thither. "Like a Cerberus, he counts the blades of grass," said Fräulein Lindenmeyer, the former mistress's waiting-woman. She likewise had been assured a shelter in the Owl's Nest for life. She occupied the best room on the ground floor, a pleasant corner-room, where she could sit with her knitting and library-book day after day at the window and watch the road.

These two old people lived in harmony side by side. They cooked at one hearth and never disagreed, although Fräulein Lindenmeyer, with secret indignation, often moved her chocolate cup and wine-soup bowl farther away from the penetrating odor of the gardener's sauerkraut and leeks.

Claudine had notified the couple of her and her brother's intended arrival, and now with satisfaction saw a cloud of smoke ascend and slowly dissolve above the tree-tops. Fräulein Lindenmeyer at any rate was preparing "coffee," and would make the "poor Job" forget his last potato soup at Geroldcourt which had changed so for him. There could be heard the crow of the cock, which with his six hens nested in a corner of the ruined archway, and high above the smoke from the chimney circled Heinemann's white doves, as tiny and bright as silver spangles in the blue, spring sky.

The road-line made one more turn to the right, and gradually could be distinguished the ruin-adorned, small meadows and garden-island in the shade of the woods. There lay the house built of quarry-stone which once had bravely withstood the torches of the rebellious peasants, its rough and smoke-blackened walls covered with a network of fresh mortar lines. It was surely not a mansion, and the gray-coated owls, driven back into the ruins, would have been more appropriate there than the court-trains of a maid-of-honor. Well and good! It was, notwithstanding, a cosy nest for frugal human beings ; it lay in the midst of undulating lawns, and its new windows with their clean curtains were set in the old-fashioned frame-work like youthful, clear eyes.

2

" Just at the very nicest time, gracious Fraülein ! " said Heinemann, opening the carriage door.   "The beds still full of narcissuses and tulips, and the roses budding ; besides, the children are finding May-flowers in the woods."

On the approach of the carriage he had gone out on the road.   Bareheaded, the hot afternoon sunshine falling upon his grayish-yellow wilderness of hair, he helped the arrivals to alight.

"Does it not smell sweet here, little Fräulein ?" laughed he, as he lifted Elizabeth from the carriage and for a moment held her in his arms.   The child inhaled the air with delight : " Nothing but fragrance, nothing but blossoms, wherever one looks, child ! Yes, the dear Lord is kind to old Heinemann !"

He was right.   A veritable wave of narcissus perfume and the intoxicating breath from a thousand chalices of Persian lilacs filled the air.

"Shall we now go to Fräulein Lindenmeyer ? " he asked the child, with a merry twinkle in his eyes and a broad grin about his thick, straw-colored beard.   "There she stands with her finest cap on her head !   She has been baking cake all morning and has not left a whole egg in the house ! "

Claudine, with a smile, passed him and advanced towards the gate in the picket-fence where, between two oaks which flanked the entrance, was to be seen the old-fashioned head-dress with its garnet ribbons upon Fräulein Lindenmeyer's gray puffs of hair.   This worthy old maid had always ready on such occasions a solemn quotation from Schiller or Goethe.   But to-day her sunken lips trembled in the struggle with inward agitation,—for the handsome, noble man, her pride, the former owner of the finest estate far and near, came to seek shelter—in the Owl's Nest.

Gayly he took her trembling right hand, which was on the point of pressing a cambric handkerchief to her tearful eyes, with a warm pressure in his.

"I should like to know if Fräulein Lindenmeyer still understands me so well and will intercede for me as formerly, when it was a question of obtaining some favor from grandmother ? " said he in a light, jesting tone, as he bent over her to look in her face.

Her eyes brightened. "Ah, yes, I think so ;" she replied as if ashamed and yet with triumphant certainty. "The bell-room is ready ! It is beautiful. up there ! A veritable poet's corner ! What sympathetic soul would not appreciate it ? "

He smiled and once more pressed her hand, while his beaming eyes wandered over the garden. Opposite the south gate of the church ruins and in a direct line with the former nuns' dwelling, at quite a distance, rose the bell-tower of the cloister chapel. Fire, storm, and weather had by degrees reduced the proud edifice, its spire once reaching high into the heavens, to a blunt tower. It had fallen into a state of decay even to the bell-tower, where the mason's hand checked it. The late owner had connected the tower and the house by a small building, which on the first floor was arranged for the reception of plants in winter, but in the upper story formed a gallery inclosed on both sides by a balustrade and leading to the rooms of the house, as well as to the opposite tower by means of glass doors. But far above everything gleamed the windows of the bell-room which had preserved its name.

And now, into the last place of refuge of the impoverished !

While Heinemann lifted trunk and basket from the carriage, the others approached the house. For a moment Claudine paused alone at the door, she turned to one side, apparently to inhale the perfume of the syringa blossoms which brushed her shoulder, but her thoughts were far away. Across that threshold three years before she had gone into the world filled with hope and intoxicating pleasures. At her grandmother's desire and request she became lady-in-waiting to the Dowager Duchess. It was not easy for her to give up the enviable position, no, indeed not ! Her absent eyes grew dim and her lips quivered. She had been her aristocratic mistress's acknowledged favorite, and the noble lady had known how to protect her in secret from those who envied her and from her many enemies ; so she had learned to know only the bright side of Court life. Now it lay behind her never to return, and a deep yearning for the mild, gentle old lady, whom she had served, already burned in her heart. The new life she had planned was not easy, either. To be a faithful mother to her brother's child, for him to

take upon her shoulders the cares of life and to count
every penny carefully, that want might not creep into the
Owl's Nest,—that she intended 'o venture upon, she, the
unsophisticated, the inexperienced in all that concerned
the necessitier of life ?—But *must* it not be, as her hasty
departure from court had *had* to be?

She lai ' her hand upon her anxiously beating heart and
slowly crossed the threshold and ascended the narrow
but neatly-scoured wooden stairs.   As she entered her
grandmother's former sitting-room, she breathed more
freely and told herself that it was a shameful weakness of
character to allow her courage to fail *here*, here, where
the quiet, sober life of a gentle yet energetic woman spoke
from every article of furniture, where the dear old pictures
of good people greeted her cordially from the walls.   At
Court, to be sure, mirrors reaching to the ceilings and
silken hangings had decorated the walls of their *salon ;*
her feet sank deep into the velvety carpet, and a richly
carved canopy with rich draperies had shaded her bed in
the adjoining room.   But the same Venetian mirrors had
reflected the, form of her predecessor, the same canopy
had guarded her slumber, and in a few days a successor
would enter the pretty rooms—they were merely loaned.
The spot on which she now stood and laid aside hat and
traveling-cloak, in order to remain there, was her own,
her home with the simple, comfortable furniture, the antique bookcase and the old-fashioned china closet which
contained grandma's china and porcelain.   Little Elizabeth with a piece of cake in her hand came toward her
with a beaming face ; on the table steamed grandma's
brass coffee machine, the door leading to the platform of
the middle building was wide open and allowed the scent
of the flowers in the garden to enter, and on the other side
of this platform, only a few feet long, one could look
through the narrow glass door into the tower-room, once
her own chamber during her vacation, which she always
spent with her grandmother.   But more than this delightful meeting again did a glance at her brother comfort and
encourage her.   He had stepped as lightly as if a hundred-
weight were removed from his mind, and when later on
she ascended with him to the bell-tower and he laid his
manuscript upon the oilcloth cover of a simple table by
the window, he said :

"It is a hackneyed comparison, but its appropriateness moves one deeply at this moment —I feel like one, who, after a stormy voyage, reaches his native heath and would like to fall down and kiss it gratefully."

Two weeks had passed since then, days filled with labor and duties, but, too, full of satisfactory reward. Yes, she succeeded, if here and there a scorch disfigured the new kitchen aprons, a few vessels proved the maxim of the apprentice's fee, and the soft hands of the newly-fledged cook were still very sensitive to hard work. Claudine had from the first refused Fraülein Linden-meyer's kindly offered aid. The delicate, frail little woman was unreliable, and often herself needed help. For that, however, Heinemann was an excellent support; he did all the heavy work.

So by degrees the new household was brought into its rut, and to-day, for the first time, Claudine found a free moment to ascend to the battlements of the tower. The morning sun lay upon the old bell, whose iron tongue, which had rung out through the woods, was once flung into the depths by violent peasants' hands. To-day the walls were covered with yellow flowers, which peeped forth from every crevice, and, although it looked so old, it gladly harbored young, awakening life—the birds nested under the hedges and projections of the wall, and the twittering and piping was incessant. And from the garden and the resinous firs, whose dark, waving branches, like mourning-banners, draped in the ruins of the chapel, came a dreamy hum—absolutely insatiable. Heinemann's bees and the wild bumble-bees of the woods hovered about the sweets which Prince May gives from out the chalices of the blossoms.

Above all stretched the blue ether, across which occasionally a bold bird winged its flight, as high as a thought of God above human aspirations, unapproach-ably high above the earth, with its blooming existence and fading life; but over there, on the distant horizon, it met and merged into the horizon. There the Paulinen-thal widened into a flat plain in the distance, to be again merged into the heights. Over the flat land lay a fine

golden veil of mist. It concealed the ducal castle; nothing was to be seen of the proud structure, its purple-
beflagged towers and marble stairs, at whose base the
swans sailed, while silvery ripples passed over the pond;
nothing was to be seen of the magnolia and orange trees
in the magical gardens, which with their perfume-laden
breath caused the blood to course through the veins;
nothing of the tower-high, gleaming windows, behind
which a young woman, a child of royalty, dainty and
snowy white, walked to and fro, yearning for one glance
of the lovely dark eyes which sought—*another.*

Claudine drew hastily back from the balustrades, pale
to her lips. Had she ascended to the cool, blue heavens
in order to be met by the sultry air over there? Yes,
how were heaven and earth mingled in the human breast
there on the horizon. She averted her eyes from the
sunny distance and turned them northward. Wheresoever she looked, woods, nothing but green woods! Only
there, where the broad drive separated the trees, lay in
the distant perspective, like a tiny picture, the Neuhaus
manor; its façade, rich in windows, stood out clearly in
the dusky circle of lindens. There blew a rude, severe,
but pure atmosphere under Beate's discipline. For some
time an estrangement had existed between the two
Geroldcourts. The Neuhausers had expressed themselves
frankly with regard to the Colonel's "godless passion for
gaming," and thereupon all intercourse was broken off
between the two families, which had intermarried several
times. There was not the slightest intercourse between
them; Lothar and Joachim, the two sons of the same age
of the families at variance, had purposely avoided one another, although Claudine and Beate, pupils at the same
school, were on friendly terms.

So it was not surprising that the two Gerolds, thrown
together at court, glanced at one another distantly and
coldly—Lothar, the elegant, dashing officer, and Claudine, the new maid-of-honor. Haughty in the proud consciousness of the high position attained by him, a brilliant
man, flattered and petted by the entire Court circle, he
had impressed and awed her. It was shortly before his
marriage with Princess Katharina, the cousin of the
reigning Duke. She did not blame him, that he, from his
dizzy height, looked scornfully upon the daughter of the

poverty-stricken branch of his family. That branch had almost extinguished the fame of the name, while he could add to it the title of "baron," bestowed on him by the Duke. Her appearance had cast a shadow across the path of the bright Court star, and this thought had sufficed to cause her to avoid all contact with him with sensitive timidity.

How incredibly simple and plain seemed to her at this moment the house in which he was born beside the glory of the event which had been the crowning-point of his unparalleled success, beside his marriage! She saw him before her, standing at the altar-steps beside the Princess, surrounded by the brilliant court. The bride's tiny form, almost hidden in laces and satin, had pressed closely to his side, as if he, for the possession of whom she had struggled so energetically, might here be torn from her, and with her sparkling black eyes she had glanced up at him with passionate tenderness. And he? He was deathly pale; his binding "yes" had sounded harsh, almost violent. Had he been seized with dizziness on the pinnacle of his good fortune, or had he a sudden presentiment that he would not long enjoy this happiness—that the black eyes beaming with affection would close forever after a brief year, under the pines and palms of the Riviera, whither the traveling-coach of the newly-wedded pair went at once after the ceremony? Yes, there in her magnificent villa, the Princess had died, after giving birth to a daughter, and there still lived the forlorn husband, keeping the delicate babe in the mild climate until it should become stronger, so they said; but, too, because it was hard for him to leave the scene of his fleeting happiness. He had not returned to his native land, and he would surely not occupy the quiet, lonely house over there were he to return, which fact was very acceptable to the hermit at the Owl's Nest, and to the sweetly beneficial peace of the tiny oasis in the woods.

Claudine leaned with a smile over the balustrade of the tower, and looked down into the garden, which with flower-beds and vegetable garden lay below like a gay chess-board. "Hush-a-by!" sang little Elizabeth. She was nursing her doll in the pink cotton cloak, and was toddling along the garden-path. Heinemann had fastened a bunch of May-flowers upon her straw hat, and

Fräulein Lindenmeyer was watching the happy little creature from the arbor, where she was tying together asparagus into bundles for Heinemann. The old gardener sold a great many vegetables and flowers in the neighboring small towns, and the profits were his, by virtue of the testamentary disposition of his late mistress.

At this moment he issued from the ruins with an armful of kindling-wood, and through the open glass doors of the sitting-room came the deep tones of the large house-clock, which struck eleven—it was time to light the fire.

"Work is no disgrace," said Heinemann, soon after in the kitchen, with a side-glance at the iron pan which Claudine stood upon the fire. "No, indeed, not, and a few stains do not disfigure dainty fingers, any more than my white narcissuses bear blemishes because they rise from the black earth. But from the ducal court direct to the kitchen fire—it is as if my beautiful Gloxinias were to suddenly dncamp to the wood-house or the hen-pen. Ah, poor thing! it grieves me to see it. Yes, if it had to be! But it does not have to be, absolutely not. I know better. . . Economy is a fine thing, too. I do not squander my few pennies. God forbid! But, Fräulein Claudine, moderation can be exercised in everything." He cast a meaning glance at the small piece of butter which Claudine had put in the pan in which she was preparing to broil a couple of pigeons. "That might be for a Carthusian friar." . , He shook his head. "No, we need not be so sparing. We have more than you think, Fräulein."

He uttered the last words with noticeable slowness, with emphasis. His young mistress looked at him in astonishment.

"Have you found a treasure, Heinemann?" she asked, with a smile.

"Well, that depends on how you view it," said he, shaking his head, while about the corners of his eyes appeared innumerable wrinkles, from which laughed something like suppressed delight. "Not gold or silver, to be sure. Good Lord! one might look oneself blind in the ruins and not find the tiniest speck. No, it is not that. That all adhered to the incendiaries' fingers. They even tore the gold ornaments from the silken gown of the infant Jesus! But need it be a savings-box, silver jugs, or

communion cups? . . You see, the convent owned a great
deal of land once. Nuns came in, who brought with them
possessions, mostly land, and it all became convent
ground. Then there were tithes of corn, poultry, honey,
and God knows what besides, in abundance, and the convent property was well cared for. Then milk and honey
flowed in the ruins, as in the land of Canaan, and the
nuns are said to have understood how to make money,
out of the abundance. Many a time wagons drew up at the
convent door and bore boxes and chests out into the world.
Yes, these little women were not stupid.—Heather,
whortleberries and raspberries, the best food for bees,
was to be had here and on the convent lands in abundance, and they had an apiary such as in our time can
scarcely be found in the large estates in Hungary. Well,
last night I was in the cellar. For some time I had noticed
several loose stones in the walls; but in the spring of
the year there is always much to be done, and in addition,
we had to arrange and clean the rooms on the upper
floor, and so I put off mending them from one day to
another. But yesterday I thought I ought to be ashamed
of myself, that you would think me a careless manager if
you were to see it, and so I at once fetched trowel and
mortar pail. As, however, I touched the first loose stone,
Lord of my life, it became actually alive beneath my
touch! It moved, it stirred, no wonder; and before I
could collect myself, the loose stones fell away and I looked
into a hollow as high as a man—yes, into a vault of which
no human being any longer knew. And what was in it?
Wax!"

He paused an instant, as if still reveling in the remembrance of his discovery. "Yes, wax, beautiful, pure, yellow wax," he repeated, emphasizing each word. "Layer
upon layer, a whole dry cellar full, lying just under the
tower." He shook his head. "A veritable fairy story!
An old fellow like me still reads such fairy tales as 'The
Arabian Nights,' with so much enjoyment, and since yesterday I feel as if I had myself looked into a Mount Se-
same, for what lies below is, too, as good as a chest of
money. The nuns must have worked at it and saved for
many years. There are several hundred-weight, and
they knew what the whole lot was worth, or else they
would not have walled it up before they went away. And

do I not know ?   I am myself a bee-keeper and sell what
the industrious little insects bring into my hives."

Involuntarily Claudine had set aside the cooking-utensil
she held in her hand and listened with evident interest to
the animated recital.   Over the good, broad, kind face of
the old man flitted, in changing lights, delight, pride in his
discovery, and roguishness.

"Yes, yes, it means surely a few thousand dollars !"
said he, after drawing a deep breath, with a merry twinkle
in his eyes.   "Hm ! a nice little dowry, which the nuns,
good souls, who are still said to wander about, guarded
and saved particularly for our Fräulein."

The pretty lady-in-waiting laughed.   "I do not think
we can take possession of the wax without any further
ceremony, Heinemann," said she, then, seriously with a
shake of her head.   "The former owners have no doubt
the same rights."

The old gardener looked perplexed and startled.   "They
will surely not——? " he began with hesitation.   "God
knows, that would be a sin and a shame !   The Neuhauser
over there, into whose pocket such a royal fortune fell,
would surely rather lose his right hand than touch this
paltry bit here !   But, of course,"—he shrugged his
shoulders with a dejected air,—"who can tell ?   Some of
these gentlemen can never get enough ; one finds that out
every day, and it may be that the Baron will hold out his
hand and not say 'No' when it comes right down to it.
Ah "— he irritably scratched his head—"I would sooner
have believed in the heavens falling, than that the Neuhausers could put any obstacle in our way !—Well, that
means we must wait and perhaps see the butter taken
from your bread."   He sighed and went towards the door.
" But you must see it, nevertheless, Fräulein !   I will go
down and clear away the stones lying in the way—and I
must first see if all is in order overhead that no accident
may happen—and then I have nothing more to do with
it."

Soon after, Claudine descended in his and her brother's
company to the cellar.

It was a fine, cool, dry vault, upon which the light of
the lantern in Heinemann's hand fell.—Yes, those were
walls of the period when building made no large hole in
the patrician treasury, when the peasants in their positions

as serfs brought the building material from the stone-quarries and lime-pits,—which material was formed into even, firm, thick walls, through which not a vestige of dampness could penetrate. It was no wonder that the waxen treasure of the nuns lay there just as the hands, long since dust, had placed it. . . Yes, there were layer upon layer, the rind brown with age, but when broken just as yellow and fresh as if it had recently gone through the melting and purifying process.

"As good as gold!" said Heinemann, pointing to the layers. "And all this has been gathered by those little things in yellow jackets."

"And the chalices from which they obtained the pollen bloomed centuries ago," added Herr von Gerold with agitation. "Had I anything to say about the discovery, it should not be touched?"

"God forbid!" protested the old gardener quite terrified.

"Although no style has immortalized any thoughts upon the comb as we find them upon the wax-tablets of the ancients, still here a remnant of cloister-life speaks to us," said Herr von Gerold, heedless of the interpolation. "What may have passed through the minds of the nuns while their busy hands molded into the shape in which it lies before us, what the buzzing honey-bees brought from the blooming, sinful, lovely world without the walls! Of what did they think——"

"With your permission, gracious sir, I can tell you exactly—they thought of how much money there was in it, of nothing else!" replied Heinemann in a respectful tone, but with such a roguish glance that Herr von Gerold was forced to smile.

"In convents at all times they have been bent upon accumulating money; one has only to read the old writings to find out to a nicety how the pious virgins grabbed everything there was to grab. They took the last penny and the last bit of land for their prayers from the poor souls who left the world with fear and trembling. It was no different then from now—man takes where he can. Well, he is but mortal, and he is yet to be born who will bring into temporal life an angel's wings! Only the good people should not make so much ado and pretend to be so pious, as if they had no other thoughts than those of piety and godliness."

He threw the light of his lantern upon all the walls.
"What a lovely cellar this is ! There is not a trace of the
flames which once raged everywhere to be seen. We can
use the cellar, Fräulein. All the other subterranean places
are totally filled up with rubbish, as far as that miserable
corner"—he pointed to the adjoining cellar under the
dwelling—"where there is barely room for our few pota-
toes. Therefore, the stuff must be removed as soon as
possible, Fräulein ! "

"That cannot be, dear Heinemann," decided Claudine.
"The wax must remain where it is, untouched, until one
of the Neuhausers has seen it. Will you write to Lothar?"
she turned to her brother.

"I ? " he cried with a sort of comical horror. "Dear
heart—anything you like—but not that ! You know——"

"Yes, I know," said she, smiling. "Nor do I care to
have anything to do with the Baron at Neuhaus. . . I will
put the matter in Beate's hands. She can come herself, or
send some one."

Herr von Gerold nodded. "It can do no harm to notify
them," said he. "The world is bad; it will hear of the
discovery, it will be magnified tenfold, and it will whisper
of secrecy and so forth. But no breath must fall upon my
little sister. Lothar will, moreover, think as I do. The
nuns' wax-treasure has long since become abeyant property and belongs to him upon whose land it is found—
nota bene, according to Roman and common law, only
half of it ; for the other half belongs to the one who
chances on the treasure, and that is Heinemann."

The gardener drew back and raised his hands as if to
ward off a blow. "To an old fellow like me? Half falls
to me of what lies on the Gerold estates ? Ah, that would
be a fine fashion ! How can I help it if a few loose stones
fall out of the wall? Is there any merit in that ? And do I
need Mammon?" He shook his head energetically. "I
have enough and more than enough to live on all my life
—want I do not know, and that I owe to my dear mistress.
No, do not speak of it, sir. Not a crumb, not as much
as it would take to wax a piece of linen-thread will I take
of the stuff! But I believe it would be wise to be cautious. If some one comes over here and looks at it, then
afterwards there will be no scandalous talk."

On the afternoon of the following day, Claudine strolled
through the woods to the Neuhaus Geroldcourt. She
wanted to speak with Beate herself. She had chosen the narrow foot-path which, after several turnings, merged into the
broad high-road branching off the *chaussée* in the neighborhood of the Altenstein Geroldcourt.

She had to go quite a distance ; but she trod upon moss
and grass as soft as velvet, and above her were interwov-
en the green boughs of the gigantic trees. She, the beautiful swan of the Gerolds, as her brother so tenderly called
her, flitted in her light summer dress with her white straw
hat over her brow, like a sunbeam through the delightfully
cool, green semi-darkness which surrounded her, until she
reached the highway. From this point the land grew
gradually higher and the woods thinner, the clover and
corn-fields innumerable, and the entire country fruitful
and prosperous.

Involuntarily she stooped to pick a handful of buttercups which gleamed like golden eyes amid the meadow-
grass. It was not long before the windows of the manor
could be seen. It lay upon a gentle eminence ; the
grass upon the terraces was short and velvety, cared for
for beauty's sake, not for use.

Claudine walked along one of the narrow paths which
intersected the lawn. She walked with bowed head, and
only looked up when she stepped upon the gravel under
the lindens on the west side of the house ; there she started
and, unpleasantly surprised, paused a moment undecided
what to do. Neuhaus had guests.

A lady, evidently, walking to and fro in the shade of the
lindens,—advanced, a stately lady with a very pale complexion and blazing, Southern eyes. Her elegant gray
silk train swept the gravel, and in the comb, which held
her luxuriant hair dressed high upon her head, costly
stones glittered at every turn. She carried a child upon
her arm, a thin, sallow, little creature in a white dress,
the lace upon the edge of which almost touched the
ground.

Claudine's eyes were fixed as if spellbound upon the
child's tiny face. She knew those large, sparkling eyes,
the arched nose above the full lips, the low brow upon
which the thick, black, glossy hair bristled so stubbornly—
it was the type of the side-line of the ducal house.

"I want them!" stammered the little one, reaching for the buttercups in Claudine's hand.

The young lady with a pleasant smile was about to put the bunch of flowers in the outstretched hand; but the lady carrying the child drew back hastily, as if the proposed contact might be contaminating. "If you please —no! I cannot allow it!" she protested, while her eyes haughtily glanced at the young lady's simple attire. The woman had something decidedly hostile in her glowing eyes.

At the refusal the child began to scream lustily.

At the same moment a gentleman turned a corner of the house. "Why is my daughter screaming so?" he exclaimed, advancing hastily, with evident impatience.

Claudine involuntarily assumed the cold, reserved manner which at court had been to her buckler and coat of mail. Baron Lothar had returned to Germany, and the wayward child was his.

"I want them!" repeated the child, still crying and pointing to the flowers.

Baron Lothar gravely shook his finger at her, whereupon she ceased. A sudden glow suffused his bearded face, and from his eyes he shot a hasty glance at the composed lady-in-waiting.

None the less did he bow low and courteously before her. "Child," said he, smiling mockingly, while with his handkerchief he wiped the tears from the little one's thin face, "who wants flowers others have picked? And do you not know that the hand of woman refuses the most gladly where an object is most desired?"

Claudine looked at him, the petted, admired favorite of all women, with incredulous astonishment; but his sharp remark did not seem to disconcert her. "Through me the child shall certainly not have this first, hard experience," she replied, gently. "Nor have I scarcely a right to these flowers—they grew in your fields. Permit me now?" She turned to the lady carrying the little girl.

Baron Lothar turned as well, and fixed upon the woman a glance of angry surprise. "Now?" he repeated. "How so?"

"I was afraid Leonie might put the flowers in her mouth," answered the person addressed with hesitation. Confusion and irritation struggled in her voice.

He curled up his lips contemptuously. "And the field flowers lying there ruthlessly torn to pieces beside the carriage and on the cover, who gave them to her, Frau von Berg?"

The lady maintained silence and turned away her head. Claudine hastened to give the child the bouquet, for the scene was becoming embarrassing. At the same moment two tiny hands were preparing to tear to pieces the poor yellow blossoms. Claudine thought involuntarily of the mother of the child, Princess Katharina, of whom they said, that in the early days of her love she had torn to pieces all flowers with passionate anxiety, murmuring, "He loves me," and so forth. The prettiest rose on the stalk, even the rarest buds in the conservatory, were not safe from her.

Baron Lothar perhaps thought the same. He looked with a frowning brow at the little vandal hands and shrugged his shoulders. "I beg of you to let the child resume a recumbent position," said he to Frau von Berg. "She has been sitting up too long and is tired—it can be seen by the droop of her shoulders."

The lady, with head thrown back, rustled toward the child's carriage, while Claudine with a bow prepared to take leave of the master of the house; but he remained by her side.

At a turning at a corner of the house a gentle breeze stirred the leaves of the lindens above them.

"How mysteriously they whisper up above there!" said Baron Lothar. "Do you know of what they whisper? —Of the Montagues and Capulets of the Paulinenthal."

Claudine smiled coldly. "At a girl's seminary they rarely think of the family disputes at home," she replied, calmly. "They love one another and do not ask if they may either; and if to-day I tread the ground avoided by my relatives, it is for my schoolmate's sake. I was at Neuhaus once during my last school vacation,—the fine, old trees know me."

He bowed silently and went on his way, while she entered the hall. She did not need to ask for Beate; behind the nearest doors, which led to one of the rooms situated on the side of the court, could be heard the energetic, commanding voice of her "schoolmate."

"Come, do not resist me, childish thing!" she scolded

within. "I have no time to waste—give me your hand !"
A moment's pause. "See how finely the cut is healing !
Now we can take out the stitches again !" The slight
outcry of a youthful voice followed, then all was still.

Claudine opened the door noiselessly. The vapor of the
ironing-room met her. At a long table stood three women
ironing industriously, while Beate at the window again
wrapped the bandage about a maid's injured hand.

She did not see her who entered, but her keen eyes
turned from the bandage to the ironing-table. "Louise,
you saucy jade, what are you doing?" she cried, with a
suspicious gleam in her eyes. "Lord, my very best col-
lar in your clumsy fingers ! That is more than bold in
such a greenhorn as you are !" She snatched the embroidery from the girl, sprinkled and rolled it up. "I will
correct the error later myself," said she to the others, pointing to the small bundle. With those words she went to
the door and paused in surprise before Claudine. It was
genuine delight which suddenly lighted up her severe
features. "Hot water in the coffee machine !" she
ordered concisely, put her arm around the girl's shoulders,
and led her into the sitting-room, into the beautiful, large
corner room with its dark brown, old-fashioned mahogany
furniture, its white pine floor and tastefully draped curtains.
The room had looked just so before Lothar and Beate
were born, at the time when the spinning-wheel still
whirred by the window.

At the three windows on the south side the shades were
drawn ; on the other hand the two looking toward the east
needed no protection against the bright afternoon light.
There the lindens afforded shade, and from under their
magnificent, impenetrable canopy, one could look out
upon the blooming, sunny land.

"Now make yourself comfortable, dear old schoolmate," said Beate, leading her visitor to a seat in one of
the windows. She removed her hat and softly passed her
hand over the wealth of hair which, carelessly knotted,
had become somewhat disarranged under her hat.

"It is the same hair we all admired, the wavy curls
about the brow and on the neck ! You do not wear false
rolls, and the court hair-dresser has not harmed your hair
with his curling-tongs—you have come to us tolerably
sound from—Babel !"

Claudine laughed softly and seated herself at Beate's sewing-table. There lay, beside her mending, a neatly-bound copy of Scheffel's "Ekkehard."

"You see, dearest," said Beate, who fetched various things in order to set the table for coffee, with a glance at the book almost apologetic, "a mortal such as I am, who has to be daily like a gendarme behind idleness and indolence, and who therefore must be a worker herself, is so much the more attached to her rare enjoyable hours of recreation, and for that reason I collect the best and newest literature in my corner."

As she spoke she swept book and mending into her work-basket, and laid a napkin upon the table; then she brought the sugar-basin, an old-fashioned japanned box with a stout lock. She opened it, and made a wry face. "Well, now, there it is! It is, no wonder, in the topsy-turvy! Common sugar in the good basin! That has never happened to me before! But Lothar played me a trick, a trick!—In answer to my letter in which I told him of the purchase of your plate, the man wrote me he should return. I thought in July at the earliest, and took my time, when lo and behold! he arrived the day before yesterday, bag and baggage, in the midst of our large wash! It was terrible! I needed all my self-possession, for the housekeeper lost her head altogether, and made one blunder after the other."

She lighted the spirit lamp under the coffee machine and cut a piece of cake in small strips. As she did so, Claudine thought how remarkably well the tall, strong form in the large white apron and spotless linen at throat and wrists appeared in the rôle of hostess. Her composure was perfect and very different from the awkward, insulting manner which a few days before had been so noticeable in the "barbarous woman" at Altenstein-Geroldcourt.

"Lothar alone would not have inconvenienced us," continued she, taking a small basket filled with early strawberries from the cupboard, "although he is very much spoiled. But this *caravan* he has to drag around with him! There is Frau von Berg, her maid, a nurse, and several men-servants—they all had to be brought along. And the child! Such a miserable little creature has never screamed within the Neuhaus walls—no, never! Heavens! the late

3

Ulrich Gerold, my severe grandfather, should see her !
He would open his eyes ! Such little folks without blood
and bone were to him 'a worthless brood.' The child
cannot stand on its slender legs and is almost two years
old. Baths of wild thyme and unadulterated milk would
do the puny thing good, but we dare not interfere with
Frau von Berg's program,—she is as infallible as the Pope.
Lothar's mother-in-law, old Princess Thekla, engaged her
as nurse and is completely infatuated with the distasteful
person, who is as repulsive to me as she can possibly be."

She shrugged her shoulders, poured the coffee, now prepared, into the cups, and seated herself at the table. It
was then Claudine ventured to broach her errand.

Beate stirred the sugar in her cup and listened silently.
At the point of the discovery she looked up and laughed
in surprise. "What—*wax?* In my mind I already saw
old Heinemann clearing out a chest filled with mon-
strances and all sorts of valuables ! Wax ! See, see, Ben
Akiba is not right—that is new ! And these nuns ! According to the lyric poets they are mostly white roses
which, pale and grief-stricken, look out yearningly through
the window into the prohibited, beautiful world." She
laughed. "For that the Walpurgis nuns surely had no
time,—they must have been economists and housewives
pure and simple !.. According to our old book of chron-
icles, two of the Gerolds must have been among the nuns
who were driven away. Who knows, perhaps those two
with leather apron and trowel went down into the cellar
to hide the booty from the rebels' sight ! Who knows, I
might have done so too !" She shook her head with a
smile. "A wonderful story ! And it is almost as wonderful that the honest and true-to-the-backbone descendant
is seated before me, and in a serious manner wishes to
divide the discovered treasure with us, layer for layer !"
A charming expression of humor flitted across her serious,
severe face. "Well, now, one can always use wax, and
were it only to grease a table or to wax a strand of thread.
But in that I am not the ruling power, dear heart ! You
must consult with Lothar." With those words she rose
and went out.

Claudine made no attempt to detain her. Though she
desired no farther meeting with the "Baron of Neuhaus,"
she was forced to confess that in this way the matter

would be settled at once, and therefore she rose, calmly, when after quite a long while she heard his steps in the hall.

He entered with his sister. Claudine had only seen him at court in his uniform, brilliant and triumphant "as the god of war ! " the other ladies-in-waiting had whispered. To-day he was attired in a neat, gray civil suit, and she was forced to confess, as she had before under the lindens, that it was not principally the striking brilliance of the soldierly appearance, which, even by the side of the handsome, imposing Duke, made him the most noticeable figure at court.

She left the window and was about to speak ; but with a smile he raised his hand. "Not another word is necessary," he hastened to say. "Beate has already told me that your romantic Owl's Nest has given out its treasures —the ancient property of a convent ! How interesting ! At any rate it was the spirit hands of the nuns themselves which loosened the masonry, probably because the 'right one' had finally come."

Involuntarily Claudine glanced at the dark, bearded lips which knew how to speak so kindly. It was no longer the man who by the Princess' side never spoke a pleasant word to his cousin, whose eyes had looked at the new maid-of-honor with ill-concealed vexation.

Without any more words Beate drew her towards the coffee-table.

"Come, do not be so ceremonious, Claudine ! We are not at court ! " said she. "Sit down ! Your 'Cinderella feet,' the admiration of the school—do you remember ?— have probably been surprised that such a walk fell to their lot."

The young lady, with a blush, sat down, and Beate likewise seated herself, while Baron Lothar, his hand resting upon the nearest chair-back, stood opposite them.

"It surely is a long walk through the wood," he agreed with his sister,—"a walk which no lady should venture upon alone ! Did you not fear you might meet with some insolence ? "

"I have no fear. I was always more at home in the woods than in our nursery. I feel sure that they will pro- ·-ct me like an old friend."

Yes, I am, too, a lover of the woods through thick and

thin, in night and mist!" laughed Beate. "We are children of the Thuringen forest. But for your delicate, little feet, Claudine, the road is surely too fatiguing——"

"And you have made an unnecessary sacrifice to your over-scrupulous sense of justice," interrupted her brother. "For it certainly does not require the wisdom of a Solomon on our part to decide immediately that we have not the semblance of a claim upon the discovery. The Owl's Nest has for years been in the possession of the Altenstein line—how should we go so far back into the past with claims which we should not make, though we should make good a wrong? I have, for instance, never understood how my grandfather could have agreed to the exchange, according to which an excellent piece of land fell to him in place of the worthless ruins."

"I am of the same opinion," said Beate with an energetic shake of her head. "Now old Heinemann can prove if his valuation is correct. An addition to your revenue will not be unwelcome."

"Practical as usual, dear Beate!" said Baron Lothar. "But I should almost like to protest against this disposition of the nuns' bequest. Would it not be more poetical were the pollen, which the bees of ancient days gathered together, to be converted into precious stones? Perhaps into a necklace of brilliants, which the heiress could wear on her first reappearance at court?" said he lightly, glancing half-covertly at the former lady-in-waiting.

She raised her lashes; her sad eyes met his. "Precious stones for bread?" asked she. "The happy sensation of being able to banish want from my home is more valuable to me, and therefore I think 'practically' like Beate, what should I do at court? You do not seem to know that I have resigned——"

"Yes, the sparrows pipe it from the roofs of the Residence. But do not your name and your much-envied position as favorite of the Dowager-Duchess accord you the right to go to court at any time——"

"From the humble Owl's Nest?" she interrupted with quivering lips and sparkling eyes.

"Besides, the distance is too great," he agreed; but as he spoke the words, his voice sounded as harsh and merciless as if he had a victim in his grasp whom he desired to hold fast at any price. "Eight good miles!—

Well, perhaps the court itself will find some expedient—it would need to come only a little nearer you."

"How would that be possible?" she cried with a sudden start, and in a half-suppressed voice. "With the exception of the old shooting-box, 'Waldlust,' the ducal house has no habitable possession in our vicinity."

"And in this famous 'Waldlust,' with its three small rooms, the water runs down the walls," said Beate with a laugh. "The wind will blow the tumble-down place over the next we know."

Baron Lothar made no reply at once. He began to pace the floor. "The day before yesterday, on my way I stopped for a few hours at the Residence, to take her little grandchild to Princess Thekla," he began again after a few moments' silence, pausing as he spoke. "I there heard casually of such a project on the part of the Duke." At the mention of this name he fixed a glance, firm, keen, yes, almost hostile, upon the lovely face of the former lady-in-waiting, over which a bright blush spread. "They talked so much nonsense," he continued, with a bitter, mocking smile, removing his eyes from her crimson cheeks. "You know the court gossip. It rushes from a corner like a moth, and is difficult to catch and hold fast, but its traces are left in a sullied name."

At those words Claudine raised her bowed head.

"I know the 'court gossip,'" said she, "but I never stooped so low as to allow it to bias my opinion."

"Bravo, old schoolmate!" exclaimed Beate. "You really escaped unscathed!" Her clear eyes had keenly examined the excited countenances of both speakers. "But now, let these court reminiscences rest!" she added, with a frown upon her brow. "I despise gossip, whether it be at the well and wash-tub, or at court; it is vulgar everywhere. . . . Rather tell me, how are you progressing with your new task, Claudine?"

"The beginning was difficult," replied the young lady, with her pretty, gentle smile, with which was mingled a tinge of melancholy. "Hands and aprons bear the traces of awkwardness at the kitchen fire. But this first step was happily overcome, and I now find time to rest and enjoy our solitude and Joachim's happy, contented face."

"Indeed? He sees you do a maid's work with a happy face?" He glanced at her mockingly.

"Do you think I would not manage to prevent him from seeing me at my domestic work?" she returned, with a gay smile, ignoring his scorn completely. "For this, no extraordinary craftiness is necessary. Joachim writes from early until late, upon his travels through Spain, into which he is weaving his finest poems. And at this delightful work he is beyond real life with its petty cares and trials. He is a man who can sleep as soundly on hard boards as on a soft bed, who can live contentedly on milk and brown bread. But his tender nature requires love, loving comprehension—and that he always finds, when he comes down from his quiet bell-room to his family. Oh, yes, I may say that I have grasped my new life's work—Joachim has a true poet's nature, and was entrusted to me by no less a person than the goddess of poetry." She rose and took up her hat and gloves. "Now, I must go home and make an omelette for supper,—do not laugh, Beate,"—but for a moment she herself joined heartily in her schoolmate's laughter—"my good Lindenmeyer is quite proud of the apt manner in which her pupil can turn an omelette."

"Her Highness should see that!"

"It would please her, I know. She is a German; the housewifely element is in her blood, if she was born a princess."

"But would it please her if bitter necessity should suddenly transplant her from her audience chamber to the kitchen hearth. The contrast between light and shade, which you have taken upon yourself, is too severe—my heart aches to-day."

"Make yourself easy, Beate!" interrupted her brother, with evident irony. "This trial will not last long. It is only a transition-stage, a sort of fairy episode à la King Drosselbart. Before you can realize it, radiant sunlight will illuminate the flower now shaded, a radiant sunlight which all the roses of Schiraz would envy."

Brother and sister unperceived exchanged a glance of understanding, and with those words Baron Lothar bowed and left the room hastily. As she approached the door which led into the adjoining room, Beate said, shrugging her shoulders: "Patience one moment, Claudine, I will make a trifling change in my toilet, for I should like to accompany you."

In the meantime, Claudine again stepped to the window.
Her cheeks burned, and her fine brows were contracted
in moody meditation. How excessive must be the malice
and wickedness at the ducal court to cast stones at her,
who had bravely taken a step to save her better self!
And how had she ever injured the man who had just gone
out, that he should, in an apparent jest, but in earnest,
utter insulting remarks which agitated and embittered her
scarcely quieted heart? Without, quite near the window,
stood the carriage with his child. Was he embittered,
and did he bear others ill-will because the wife had gone
from him who had lent his life such brilliance? His
fate was indeed hard to bear. She had been taken away
forever, and what remained of her lay there, frail and
helpless, while the immense fortune which the Princess
had left could not obtain for her child sufficient strength
so that it could stand upon its feet! . . . How much strife
had there already been about the feeble little creature!
The grandmother, Princess Thekla, who could not become
reconciled to her favorite daughter's death, had gone to
Italy to beg for the child, but Baron Lothar had sharply
and decisively refused to give her up. It was then
rumored at court that the old lady cherished the plan of
giving her remaining daughter, Princess Helene, to her
son-in-law as his second wife, that her beloved grandchild might not fall into the hands of a strange step-
mother, and a few clever ones alleged that the young
Princess would not say "No," for since the time of her
sister's betrothal she had nursed a secret preference for
her brother-in-law. Princess Helene was prettier than
her deceased sister, but she too had the large, peculiar
sparkling eyes, with which the child without stared up
into the linden boughs. She lay among her white pillows,
her thin, little fingers plucked nervously at the blue satin
coverlet, while an old nurse sat beside the carriage knitting, and as she did so, with animated gestures telling the
child stories.

The rumbling of wheels shook the ground beneath the
young lady's feet, and immediately thereafter Beate, dressed
to go out, re-entered the room. She took the basket
with the strawberries from the table and hung it on her
arm. "For your little Elizabeth," said she to Claudine,
and a rosy flush flitted across her face.

The sugar-basin and the remainder of the cake were
hastily locked in the cupboard, then they set out.

An open carriage stood at the door.   Baron Lothar sat
upon the box and held the reins.

"Forward, dear!" urged Beate, when Claudine in
affright hesitated on the doorstep, and evidently did not
wish to accept such an attention at Neuhaus.   "These
fine fellows"—she pointed to the horses, magnificent,
young animals who were held in with difficulty—"snort
like sun-horses.   They would like to run away with us."

Soon after the carriage rolled under the lindens and
down the main road.   Baron Lothar easily managed the
fiery team.   From time to time he glanced at the rye and
wheat fields, and the boughs of the fruit-trees on both
sides of the road with their green clusters.   Not once
did he turn towards the occupants of the carriage.   He
had noticed Claudine's hesitation, had read resistance in
her face ; she knew it, for her eyes had met his mocking
ones, which drove the blood into her cheeks ; still *nolens
volens* they now were forced to drive together.   "Montagues and Capulets" in one carriage, which with its light
satin cushions, its glittering, gleaming equipment, flew
through the Paulinenthal like an embodied bit of court
brilliance.

So to speak, flooded with the aromatic perfume of field
and wood, and bathed in the golden glory of the setting
sun, the beautiful, broad valley lay there, a magnificent
panorama which the small stream, springing merrily from
the mountains far above, intersected.   Sparkling, flowing
on, now shaded by the willows, now in the bright sunlight, lapping the flowers on its banks, it came, the gentle
stream, which, in conjunction with violent thunder-showers,
had repeatedly become a beast of prey.   Who could tell
by its appearance that it had swallowed a part of the
Gerold possessions ?

Round about, wheresoever one looked, work was being
completed before evening tide.   The mower's scythe, with
a dazzling glitter, ran through the meadow grass ; in the
furrows of the potato fields whole columns of women
worked with hoes, while between the wild sloe-bushes
of the grassy commons, knitting as they went, barefooted
maidens drove before them their geese and goats.   From
the woods came the rhythmical strokes of the ax.

Hearty cries of greeting met those driving by on all sides, and these greetings were genially returned. Claudine for the first time acknowledged that the occupants of the fine carriage needed not to be ashamed in the face of the industry of the workmen : they were not like the useless lilies of the field, not like the drones in the hives ; they worked too, the one from native love of activity, and the other for the sake of satisfaction, to preserve self-respect, to be useful, and to promote the welfare of others.

For a brief second, far beyond the tree-tops of the gardens, was visible the slate roof of the Altenstein Manor. The flag-staff still rose in the air bannerless—the deeply-mourned ancestral home did not yet shelter the new owner. But up the road came slowly a heavily-loaded furniture wagon, followed by a low vehicle which contained the case of a grand piano.

"Our new neighbor is moving in, it seems," said Beate, as if to herself, glancing keenly at the carriage passing by. At that moment Baron Lothar turned hastily to Claudine.

"Do you know who has bought the estate ?" he asked, breaking the silence as suddenly as a judge who seeks to confuse the delinquent in an unguarded moment.

"How should I know ?" she said, somewhat sharply, surprised at his tone. "We are trying to forget that we ever lived on this side of the forest, and do not ask who is to succeed us."

"No one in the valley knows yet, Lothar," said Beate. "Our greatest gossips in the village are trying to solve the mystery. I am occasionally possessed by the secret fear that some wealthy manufacturer is the purchaser ; what I have just seen on the wagon strengthens me in the belief,—such people can never have things elegant and gorgeous enough ! Terrible ! Smoky factory chimneys in our lovely, pure valley !"

Baron Lothar had long before turned around ; he did not reply, and his whip played upon the backs of his horses. Again the carriage rolled on, now in the wood, and Beate said, with a glance at the underwood which was spread over the mossy ground, strewn with starry blossoms and bracken, she believed those at the Residence with their dust-filled lungs would gladly stretch themselves upon such a green couch. She had the basket with the strawberries on her lap, and had spread a

small napkin over the deliciously fragrant fruit as protection against the sun. This time the pace was quicker
than it had been recently with the tired horses.

"Why, how beautiful your Owl's Nest has turned out!"
exclaimed Beate in surprise, as the small estate came in
sight. "Since my last visit to you and your grandmother, I have not been here. It is entirely enveloped
in a green mantle!"

She was right. During the last years of her life, the late
owner had planted wild vines about the tower. Fourteen
days before the vines covered with undeveloped leaves
had clung to the walls like a thin, almost imperceptible
net-work, but to-day the luxuriant foliage left only a few
window-arches free. The vines crept as far as the lower
room in the tower; they framed the glass-door leading
to the platform and hung over the balustrades like a
carpet.

Heinemann had just pointed out a bird's nest high up in
the trees to little Elizabeth; he carried the child upon his
arm as he advanced to meet the carriage. In anxious
agitation he raised his bushy, yellow brows—were they
coming to claim their share of the wax?

The carriage halted. The old gardener, with a polite bow,
opened the door; but only his young mistress alighted.
Beate remained seated, and offered the child, still in
Heinemann's arms, the strawberries. With surprise Claudine saw a beautiful, tender smile flit across the grave
face of her schoolmate, and the child, too, must have instinctively felt that the sunbeam was a rare one, for she
suddenly leaned forward and threw her arms around
Beate's neck; then, laughing with delight, she took the
basket from the "big hands" which recently she had indignantly warded off from her favorite doll, and tried to
escape from Heinemann's arms, in order to run home.

Beate and Claudine then planned another visit to be
made shortly—a walk through the woods which would
relieve the mind of all domestic troubles. Soon after the
carriage turned and drove homeward.

Baron Lothar did not speak another word, but he took
leave of Claudine with a deep bow, and of Heinemann
with a pleasant word.

"Zounds! by all that is true! I am no friend of the
Neuhausers,—indeed not; on the contrary, they have

more luck than merit, and the Altensteiners have to lower
their sails before them—unfortunately," said the gardener,
as he shaded his eyes with his hand and looked after the
equipage with the greatest interest. "But even envy
must acknowledge that he is and will remain a handsome
soldier, even in his simple gray coat. I, too, was a soldier
—a shrewd one, Fräulein—and I know how to sum up
the officers. I believe that when he rides at the head of
his squadron, the fellows will sit still more erect and
proudly upon their horses. We know what he is at heart
—haughty, to be sure, and vain of his aristocratic con-
nection ; and with regard to this "—he made a motion as
if counting money with his thumb and forefinger, and
with an anxious, questioning side-glance examined the
face of his young mistress,—"ahem ! they will take too
what is to be had ? "

Claudine smiled. "Make yourself easy, Heinemann ;
the wax is to be left in your hands ! You can do with it
what you like ! "

"How ? Really ? These people will take nothing ? "
He was on the point of leaping with delight. "A weight—
a hundredweight is removed from my heart. I was in
agony until you came ! Well, that is over, thank God !—
Now, you shall see what old Heinemann can do, Fräulein !
I will obtain money from that fellow in town, rich Volz,
for whom the bee-raisers in the district cannot get enough
wax. We can find use for it, Fräulein ; we can use it more
particularly now, as we shall surely have fine visitors occasionally. And then it must not be too poverty-stricken
in the house,—surely not ; we owe that to our good mistress under the sod ! To-morrow I shall take the pewter to
the pewterer, it must be brightened up ; and we need a
new cream jug with the coffee set ; how would it do if we
were to buy new curtains for the best room ? After the
last washing Fräulein Lindenmeyer mended and darned
them carefully, but one can see——"

"But, wherefore all this ? " asked Claudine in surprise.
"Fräulein Beate——"

"Ah, what of her ? She herself mends and darns all
sorts of old rags and hangs them at the windows ; she is
very domesticated and saving and would not scoff at a
darned hole ! " He pointed with his thumb towards Fräulein Lindenmeyer's room. "There she is in there, the

village gossip, the forester's wife from Oberlaute, who
obtains all the latest news fresh from the Residence and
carries it afterwards in her knitting-bag from house to
house, until it is stale.   When we are nearer the house
you will smell it, gracious Fräulein,—pure cinnamon and
vanilla !   Fräulein Lindenmeyer in her delight at the rare
visit has made chocolate, thick chocolate—the spoon sticks
in it—B-r-r !   And to-morrow our old Mamselle will be laid
up with her very worst stomach trouble—well, for my
part !   the news which the brave postilion in petticoats
has brought us is in the end worth a little suffering ; it is,
that our Duke has bought the dear, beautiful Altenstein
Geroldcourt."

Claudine was standing beside the yew-tree at the entrance to the garden.   With a sudden movement she
grasped a branch of the tree, as if seeking support.   The
blood rushed to her face to give place immediately to
ghastly pallor.

"Good God, how it affects you ! " exclaimed Heinemann
in affright, lending her his support.   "What an old block-
head I was to blurt it out so abruptly !—But the fact remains."   He shook his head sadly.   "Yet, is it not a thousand times better for Geroldcourt to fall into such hands,
than that perhaps a wealthy manufacturer should have
reeling and spinning done in the rooms?   And your youth,
Fräulein !   Ask those below "— he pointed to the ground
beneath his feet, to the nuns' cemetery—"if each one
would not with delight have slipped out of the solitary
forest had they only been able to find a crevice in the
high walls ? . . . You see, that is the best part of it—you
will again have society, you will be in your proper element.
Every flower needs especial soil.   The entire court will
move to the Altenstein Manor for the summer.   The Duke
wants to have a dairy especially for his young wife ; she
is said to have consumption, poor little woman, and the
air of the cow-pen is supposed to be beneficial."   He
scratched his head.   "Good Lord, that is a remedy such
as musk would be for a general breaking-up."

The young lady continued slowly and silently on her
way.   Her pale lips were compressed convulsively.
Heinemann looked at her timidly.   In that gentle, lovely
face which he had known since the first time the deep,
blue eyes had opened, was reflected a struggle which he

could not understand. It was not grief for the lost home, as he had thought at first; it looked rather as if she were struggling inwardly with a foreign power which rushed in upon her, as if a struggle were taking place in her soul, while her lips remained mute. He saw it by the way in which her head was thrown back, by her outstretched, evading hands. She seemed to have forgotten his presence altogether. He therefore said not a word and busied himself with the nearest vegetable patch; and only when she was about to enter the house did he follow her and ask leave of absence for the next day, "on account of the wax business." She accorded him permission with a faint smile and ascended the stairs:

Above, in the seclusion of her room, she sank into a chair and buried her face disconsolately in her hands. Had all been in vain? Would temptation really follow her, wheresoever she went? No, no, her position was not so helpless and unprotected as it had been a few weeks before! Was not her brother beside her? And could she not say too :—My house is my citadel—I can and will close it against every one who should not cross my threshold?

The next morning Heinemann went into town very early. By his side trudged a village urchin with a barrow, which the old man had filled with early vegetables for his customers; the business trip to town must be turned to profit! The pewter had to be left at home, nor did he obtain permission to buy new curtains. Not without anxiety did Heinemann occasionally look back at the house, until the trees prevented him from seeing anything more. What he had predicted had come to pass—Fräulein Lindenmeyer had a sick-headache. She was in bed and needed nursing. Gladly would he have remained at home, but at daybreak he had cut the vegetables, and they must be taken away.

His young mistress was alone; for the master up above in the bell-room did not count. With his pen in his hand he was never in the real world; everything around him might burn up if only the bell-room remained standing and the ink did not dry. This opinion arose in no way from contempt; on the contrary, Heinemann was filled with admiration, but in his eyes his learned master was one for whom one must think and care in common things as they did for the dear, innocent creature, little Elizabeth.

Well, he had done his utmost to lighten the day's work for the young mistress. He had milked the goats, had taken fresh eggs from the hens' nests and picked peas for dinner; kindling wood lay on the hearth, the staircase was swept clean, and the homœopathic medicine chest with directions written in his hand stood in Fräulein Lindenmeyer's room—he understood the healing art as no one else did, Fräulein Lindenmeyer always maintained.

As he never through the day latched, much less locked, the garden gate, he did not do so to-day. The mastiff stationed there barked promptly, as soon as the gate swung upon its hinges from without. The poultry roosted behind an inclosure set apart for them, and the cat always effected her visits to the woods through the windows of the church ruins. Of the child, of little Elizabeth, the old man had not thought. She was indeed generally his inseparable companion in the garden; she followed him and chattered constantly, while his large, callous hands worked busily, and he readily replied to her questions, occasionally wiping his earth-stained fingers on his apron, in order to put the child's hat over her forehead or to carefully "plait" the doll's loosened hair. Under his watchful care Elizabeth had never gone as far as the gate, and Claudine too knew she feared the dog. Therefore she went about her household duties with unconcern, leaving the child playing in the garden.

Through the open windows she could hear the doll's carriage rolling over the gravel, and had frequently smiled at the modulation of the sweet, childish voice according as she scolded her dolls or lavished caressing names upon them.

Noon came. The heat increased. Occasionally a single cloud floated idly across the sun's disk and cast a momentary shadow over the garden—a shadow agreeable and obscuring, as if a gigantic bird were soaring compassionately above all the drooping and dying flower-chalices.

Claudine stepped to the window and called the child; but she was startled at her own voice, so quiet was it without. Only the dog with his rattling chain crept from his stifling kennel and looked attentively at the window whence came the call. The child did not reply, nor was her light frock to be seen either among the bushes or in the arbor.

As yet Claudine did not feel uneasy. The child often went from the garden direct to the bell-room, to take her papa a couple of flowers or an apron filled with "beautiful stones."

Claudine hastened up there, but her brother was seated at the northern window, in the cool room darkened by the drawn green blinds, so engrossed in his work, that at her question he only looked up with an absent, but affectionate glance, shook his head with a smile and continued his writing assiduously. Nor was the child with Fräulein Lindenmeyer. Claudine now rushed anxiously into the garden.

In the arbor stood the doll's carriage with her favorite doll, the wax face carefully covered with a child's pinafore ; but the little nurse was not there. Nor was she in the corner of the archway with the goats and hens, nor in the chapel ruins where she liked to play upon the green lawn and hunt daisies for the "poor ladies," as she called the carved forms of the abbesses upon the mossy grave-stones now leaning against the walls. All Claudine's anxious calling and searching were in vain.

Then she saw lying, on the road outside the gate, a glowing, red peony, and she knew that the child, a posy in her hand, had gone out of the garden. Without any meditation she hurried along the *chaussée*.

Deserted, silent, the white road-line lay before her. Since the highway was in such close proximity, this means of communication was almost entirely forsaken ; rarely did the rolling of wheels break the stillness—so there was no danger of the child being run over. Moreover, she must have robbed Heinemann's bed arrantly, at any rate the tiny hands could not hold all the blossoms, for here and there a stray pansy or a sprig of jessamine marked the way she had taken.

She must have been gone quite a time ; at least the stretch of ground which she had already covered seemed endless to Claudine, tears of anxiety filled her eyes and her heart throbbed wildly. Finally she found the hat of the child's pet *Lenchen*, near the thicket which bordered on the drive ; her blood curdled at the thought that Elizabeth had gone into the woods and was wandering about there ;

she was on the point of calling aloud, when the prattle of
the child, with which were mingled a man's tones, reached
her—the sounds came from the spot at which the road
turned so sharply that the dense forest suddenly interposed
and hid it from view.   Involuntarily she pressed her
hands to her throbbing heart and listened.   Yes, it was
Baron Lothar who just spoke; the child was with him,
and after a few more hasty steps she saw the speakers
advancing.

With his left hand Baron Lothar led his horse by the
bridle, and upon his right arm he carried the runaway.
Her round hat hung about her neck, and her thick, fair
hair fell in confusion low upon her brow and about her
flushed cheeks.   She must have already deeply repented
her bold act, for she looked as if she had been crying,
but she had not yielded up her *Lenchen ;* in her fear
and helplessness, she held the doll convulsively to her
breast.

She cried out as she saw her pretty aunt advancing upon her so precipitately.   "I wanted to take the *strawberry lady* some flowers, and it took so long, ah, so long !
And *Lenchen* has lost her new hat, aunt !" she exclaimed,
taking her left arm from her bearer's neck, as if she wished
to return to her aunt's protecting care ; but he held her fast.

"You will stay with me now, child !" he commanded.
She cowered like a frightened bird and looked shyly in the
bearded face close to hers—the commanding tone was
new to her.   "You are responsible for this, little runaway !" he continued to the child, while his eyes expres-
sively examined the beautiful lady-in-waiting's agitated
face and her tearful eyes.   She now stood before them and
vainly strove for breath and words of thanks. —"Now you
would like to dismiss me hastily and do not ask if those
arms can carry you ?   For you surely cannot walk with
your tired little legs ! No, no, do not !" he said, ward-
ing off Claudine, who indeed raised her arms to relieve
him of his burden.   "It is scarcely more than if I had a
hedge-sparrow on my arm ! Come, child, put your arm
around my neck again and do not look at me so timidly—
you were not afraid of my beard before !—See, how finely
my chestnut horse goes with me and allows herself to be
led !   And there is, too, the unfortunate hat about which
you have shed such bitter tears ?"

The child laughed gayly when Claudine put the hat upon the doll's head and tied it firmly.

Baron Lothar looked fixedly at the two slender hands, the hands so greatly admired at court, which were so near his eyes. A broad, dark streak was visible around the thumb and forefinger of the right.

"Rust-stains are no disgrace, says my old Heinemann," she stammered, coloring beneath his gaze and quickly letting her hands fall from the tied strings.

"No, they are no disgrace, but that they should exist! Is there no servant to be found at the Owl's Nest who could save you such work?" A mocking, incredulous smile trembled about his lips. "*Must* not a time come when you will look upon the memory of these spots with something like reproach?" His fiery eyes were fixed upon her face.

She returned his glance with haughty indignation.

"Has court scandal whispered to you that I am untrue and inclined to comedy?" she asked, smiling bitterly. "Must I tell you plainly the painful fact that my brother, although an honest man—tor, thank God, the creditors are paid!—left house and court a beggar? We can no longer be waited upon, and I am quite convinced that this is no great trial. These stains"—and she looked down at her blackened fingers—"I shall only look upon as reproaches when they are proofs of my awkwardness. But that too improves from day to day." She again smiled with her gentle cheerfulness; she, however, saw a dark flush mount to his face; she dared not rebuke him who bore her tired darling upon his arm, more severely. "I shall not need to be ashamed, and last night I could have comfortably invited strict Beate to partake of the scorned omelette."

"I am convinced, and herewith ask your pardon!" he interrupted, bowing his head low in sarcastic submission. "You do not merely seem to be a Cinderella, you are one in reality. . . . A man can scarcely understand such a situation, but it may have a piquant charm for the moment to disappear in the gray chrysalis, and later to ascend into the sunny heights with glittering wings."

She compressed her lips and was silent, because she knew she would be horrified at her own voice if she touched upon a theme, with a single word, which she carried hidden deep in her breast and which he constantly

4

renewed with a sort of stubborn persistence. The expression of his bold, energetic face excited her against her will.

She stepped aside to make way for him, and he walked on beneath the overhanging beech boughs. For quite a while there was only to be heard the man's footsteps and the clattering of the patient horse's hoofs as it walked by his side, until Elizabeth broke the impressive silence with a caressing name for the "dear, good chestnut."

"This little German blonde does not bear the least resemblance to her dark, Spanish mother," said Baron Lothar, as he gazed upon the child's charming face, looking past him at the horse's head. "She has the Altenstein eyes. At Neuhaus we have the picture of our great-grandmother, who was an Altenstein. Although I was so wild a boy and took so little interest in the stiff portraits on the walls, I always paused in front of that beautiful, large oil painting when our state-rooms were open. The lily of the valley, Duke Ulrich called her. She was a lovely woman; she never returned to court after His Highness once kissed her hand too ardently."

A pause again ensued, and with the crackling of the pebbles beneath the feet of the pedestrians were mingled the piping and twittering in a bird's nest above their heads.

"Young birds are in that tree, I know; Heinemann always holds me up and lets me look into the nest," said the child, with a longing, upward glance.

Lothar laughed. "This is too high, little rogue, we cannot reach so far. But see, how these blue eyes can sparkle!—I do not believe the light in my handsome great-grandmother's eyes could have changed thus. . . In the Neuhaus Gerolds the woman's head with the pale golden curls has not reappeared; not one of the female descendants has inherited that face, though so many daughters have been married in Neuhaus. I, therefore, always thought that style unique. Only later, much later, was I convinced that this face was a peculiar inheritance of the Altensteins,—it was at our court. I was out hunting with the Duke, and we came into the Dowager Duchess's salon late, just at the moment when the new lady-in-waiting stepped to the piano to sing 'The Violet' by Mozart."—He leaned forward in order to look into her face. "You, of course, do not remember the evening?"

She shook her head with a vivid blush. "No, I have

had to sing 'The Violet' so often, that no especial memory is attached to it for me."

For a moment he had paused, but now he proceeded at a quicker pace. To an artist's eye this group upon the forest road would have been an attractive bait for the picture of a fleeing family. The handsome man leading his horse by the bridle, who so firmly and unwearyingly carried the tired child upon his arm, and the feminine form walking beside him, the clinging gown, to aid her in moving with more ease, half tucked up in the girdle, the wealth of wavy hair uncovered so that through the beech boughs every stray sunbeam charmed forth golden lights,—these two looked as if they belonged to one another, to share joy and sorrow, like those "whom God hath joined together."

In a short while, the gay flower garden shimmered through the underwood, which was growing less dense, and the barking of the dog was audible. . . Herr von Gerold had been, though somewhat tardily, recalled to consciousness by the sudden appearance of his sister in the bell-room and her hasty inquiry after the child; he had, too, heard her anxious call, and had at length determined to hunt for her. For he now came hastily forward, and through the yew-trees at the entrance to the garden could be seen a woman's head timidly peeping out in a night-cap, and bound with compresses. Fräulein Lindenmeyer in her uneasiness had forgotten herself so far as to venture to the furthest limit of the ground ; at the sight of the tall, strange, manly form, however, she ran towards the house as if possessed, with flying skirts and a shawl hastily thrown over her head.

A few days before Herr von Gerold would have passed the scion of the Neuhaus branch as a stranger and unmoved by any feelings of relationship, as he had always done at the University ; but yesterday Baron Lothar had rendered his sister a courteous service, and to-day he brought him his missing child.

He therefore hastened towards him with an expression of warm gratitude, and after a few introductory and explanatory words on Claudine's part, both men shook hands cordially. Indeed Baron Lothar made no preparations to again mount his horse and to ride away, after Herr von Gerold had taken the little one from him. As they conversed, he walked between brother and sister to the garden-gate, and there too he accepted Herr von Gerold's invitation to proceed and to look at the interesting wax-find, without hesitation, quite as a matter of course. He had, as he said, purposely ridden that way on account of the Owl's Nest, which yesterday had charmed him.

Claudine preceded the others to the house. Upon the threshold she turned once more ; she had to smile. Baron Lothar had spoken of King Drosselbart and Cinderella, and was not their walk indeed like a fairy-tale? There he went, in his civil dress, leading his horse past Heinemann's flowers cultivated for sale, paying careful attention that the hoofs should in no way come in contact with the valuable petals,—he, whose gallant form she had last seen at court surrounded by a brilliance which rarely falls to the lot of mortals,—and she, the then so-called fondling of the Dowager Duchess, who walked as if on velvet and who could be touched by no rough breath of air, now hurried down the dark, worn stone steps in order to fetch one of the few bottles of wine still in the cellar, of her grandmother's store.

He led his horse to a cool, shady corner of the chapel ruins and fastened it to a strong elder-bush which had nestled there and spread its dark green foliage lovingly over the desecrated walls ; then he entered the house.

He cast merely a cursory glance into the wax-cellar. It could easily be seen that it was not the prosaic bequest of the nuns which suddenly showed the Owl's Nest in an interesting light ; indeed, he confessed quite frankly that in preference to the nuns' thrifty accumulation he chose the gallery with its clinging vines and the bell-tower.

Claudine therefore set a small table, with bottles and glasses and a fresh bouquet, out-of-doors by the glass-door which led from the sitting-room into the open air. Close to the wall of the middle building stood the last remnant of a former avenue, an old stone-linden, its summit almost dead. The only branches in which the sap still flowed overhung the balustrade ; these were, however, covered with thick foliage and formed a shady corner in conjunction with a small awning. From this point they could see two slender pillars, the last of the magnificent ones, which once had supported the nave of the church, and behind them arched a paneless, painted window in the east side-wall. Through the other windows the forest of trees, which in the course of time had pressed closely to the wall, forced their branches, and from the base crept numerous vines, on this side climbing over the walls curiously with a firm foothold into the deserted house of God. On the other hand, the pillars and the arches of the windows looked upon a narrow, shaded strip of forest meadowland without, a peaceful green island across which game wandered heedlessly.

With crossed arms Baron Lothar stepped upon the balcony and looked out upon the charming perspective.

"The German woods are pretty, too," said Herr von Gerold the much-traveled, with his mild, soft voice, beside him. "What!" cried the person addressed. "Too? I say : *only* the German woods are pretty ! What care I for palms and pines. for the soft, southern breeze, caressing my face, like the caress of an unloved hand ! I longingly pined for the Thuringen forest and its bracing air, for its deep shades and humid copse, which rises defiantly against the huntsman. —I have pined for the wintry storm which drives hostilely through the branches, which lays hold upon me and calls into play all my strength. —No. . . And I confess, even at the risk of being stamped as a barbarian, a German bear, even the art treasures could not help me to conquer my homesickness ; for I do not understand them. I understand them as little as the majority of the annual tourists to the south, though they gush and are almost beside themselves with enthusiasm."

Herr von Gerold laughed an amused laugh ; he was thoroughly familiar with this hypocrisy of the ignorant ; but Claudine, who was pouring the wine in the glasses, said with a glance at the person standing upon the balcony : "You understand more about music ? "

"Who tells you so ? " he asked, with a frown. He advanced to the table. "To my knowledge I have never allowed my light to shine at court. Have you ever seen me touch the keys of the piano in the presence of the courtiers ? But you see," he turned to Herr von Gerold— "because a mere report is circulated, that in the seclusion of my chamber, I sacrifice to my gods, Bach and Beethoven—they are trying to bind me in this weak spot ; not for my sake—God forbid ! Were it not for my little daughter

I could live comfortably among the heathen or elsewhere. They would not seek for me ; but they want the child in the Residence, and therefore His Highness graciously wishes to make me intendant of the court theater." He laughed in a forced manner. "An excellent idea !—I am to take into my hand the wires of the visionary world of boards and pasteboard ; am to swallow the dust of scenery and theatrical government ; am to contend with refractory singers and dancers, in order to keep myself above the waves of intrigue—God forbid ! I would rather retire altogether at Neuhaus or to my estate in Saxony, hunt, sow, reap, and go, if must be, behind the plow ; then I can at least say, I am healthy in body and soul."

He took one of the filled glasses from the salver which Claudine offered him. "And you? I only see two glasses," said he to her. "At court you always cleverly managed to avoid clinking glasses with me—I understood it, the Montagues and Capulets were face to face ; but to-day it is different. I am here as your guest, and if you will not allow me to drink your health, I must beg of you to clink glasses with me in memory of a lady whom we both love, to the well-being of our revered Dowager Duchess !"

Claudine hastened to fetch a glass, and soon after through the garden rang the silvery tone of the three glasses.

"The old trees will be surprised," said Herr von Gerold merrily, with a glance at the highest tree-tops, which had witnessed the burning of the cloister of St. Walpurgis and of the patron saint.

"Since the Bacchanal which the iconoclasts celebrated at the wine-butts of the burning cloister, no clinking of glasses has surely been heard here. But it sounded so clear and pure, so delightful, that I should once more like to clink, and to one whom I honor very much, though I have not been personally near him. He is a noble man, a zealous patron of the arts and sciences ; he loves poetry —our Duke, God save him !" At this instant the golden Rhine wine spurted like a gleaming ray of sunshine in the air, and Baron Lothar's glass lay shivered upon the stones.

"Ah, pardon, I was very awkward ! How clumsy I am, to be sure !" He apologized with a sarcastic smile.

"The old fellow there"—he pointed to the linden-bough against which his arm had struck,—"is wonderfully strong, he does not give way. . . Well, His Highness will live without my wishes." He drew on his glove and extended his hand for his whip. "I have repaid your hospitality badly ; my immediate self-exile shall be my atonement. . . I should gladly have remained in this delightful retreat, and I should have liked to have obtained a glance at the bell-room, but we will leave that for another time, if I may. . . And now come here, little vagabond. . ." He raised Elizabeth, who sat quietly upon a willow-chair on the balcony and watched with astonishment the unusually loud conversation upon the platform, and kissed her. "You will not go out there again." He pointed to the garden gate with a severe air. "When you want to visit the 'strawberry lady,' send me word : I will fetch you with the carriage as often as you like.—Do you under- , stand me ? "

She nodded silently, with a timid glance, and again tried to reach the ground.

"Was uncle angry ? " she asked her father, when he returned from the entrance to the garden to which he had escorted his departing guest.

"No, my child, not angry, only somewhat whimsical," he replied. "The poor glass and the fine Rhine wine ! " He looked with a sad smile at the remnants. "And the poor slandered linden branch, which really did not do it ! " he added, roguishly. "But say, Claudine,—was not Lothar the Duke's favorite ? " he asked his sister, who stood quietly by, with head slightly bent forward as if still listening to the tramp of the horse's hoofs, which had long since died away.

"He is still," she replied, with averted face. "You hear, they are trying to attract him to the Residence."

Her voice sounded unsteady, and about her quivering lips hovered a forced smile, as she passed her brother on her way to the kitchen to prepare the noon meal. In the center of the sitting-room stood the table already set with its three covers. Yes, they were old-fashioned, bent pewter plates from which they ate. At the time of her removal to her widow's seat, the grandmother had left all her silver-ware behind her—the large, fine, silver treasure should not be divided—and she took with her only her inherited old English pewter, "just right and suitable for a widow living alone in her last days on earth," she had said. And with her scanty income, to which she later on limited herself in the face of the pecuniary circumstances of her grandson, it was practical to use unbreakable ware. The knives and forks beside the pewter plates had black, worn-off, wooden handles, and, as a protection for the table-cloth, an oilcloth cover lay in the center of the table—all simply plain and economical, though scrupulously clean.

He had noticed that in passing, and it was well so. No comedy could be thought of there ; the entire drift of the household proved the adaptation of the possessors to their circumstances ; he now knew that her flight had been serious.

The ducal house possessed various castles around the country, beautiful, old-fashioned castles with magnificent gardens and fine grounds ; but they lay principally in the neighborhood of the cities, or upon flat land, where the extremest park roads bordered upon broad fields, and the woods began so far away that they seamed the horizon like a dark streak. The ancestors loved the sunny plain, and avoided the dark mountain forest in the buildings, and, though the majority, too, were enthusiastic sportsmen, and, for the sake of shooting, often remained for weeks in the forests, a few had, scattered here and there, very primitive little hunting-boxes for their night-quarters and for their meals taken at such times.

The Altenstein Geroldcourt, with its neighboring forests and bracing mountain air, was a valuable acquisition for the Duke, as all in the country agreed. For the three delicate young Princes, the Duke's sons, and the extremely delicate health of his wife, such a place in the heated season was very desirable, and therefore did they understand the zeal with which Geroldcourt was prepared for the reception of its princely owners. The young Duchess herself seemed in passionate haste ; no baths, no change of climate had been able to improve her failing strength ; she now hoped everything from her stay in the forest. Therefore, too, at the command of the Duke, all the

buildings were simply furnished on the outside; not a
stone in the walls should be touched, not a garden-bed
changed, and when a plan was presented to His Highness
of a fine fountain, in place of the still excellent but
too "countrified" one in the court, he had rejected it with
a frown, and had given strict orders that the fountain remain as it was.   He was, too, very angry when he
learned that the hawthorns and syringas in the corners of
the court had been extirpated, root and branch, to make
more light for the darkened rooms of the ladies-in-waiting,
and there were many envious ones among the court
servants when the Duke named old Friedrich Kern, who
had been coachman, gardener, and lackey, in one person,
to the last Altenstein Lord as *Castellan* of Geroldcourt.
His Highness rightfully thought that such a faithful servant would be the best guardian of his new possessions.

So Geroldcourt remained practically unchanged; for
in the interior, too, many a costly piece of furniture which
the Duke had bought in through a third hand was again
put in its old place; it was so with the fine Meissen
porcelain set, with its much-admired candelabra, in one
of the handsome salons; so with the Rococo furniture,
which bore the initials and the arms of the Altensteins
wrought in mother-o'-pearl and silver.   To be sure, all
the rest was new, and the silent sleepers beneath the
house chapel would have, had they wandered about in
spirit, had difficulty in finding their way around their
former home: princely wealth and artistic taste unfolded
such refined luxury in all rooms.

Day and night work was done at Geroldcourt, and
the trains had promptly brought what Paris and Vienna
could offer in furniture and objects of decoration.   It was
possible that the Court would remove to the Paulinenthal
at the end of July.

In the mean time, changes were made at the Owl's
Nest.   Heinemann had done "a fine business," he said,
rubbing his hands with delight.   One day a wagon drew
up at the garden gate, and that which the industry of bees
and nuns had gathered together ascended from the night
of centuries in the depths of the earth to God's free sunlight, and went out into the world, to be of use to mankind; and when, afterward, Heinemann laid a large number of bank notes upon the table in front of his young

mistress, he said, with the roguish twinkle in his eyes
which suited his broad, true-hearted face so well : "One
might now spread the butter upon the rolls at tea-time
somewhat thicker, and put a larger piece of meat in the
kettle, not to speak of the new curtains which must now
be obtained, for so many eyes were turned from the road
towards the best corner-room.

Yes, there was more passing by, and Fräulein Lindenmeyer had her spectacles pushed up more frequently on
her brow than they sat on her sharp nose. She now often
dropped stitches, and could not read uninterruptedly any
more, so much was passing on the road, she complained ;
but at those words her whole face beamed, for although
the solitude of the woods was so beautiful, so celestially
beautiful, the poets would not have sung them so entirely
without reason ; but certainly at times, when for a whole
day not even a cartload of wood, nor even the butter-
woman, came past from the village, it was "a very little
bit lonesome."

The three little Princes arrived first with their suite and
servants, and the road to the Owl's Nest must have
pleased them especially, for they passed daily. It was,
indeed, a delight for the old Mamsell, knitting at the window, to see the young Princes riding past on fine ponies ;
and it was almost as delightful when the magnificent
equipage came in sight from Neuhaus ; one could watch
them comfortably and with enjoyment, for they rode
slowly, very slowly. Inside sat handsome Frau von
Berg, with the poor little shadow, the daughter of Princess
Katharina, upon her lap, and Baron Lothar drove his child
himself.

On the other hand, Heinemann was always busy with
his rose-bushes when the carriage came in sight ; then he
neither heard nor saw, and persistently turned his back to
the chaussée, for he detested the corpulent woman who
reclined among the silken cushions, as if she were a
Princess herself. He had seen with his own eyes that, as
his young mistress in her white "Sunday gown," as
beautiful as an angel, stood upon the balcony, she turned
her head away as quickly as if a poisonous toad had
leaped in her fat face. And had she not, on passing the
first time, examined the dear old house in the garden
scornfully with her eye-glass, and stared at him (old

Heinemann), from head to foot, haughtily, as if he must,
at once, upon the spot, make his most submissive bow to
her? Well, she might wait for that.

Things were surely very different when the lord of
Neuhaus came riding by upon his fine chestnut. Then
the finest rose on the bush was mercilessly cut off and
handed over the hedge to the horseman, who always put
it in his button-hole. And Heinemann honestly confessed
he no longer understood his own thick old head; but with
the best of wills he could not be vexed with the owner of
Neuhaus; he liked to look in his fiery, commanding, soldier's eyes as he talked with him from the saddle over the
hedge.

Beate, too, had been to the Owl's Nest several times.
She always came on foot and remained to coffee; and,
though she was, as a rule, reserved with regard to her
feelings, she acknowledged repeatedly that she enjoyed
such visits the whole week. Then the two schoolmates
sat together and drank their coffee out of the "pewter,"
while little Elizabeth played around them. And, although
Herr von Gerold could not make up his mind to come
down and greet the visitor—he shuddered whenever he
thought of the meeting on the staircase at Geroldcourt—
he looked out of the window of his bell-room, and saw
how cozily his child sat on Aunt Beate's lap, how affectionately she stroked the large brown hands and let them
spread a piece of bread and butter for her. At such times
Baron Lothar came promptly, towards evening, to fetch
his sister; Heinemann had to remain with the horses
while the lord of Neuhaus greeted the ladies, and
ascended, as well, to the bell-room to bid the hermit good
evening.

Now the owners had taken possession of Geroldcourt
and the bright flag waved high above the roof of the house.
The villagers stood by the wayside and admired the magnificence of the ducal equipages rolling by and the servants who followed in less elegant carriages. Surely
there would be no vacant room at Geroldcourt! But the
Altenstein manor was a spacious building; every genera-
tion had added to the old seat according to their needs.
From its dimensions and architectural beauty it could be
given without hesitation the designation of "castle."

The afternoon sun fell full upon its imposing façade,

flanked by two octagonal towers, and caused the decorated molding in all its strong, and yet so finely-drawn lines, to stand out sharply ; and, through the high, wide-open windows the air, laden with the aroma of pine wood and forest moisture, entered the house,—truly delightful air ! "My spring of health !" said young Duchess Elizabeth in her low husky voice.

It was the second day after her arrival. The day before, at the physician's orders, she had kept her bed after the trying journey. But on this day "already wonderfully strengthened," she walked through the rooms on the upper story leaning on her husband's arm. And one recalled with a shudder the heated plain without, here where the sun did not burn, where his beams fell with emerald hue and softened by the green masses of foliage.

"Here I shall again be your nimble doe, your gay Liessel, shall I not, Adalbert ? " said the Duchess, seeking her handsome husband's eyes with a tender glance. With an effort she stood erect and tried to walk with a firm step beside him. Yes, although she looked so shadow-like and frail in her white house-dress, in her reflection in the high pier-glass, she speedily grew stronger here ; the feeling of strength returned, the pointed little face became rounded, and her form again assumed its delicately rounded proportions and elastic grace, this form which had once been called nymph-like ! Only two months in this invigorating forest air and all was again well !

She occupied the rooms in the eastern wing, adjoining which was the dining-hall opening on to the court, and only a common reception-room separated these apartments from those of her husband in the western wing. The last chamber of the long suite was his sitting-room, one corner of which opened on the tower balcony. It contained valuable paintings, Spanish landscapes, which gave out simultaneously the golden light and the glow of the southern sun. A curtain of violet plush falling on both sides in heavy folds shut off the door just mentioned.

In the center of the room stood a step-ladder. Old Friedrich, or rather, castellan Kern, as he was called, had been fastening a lamp, which had just arrived, to the ceiling, and on the entrance of the couple hastily descended the stairs. The Duchess paused involuntarily in the doorway.

"Ah, the poor, beautiful Spaniard lived here," cried she, in a low, vibrating voice. "And here she probably died?" She fixed her large, feverishly gleaming eyes with anxious inquiry upon the face of the old man who bowed low.

He shook his head. "No, your Highness, not here. To be sure, the gracious master had the room painted for her, and it cost a large sum of money; but she could not stay here two hours. The farmyard was too near. She could not hear a cow low, and if a lumber-wagon rattled over the stones, and the threshers worked in the barns, she stopped up her ears and ran through all the rooms and corridors, until she found a quiet corner into which she could creep like a timid young kitten. Yes, she was not fitted to be a housewife! She was always quiet and sad and would not eat; only occasionally did she break off a bit of chocolate, on which she lived. Towards the last, she occupied the summer-house, and, when the weather was fine, she was carried out in silken covers and laid upon the mossy ground, there where the forest trees adjoin the garden. Yes, there she liked to be, in the 'pale land,' as she called our good Thuringen, and there on a lovely August day she fell asleep, her life went out.— Homesickness was said to be the cause."

The Duchess entered the room, and her eyes wandered over the paintings.

"Homesickness!" she repeated, with a slight shake of her head. "She should not have married the German husband, for she could not have loved him. I should not have died in the remotest ice-desert, were I with you!" she whispered tenderly, looking again into the face of the tall man at her side, as with him she approached the door.

He smiled kindly upon her; she sank on one of the small, violet velvet chairs without a back and looked with delight at the landscape without.

"A fine view!" said she, folding her small waxen hands in her lap. "The Gerolds understood the choice of their family-seat better than our house, Adalbert," said she, after a momentary silence. "In all of our castles and country-houses we have not one view like this. Who occupied this wing?" she asked the castellan, who was noiselessly closing the step-ladder in order to carry it away.

"Only ladies, as long as I have been at Geroldcourt, your Highness," replied the old man, setting down the ladder carefully. "First the deceased councilor's wife until she went to the Owl's Nest, and then the Colonel's wife. Two rooms further on,"—he pointed to the door which led to the side wing,—"were our gracious Fräulein's."

"Ah, pretty Claudine's?" cried the Duchess, in a half-questioning tone.

"Yes, your Highness, Fräulein Claudine von Gerold. She was born in that room too. I remember when the little angel was shown to us on her white pillow."

"Mamma's favorite; do you hear, Adalbert?" said the Duchess smiling at her husband, who stepped to one of the windows and, apparently rapt in thought, gazed into the distance. "The swan, as her poetical brother calls her in his poems, the remarkable girl who left court to go into poverty, to be a support to her brother.—The Owl's Nest is the name of the woodland corner in which Fräulein von Gerold now lives?" she asked the castellan.

The latter bowed. "Originally *Walpurgiszella*, your Highness. 'My Owl's Nest,' the councilor's wife said, when for the first time she went through the ruins at midnight, and from all sides came screams and the clapping of wings, as if all the corners were filled with children. The Owl's Nest remained, although the rascals no longer hold sway here. In the tower which was filled with them from top to bottom, it is now quite cosy. Ah, yes, the tower"— he involuntarily stroked his faultlessly shaven chin—"the entire neighborhood has been talking of the old walls for a few days. There is the rumor of a large discovery, which they are said to have made in the cellar——"

"A discovery of money?" asked the Duke abruptly and anxiously, as, with a firm hand, he pushed back the violet plush curtain in order to see the castellan's face.

The old man shrugged his shoulders. "Ready money? I hardly think so. They tell of an enormous treasure, of gold, silver and precious stones in abundance. But"— a sly smile flitted across his face—"I know my good friend, old Heinemann, the scamp, he tells those who question him, so much that they cannot remember it all, and perhaps the whole thing is only a communion cup."

The Duchess' large, bright eyes looked in astonishment at the old man, like those of a child to whom a fairy-tale is told.

"A treasure?" she asked. Then she paused, and her smile gave place to a proud, cold expression; under the velvet curtain of the door opposite a gentleman appeared, who, coming nearer, bowed respectfully.

The lady bent her head almost imperceptibly and turned to the window; her delicate lips quivered nervously. The Duke's voice, however, rang pleasantly through the room.

"Well, Palmer? What have you again disagreeable to announce? Is it the fungus in the old rafters, or is your room haunted?"

"Your Highness is pleased to jest," replied the person addressed, "I merely gave you my opinion in respect to the purchase of Altenstein as in duty bound, and I trust your Highness did not misinterpret my intentions. However, just now I have only pleasant things to relate; Baron Lothar Gerold begs the honor of being allowed to greet his neighbor."

The Duchess turned quickly. "Oh, a hearty welcome!" cried she, and when, in the course of a few moments, Lothar entered the room, she extended her slender hand to him: "My dear Baron, what a great pleasure!"

The Baron took the offered hand and pressed it respectfully to his lips. Then, bowing in front of the Duke, he said in his deep, musical voice: "Your Highness will permit me to announce to you that I think of acclimating myself here again."

"It is high time, cousin; you let us wait a long time," replied the Duke, offering his right hand to the stately man.

The Baron smiled; the Duke seemed in an unusually good humor.

"Unfortunately, you had to come alone, dear Gerold!" cried the Duchess, again extending her hand, while in her lovely, fiery eyes tears glittered. "Poor Katharina!"

"I have brought my child home with me, your Highness," said he gravely.

"I know, Gerold, I know! But a child is a child, and only in part takes the place of a life-companion."

She spoke almost passionately and her eyes sought the

Duke, who leaned against a costly inlaid cabinet and, as if he had heard nothing, looked out of the window upon the linden branches which waved in the afternoon sunshine.

A pause ensued ; slowly the young Duchess lowered her lashes, and down her checks rolled a few tears which she hastily dried. "It must be so hard to die when one is supremely happy," she murmured.

Again a pause. These three were alone in the room ; the old castellan had long since crept away with his step-ladder, and Palmer, the Duke's private secretary, a much-envied favorite of the reigning lord, stood in the adjoining room behind a portière, as motionless as a statue.

"Apropos, Baron Gerold," the Duchess spoke eagerly,— "have you heard the story of the valuable discovery said to have been made at the Owl's Nest ?"

"Indeed, your Highness, the old walls have yielded up their treasures," replied Baron Lothar, visibly relieved.

"Truly ?" asked the Duke, with an incredulous smile. "What is it? Communion cups—gold ?"

"Nothing like that, your Highness. It is wax, pure, yellow wax, which the nuns walled up there when the enemy advanced."

"Wax ?" exclaimed the Duchess with disappointment.

"Your Highness, pure, unadulterated wax is as good as money. Nowadays——"

"Have you seen it ? " the Duchess interrupted.

"Surely, your Highness ! I saw it on the very spot where it was discovered."

"Then the feud between the Altensteiners and the Neuhausers has been done away with," the Duke said nonchalantly.

"Your Highness, my sister Beate, and Claudine von Gerold have been friends since childhood," replied the Neuhauser with equal nonchalance.

"Is that so ?" These words were a shade more indifferent, and the Duke again looked out of the window.

"Do you know, dear Gerold, I should like to see the wax ! " cried the Duchess.

"Then your Highness must hurry ; for the dealers are after it like wasps about ripe fruit."

"Do you hear, Adalbert, shall we not drive over ? "

"To-morrow, the next day, Elise, whenever you like— after we have assured ourselves that we are not intruding."

"Intruding? Intruding on Claudine? I know she will be delighted to see people in her retreat. Please, Adalbert, give orders for the carriage at once."

The Duke turned. "At once?" he asked, and a slight pallor overspread his handsome face.

"At once, Adalbert, if you please!"

She rose eagerly and approached her husband; she laid her hand beseechingly upon his; her unnaturally brilliant eyes looked at him with an expression as imploring as those of a child.

He looked out, as if he were examining the weather. "But the drive through the chilly night air?" he murmured.

"Oh, the delightful air of the woods!" she besought. "I am quite well, Adalbert, really quite well."

He bowed assent, and turning to Palmer, who entered at that moment, he gave orders for the carriage. Then, after having invited Lothar to accompany them, he offered his arm to the Duchess, who withdrew to her room to prepare for the drive.

The Neuhauser looked moodily after the pair; what had happened to the Duchess during his absence, to that, though frail still energetic, elegant woman with the tender, sentimental nature, inspired with a love of the beautiful? The woman who had assumed the duties of her position with almost fanatical zeal? She was merely a shadow of her former self, and the fire which gleamed in her eyes was the glow of fever; her once so charming vivacity had given place to a nervous unrest, which was proof of her ill-health. And he? The folds of the curtain had just fallen behind his tall, imposing, handsome form, the type of manly strength; a veritable ancient German, with his fair hair, with his calm composure and blue eyes; stubborn to an extreme in what he once resolved upon. Baron Lothar could not account for it, but he was reminded of a chase in which they had both participated. The Duke had seen a fine stag which constantly evaded him; day and night he hunted the game, accompanied only by one forester, and with unparalleled endurance he bore the fatigues of the sport. His suite did not see him until the morning of the fourth day, when he appeared in soiled, drenched garments and with muddy boots—during the night there had been a severe storm—he having shot the stag early in the morning.   Yes, he was stubborn in the extreme, and therefore——

The Baron's eyes were still fixed upon the violet portière : he only looked up when Herr von Palmer entered and advanced towards him with elegant ease.

"Permit me, too, Baron," began the dapper little man upon whose temples many gray hairs were visible, "permit me, too, to greet you upon native soil.   You have been too sorely missed in the Court drawing-rooms, for us not to be delighted to have you again."

Baron Lothar, from his stately height, looked down upon the speaker's sallow face, without the quiver of a muscle.   "A peculiar, a cunning face," said he to himself, as he gazed at the southern, sallow countenance, overshadowed by heavy brows, and the forehead which already extended over half of his head.   "I am very much obliged," said he coldly, turning from the little man to one of the brilliant paintings on the wall.

"How do you think Her Highness looks, Baron ?" asked Palmer, assuming a mournful expression.   And as the tall man, so absorbed in examination of the pictures, seemed not to have heard his question, he added : "We shall have a quiet winter, for she is a dying woman.   And then——" Lothar turned abruptly and gazed at the speaker.

"And then ?" he asked, while over his face with its regular features, flitted an expression so threatening that Palmer made no reply.   "And then ?"

At this moment the carriages were announced, and Baron Lothar passed Palmer without insisting upon an answer.

He sat opposite the ducal pair with pale cheeks.   The carriage rolled along the well-kept main road into the magnificent, fragrant pine forest.   The Duchess' pallid, sunken cheeks contrasted strongly with her dark red silk gown, and yet this face wore a look of delight in life, of a longing to live, of a thirst for enjoyment ; her colorless lips were parted over her small, white teeth ; from beneath the simple sailor hat, with its red ribbon, her glowing eyes sought to pierce the mysterious depths of the pine-forest ; her bosom rose and fell as if every breath must be beneficial to her.

"Yes, indeed, a dying woman !" said Lothar.   "And then—then ?"

The Duke, who leaned back among the cushions beside his wife, seemed to have eyes for nothing but the game-fence which stretched along the forest.

And then ? Baron Gerold knew only too well the secret which the world already knew ; it had taken unto itself wings and had flown to him in the secluded villa on the Mediterranean. He was not surprised to hear of the Duke's passion ; he had foreseen it and had clinched his fist on hearing the name of the reigning Duke coupled with Claudine's for the first time.

Her Highness began to chatter ; she talked incessantly of Claudine ; he was forced to reply, although he would have liked to have pressed his hand against her lips.

Behind them came the carriage which contained the Duchess' oldest maid-of-honor, Baroness von Katzenstein. Beside this affable old lady sat Palmer, smiling maliciously. That the Duke should already be upon his way to the Owl's Nest seemed to him over-hasty.

Suddenly the vehicle stopped. He leaned out of the window and his smile grew more malicious. At some distance in front of them stood the ducal equipage ; at the side of the road another, the Neuhaus carriage ; Palmer recognized it by the fiery steeds and the coachman's black and yellow cockade. Baron Gerold now alighted and handed the Duchess something white, covered with blue ribbons—his child.

"Ah, Frau von Berg with Princess Katharina's child," said the Baroness, raising her lorgnette ; " it is said to be a strange little thing. I am sorry for poor Berg."

Herr von Palmer sat down again ; he made no reply to the last remark, but still smiled. How rustically delightful it all was !—At length the horses started off and the Neuhaus carriage rolled past them. With incomparable politeness the swarthy little man bowed to the handsome lady under the gay parasol. She held the child upon her lap and her blue-gray eyes gleamed strangely.

"She is still good-looking," murmured the Baroness, returning her bow somewhat stiffly, "and, gracious heavens, she cannot be very young ! Why, Palmer, I think it is thirteen years since we first met her at Baden-Baden, when I was there with the Dowager Duchess and the Duke—it was at Countess Schomberg's. She came to the Residence with her husband; for change of air, she said." A roguish glance flitted over the old lady's kindly face. " I will say nothing wrong of her; it was but short-lived glory, Palmer; one year later the Duke married, and from that day forth he was a model husband."

"Ah, madame, His Highness has always trodden the path of virtue, as he does to-day, at this moment; who could doubt it?"

The old lady glanced at her neighbor's smiling face and a flush of vexation dyed her cheeks. "Spare me your sarcasm, Palmer!" cried she. "I know what you mean, but there is not a spark of truth in it. Claudine Gerold——"

"Ah! who is saying anything against Claudine von Gerold, the purest of our pure women?" he responded, raising his hat from his bald head.

Frau von Berg colored still more, bit her lips and was silent. That Palmer was an eel, he could never be caught, a Mephistopheles, a Tartuffe.—In her anger, she could not find enough epithets to bestow in her heart upon the generally detested favorite.

"Here we are," said he, pointing with his gloved right hand to the pediment of the chapel, ruins whose sandstone arabesque appeared like lace upon dark velvet. Above the tower of the dwelling-house, which rose from the mighty tree-tops, Heinemann's doves circled like sparks of silver, and under the drooping beech boughs gleamed the flowers in the tiny garden.

"Truly, madame," said Herr von Palmer, "this Owl's Nest is an idyl; a nook created as if for undisturbed dreams of future happiness."

On the gallery of the middle building a laugh was heard. It was not exactly melodious, like the laugh from a lovely woman's lips; it was rather too loud, but so hearty, so clear that even the man writing so diligently in the bell-room listened, and a slight smile flitted over his at first impatient face.

How it sounded!—So bright, so true, so sincere! It stimulated him strangely; he was reminded of a cool woodland spring which bubbles over stones and rocks. Remarkable!—and it was Beate, the "barbarous woman," who was laughing thus. He shook his head and seized the pen, but he could still hear the laughter. Below, in the shadow of the ilex, Beate was drying the tears which merriment had called into her clear eyes.

She was sitting beside Claudine on the bench which old Heinemann had skillfully fashioned out of birch-trunks, and was giving a lesson in the use of the sewing machine which stood before them on a green garden-table, and the former maid-of-honor's pretty, slender fingers were trying to manipulate the complicated mechanism.

"You look so comical, Claudine," laughed Beate. "Why, dear child, you have not had any thread in your needle for some time, and you are sewing with genuine fanaticism. Here it is—now, that is right."

The cheeks of the beautiful girl in the simple, light gown were crimson with excitement.

"Have patience with me, Beate, I shall soon learn," said she, looking at the seam. "After awhile I will be able to help you with your sewing."

"That too, no!" said Beate. "A house filled with women who have nothing to do, and *you* to help me, with all the work you have to do? The few leisure hours left you should be devoted to your piano and your easel. But I have designs upon some one else, and that is Frau von Berg. Do you think that person would knit a stocking for the child? And when one day I took her some of our finest home-spun wool and said: 'Here, my dear, you can make preparations for the winter; it is cold in the mountains,' she turned up her nose and said: 'Her Excellency, Princess Thekla, always saw to the slightest details of her grandchild's wardrobe, and woolen stockings were moreover unhealthy.' 'Is that so?' said I. 'Do I look ill? Or does the child's father? And we, my dear, wore nothing else when we were children but homespun wool and linen, and we thrived.' She did not venture to reply, but—her face! She sought to conceal her vexation, and then remarked very coldly that she had strict orders from the Princess. Lord! Why was Lothar so stupid? He is the father! But when I told him the whole affair afterward, he shrugged his shoulders and made no reply. If I had the over-fed child four weeks, you would see a wonderful change, Claudine; it would be as fresh as this little, plump thing here." She pointed to the child playing at her small table with a cup and plate which Aunt Claudine had given her from her own doll's house.

"Besides," continued Beate, "the healthy, natural mode of life is doing *you* good too ; you should just see yourself. Your eyes are so bright—and you have regained the pink tinge in your cheeks which you lost entirely at court. It is fortunate, my dear, that there is no one here whose head you can turn, you——"

With a smile Claudine bent over the machine and turned the wheel. She did not notice Beate's sudden pause, nor the surprised, almost terrified glance which the latter cast upon the road. Merciful Father, that was the red and gold livery of the court which was to be seen under the trees ! "Claudine !" cried she, "the ducal party ! Indeed, they are coming here ! "

Claudine, on the verge of a swoon, leaned against the seat ; with startled eyes she looked at the carriages, which were just stopping ; through the middle path rushed Time in his shirt-sleeves trying to take off his working-apron ; probably in order to don the old livery. Fräulein Lindenmeyer's windows were hastily closed, and Beate turned to fly, when her eyes fell upon Claudine.

" What ails you ? " she whispered, seizing the girl's hand. "Come, we must go to meet them, or are you too ill ? "

The lovely girl had, however, risen ; she hastened down and advanced to the garden-gate—with as much composure as if she were walking upon the polished floor at a brilliant court ball, as if, instead of her simple dress of raw silk and her black taffeta apron, she was attired in the court train of light blue velvet in which a short while before she had enchanted all who beheld her. Beate watched her with admiring eyes.

How gracefully her form bent in courteous deference, how humbly she submitted her brow to the Duchess' kiss !

Beate leaned forward in order to see the men. There stood Lothar, indeed, by the side of the Duke, and they were just preparing to proceed to the house, the Duchess on Claudine's arm. She quickly glided through the glass doors into the sitting-room, and from thence into Fräulein Lindenmeyer's room. The old lady was beside herself with excitement ; she was standing before the mirror, arranging her cap with its red ribbons, which made as desperate an effort as its owner, whose hands trembled so they could not pin it on. Fräulein Lindenmeyer presented a comical appearance ; she had put on her black bodice, but the skirt still hung forgotten in the press, the doors of which were wide open ; she trembled like an aspen leaf.

"Fräulein Lindenmeyer, do not excite yourself so ! " cried Beate merrily ; "tell me rather where the china plates are kept which belonged to grandmamma, and where Claudine keeps the silver spoons ? Then you may sit in the easy-chair by the window ; your toilette is just right for that ; and later on you can watch the guests promenading in the garden."

The old lady, however, was so completely confused that she assured Beate she could remember nothing at all that moment, and were her life to depend on it. With a smile Beate closed the door and ascended the stairs to the visionary, who had no idea as yet of the honor shown his house, and who saw and heard nothing but his own thoughts. She shook her head and hesitated at the door which led into the bell-room. A deep flush lay upon her cheeks as at his "Come in ! " she turned the knob, and suddenly her severe face with the marked lines was transformed into one of maidenly beauty.

"Joachim, you have guests," said she ; "put on your finest clothes and come downstairs ; the Duke and Duchess are below."

When he raised his head and looked at her with irritation and surprise, she laughed the same laugh he had heard before.

"Come, make haste ! Their Highnesses will miss the master of the house. I will come afterwards with refreshments."

Involuntarily he ran his hand through his thick, brown hair. That was still lacking at the Owl's Nest. . . Distinguished visitors !

What did they want with the poverty-stricken ? Ah ! Claudine—they had come to fetch Claudine !

He hurried out with a gloomy air. She paused a moment in the room and looked around, as timidly as a child entering a church for the first time. · Then the tall, robust girl stole on tip-toe to the writing-desk, and with a throbbing heart and crimson cheeks glanced at the open book upon which the pen lay. The fine characters were not yet dry ; there was the title : "Some thoughts about laughter." As if in surprise she shook her head and turned from the MS. to the open bookcase, when a smile again hovered

about her lips, but this time it was not roguish; it was a
smile of inward contentment, and smiling thus she descended to the dining-room, arranged fresh, fragrant wild
strawberries and pulverized sugar upon a tray, and, followed by Heinemann, who looked somewhat odd in the
long since cast aside livery of the Gerolds, but whose old
honest face was rendered solemn by respect, advanced
to the table on the gallery, just as the Duchess rose to
visit the wax-cellar, in which there was but very little of
the wax left.

Beate von Gerold had met the Duke and his wife;
when her brother married a Princess of the ducal house,
she spent three of the most wretched days of her life at
the Residence, where she was forced to pay and to receive
calls, to dine at Princess Thekla's, and, as she expressed
it, to "live through" a ball at the castle. Once she had
worn light-blue silk, once yellow satin, and had been extremely miserable in both, for the bodices were too tight,
the dressmaker would have it so. When she returned to
Altenstein she immediately put on her comfortable woolen
gown and declared she had rather break stones than
live at court. In consequence of the remembrance of her
experiences her curtsey was less low, and her face wore
the expression which Joachim described as "barbarous."

"Now to the wax-cellar, my good people," admonished
the Duke, carefully placing about his wife's shoulders her
red mantle embroidered with gold. Claudine took a large
key from the basket on the table standing by the sewing-
machine, and bade Heinemann precede them; Joachim
escorted the guests. She hurried into the house to get
out the spoons, plates, and a tablecloth.

She performed her duties with trembling hands and a
sorrowful expression about her mouth. "Why?" she
said, half-aloud, "Why hither too?" And she leaned her
head against a post of the old oaken chest which held her
grandmother's linen, as if seeking bodily support in the
storm which stirred her soul. "Be still!" she whispered, pressing her hand to her breast, as if she longed to
force her wildly beating heart to obedience. And she
accomplished her desire. When, a few moments later,
she prepared to follow the visitors into the cellar, her
grave, beautiful face was as calm as ever.

"Halt!" said a deep voice in the vault. "So far and

no farther ! You have nothing around you, and it is cold
down there."

Baron Lothar was standing in the dimly-lighted archway and extended his hand to her. "If you can conquer
your impatience a while longer, cousin," he continued,
and his words sounded almost ironical, "I hear the guests
ascending the stairs. Was not that His Highness' voice ?
Or am I mistaken ? "

She gazed fixedly in his face and he merely shrugged his
shoulders slightly. He looked at her so strangely, almost
threatening.

"It is better we should await them above," said he,
"for here——" He paused, for she had turned and ascended the steps which led into the house, and from thence,
without looking around, to the pleasant square. He followed her and leaned against the casing of the glass-doors
while he glanced at the simple table. Nothing there
recalled an ancient, wealthy family ; upon it were only
simple glass plates and thin, worn spoons. The family
silver was in *his* cupboards ; only the damask tablecloth
bore the arms of the Gerolds in the corners, a masterpiece
of the art of weaving. The old Frau had brought it with
her as a souvenir of the day on which it had been used
for the first time, on the day of her son's christening.

"Our arms," said he, pointing to the leaping stag which
bore a star between its antlers and which stood out like
satin from the texture. "This escutcheon has remained
unsullied for centuries ; not once has the brilliance of the
star been dimmed! To be sure, misfortune befell the
family ; to be sure some succumbed to the power of
Fate ; but up to the present day the men and the women
maintained their honor immaculate."

The beautiful girl started as if a viper had stung her,
and a heartrending glance was cast upon him from her
blue eyes ; but the words died on her lips ; just then the
guests returned, and Lothar hastened to meet them. The
Duke, walking beside Joachim, followed his wife, who
had taken the old Baroness' arm. Behind them came a
strange couple, Beate with Palmer, whom she overtowered
by a head's length. She listened to his eager words with
an expression of smiling contempt, and, arrived at the table,
she sought a chair as far removed from him as possible.

"And the whole cellar was full ? " asked the Duchess,

seating herself, and continuing, without awaiting a reply :
"Oh, wild berries, how I like them ! How much more
spicy they are than those which are grown in the gardens
or hot-houses ! Do you know, my friend," she turned to
the Duke, who was still standing conversing with Joachim,
"we will go into the woods with the children and
hunt berries ; a delightful picnic can be arranged. Herr
von Palmer, do you see that a spot is found where strawberries are to be had, but soon, soon ! We wish to enjoy
the fine weather here ! "

They seated themselves around the table and Claudine
passed her guests the saucers filled with fruit. She was
now at the Duke's place ; with a curt wave of his hand he
refused them, without glancing at her, and seemed to be
listening attentively to Joachim's words. She approached
the Baron. He too refused the fruit. Silently Claudine
returned to her seat and looked down upon the child, who
had stolen up to her and was leaning against her knee ;
she, however, did not start from her reverie until the
Duchess addressed her.

"My dear Fraulein von Gerold, you must come to
Altenstein often; we, my husband and I, have firmly
resolved to lay aside all etiquette here; we will live together as genial neighbors, have parties and pay visits.
We shall surprise the Neuhausers too ; yes, yes, Fräulein
von Gerold," she turned to Beate, "I must see your famous model household, and hope we shall likewise be able
to welcome you at Altenstein."

"It will afford us great pleasure to have your Highness
honor us with your presence, but you must kindly excuse
me," said Beate, in her deep voice, which sounded hard
and not very courteous. "My household duties will not
permit me to leave home often or for long ; it is only
entrusted to my care, I am merely there as my brother's
housekeeper. When acting for *another* one should be
doubly conscientious, your Highness."

The Duchess for a moment glanced at the speaker in
surprise; then her usual amiable expression returned.

"The Gerolds have all been faithful to their duty," said
she pleasantly ; "that is excellent and praiseworthy, and
I must accept your refusal. But you, Fräulein Claudine
von Gerold ! We can surely count on you, can we not,
Adalbert ? "

"Pardon me! What did you say? I did not hear, Elise."

"You are to second me," said she, "in maintaining that we count upon mamma's favorite during our stay at Altenstein, that we wish to have Fräulein Claudine von Gerold with us a great deal. Do we not, Adalbert?"

For an instant there was silence under the oak-tree; the setting sun gilded every leaf with a purple light; flickering lights glinted through the branches, and it was doubtless those which caused the sudden changes from white to crimson in Claudine's cheeks. "Indeed, Fräulein von Gerold," sounded in her ear in a voice which suddenly stilled the conflict in her breast, so calm and indifferent did it sound. "Indeed, the Duchess has talked of practicing with you in the Altenstein music-room." And turning again to Joachim, he asked: "Well, how was it? Did the man die of the wound—or——?"

"He is alive, your Highness, and as ardent a sportsman as ever."

When the Duke talked of the chase and such things, he was deaf to all other topics, as all knew. Palmer alone smiled incredulously, and looked at Claudine, who breathed with relief.

"If your Highness wishes it," said she, in a low voice, "but I have not sung a note for a long time; I have not the leisure."

A slight cough caused her to pause; through the trees came the first cool breezes of evening; the sufferer's usually so pallid cheeks glowed.

The Duke sprang up. "It is time for the carriage!" said he.

The ducal servant, who had been standing motionless at the garden-gate, watching the carriages slowly driving to and fro without, received a sign from Palmer, and very soon the guests were seated and the vehicles rolled along the street.

"We too must think of going, Lothar," said Beate to her brother. He nodded assent and shook Joachim's hand. When he turned to Claudine she had vanished.

Beate, who went in search of parasol and hat, found her apparently composed in the kitchen, busy filling a saucer with strawberries for Fräulein Lindenmeyer, as, she said.

"Well, where are you? We are going, Claudine," began Beate, drawing on her silk gloves. "To-day has been a lively one; I congratulate you on your neighbors; they will be very pleasant. Keep something in the house all the time, a few small cakes or some such thing; the mistress of Altenstein will come often; she likes the rôle, as did Queen Louise at Paretz. Ah, Claudine, I believe with the poor woman that it is fear, fear of death, which causes her to do everything she possibly can; did you notice, she can scarcely breathe? But I must go; corpulent Berg will be hungry and they cannot get into the dining-room; I locked it. Good-bye, Claudine, come soon and bring the child with you." She pressed her hand and left the room.

Claudine took the strawberries to Fräulein Lindenmeyer, whom she found still in her petticoat and cap with red ribbons; she had the little one upon her knee and was telling her a story of a wonderfully beautiful maiden who had wedded a prince.

"A Duke," corrected Elizabeth, and seeing Claudine she asked: "May I stay here a while longer, aunt?"

But her aunt did not hear her; she was listening to the rumbling of the wheels of a carriage, which rumbling grew fainter and fainter.

"Oh, Fräulein Claudine!" exclaimed Fräulein Lindenmeyer, delighted to at length be enabled to speak of the great event, and letting the child glide from her lap, as she rose, "what a handsome man the Duke is! Every inch—a Duke! As he walked through the garden beside our master, Schiller's words occurred to me: 'Es soll der Sänger mit dem König gehen, sie beide wohnen auf der Menschheit Höhen.' Ah, Fräulein, could but your grandmother have seen you sitting like *one* family in the gallery eating strawberries. Ah, Fräulein Claudine!"

"Aunt Claudine, I like Uncle Lothar better," chatted the child. "Uncle Lothar has kinder eyes."

The young lady turned suddenly and without a word walked to the door; then she ascended the narrow stairs and knocked at Joachim's door. She found him pacing the floor with an almost helpless expression upon his face.

"I have been completely disturbed in my line of thought," he complained. "Oh, my lovely solitude!—

Claudine, do not misunderstand me! You know how much I think of our ducal family and how much I honor them, how proud I am that my beautiful sister attracts them to our forest-nook. But, Claudine,—are you angry that I say it?" he asked, noticing the shadow on her face.

She shook her head. "No, Joachim, why should I be? But I am sorry for you, and we will tell them frankly that you must not be disturbed at your work by anything—do you hear?—by anything."

He paused and patted her cheek.

"No, child," he replied, "as a former maid-of-honor you know better than any one that such a thing is impossible. It was exceedingly kind of the Duke and Duchess to visit us here. A refusal, such as Beate made in her rough way, must not come from us. Beate," he continued, "took my breath away when she blurted out the reply. I cannot conceive how Lothar can listen so quietly; it would cut me to the very heart."

"But your work, Joachim? Rest assured, the Duchess would be inconsolable were she to learn later on that she had hindered you."

"She has a sweet disposition, Claudine, and is inspired with a love of the beautiful, and she is ill—very ill. Did you hear her cough? It made my heart ache. *She* coughed like that too, Claudine—oh, that dread disease! No, no, Claudine, on account of the ebbing life may the Owl's Nest be open to her at any time."

His sister made no reply. She stepped to the bay-window through which the ruddy evening light gleamed and looked anxiously over the tree-tops. No, she could, she dared impose upon him no fresh cares, she could not render him uneasy; perhaps the blind, all-oblivious passion was dead too? None of those ardent glances had followed her to-day, he had scarcely noticed her. She mechanically nodded her head, as if to oppose an inward voice. "Perhaps his gallantry, his magnanimity, have conquered, and the sight of the fading life——"

She might be comfortable, she might hope.

Her brother approached and took her hand. "Does the solitude make you sad, Claudine?" he asked, tenderly. "To-day when a bright gleam of your past life entered our house, it seemed to me so unspeakably pitiful; then the thought occurred to me that it was a sin to fetter you here, proud swan ! "

"Joachim," cried she, laughing, but her eyes were filled with tears, "if you knew how gladly I stay here, how cosy, how delightful this 'poverty' is to me, you would never mention such a thing again ! No, I am not sad, I am happier than I have been for a long time. And now I must go downstairs and prepare our supper, which consists only of salad and soft-boiled eggs, but you do not know, Joachim, how tender Heinemann's lettuce is."

She offered him her cheek for a kiss, and nodding to him once more, left the room. And the tapping of her heels upon the stairs and the fresh, metallic ring of her voice resounded in the ears of the man who stood at the window. Ah, if only her mournful eyes had not contradicted her words !

A few hours later on, the Owl's Nest lay silently and calmly there, as if the forest with its rustling had lulled it to sleep ; only in Claudine's room did a light glimmer. Its occupant sat at the old-fashioned writing-desk, which stood upon absurdly slender legs and had once been used in grandmamma's servants' room at the manor far away in Prussia. She had unlocked several drawers, and was examining letters, dried flowers and all sorts of boxes. Yes, this proud, beautiful maid-of-honor with the composed manner was but a girl like others, a veritable girl, with an uncertain heart and secret fears and hopes ; how could she otherwise have pressed to her lips, as she now did with tearful eyes, a scrap of paper upon which a few notes were written ?—They were only a few measures of hastily written notes and below them the words : "Wouldst thou give me thine heart, our secret should be kept." She was once to sing it at the request of the old Princess, and the music was not at hand ; then some one in the select circle rose to write down from memory the sweet melody, and she sang the song. She felt that she had sung well that evening. And when she finished she saw two manly eyes fixed upon her with admiration ; only that one time, never again. The glance had lasted but an instant ; then his eyes turned to Princess Katharina, beside whose chair he stood ; a gallant knight, always obeying the whims of his lady-love with smiling nonchalance. And the keen, black eyes of the little Princess looked at him so tenderly, as if they wished to repeat the words, but as a question : "Wouldst thou give me thine heart ? "

He had probably forgotten the circumstance long since ; or he would not, when she had spoken of his love of music, have been so hostile ; she, however, could never forget that night. It was then, too, that another pair of eyes had for the first time sought hers with that ardent, glowing glance, frightening her almost to death.

"Wouldst thou give me thine heart ? "

She sprang up and went from the writing-table to the window and back again with the old tormenting restlessness. Her eyes roved through the room as if seeking help, and she paused at the desk and looked at the tiny pastel of the cherished female face which hung there in the richly carved frame, above which was the stag, the star between its antlers, which, made of metal, gleamed weirdly in the flickering light. A bitter, melancholy expression hovered about her mouth.

"Mother," said she softly, "were you still living, I could tell you all ! "

She clasped her hands and gazed fixedly at the picture, as if she were uttering a prayer.

The next afternoon a severe storm rose from beyond the mountains and broke over the Paulinenthal. Old Heinemann with many a sigh saw his carnations torn to pieces by the storm, saw the water flood his beds and loosen and wash away the young roots of the newly-planted vegetables.

"Oh, Lord ! " he sighed in the kitchen, where he was, washing the dishes like a scullery-maid, "Only see, Fräulein, how hard it rains." He pointed through the window toward the mountains wooded with pines, where in several places a white column of smoke rose now and then. "The stag is smoking his pipe ; it will not cease raining for three days, you may depend upon it. If it only stops then ! It is raining very hard over there, and is very dark over here."

The child stood with her doll at the window in Fräulein Lindenmeyer's room, pressed her tiny nose against the

panes, and asked if it would ever cease raining. It was
nicer in the garden.—And the old lady sat beside her knitting busily, turning her head from force of habit to look
for passers-by, but in vain. Only the lame purchasing
agent, wet to the skin, drove past with her jaded horse ;
she had her dress-skirt thrown over her head and an oilcloth cover over the horse's back, and the water was drip-
ping from the vehicle.

In the sitting-room Claudine was practicing on the sew-
ing-machine, and her cheeks flushed with delight when
she finished one faultless seam. Yes, work, even the de-
spised, mechanical feminine needlework, is a blessing ; it
passes away many an hour of care.—Joachim was deep
in his books. It was ideal weather for composition, he
said at dinner ; and, as soon as he had finished his meal,
he returned to his MS. and heard and saw nothing more.

On the following day it still rained, and on the third
day still more. At the Altenstein manor it looked as
gloomy as did nature; the Duchess felt weak and ill and
coughed ; the dreary weather inspired her with dreary
thoughts of the future. She had essayed to overcome her
feelings by writing letters to her sister, but suddenly tears
had fallen upon the paper, and she did not wish the sorely-
tried young widow to be rendered sadder by word of her
troubles. She had then descended to the large middle
room where her two sons were taking fencing lessons.
For a moment the bold passes of the handsome, fair-haired
boys delighted her ; then the old faintness stole over her,
and Frau von Katzenstein was obliged to lead her back to
her couch. After a while she sent for the youngest
prince, a fine boy, glowing with health, who had taken
the last remnant of her strength by his appearance in the
world, and she gazed with blissful delight in his laughing
blue eyes. How much he resembled his father, the husband beloved above all others ! Suddenly she rose, and,
the child upon her arm, passed through the room to the
door.

Frau von Katzenstein and the maid followed her and
offered to relieve her of the boy ; with a smile she evaded
them. "I want to surprise the Duke ; stay here, if you
please." And on tiptoe she stole over the waxed floor of
the salon, which separated her apartments from her husband's, and paused panting at the door of his study.

It was delightful to have him so near at hand, to be able to go to him, like any other happy wife who carries her child to his father. She took the little one's hand and helped it to knock at the door. "Papa!" she cried, "dear papa, open the door, we are here, Liesel and Adi!"

Within, a box was hastily closed and the door at once opened; the Duke, in a black velvet house-jacket, appeared upon the threshold, evidently surprised at the visit. At the writing-table stood Palmer, papers in his hand; and on the surface of the table several sheets were spread.

"Am I disturbing you, Adalbert?" asked the young wife, coughing as she spoke. The room was filled with the strong, bluish smoke of Turkish cigarettes.

"Would you like something, Elise?" he asked. "Excuse this smoke, it makes you cough; you know I have this bad habit when I work. But come, I will go with you, this is no place for you."

She slowly shook her dark head. "I wanted nothing," and with a glance at Palmer she suppressed the words: "I merely wanted to see you, to bring the child to you."

"Nothing?" he repeated, and a slight impatience was visible in the movement with which he took the child from her. "But, first of all, come away from here!"

In a few moments she was again seated alone upon her lounge. He had work to do: he was listening to a proposition regarding the construction of a new academy to be founded by him at Neurode: it was very important. To her question: "Will you not take five o'clock tea with me, Adalbert?" only an absent: "Perhaps, my dear, if I can find time. Do not wait for me," was the reply.

It struck five and she still waited; then over the graveled garden-drive a carriage rolled. It was the Duke's; he was going out and in such weather! Oh, yes, she had forgotten; he had spoken the day before of driving to Waldlust, to the old ducal hunting-box which was to be renovated. Sadly she laid her head back on the cushions. How desolate it was in the strange rooms with the rain pattering against the windows, and so lonesome! The child was playing in his room with the governess; the Duke did not wish her to keep him with her long, lest the noise he made might disturb her. To be sure the doctor forbade any strain; but, when one is a mother, such an order is hard!—Frau von Katzenstein sat in the next room,

6

dozing or reading, but no one might just as well have been there; the kind-hearted old lady did not understand her, she cared only for the physical comfort of her "dear Highness," in this vieing with the maid.—Ah, that loneliness! Once more she took up the book which had slipped from her fingers, but her eyes ached; she could not read, it was such a dreadful story; one knew beforehand that the heroine would commit suicide, as was the fashion. But when one is sad oneself, and when the rain falls without so monotonously, as though it would never cease, one must not read anything that makes one sadder. Yes, if there was one soul to whom one could speak, as she formerly spoke with her sister, when they were still at home, from the heart. Yes, then it is cosy, when the storm rages without, the twilight shadows fill the room, and a bright fire crackles in the grate.

Suddenly a form rose before her eyes—the form of Claudine von Gerold in a simple gown, the basket of keys on her arm, gracefully managing her brother's small household. How calm she appeared, how happy, and happiness-bestowing! Claudine had always excelled the other ladies-in-waiting; not for the world would she have had little Countess H—— with the soubrette face and the supercilious ways about her at quiet Altenstein, much less Fräulein von X——, who scarcely ever raised her eyes, and never smiled; never could one feel a desire to form any intimacy with one of them. But Claudine—Claudine Gerold.—Suddenly she was possessed by a longing for the presence of the maiden with the grave, blue eyes. She pressed the button of a silver-bell which stood at her side, then she walked to the writing-desk and hastily scribbled a few lines.

"This letter is for Fräulein von Gerold. A carriage must go over to fetch her; hurry!"

She now grew feverishly restless. It might be an hour before she would arrive. She ordered a fire to be kindled in the grate and had the tea-table set near the leaping flames.

Then she wandered about the room, stepping occasionally to the window to look out at the rain. One hour passed, still she came not. There, hark, a carriage! She drew back, her heart palpitated like that of a young bride who hears her lover's footstep, and she was forced to smile at herself. "Christine would call me 'fanatical' again," she murmured, when to her astonishment Baron Gerold was announced : "By her Highness' request." She had entirely forgotten it. To-day?—Yes, it must be so ! Indeed she had asked him to bring her news of the rumored poverty-stricken condition of Wahlenrode, the village near by.

She was pleased to see him, and questioned him carefully —but between times she listened for sounds in the distance.

"You find me somewhat absent-minded, Baron ; I am expecting company," said she with a smile, as in the midst of an explanation with regard to the erection of a poor-house, she turned hastily to the window. "Guess, whom ? But, no, do not guess, then you will be surprised. Well, my dear Gerold, if you want to undertake the building, you can count upon *my* help."

"Your Highness is, as usual, kindness itself," said Lothar rising.

"His Highness," suddenly said the voice of Frau von Katzenstein, and immediately thereafter the Duke entered.

"Ah, how cosy, Liesel," cried he gayly, kissing his wife's delicate hand, .which was extended to him. "And you, dear Baron, do you know I just sent a forester to you? I fancied a game of *ombre* to-day. It is the very weather for the game—eh?"

"Your Highness has but to command me."

The Duke suppressed a slight yawn and seated himself at the fireplace ; old Frau von Katzenstein was busy at the side-table preparing tea ; a lackey went to and fro cautiously, and now took his station at the door like a shadow, awaiting the moment when he should pass the cups. Twilight came on quickly ; the faces of those present could only be indistinctly distinguished ; now and then a ray of light darted up from the fire in the grate and lighted up the Duke's face. He looked tired and his large, white hand stroked his fair, full beard regularly and repeatedly.

"It is really very lonesome here on such days," he began at length. "For a fact, the whole way, dear Gerold, we did not meet a soul excepting your sister. The resolute lady was walking, armed with umbrella and waterproof, as comfortably along the deserted, wet road, as if it were the finest May morning. No doubt she was going to the Owl's Nest, for she took the road to the right."

"Probably, your Highness; she does not allow the weather to prevent her paying her cousin a visit."

The Duke took one of the cups with the arms upon it. "Enviable!" said he half-aloud, putting an enormous piece of sugar in the fragrant drink.

"Her health, your Highness means? Indeed, none of the Gerolds know what nerves are; they have, as your Highness' favorite author said to his Uncle Brasig: 'Nerves like steel and bones like ivory.'"

"Of course I meant that," came from the Duke's lips. And quickly draining his cup, he asked : "Is it now your custom to sit in the dark, Liesel? Formerly you had to have light at any price."

"Fraulein Claudine von Gerold!" announced Frau von Katzenstein suddenly; simultaneously was heard the rustling of a silk gown ; a form glided through the shadowy room, and a vibrating, musical voice said:

"Your Highness wished to see me!"

"Ah, my dear Claudine!" cried the Duchess with delight, pointing to a chair. "Did my impatient request inconvenience you?"

At this moment the lamps were turned up, disclosing the handsomely hung apartment and those gathered around the fireplace.

The Duke as well as Baron Gerold rose, and both looked at the lovely girl with an expression of surprise. His Highness' eyes for a moment gleamed, then became as apathetic as before. But upon the Baron's brow was a dark frown which, too, speedily disappeared. There she stood beside the Duchess' couch, the simple black silk dress set off her slender, well-proportioned form to advantage. She had scarcely any color in her cheeks, and after a low bow to His Highness, she looked down at his wife with composure.

The Duchess pointed to a chair which had been pushed forward, spoke of the pleasant evening, and asked Claudine if she was well, she looked so pale. With her own hand she passed the young lady a crystal *flacon.*

"Only a few drops, dearest Claudine ; a little *Arrak* will warm you up after the cold drive."

The Duke did not resume his seat ; he leaned against the mantelpiece and watched, apparently with the greatest interest, the movements of the old Baroness who just approached her mistress with a basket filled with gay strands of wool, and who withdrew upon a wave of the eager speaker's hand.

He did not participate in the conversation into which the Duchess drew Lothar who was stationed behind Claudine's chair, facing the Duke, and who spoke with a peculiar accent as if some emotion prevented him from talking as usual.

"I think the *ombre* table is awaiting us," said the Duke suddenly, lightly kissing his wife's brow, and, with a slight bow to Claudine, leaving the room followed by Lothar.

"Dearest Katzenstein," said the Duchess, "I know you have letters to write : do not let me keep you from doing so ! You see, I have the most delightful company. Have the curtains drawn, the tea-things removed, and my couch pushed up here ; it is so cosy at the fire-place, notwithstanding the fact that it is the 6th of June. And, dearest Katzenstein, lights on the piano. You will sing for me ? " she turned to Claudine.

"If your Highness wishes me to——"

"Oh, I *beg* of you to do so. But first let us cnat ! "

The nervous woman, lying upon her couch, sought by means of the most charming amiability to induce her quiet companion to talk, but the girl seemed dazed. She felt as if she should suffocate in those artificially warmed rooms, with the memories of past days which peeped forth from every corner, which looked down upon her from every arabesque. In that large, handsome room, when children, Joachim and she had always received their Christmas gifts ; there the ball had been given in honor of her eighteenth birthday ; there, in tears and deep mourning, had she received her brother, who returned home with his pretty young wife, while downstairs lay their father's remains. At that time the octagon window had been transformed into a garden ; tender, blooming pomegranate trees had been placed there, that the northern home might not seem so dismal to Joachim's wife ; the purplish-red blossoms should be a greeting from her distant land, Claudine had thought ; and she had but succeeded in causing her young sister-in-law's lovely eyes to fill with tears. "Oh, how small these buds are—how fragile they look ! " she had lamented. How trying that time was !

Claudine's eyes turned from her reverie to the present; the Duchess' voice had awakened her, and these eyes were so fearful and heavy with unshed tears, that the lady was silent ; but a timid hand sought the girl's and held it fast.

"I forgot that it would sadden you to see strangers in your ancestral halls."

The words sounded so tender, so gentle, and the pressure of the tiny, feverish hand was so sincere ; Claudine turned away her head in order to hide the tears which dimmed her eyes.

"Weep on, tears relieve," said the Duchess simply.

Claudine shook her head and made a powerful effort to regain her composure, though she did not succeed altogether. What a conflict was taking place within her, and in addition to it, all the Duchess' kindness !

"Pardon, your Highness, pardon !" she cried at length. "Permit me to return home soon ; I feel that to-day I *can* not be the company your Highness requires——"

"No, indeed, my dear Claudine ! I will not let you go ! Do you think I cannot understand you? My dear child, I too have wept to-day." As she spoke the tears trickled down her hectic cheeks. "I feel so sad to-day," she continued ; "I feel so ill, I think of death constantly ; I cannot forget the terrible vault under the castle, the chapel at the Residence, and then I think of my children and the Duke. Why must one have such thoughts when one is still young and as happy as I am? Only look at me, dearest Claudine. I am happy—with the exception of my ill-health. I have a husband to whom I am dearer than all else, and such sweet children, and yet these dark, these horrible fears ! I breathe with such difficulty to-day."

"Your Highness," said the young girl with emotion, "it is the sultry air."

"Of course ! I am nervous, it will pass off, I know ; since you are here I feel better. Come often !—I will confess to you, my dear Claudine. Mamma knows my secret —since I have seen you I have longed to have you near me. But mamma herself was so charmed with you, that she would not listen to thoughts of a separation from you ; I cannot blame her, indeed. The Duke even begged for me, but she refused point-blank."

Claudine did not stir ; her eyes were cast down, and over her face for a second flitted a crimson glow.

"It is strange—dear mamma never refuses me anything! Yes, and now, dear Claudine, I have a favor to ask: Remain with me, at least while we are here!"

"Your Highness, it is impossible!" exclaimed Claudine, almost harshly, adding imploringly: "My brother, your Highness, his child!"

"Oh, yes, I understand; but you must at least spare me a few hours daily, Claudine, only a few hours! Give me your hand upon it. Only a few songs occasionally. You do not know how your singing delights me."

The Duchess' thin, feverish face was near hers, and the unnaturally bright eyes looked beseechingly into those of the girl. There was so touching a reminder of the dying life in that face.—Why did the woman make the request? And what did she ask of her? If she suspected—but no, she must not suspect it!

"Your Highness!" stammered Claudine.

"No, no! I cannot be put off so easily. I want a friend—and a nobler, a better, a truer one than you, Claudine, I cannot find. Why do you let me beg so?"

"Your Highness!" repeated the girl with emotion, bending over the hand which still held hers. But the Duchess raised her head and kissed her brow.

"My dear friend!" said she.

"Your Highness! For God's sake, your Highness!" rang through the room. But the Duchess did not hear the words; her head was turned towards the old Baroness, who in a low voice announced that the Duke would sup in the salon adjoining the card-room and asked where Her Highness would like supper served.

"In the small drawing-room up here," commanded the Duchess, looking with disappointment at Claudine. "I had anticipated our evening meal so much! We would have made such a nice *partie carrée*, the Duke, your cousin and ourselves!" adding playfully: "Yes, yes, my dear Claudine, we poor wives have to share the hearts of our husbands with a few passions: hunting and ombre have cost me many a tear; but—happy the woman who has nothing more important to weep about!"

It was nine o'clock before Claudine received permission to drive home. As she, escorted by the Duchess' waiting maid, descended the broad familiar stairs, she met a lackey with two silver champagne coolers, ornamented

with the arms. She knew that His Highness was fond of
impromptu card-parties with an abundance of *Heidsieck
Monopol* and cigarettes ; these parties frequently lasted
until morning dawned.   God be praised that such was
the case on this day !

Claudine hastened down the steps covered with a red
carpet ; at the door stood her father's old servant, Friedrich
Kern, now in the ducal livery, his honest face puckered
into a thousand wrinkles with delight.   She nodded
pleasantly to him and hurried out.   With a sigh of relief
she sank back among the silken cushions of the carriage ;
she had been as timid as a child lest some one might
come upon her in the corridor, or on the stairs !   No,
thank God ; she was alone in the ducal carriage, and it
was bearing her to her home, to her very own home !
Never had she felt such a yearning for the simple little
room.   For a time she yielded to the sensation ; then suddenly she opened the window and passed her hand over her
forehead ; the perfume from the scented cushions brought
back to her painful memories from the capital.   It was
the Duke's favorite perfume ; the heavy, fragrant scent
came from all his garments, surrounded him like a cloud ;
it had often made her dizzy when His Highness had flown
over the floor with her in the mazy dance.   Suddenly she
clinched her fist, and the blood rushed to her brain.   Nothing in the world brings back the past so vividly as perfume.

She opened the other window as well, and sat in the
direct draught occasioned by the rapid drive, her lips
compressed and her eyes sparkling with tears.   She had
nevertheless crossed that threshold again, she had been
forced to do so !   What had flight availed her ?   Nothing !
Nothing at all !   Were he to prove his words, he would
know where to find her anywhere ?

Her thoughts grew confused ; she seemed degraded in
her own sight ; should she not have repulsed the Duchess'
hand as abruptly as Beate had ?   Ah, Beate !   How
calmly and clearly she proceeded on her way !   At that
moment the windows of the Neuhaus dwelling glimmered
through the boughs of the lindens ; a sudden longing for
her frank cousin possessed her,—a longing to hear only a
word from her, to read in her eyes if she had really done
anything so wrong.   She pulled the silken cord fastened to
the servant's arm, and bade him drive to the Neuhaus manor.

Beate had just entered the large hall, a bunch of keys jingling in her hand, and behind her a maid carrying a piece of linen fresh from the spindle.

"What, is it you?" cried Beate in her loud voice, which echoed through the room. "Heavens, where have you come from this evening?"

She stood under the wrought-iron hanging lamp ; from under the black lace scarf which she wore over her head, her face looked out as pale as marble. "I wanted to bid you good-evening as I passed," said she.

"Ah, then, come in ! Where have you come from? Surely from Altenstein, judging by your dress ? I thought of visiting you to-day ; but in the neighborhood of your house I met Berg with the little one, and guess who else was in the carriage? Herr von Palmer ! Well, that aroused my curiosity. I called the coachman and asked to be allowed a seat on account of the weather."

"The couple were very pleased, it seemed to me. Listen, Claudine ; I do not know much about love-affairs, I have had no experience, but—I'll wager my head, these two will make a match."

As she spoke, she led her cousin into the sitting-room, and seated her in one of the stiff arm-chairs covered with brown repp.

"Tell me," she called from the other end of the room, where she was looking for scissors, thread, and needle at her work-table, "have you come from Altenstein? Is the ducal carriage outside ? Yes ?—Then, my dear child, we will send it away ! Our Lorenz will consider it a pleasure to drive you over later on." She cast a glance at the regulator which hung over the sofa between her parents' portraits. "Half-past nine in five minutes ; you can certainly remain until ten ? " Already she was at the bell-rope near the door and giving her orders to the house-maid who came at her call.

"Did you not see Lothar ? " she then asked. "The Duke's forester was here to summon him to Altenstein. They sent for you as well ? "

Claudine nodded.

"You are pulling a very miserable face, dearest ! " said Beate, laughing and seating herself with her needlework.

"I am not very well ; I would have preferred to have remained at home."

"Why did you not say so frankly?"

Claudine blushed. "I dared not—the Duchess wrote so kindly."

"Well, yes, Claudine, of course you could not do so," replied Beate, waxing the thread with which she was sewing on a loop torn from a servant's towel. "They have always been very kind to you," she added, "and the little Duchess is, notwithstanding her enthusiasm, a sweet woman—and so ill! Do you know, it would really have been unkind had you refused to make so slight a sacrifice for her. If you are afraid that your household will suffer during your occasional absences, make yourself easy, child, *I* will see to it."

With these words, she rose and busied herself at her sewing-table, as if she did not wish to look at Claudine.

"You are so kind," murmured the girl. Even the excuse that she could not leave her duties at home was taken from her. It was as if all were allied against her.

"But you have not yet told me if Lothar was at Altenstein," asked Beate, returning.

"He is playing ombre with His Highness."

"Gracious, that always lasts a long time! Who are the rest of the party?"

"Probably the adjutant or the chamberlain and—another, possibly Palmer."

"Ah—he! You are right! He said he was in haste when he took leave of me in the carriage. I offered to drive him to Altenstein, but he thanked me, he was about to take a walk—in this rain, Claudine,—when he accidentally met Frau von Berg. He preferred to walk. 'Very well,' said I, and let him walk. I was amused at good Berg's face when I came upon them; she looked as if she would have liked to annihilate me! The coachman and the nurse told me afterwards that Herr von Palmer had often 'accidentally' met Frau von Berg, and the nurse added: 'Then they speak *Welsh*'—meaning French—'of which I do not understand one word.' But, there comes Lothar! See the dog!"

The fine spaniel sprang up and stood at the door of the room, wagging his tail, a quick, elastic step drew near, and soon the Baron entered. For a moment he looked in astonishment at Claudine, who had risen and thrown her lace scarf over her head.

"Ah, my gracious cousin," said he, bowing, " I thought you still in the Altenstein drawing-rooms. His Highness broke up the game so suddenly that I supposed he wanted to spend an enjoyable hour with the Duchess. Moreover His Highness was exceptionally unlucky at cards," he continued, "which he took as a good omen : he is superstitious, like all intelligent people ! At any rate he called me 'Cousin' this evening, and that he only does when the barometer is very high."

While uttering those words he laid down his hat and drew off his gloves.

"Give me a glass of pure, cool beer, sister," said he then in a changed voice; "that sweet French Sekt and those strong cigarettes are horribly unpleasant. Are you going so soon, cousin ? "

"Stay a while ! " said Beate, and turning to Lothar she added : "She is not very well, but as the Duchess sent the carriage almost to her room, she could do nothing else but drive over." Herr von Gerold smiled and took the foaming glass brought him by a servant. "Of course," said he, as he drank.

Claudine, who, as he spoke, rose and drew her scarf around her shoulders, when she saw that smile, turned as pale as death. Suddenly she stood before him, erect and proud.

"Of course," she repeated with quivering lips, " I could not disobey Her Highness' commands. I went to her to-day, and shall go again to-morrow, the day after and every day, if Her Highness bids me ! I know I shall please Joachim by helping to shorten a few hours of suffering for an invalid, were she the Duchess or the poor woman who works by the day in our garden."

She paused abruptly, but it was as if she made an effort to keep from saying more.

"Send for the carriage, Beate," she then besought, "it is time for me to go."

For a moment the smile had vanished from Lothar's face, but it now again trembled about his mouth. He bowed low in token of assent. "Permit me to accompany you," said he, taking up his hat.

"Thank you, I prefer to be alone ! "

"I regret that you must bear my presence another fifteen minutes, but I cannot allow you to drive alone."

She threw her arms about Beate's neck and kissed her.

"What ails you?" asked the latter. "You are trembling."

"Oh, nothing, Beate."

"Let me know if you are not at home; I will fetch the little one."

Again she drove into the silent forest. She leaned back in a corner of the carriage, she drew her dress closely about her and held the folds tightly in her hand, as if she wished to crush something in order to calm her inward agitation. Beside her sat Lothar; the light of the carriage-lantern fell upon his right hand, on which gleamed the broad golden wedding circlet; it lay there quietly, as if he to whom it belonged were sleeping. Not a word was spoken in that cosy, silken, upholstered space which shut in two human beings from the storm and the darkness of night. A storm of anger and pain raged in the girl's heart; what did this man think of her, what was she in his eyes? She could not form any opinion, for her own words sounded startling in her ears: "I shall go there again to-morrow, the next day, every day!"

The die was now cast; what she had said she would do, and she did what was right.

She leaned forward; God be praised! There gleamed the light from Joachim's windows. The carriage stopped and the door was opened. Baron Gerold sprang out and offered her his hand to help her to alight. She did not notice it and advanced to the gate. With a haughty turn of her head she looked at him once more, and by the light of the lantern which old Heinemann held aloft, she thought she saw him looking after her with a grieved expression. It was probably only imagination called forth by the lantern light. So grieved, grieved about her!

She reached the house breathless, and behind her she heard the rolling of the equipage in which he was returning to Neuhaus.

"They are all asleep," whispered the old man, as he lighted his mistress up the stairs, "only master is still working. The little one played in Fräulein Lindenmeyer's room and then we ate strawberries with cream; everything went finely."

She nodded to him with her grave, pale face and closed the door of her room behind her; there she sank into the nearest chair and buried her face in her hands—and so she sat a long, long time.

"He is no better than the other," said she at length, preparing for bed. "He too no longer believes in woman's honor and purity!"

What had her flight availed her? Did not he—just he—believe the worst of her? His smile—his words that evening would have proved it to her, even had she not already known it. Oh, the whole world might think of her what it would—if only her heart, her conscience remained pure! She would see that she need not cast down her eyes in shame. She compressed her lips. Well and good, she would show him that a Gerold could even tread the dirtiest, muddiest road, without soiling even the soles of her shoes. And hastily she turned to where the star gleamed between the stag's antlers ; *for her sake* its brightness should never pale!

She rose, lighted the candles, and looked around her room. How it looked! The traces of the struggle within her soul, her disordered thoughts, were startlingly evident in the usually so tidy room ; there a cupboard door was wide open, on the chest of drawers lay ribbons, needles, and combs in confusion, while several dresses were on the bed and chairs ; everything bespoke so clearly the hour of indecision through which she had passed before she drove to Altenstein. Aimlessly she had taken the articles from their places and flung them aside ; she did not, no, she did not want to go, and yet she had not the courage to excuse herself by a falsehood. Outside the horses pawed impatiently, and one fifteen minutes after another passed, until Joachim finally came and asked : "Why, sister, are you not ready yet?"

Then she went.

She began to put things to rights ; she heaved a sigh of relief when order again reigned around her. Yes, everything was in order ; she herself had decided in a moment of anger, of bitterest pain. But had she made the right decision?

Frau von Berg sat in her room at Neuhaus, at her writing-table. The door of the adjoining room was open ; within that room was the child with a nurse. The rain

pattered against the windows and the wet linden boughs
nodded ; the lady was wrapped in a heavy woolen shawl
and was writing ; excitement probably inspired her pen,
for it fairly flew over the cream-colored paper ; and the
characters were remarkably small and running ; a peculiar
handwriting, like the neat chaste-weed.

She was exceptionally ill-humored, and when Beate's
loud voice resounded from below, she clinched her fist
and glanced, with eyes sparkling with anger, at the door.
Who could promise her that the shrew would not, by virtue of her position, obtrude herself upon her again, to
assure herself that all was in order? Just as yesterday,
by virtue of her authority, she had forced her way into
the carriage and had interrupted an enjoyable conversation. And the worst of it was, that one was so powerless
there. The Baron had scarcely eyes for his daughter, and
where those eyes were she knew only too well. The
evening before he had accompanied *her* at night to the
Owl's Nest !

She glanced out of the window ; then she nodded as if
something especial had occurred to her and wrote on :

"Yesterday I gave various hints to Princess Thekla in
my weekly bulletin of the condition of her grandchild,—
hints, which, after all I have already told you, will throw
Princess Helene into one of her famous paroxysms of rage.
This young woman's jealousy is almost incredible ; I have
often told you of it.

"Moreover, my dear Palmer, I heard last night on
passing the sitting-room—I was coming from the laundry,
where I had a dispute with the housemaid,—you cannot
fancy the annoyance to which one is exposed when one
asks anything outside of the ordinary routine in this
model household,—as I passed, I heard the little simpleton, the *ci-devant* swan, maintain in a loud voice to her
faithful admirer, that she proposed to go to Altenstein
every day ! Consequently your prophecy has proved to
be true. How did you say? There is no better means
of depriving a timid lover of the last remnant of reason,
than by playing at hide-and-seek with him ! It would
never have occurred to me ! You say the Duke has
grown colder—*tant mieux !* But permit me to doubt that
somewhat ; I think I know him better than you.

"I hope to see you to-morrow. Mlle. Beate has an-

nounced a general house-cleaning. At such times she
puts a white cloth on her head and dusts off the family
pictures with a long brush. It is a fête day; there are
potato-dumplings with dried fruit for dinner; ah, the life
here is idyllic! I cannot stand it much longer, my dear,
I assure you. See to it that they do not remain here
forever; then my imprisonment will be over too. Say
that there are cholera bacilli in the spring water at Altenstein, or put a few dozen rats and mice in the upper
rooms; say that the ghosts of the late Colonel or of the
beautiful Spaniard walk, or that the lightning strikes; I
care not what, if it only drives out the occupants and I can
see the roofs of the Residence again; I cannot breathe in
this cow-pen air."

She paused here and turned her head towards the adjoining room, where the pitiful whimpering of a child could be
heard. An angry expression flitted across the full, white
face of the listener. "Oh, Lord, I wish I——" she muttered
as she rose.

"Frau von Berg, the child is very restless," said the
nurse.

"Then give her some milk; she is no doubt hungry.
What else can it be?"

"She will take nothing, madame——"

"Then walk up and down with her; she *must* be
quiet."

"I dare not take the child up as long as the wet compresses are on; the doctor has——"

Frau von Berg threw her pen upon the table and rushed
into the nursery.

"Be quiet—be quiet!" cried she in her loud voice,
clapping her hands as she approached the bed; her eyes
looked so threatening, so angry, that the child ceased its
noise only to scream the louder a few seconds later. The
cries sounded so pitiful, so beseeching, that the nurse
turned from the spirit-lamp at which she was preparing
the prescribed food, to the bed, while in the corridor steps
were heard, and the next moment Baron Gerold stood on
the threshold.

"Is Leonie ill?" was his first question, and his eyes
sought the bed of the child, who extended her arms to him
and became quieter.

Frau von Berg was confused, but she remained at the

foot of the bed. "No," she replied, "only either hungry or obstinate."

"That was not the cry of an obstinate child," said he, shortly and firmly.

"Well, it is possible she does not feel well," said the handsome woman ; "it has seemed to me for some time as if the child could not stand the air here ; just think, from the soft, warm climate of the Riviera to the climate of the German forests, to this keen, cold mountain air."

He looked at her gravely.

"You think so?" he asked, and his tone drove the blood to her cheeks ; she feared his sarcasm. "I am sorry," said he, "that the poor child was sent by the first physician of Nice, direct to this keen, cold air. She must, unfortunately, become accustomed to it, for Nice is out of the question, as her father is at present obliged to remain here. Moreover, my dear Frau von Berg, the 'keen, sharp air' seems to agree with her very well ; yesterday I saw the child creeping through the room and drawing herself up all alone by a chair."

Frau von Berg shrugged her shoulders slightly.

"What is that for a two-year-old child?" said she.

"Be logical, madame ; what we are talking of is, if the child's health has improved or not. The *age* of the child has nothing to do with this.—I should now like to give you some information which will surely interest you. Their Excellencies, Princesses Thekla and Helene, will shortly come to Neuhaus for a few weeks, to convince themselves personally of the condition of the grandchild and niece. How does Her Excellency know that the Reitenbach doctor is now treating my child? Have you any idea?"

Frau von Berg changed color. But she did not lose her self-possession and shrugged her shoulders.

"I have made no allusion to it in my letters to Her Excellency," he continued, walking from the bed to the window ; "I do not like this interference in the arrangements I make. Besides—Princess Thekla is a homœpath and has every pocket filled with pellets and drops. Have you really no idea, Frau von Berg?"

She shook her head. "None!" she replied.

He was not paying any attention to her words ; he pressed his brow against the window-pane and gazed out upon the road which crossed the forest like a gleaming white strip. There came the ducal carriage driving rapidly along. For a moment a woman's face was visible through the window, then the equipage disappeared.—Claudine was driving to Altenstein.

When he turned, he was strangely pale. Frau von Berg looked at him with a malicious smile about the corners of her mouth ; she too had seen the carriage. He did not notice her ; he stepped to the bedside of his child, who now slept, and gazed for a long time upon the frail, little creature.

As Frau von Berg softly stole into the adjoining room, he paused there. A hard, bitter expression gathered about his mouth. The old nurse behind the bed with its blue hangings stared fixedly at him,—did the master dislike his child, because she had cost the life of his adored wife, when she was born ? Yes, yes, it frequently happened so ! Poor thing ! such an innocent creature destined to be always looked upon with reproachful eyes ; poor thing !

The man at the tiny bed suddenly turned and went out hastily. The old woman bent over, and put her hand soothingly upon the child, who was sleeping soundly. She thought the door would slam, so fierce had he looked. God be praised ! although he indeed closed it noisily, the babe slept on.

Yes, Claudine was driving to court. She sat in the carriage with the calm, proud expression which her features usually wore. She had that morning attended to her household duties early, and after breakfast had slipped out of her Cinderella garments to don the simple but elegant toilette of soft, dark blue silk which had come home from the dressmaker's a few days before she asked for her dismissal. She was not vain ; she was forced to select that dress, for Her Highness had the day before mentioned in the course of conversation that she did not like black.

When Claudine entered the tower-room to bid her brother good-bye, he looked at her in surprise.

"How lovely you are ! " said he proudly, kissing her brow.

She looked at him anxiously and in perplexity.

"I have no other dress, Joachim,—and in this miserable weather——"

"I am not finding fault," replied he kindly. "I like the harmonious effect of your fair hair with the deep blue. Farewell, little sister ; go with a light heart ; Elizabeth is well taken care of by Fräulein Lindenmeyer, and I am writing. Why do you still hesitate, darling ? Have you any trouble ? "

She took a few steps forward and her lips moved slightly, as if she wished to speak. Then she turned hastily, murmured an "Adieu !" and left him. To him, the visionary, with the gentle nature, she could not present her case for decision. She must act for herself, that was the only right way. So she entered the carriage, with the sense of discomfort which possesses all noble characters when everything about them does not seem clear and plain, and yet with the firm determination to make her way through the perplexities by her own strength.

But what should she do ? The Duchess called—and she must go. If she were not confined to her bed, she had no reason to refuse ; a falsehood she *would* not tell, and the truth she *could* not. And was she not safest beside the Duchess ? In her *boudoir* no ardent, beseeching glance could fall upon her ; in the presence of the charming woman all selfish desires would lie dormant. She pressed her handkerchief to her throbbing temples, as if she could lessen the pain which had been there all day.

The high gabled roof of the Altenstein castle now rose above the summits of the trees, and, just at that moment, after many dreary, rainy days, the first rays of sunlight broke through the clouds and gilded the top of the tower, as if the old homestead was sending her a greeting of welcome.

"Her Highness has been awaiting you impatiently," said old Frau von Katzenstein in a low voice in the anteroom.

"Her Highness wishes to hear you sing a new song by Brahm, and she practiced two hours on the accompaniment this morning. She is terribly nervous and excited, dearest Gerold ; she has had a slight dispute with His Highness."

The young girl looked inquiringly in Frau von Katzenstein's face.

"Between us, dearest Gerold," she whispered, "Her Highness desired that the Duke take tea with her this afternoon, and he refused in a curt manner which might almost be termed unkind.—'We are to have some music,' said Her Highness timidly, 'and I thought, my dear, you were very much interested in singing last winter. I do not think you missed one of the small *musicales* at mamma's?' His Highness replied : 'Yes, yes, to be sure, my dear—but—I have summoned Palmer for a consultation, and as the weather is finer, I shall go to Meerfeld this evening ; you know, the doctor has strongly recommended me as much fresh air as possible.'"

Claudine turned her music-book in her hands ; she colored and seemed exceptionally agitated by the information. "Will you announce me to Her Highness," she asked.

"Immediately, dearest Gerold ; but let me tell you this ; the Duchess turned her back to him and said softly : 'You do not *want* to, Adalbert?' and he went away without replying and she wept."

The Duchess was seated at her writing-desk when Claudine entered, and she extended her hand to her. "It seems as if the sunbeams, shining without, entered my room with you, dear Claudine," said she in her faint, languid voice. "You cannot imagine how lonely one can occasionally feel among people, even those who should be—who *are* indeed all in all to one.—Just now I became restless and fetched my diary ; I turned over the leaves and felt soothed. I have had a great deal of happiness ; that is a consolation, and I am grateful. Sit down ; are those the songs of which I spoke?" She seized the notes and turned over the pages. "Ah, yes—*Constant Love!*—You must sing it for me afterwards, dear Fräulein von Gerold. Now I am going to ask you to take a short drive with me ; I long so indescribably for fresh air, and—thank Heaven !—the sky has cleared."

When, in the course of an hour, the ladies returned, they partook of tea and Claudine stepped to the piano. The Duchess lay upon her couch and listened ; the maid-of-honor sat at the window behind her royal mistress and watched her slightest movement.

Claudine's beautiful, soft, alto voice filled the room, which was in semi-darkness ; she had the notes before

her, it is true, but she did not use them. And so she
passed from song to song with melancholy delight. The
costly instrument stood, strange to say, in the same room,
on the same spot where once *her* instrument had stood.
The full, sweet happiness of her youth was revived amid
these surroundings. She did not know how it came that
Joachim's favorite song escaped her lips :

> " Aus der Jugendzeit, aus der Jugendzeit,
>   Klingt ein Lied mir immerdar—
> O wie liegt so weit, O wie liegt so weit,
>   Was mein, was mein einst war."

She sang the sad, simple strain with deep feeling, and
in the middle of the last strophe she stopped with a tone
which sounded broken, and after a couple of discordant
chords, struck mechanically by her accompanying fingers,
she ceased.

Then these words rang through the room, soft and
low :

"Adalbert, I knew you would come !"

Claudine rose and gazed at the tall man who was
stooping to press a kiss upon his wife's hand. She bowed,
at the same time grasping the arm of her chair, as if in
need of support.

"Sing on, Fräulein von Gerold," said the Duke, "it is
a long time since I had the pleasure of hearing you."

He sat in the deep shadow beside his wife's couch, his
back to the window. Claudine did not see his face ; but
she knew that the last rosy light of the setting sun was
falling upon her, which added to her confusion. She
made a mighty effort for composure, but when she began
to sing, her voice was weak and husky, as if her throat
were contracted convulsively. She stammered an excuse and rose.

"How strange !" said the Duchess. "Have you been
troubled this way before, dearest Claudine ?"

"Never, your Highness !" she replied truthfully.

"There are such cases from nervousness," remarked
the Duke with composure. "Perhaps you have fatigued
Fräulein von Gerold ?"

"Oh, that may be possible ; pardon me, my dear
Claudine, and rest yourself," cried the Duchess, evidently
concerned. She called the young girl to her to take her

seat in the chair from which the Duke had just risen, in order to pace the room, almost inaudibly.

"Sit so that I can see your face," she besought. "Indeed, you look ill; but now your color is returning. My God, I believe the Duke's sudden entrance frightened you!—Adalbert!"—she laughed, turning her head—at the moment he was behind her sofa,—"you are to blame for this sudden silence—oh, you naughty man, what things you bring about!"

Involuntarily, Claudine raised her eyes to the face of him addressed thus, in order the next moment to lower them in affright,—for she again saw that ardent, beseeching glance. It had flown to her over his wife's head, while his voice said calmly: "I should be sorry, Fräulein, were such the case; but I cannot believe that my appearance here can have anything terrifying or unusual. I——"

"Certainly not, your Highness!" replied Claudine, aloud, and drawing herself up. "I was tired, I had a slight headache. I am much better now."

"I am glad!" smiled the Duchess. "Now, let us chat. You are so silent, Adalbert; how did it happen that you gave up your hunting expedition? Tell me! Was it really only because you wanted to spend the evening with me?" As he passed her again, she looked up at him with blissful eyes, and without awaiting a reply, she chatted on: "Just fancy, Adalbert, our eldest boy has written a poem, his first verse; the doctor gave it to me to-day; he found it in his Latin book; do you wish to see it? Dearest Claudine, it is on my desk under the letter-weight,—no, there, under that with the Duke's bust. Thank you; will you read it to us? It is written in such a childish vein, and yet its meaning is so grave."

Claudine took the paper, stepped to the window, and in the dusk read the large, childish characters:

> " Wenn ich ein Mann erst werde sein,
> Hab' ich ein Wörtlein mir erkoren—
> Das schreibe ich in's Herz mir ein,
> Das niemals werde es verloren:
> Treu will ich sein, das ist mein Wort,
> Treu meinem Volk, treu meinem Gott,
> Treu meinen Freunden immerfort ;
> Treu meiner Pflicht, mir selber treu,
> Das treu stets meine Treue sei ! "

Claudine could not see the Duchess' face ; but she saw her extend her hand to her husband and heard a trembling voice murmur : "Your son, Adalbert !" And aloud she asked : "Is it not fine?"

He paused in his walk. "Yes, it is, Elise ; may the good Lord lead him so that it will never be difficult for him to keep his faith."

"That *can* never be difficult, Adalbert."

"Never ?" he asked.

She shook her head.

"Never !—What do you say, Claudine ?"

"Your Highness, there may be cases," said the lovely maiden, "when it costs a severe struggle to keep faith."

"Then it is no faith strengthened by love," interrupted the Duchess, her cheeks ablaze, "it is an artificial faith."

"Yes," said the Duke, half aloud ; the simple assent sounded peculiar.

"It is not faith at all, it is merely a *sense of duty,*" said his wife warmly.

"Faith in duty is doubtless the highest grade of faith, your Highness," said Claudine gently.

"Ah, that is a fine argument, my dear child," again interrupted the Duchess ; "a faith which has first to struggle with itself has moreover lost its significance. If, for example—*sans comparaison*—if the Duke "—she hesitated a moment and a roguish smile flitted over her face—"if—well, if his thoughts were occasionally—let us say to revert to you, Claudine, his marital fidelity would be valueless, were he to be the most faithful of husbands. Do you hear, Adalbert? You would have, in my opinion, already broken faith."

The Duke turned and looked out of the window ; Claudine sat there with horror depicted upon her features ; the Duchess did not notice it ; she laughed as if her idea had been a very droll one. And she continued to laugh with childish glee, as only one can laugh who calls a great happiness his own and jestingly speaks of a possible loss because he is certain it can never be possible.

"Claudine !" cried she, in the midst of her laughter, "how you look ! Do not fear, it is no high treason ; Adalbert knows how I often jest ! My God, how my chest aches now from laughing. Claudine, Claudine !"

The words were drowned in a violent paroxysm of coughing. "Water! Water!" she cried.

The terrified girl sprang up and hastened to the table, upon which a water bottle always stood. Frau von Katzenstein, who had rushed into the room, held the gasping Duchess in her arms; the Duke stood beside the couch with a gloomy brow; the sufferer grasped his hand convulsively.

She was exhausted from coughing and could not drink. Softly the doctor, who had been summoned, entered the room; Claudine stepped aside to make place for the kindly old man.

"Dear Doctor Westermann!" panted the invalid, "I am better now—it is passing off—oh, my God, I can breathe again."

It was dusk. Claudine had withdrawn to a window-niche; she was upon nettles, and glanced, almost absently, at the group in the center of the room. The Duke too stepped back, and his wife asked in a faint voice: "Did I frighten you very much, Adalbert? Forgive me!"

He made a gesture in the negative, in which, however, lay much suppressed impatience.

"Your Highness must lie down at once," said the doctor.

The Duke, who had approached the door, returned suddenly. Frau von Katzenstein supported her mistress, who obediently tried to rise. She nodded to Claudine.

"Until we meet again! I shall send for you soon, dearest! Good-night, my friend,"—she turned to the Duke,—"I shall be well again to-morrow."

When she had disappeared behind the curtain, the doctor advanced to the Duke.

"Your Highness, it is nothing serious; but my esteemed patient must be careful; there must be no exciting conversation, no discussions such as she delights in. Her Highness' temperament has played me tricks before this; she must live quietly."

"Dear Doctor, you know the Duchess—she merely laughed a little."

"I simply take the liberty of impressing it once more upon your Highness," replied the old man with a bow.

The Duke waved his hand with apparent absent-mindedness and impatience. "Good evening, dear Westermann."

Claudine started ; she drew back farther into the shadow
of the window-niche and watched the doctor leave the
room with strangely fearful eyes. She was alone—alone
with the Duke. What she had always sought to avoid,
what he had unmistakably sought to bring about, had
come to pass. But perhaps he had forgotten her presence ;
he was pacing the room with such agitation. Oh, he
would not see her ; the single candle, which had been
hastily lighted, was scarcely sufficient to illumine the fireplace, and she was hidden behind the silken curtain of the
window-niche. She waited in breathless anxiety, like a
hunted doe, which does not know how to escape the
huntsman.

She could hear the pulsations of her heart as plainly as
his footsteps upon the soft carpet. Then she started—the
steps approached ; a tall form stepped under the curtain,
and a voice rendered strangely unsteady by passionate
emotion called the name : "Claudine !"

In terror she stepped aside, as though in search of some
means of escape.

"Claudine," he repeated, bending over her, so that, notwithstanding the twilight, she was obliged to see the imploring expression in his eyes, "this scene was painful
to you? It was not my fault. I should like to beg your
pardon."

He tried to take her hand ; she hid it in the folds of her
dress. Not a word escaped her sealed lips ; she stood
there mutely, gazing at him with beautiful but indignant
eyes.

"How am I to interpret this?" he asked.

"Your Highness, I have the privilege of being the
Duchess' friend," said she, in despair.

A mournful smile for a moment crossed his face. "I
know it ! You are not in the habit of forming friendships
so quickly, but—you think, one should profit by every
opportunity?"

"So your Highness seems to think !"

"I ? Upon my honor, no, Claudine ! But you fled with
veritable haste behind the barrier which this friendship
raises up between you and me."

"Yes," said she frankly. "And I hope your Highness
will respect the barrier—or——"

"Or ?—I honor your reserve, Claudine," he interrupted,

standing at a respectful distance from her. "Do not think that I shall follow you like a love-lorn page. Nothing shall remind you that I love you as passionately as ever a man loved a maiden. But permit me to remain near you without being forced to encounter this icy coldness ; leave me the hope of a future in which the sun will shine for me too,—only the hope, Claudine ! "

"I do not love you, your Highness ! " said she, proudly and curtly, drawing herself up. "Permit me to retire."

"No ! One word more, Claudine ! I ask no confession of love ; this is neither the time nor the place for it ; you are right to remind me of it ! Can I help it that I did not choose the Duchess from love, that my deepest affection is yours ? I think it happens to better men than myself ! It comes without our aid, it is there and increases hourly ; yes, it increases the more we struggle against it. I do not know if you feel as I do ! I only hope so, and do not wish to live without this hope." He advanced and bent over her. "Only a word, Claudine," he implored, softly and humbly, "dare I hope? Yes, Claudine ?—Say, yes ! And not a glance shall betray how matters stand between you and me."

"No, your Highness ! By my love for my brother I swear to you, I feel nothing for you ! " she cried, retreating to the window.

"For another, Claudine, for another? If I knew that positively ! " he exclaimed, passionately.

She did not answer.

He turned with a despairing gesture towards the door opposite, then he returned once more.

"Do you think that all the considerations of honor would not have sufficed? Do you think I could degrade you?" he asked. "Do you think——"

"Your Highness is already doing so," she interrupted, "by speaking to me of love in your suffering wife's apartments."

"If you look at it thus," said he, sorrowfully.

"Yes, I do, your Highness,—I do, indeed ! " exclaimed the lovely girl, beside herself.

"Claudine, I pray you ! " he murmured, and again he paced the room so hastily that the lights upon the mantelpiece were blown hither and thither by the draught. "You know that my brother, the Hereditary Prince, died suddenly, shortly before my father's death, about twelve years ago?" he asked.

She nodded assent.

"Well; but you do not know that at the time negotiations were pending between our court and the cabinet at X——relative to the project of a marriage between Princess Elise and the Hereditary Prince, my brother. A decision had almost been arrived at, that is, my brother was to come to X——, presumably by accident, to see his prospective bride—when he died, and with the rights which I assumed, I also assumed the duties. At the close of the period of mourning, I went to X—— and married his betrothed."

"It was of your own free will, your Highness."

"Not at all. This marriage was but one more burden which the crown brought me. Princess Elise, who received me innocently and stared at me with her large, childlike eyes, was as little aware of my brother's suit as she was of the purpose with which I approached her.

"She is easily impressed, and with very little trouble I won her heart; at that time I was very indifferent to women; I did not know the best, and the others bored me. I did not fancy Princess Elizabeth from the first; I do not admire women who are always soaring in higher regions. I hate all exaltation, all these extremes of delight and sorrow. At first I was almost distracted by her tears. Later on I became utterly indifferent to what in the beginning had repelled me. I have always been an attentive husband to her, and have indulged her whims since her illness; I honor and respect her as the mother of my children; but my heart remains untouched the more affectionate she grows. I cannot help it; nor does it change upon reflection. Then I saw you. I know, yes, I know you judged that from a standpoint of heredity, and fled from my love to your woodland retreat; but it drove me after you with the old ardent longing, and I find you as unapproachable as ever, I find you the Duchess' friend." His face twitched. "Very well, Claudine, I will wait a while," he added; "only tell me, do you love each other?"

She was silent. A crimson blush mantled her brow, the blush of maidenliness. Silently she bowed her fair head.

"Say 'No,'" whispered the Duke, passionately.

"Her Highn, ss desires that Fräulein von Gerold bring Scheffel's songs into the bedroom, in order to read them aloud to her Highness," said Frau von Katzenstein, entering.

Claudine started in affright, and looked at him as if imploring mercy.

"Yes—or no, Claudine, is your heart already given?" he whispered, in a tone of command.

She drew back and bowed low. "Yes!" said she, firmly, passing him by with head erect, in her hand the book which she mechanically took from the table. She was to read aloud, now! She was half dazed.

The Duchess lay in her large French canopied bed, the heavy crimson silk hangings of which were pushed back. The whole room was flooded with a deep rosy light, the occupant's favorite color. From the ceiling depended a ruby-colored lamp. Beside the bed stood a low table covered with red silk, upon which stood a lamp with a red shade; in a folding Russia-leather frame was the photograph of the Duke and the Princess. On the opposite wall, in a heavy gilt frame, hung a fine copy of the *Madonna della Sedia ;* the eyes of the slumberer, on opening, would fall upon this beautiful picture first.

The Duchess seemed to have fully recovered; she lay comfortably beneath her crimson canopy, and smiled as Claudine entered.

"Take a seat upon this tabouret and read me the Thuringen songs, dear Claudine. Was the Duke with you?" she asked. "Was he very anxious about my attack? I am always sorry when I have to cough in his presence; I know it troubles him. Was he very sad?"

The invalid looked keenly in the agitated face of the beautiful maid-of-honor, who did not know what to reply. She seated herself, and stooped to pick up her handkerchief in order to gain time. How awkward her position was!

"Claudine!" said the Duchess, "I believe you all think me very ill, much more so than I am. Read on; I ask no answer. There, where the marker is." And Claudine read in a trembling voice :—

" Denn das ist deutschen Waldes Kraft,
  Dass er kein Siechthum leidet,
  Und alles, was gebrestenhaft,
  Aus Leib und Seele scheidet "—

"Do you hear?" interrupted the Duchess, "do you hear? I shall recover here, too! And to-morrow the sun will shine, and we shall stroll among the firs and inhale health—ah, my beloved home!"

In the evening, when Claudine descended the stairs to drive home, Herr von Palmer advanced to meet her and walked down with her. Behind Claudine's back he gave the maid a sign, and she vanished immediately.

"My dear Fräulein," he began, respectfully,—he could not have been more gallant had she been a Duchess,— "his Highness has entrusted me with the honor of delivering into your hands a note, which I do herewith."

He held towards her a note sealed with the ducal arms. "It concerns her Highness, the Duchess, and his Highness said it required no answer."

She was forced to take it, although she would have preferred to have thrust aside the man's hand. How could the Duke be so careless as to send her a sealed letter by that creature! In his presence she opened the envelope and read the few lines :—

"Claudine !

"You are an uncommon personage, and will, therefore, judge correctly uncommon things. After your last words, I have but one more request: remain true, notwithstanding, to the Duchess; do not avoid Altenstein in consequence of my avowal! It is not necessary. Upon my word, you can trust me.   Adalbert."

With note and envelope in her hand, she proceeded hastily on her way. Herr von Palmer followed her and politely helped her into the carriage; he even carefully put the train of her gown into the coupé as tenderly and cautiously as a mother caring for her daughter's ball-room finery, and only drew back, with a low reverence, when the servant closed the carriage door.

"Until we meet again!" said he, when the footman seated himself on the box beside the coachman and the horses started off. Then with a smiling face he took a paper from his right sleeve. "Such things should be held fast, beautiful Claudine," he murmured, glancing at the lines by the light of the lantern at the door.

He nodded with satisfaction, and, humming an operatic air, returned to the castle to seek his room on the ground-floor. There he lighted a Havana, flung himself upon the couch, and ran through the *billet* once more; he read, so to speak, everything that the Duke wrote, secretly, at a distance, by the motion of the pen; in an extreme case he opened the envelope. To-day, without this trouble, he had succeeded; for the Duke, before he put the note in the envelope, rose in agitation and paced the floor, leaving the billet exposed to his falcon eyes. Neverthe-less, it was well to have the original.

"His Highness seems to have taken a somewhat stormy course," he murmured; "and she—has rejected him in virtuous indignation, and threatened not to come again. And now he begs her, for the Duchess' sake, to give up this horrible resolution, and promises to do better."

"Time won—all is won!" thought he. "That is logical. Nothing can be said against it—hm! She is sensible; she will be content to crown his Highness' brow with roses; she will help rule; these women all think they can atone for their position by so-called good deeds; they wish to enrich the unfortunate whom they have in their power, wish to show the people that their beloved ruler has not fallen into the hands of an unworthy person; they are to kneel before them in adoration, and hail her as 'the country's guardian angel!' In their longing for self-aggrandizement the shrewdest of them see just what is before them, and this time *I* may be the one!"

He puffed the cigar smoke towards the ceiling and ex-amined the fresco upon it.

"She cannot bear me," said he; "she feels towards me as the innocent Marguerite felt towards Mephis-topheles; and some day she will say to her royal Faust: 'The creature in your service, I hate in my inmost soul,' and so forth. We must prevent that! I will not let it go so far, as that the Duke shall believe her or not—that I am a rogue. But now, attention! Berg will help me, she has extraordinary talent for intrigues; I am some-times inspired with horror of the woman myself."

"Supper is served," announced the lackey.

Herr von Palmer rose leisurely, cautiously locked the note in an enormous old writing-desk, which bore the Gerold arms, arranged his scant hair in front of a pier-glass, washed his thin, delicate hands in a veritable flood of *Eau de Cologne*, yawned, took his crush-hat and gloves from the servant respectfully awaiting him, and after casting a glance at the clock, the hands of which pointed to the hour of ten, he set out for the small dining-room in which were already assembled the few cavaliers whom the Duke had selected for his stay at Altenstein : old Chamberlain von Schlotbach, Adjutant von Rinkleben, who had the rank of captain, and Herr von Meerfeld,—"a fellow like a young dog," as Herr von Palmer described him.

The latter did not seem to take any especial pleasure in the friendship of these three gentlemen.

"Pardon," said he to those forming a group, "for keeping you waiting, I was busy in His Highness' service ; and a charming service, my dears. At His Highness' command, I assisted pretty Claudine von Gerold into her carriage."

"Zounds ! has she been here again ?" cried Herr von Meerfeld, with unconcealed astonishment.

"She has just left the ducal apartments——"

"You mean Her Highness' apartments," said the captain, with a trace of severity, while a slight flush mounted to his cheeks.

"I had the good fortune to meet the lovely guest in the upper corridor," replied Palmer, with a smile which spoke volumes.

"Ah, is that so ? 'Man wuszte nicht, woher sie kam, und schnell war ihre Spur verloren, sobald sie wieder Abschied nahm,'" quoted Herr von Meerfeld, laughing.

The captain cast an angry glance at him. "Fräulein von Gerold was with the Duchess, she sang in her salon, and then went into Her Highness' sleeping-apartment," said he in a loud, firm voice.

"Excellently explained !" murmured Palmer, with a low bow ; the Duke had just entered.

"I do not understand Claudine von Gerold," said the captain gravely, as after supper he walked with Herr von Meerfeld down the corridor at the end of which was their room. "It is courage in the wrong place ; she should avoid the lion's den. It is incredible with what boldness a woman stakes her good name, firm in the conviction of her safety and virtue."

"Perhaps it amuses her to dance upon the dangerous rope," replied Herr von Meerfeld; "if she makes a mis-step, arms are open to receive her; if she does not—so much the better. I think, however, it may become quite interesting: it is devilishly slow in this German Aranjuez."

"I might perhaps think so of another, dear Meerfeld; but with regard to this lady I must ask you to curb your harsh criticism."

"Well, do not be tragical, little captain," laughed his companion. "Do not lose any sleep over it, for His Highness does not now look like a happy man; he was vexed. *Ennui! Ennui!* This Altenstein was an absurd fancy. If one does ridiculous things here, there is some excuse."

Claudine reached the Owl's Nest; she had the crumpled note still in her hand. Old Heinemann, who for some time had waited with his lantern at the garden gate, received scarcely more than a bow from his young mistress. She entered the house before him, and when he followed and bolted the door, he heard only the rustle of her silken gown in the upper hall; then he heard a door shut and all was still.

In the tiny room up above all, too, was still and dark, as if no one was within; yet at the window sat a form staring motionlessly into the forest depths which surrounded the isolated house so densely, and trying to think calmly over the events of the day. "What took place?" she asked herself, to reply to her own query: "The Duke confessed his love for me and—I repulsed him forever; but at what a price!" By the avowal of her greatest secret, which she had not dared to acknowledge even to herself, because she could not realize, owing to the confusing throbbing of her heart, that she loved. Her pride rebelled at the fact; and now he, who that very day had made her an insulting confession, knew of it! Did the Duke suspect *whom* she loved? It would be unbearable!

Involuntarily she crushed the billet in her hand, and tears of shame filled her eyes. Hastily she rose, lighted a candle, unfolded the paper, and tried to smooth it out;

then she leaned heavily upon the table and stared at the
torn envelope ; it was only the envelope, nothing more—
the note was gone ! Anxiously she searched for it, upon
the table, upon the floor, on the spot where she had been
sitting ; she shook out her cloak and the folds of her dress ;
finally she took the candle-stick and hunted on the stairs
—but nothing was there ! Like a thief she stole to the
door, pushed back the bolt, looked on the threshold and
the sandstone steps—nothing there either ! In her anxiety,
she walked down the garden-path to the gate, shielding
the flickering light with her hand ; possibly she had
dropped the note on alighting. The gate, leading to the
road, creaked as she opened it ; the light looked ghostly
on the road—she could see nothing white. Carefully she
looked among the whitethorn bushes at the side of the
gate—nothing ! Suddenly the candle flickered and went
out and left her in the dark ; so deep did the darkness
seem to her eyes accustomed to the light, that for a
moment she stood there helplessly, and could not decide
which way to turn in order to reach the garden.

Ah, yes ! There above her window glimmered Joachim's student lamp, sending out a faint ray of light into
the garden and upon the road. If he could suspect how
she stood without, anguish and indignation in her heart !
She really envied him the peace of his small room, into
which no storm from without penetrated ; his tiny bark lay
in harbor, while *hers* was tossed upon the stormy sea,
and where it would at length find a haven, God alone
knew ! Involuntarily she turned and looked yearningly
over the dark mountains in the direction in which Neuhaus lay, and just at that instant the clouds broke and
one star shone forth brightly. She smiled amid her tears ;
it seemed to her like a promise of comfort, of happiness,
like a good omen.

Suddenly she started and rushed through the open gate.
Upon the road could be heard the tramp of a horse's hoofs,
coming nearer and nearer ; it was a hasty step, and now
the rider passed close by her, in the glimmer of light ; he
paused and looked up at the tower-window. As if seeking support, she clutched at the gate and looked over it—
Lothar ! What did he want ?

An almost bewildering sense of bliss stole over her ; the
candle fell from her hands, which were clasped. Did she

see aright? Was it really he? What did he want? Had
he come to glance at her window? Merciful Father, a
sign that she might know she was not dreaming, that it
was reality!

He turned his horse, and slowly rode back; the darkness again swallowed up his form : only the tramp of the
horse's hoofs resounded for some time in the ears of the
trembling girl, until she finally crept back to the house.

She no longer remembered the lost note ; indeed, she
could not think ; her eyes burned, and her lips were
parched ; her temples throbbed painfully. "Rest!
Rest!" she murmured, burying her hot brow among the
pillows, after having extinguished the lamp :—"Rest!
Sleep!"

On the following day there was unusual bustle at Neuhaus. On the ground floor next the sitting-room, to the
left of the large hall in the lofty, spacious dining-room,
stood a table which differed materially from the one usually
set there. While it, as a rule, was covered with a spot-
lessly white, but rather coarse tablecloth, with napkins of
the same quality, on this especial day it wore a dress of
gleaming damask reaching almost to the floor, which was
highly polished. The simple set of English stone-ware
with a blue border was replaced by costly Meissen china,
which for years had been the pride of the Neuhaus china-
closet ; beautifully-shaped dishes containing fruits and
confections took the place of the pewter baskets in which
dessert was generally served, did it consist of early pears
or winter apples or pastry ; and in the place of the stout
Solingen knives and forks with horn handles were silver
ones which gleamed as if new from the shop, and which
bore the arms and initials of the Gerolds, and a date which
would have told their old age, had not their odd form already done so.

The arms of the enormous crystal candelabrum over
the table, which was laid for seven, held yellow wax
candles, as did the candelabra upon the walls. On the
large, oaken sideboard silver and cut-glass sparkled and
gleamed ; in astonishment, the sun, which daily at this
hour cast a glance into the room, shone upon the splendor,
diffused many-colored lights, and played on the brown hair

8

upon the white brow of Beate, who was busy putting
flowers on the table in a couple of vases.

"Will you stand up?" she muttered angrily to herself,
as a few wallflowers fell to one side. "There, that's it!"
And amid the variegated magnificence she planted a red
rose; then examining the artistic structure, she handed it
to the housemaid standing beside her. "Take it to
Frau von Berg, Sophie; she must take it to Princess
Thekla's room; your master has given the order. Come
back immediately and dust all the chairs again and close
the blinds; the sun is coming!"

Beate now approached the table once more and paused
with a shake of her head at the seat which she, according
to Lothar's request, was to occupy by the side of Her Excellency, Princess Thekla; to-day for the first time and
then daily for four weeks. How would she stand it?—
There lay the soup-ladle, the symbol of her housewifely
dignity; Lothar desired that she exercise that office as
usual, "for we are at Neuhaus, my dear Beate, not at
court, and nothing in the world is more distasteful to me
than the carrying about of filled soup-plates, they so easily
run over."

That was, too, the only thing he had given orders with
respect to, in view of the arrival of his aristocratic visitors;
everything else he had left to her sensible head and her
skillful hands, and had replied to all questions : "You will
manage all right, do just as you please."

She had mastered the enormous undertaking. She had
tied a white cloth over her glossy brown hair, and in her
house-dress and apron, with her bunch of keys and dust-
broom, had gone about the house, and made the servants
"take to their legs," as she expressed it; move furniture,
put up curtains, spread carpets on stairs and in corridors,
and had taken the best she had from chests and presses.
Now all was done; she could rest a few hours before she
would be obliged to receive her guests.

The entire upper floor had been placed at the disposal
of Lothar's august mother-in-law and sister-in-law; the
maid-of-honor was given a neat room next Frau von
Berg, the gentleman-in-waiting with the chamberlain was
housed in the garden pavilion, and Her Highness' maid in
the neighborhood of her mistress. Lothar retained his
room to the right of the hall; Beate's cosy, old-fashioned

sitting and bedrooms were to remain entirely separate; *one* refuge they surely must have.

Beate walked down the corridor and approached the door of her sitting-room; a humorous expression for a moment lurked about her full mouth; then she took a piece of chalk from the key-basket, wrote upon the brown wainscoting "No admittance!" and still smiling, entered her domain. For a while she sat in an easy-chair; then she sprang up and hastened into her bedroom. In a few moments she came back; she had put on a large, brown straw hat and a light pelerine. As she went out, she drew on a pair of cotton gloves, and buttoning the same, she entered the kitchen where the red-haired cook was just taking cakes and cookies from the oven.

"I am glad, Riekchen, that some are baked," said Beate, taking half a dozen of the small cakes; "give me some paper—I am going to take a walk and will be back promptly. Don't make any blunders in the cooking, and do not put the green peas on too soon; the venison in the oven an hour exactly!—I must tell you again, for I shall have no chance to see to it, when I am once seated at the table, see that the trout is a nice color, and served with greens. All depends on you, Riekchen!"

She nodded again and went hastily out of the kitchen, taking a side-path through the park to the main road. To be sure, it was wrong for her to run away to-day when her reputation as a housewife was to be tried. What if anything should fail? "I don't care!" said a voice within her. "For when the whole regiment has arrived, I shall not be able to go to the Owl's Nest, to see Claudine and the child."

She went in great haste and took all sorts of cuts; her face glowed, when, after half an hour, the Owl's Nest rose from the green tree-tops; it was just three o'clock in the afternoon.

The child was playing in the shade of the old wall with her doll's carriage; she ran to meet her "aunt," who seated herself on the ground and took the child in both arms.

"It was not very nice, Aunt Beate," she complained; "it rained all the time and Aunt Claudine rode away so often."

"But to-day the sun is shining and you can play in the garden again—you like that?"

The little girl nodded and tripped beside her. "Aunt Claudine is at home, too," she chattered; "she sits in her room and writes and is dressed so fine!" At the door the child paused and shook her fair head. "I am going to Heinemann again," said she, running away.

Beate ascended the narrow staircase and knocked at her cousin's door. Claudine indeed sat at the writing-table, but she was not writing; before her lay a completed letter; the scent of fine sealing-wax filled the room.

"Oh, Beate, is it you?" she said languidly, rising to greet her visitor.

"Ah!" jested the latter. "In white with blue ribbons! What is the matter? Are you going to Altenstein?"

The girl nodded.

"I asked to remain at home this morning, but the Duchess would not hear of it. She wrote me if I would not come to her, she should come to me; she is going to drive over and fetch me." She looked past Beate with resignation. "It is so warm," she continued, "I longed for a light dress. They say the color of a dress affects the mood; well, I could just as well——"

"Wear black ribbons," completed Beate, seating herself. "What ails you? You look as if you had a sick headache!" And she glanced in surprise at Claudine's low-spirited face.

"Nothing really ails me, Beate."

"Really?—You learned that at court; an unfortunate maid-of-honor must always be well, like a danseuse who has to smile even if she can scarcely breathe."

"Beate, you exaggerate," said Claudine quietly. "No, I am not ill; but only think—perhaps I shall go away for some time."

"You?" cried her cousin. "Now?"

"Yes, yes! But do not say anything about it. Joachim does not know of it yet," she replied.

And before Beate could utter the question upon her lips, Claudine said: "Did you not meet Joachim?"

"No!" answered Beate softly.

"I believe he was going to return Lothar's visit; you know that is a resolution for him. He just left; I feel convinced he will take three hours; for, as he walks, all

sorts of things will occur to him, and then he will seat
himself and write and make notes in his memorandum
book and forget time and place."

"He will not find Lothar at home," said Beate, with
hesitation. "He has gone to Labstedt."

"To Labstedt?" asked Claudine. "Is he going
away?"

"No; he expects Princess Thekla and her daughter;
did you not know it? She is coming to spend four weeks
at Neuhaus, to be near her grandchild."

"No, I did not know it," said Claudine in a low voice.

"I thought I mentioned it to you, Claudine?"

The girl made no reply. The room was so quiet, that
even the ticking of the tiny watch set with brilliants which
hung in a mother-of-pearl case on the writing-desk could
be heard. Beate looked longingly out of the window;
she would have liked to have gone. She thought of her
household duties which that day she had faithlessly neglected, and then she saw a man's form in the dusky corridor of the Neuhaus castle, standing at a door upon which
was written in chalk: "No Admittance!" And she
saw that man shake his head and turn away again.—He
must not go away thus—no, no! Perhaps he would
never come again!

She sprang up suddenly.

"Pardon me, Claudine, I must go home; you know, so
much has to be done." The untruth died upon her lips;
she blushed. "Farewell, my darling!"

"Adieu, Beate!"

"For Heaven's sake, you are ill, Claudine!" exclaimed Beate, staring at her cousin, on noticing for the
first time that her face was colorless.

"No, oh, no!" said the latter. And a wave of crimson
rushed over brow and cheeks. "I am well, quite well!
Go!" she urged. "Go, I am perfectly well; I will go
down with you. Of course you have a great deal to do
yet, and tell Joachim, if you meet him, so that he can
go before the ladies arrive; he is so shy, you know, so
peculiar!"

"He need not see them at all! I have my own room!"
murmured Beate.

"Oh, you do not know Princess Helene!" said Claudine bitterly.

"Is that so?" asked Beate, as she descended the stairs with Claudine. "Well, then give me a few pointers on this little Princess; Lothar will not say a word."

"Beate—I—you know—I am not impartial enough to be just. She does not like me, I believe, and always shows me her flippant side. Those whom she likes think her charming. She is a little spit-fire, attractive, without being what you would call pretty, animated, capricious——" she hesitated. "Yes, yes," said she softly, "she is very fascinating, very—and now, farewell, Beate."

"Are you going to cry?" asked her cousin. "Your eyes glisten so."

"No," said Claudine, "I am not."

"Then good-bye, dearest, and think of some new costumes. Lothar wants to give a party; I believe you will then outshine this 'very charming Princess,' and will you help me with your advice? I am innocent on the subject of court etiquette as a little child. Adieu, dear, farewell!"

Claudine hastened into her tiny room. It seemed to her as if the world since yesterday had become unjointed; she knew only too well why Princess Thekla had brought her daughter to Neuhaus!

"Lost!" she whispered. "Lost forever! But can one lose what one has never possessed?"

She was no poorer than ever, and yet—since yesterday, since that terrible day a gigantic hope had entered her heart; she had involuntarily attached a thousand sweet absurd thoughts to his nocturnal ride. Hope and fear possessed her until daybreak. When, after a short nap, she awoke, his image was again before her, as she had seen him the previous night in the glimmering light of her window. What nonsense! He had not come to gaze upon her shadow with loving eyes! he had wished to find out if she was at home, as became an honorable girl! Oh, he was very anxious as to the honor of his name!

She pressed her hands to her eyes so tightly that she thought she saw sparks of fire; but in the midst of it all was a dainty, girlish form. She let her arms fall again—and looked through the window. Was she sane? Through the red sparks, which still danced before her eyes, the red livery of the ducal servant gleamed on the

other side of the gate, and now Fräulein Lindenmeyer
rushed into the room.

"Claudine! Fräulein Claudine, Their Highnesses!"

With faltering steps Claudine approached the mirror,
put on her white straw hat, suffered Fräulein Lindenmeyer
to thrust her blue parasol into her hand, and went down.
She scarcely saw that upon the high box of his fine two-
seated carriage sat the Duke *in propria persona*, holding
the reins. Mechanically she bent over the hand of the
Duchess, whose delicate face beamed with delight at the
drive.

"Thank you, my dear Claudine, I am very well!" said
she, in her weak voice. "How could I be otherwise?
Such charming weather, such fragrance of pines, the Duke
as charioteer—and you by my side! Tell me yourself,
my dear, is it not so?"

For several hours they drove through the woods; at the
isolated mill by the babbling brook, a pause was made,
and the Duchess obtained from the miller's wife a glass
of cool milk, while the Duke threw the reins to the servant and leaned chatting against the carriage-door. He
genially asked the respectful miller, who hastened up, as
to the condition of business and bade him present to the
Duchess his three boys, who were the same age as the
little princes, and the royal lady asked the fair-haired,
sunburnt children what they intended to be, and upon
the reply "Soldiers!" gave each one a silver dollar with
the Duke's head upon it, for their savings-bank. Then
they drove on, homewards; for the evening sun began to
shine through the fir-branches.

The Duchess asked a thousand questions; with an effort Claudine gathered together her wandering thoughts.

"There are guests at Neuhaus," said the Duchess;
"there is the standard of our house waving in the breeze."

"Her Highness, Princess Thekla," said Claudine in a
low voice.

"And Helene?"

"Princess Helene was likewise expected, your Highness."

"Adieu, thou beautiful solitude!" sighed the Duchess.

The equipage approached the low wall of the Neuhaus
park; towards it rolled two landaus, the coachmen and
footmen in livery. They would meet at the entrance,

and, indeed, the Duke lowered his whip with a bow, and
the Duchess waved her hand to the carriage within which
sat two ladies opposite Baron Lothar. Claudine saw how
the young Princess, in a stylish traveling cloak of light
gray silk with flowing sleeves lined with blue, shot from
beneath the dainty straw hat a glance of scornful surprise; how Princess Thekla turned her lorgnette coldly
upon her at the bow which the reigning Duchess half unwillingly gave her, and how Lothar scarcely seemed to
heed her. After a few seconds they had passed..

"There goes the future mistress of Neuhaus," said the
Duke, turning on his high seat, his keen eyes scanning
the girl's pale face.

"Do you really think so, Adalbert? What good fortune for the little thing!"

He did not reply. Claudine grasped the handle of her
parasol; she made an effort not to betray her deep emotion. Did the Duke suspect who it was whom she bore
in her heart? She could not prevent a warm flush from
suffusing her face, and now she again met the Duke's
piercing eye.

"She is a spoilt creature," said the Duchess, who reclined dreamily among the cushions. "May she bestow
and find happiness! Between ourselves, dearest Claudine, I believe Gerold's love is requited and favored by
Princess Thekla as well."

"I believe so, too, your Highness," replied Claudine,
almost startled at her harsh voice. She felt suddenly cold
and composed.

In the mean time the royal guests arrived at Neuhaus.
Princess Helene had kissed and wept over her sister's
child, which Frau von Berg carried to meet the ladies in a
white dress covered with lace. She had gone up and
down stairs, had opened doors, had looked into the rooms,
and had asked which was her brother-in-law's sanctum,
in order thereupon to enter the room which with its
trophies of the chase and its arms, its pictures, its antique
furniture and Persian rugs, was the model of a refined
bachelor's apartment, and there, as curious as a child,
she had taken in everything with her dark, sloe-like eyes.
She went into the garden and then again into the house,
and suddenly stood before a door on which was written
in a bold hand: "No Admittance!" In a trice Her

Highness had turned the knob, and her dark head peeped
inquisitively into the old-fashioned sitting-room. How
cosy it looked! How charmingly the sunlight played
upon the dark furniture! And strange to say, there at the
open window sat a man reading ; his delicate profile stood
out sharply against the dark green of the trees outside the
window. He was so deeply occupied with the old leather
volume that he did not notice how he was being examined. Softly the little Princess again shut the door and
flew up the broad oaken stairs. Up above she flung herself into an easy-chair and laughed heartily at the terrified
face of Frau von Berg, who was writing seated in her
accustomed place.

"What was it you wrote us about Neuhaus, dearest
Berg?" she asked, planting her tiny feet energetically upon
the footstool. "In your letters to mamma there was nothing but 'not at all *comme il faut!*' 'Philistine customs,'
et cetera. I think it charming, more than charming here ;
I shall not for a moment feel the *ennui* which could be
read between the lines of your letters. What is the matter with the Baron's sister? She is an original person,
but looks stately enough in her gray silk gown ; and as
far as the outward appearance of the child is concerned,
wash off the thick coating of rice powder, which you have
put on her poor little face, probably to affect mamma, and
she will look better. Just at present she looks like you,
dearest Berg, when you try to appear particularly languishing."

"Your Highness!" cried Frau von Berg in an injured
tone, coloring even beneath her rouge.

"Do not excite yourself," continued the Princess. "Do
not make any such attempt! I think it charming here,
and shall tell my brother-in-law so."

"Then your Highness will suit his taste, he too thinks
this neighborhood charming!"

"Oh, I know what you mean, my dear," replied the
Princess, "but that is absurd, simply absurd. Out with
it, dear little Berg, if you know anything positive," said
she, certain of conquest; "you surely know it is not a
matter of indifference to me who is to be the mother of
the child." She pointed to the door.

"Your Highness will not believe me," pouted the lady,

avoiding the sparkling black eyes which looked almost passionately into hers.

"Sometimes I do not! However, I know quite well how to distinguish between your truth and fiction."

"Then I will leave you to choose, Princess," began Frau von Berg eagerly, "whether you wish to believe or not. He——"

"It is not true!"

"But, your Highness, I have not spoken yet!"

"Alice, do not speak, it is not so," cried the Princess, almost menacingly. "He has never looked at her, he has studiously avoided her. You were about to tell a different story."

"Just as your Highness commands; she——"

"She is in other fetters and bonds, I have seen it," exclaimed Princess Helene. "The Duke——"

"But I have not spoken," interrupted Berg. "If your Highness is so well informed, what can *I* say?"

"Speak, Alice," now besought the Princess; "is it possible? Mamma is beside herself about it, I can see; she says nothing to me, since we saw the Duke in the carriage with *her*, but her nose is sharp; that betokens a storm, you know it, Alice."

"But the Duchess was with them, Princess."

"Ah, my God," cried the latter, clasping her tiny hands, "poor, dear Liesel! She is soaring, as usual, in the upper regions and cannot see the woods on account of the trees. I'll wager, Her Highness, my cousin, is writing another drama which is to be presented next winter for our edification. Do you remember last winter, Alice? Ah, you were at Nice! Terrible! Terrible! Several times tears filled my eyes, but on the whole—Heaven protect us! Three corpses were finally on the stage, and I heard Count Windeck say to Moorsleben: 'Now watch, madame, very shortly the prompter will stab the lamptrimmer!'"

She laughed merrily, but soon became serious.

"Nevertheless, I like her, Alice; she is lovable notwithstanding her romantic ideas. Poor, poor Liesel! Had *she* not sat beside her to-day, I would have alighted and have fallen upon her neck. Tell me, Alice, how can she have such an icicle as that Claudine for a companion?"

At that moment the dinner bell rang and Princess Helene repaired to her room in all haste to have her hair arranged by her maid. Princess Thekla was just descending the carpeted stairs on the arm of her host, when she followed with Frau von Berg and the maid-of-honor.

"By the by, Alice," asked the young Princess softly, "what sort of a man is he who lives in the room on which is written 'No Admittance'!"

"A *man*, your Highness ?"

"Yes, yes !"

"Your Highness must have seen a ghost !"

"No, indeed ! I shall ask Fräulein von Gerold." And they had scarcely taken their seats than she did so.

"That was my cousin, Joachim, your Highness," answered Beate, and the soup-ladle trembled somewhat in her hand.

"Claudine von Gerold's brother ?"

"Yes, your Highness."

"Is the Owl's Nest near by, dear Gerold?" asked Princess Thekla, putting more salt in her soup.

"Half an hour's drive," he replied ; "if you so desire, I will take you over to the ruined cloister; it is worth seeing."

"Thank you !" coldly said the old Princess.

"Thank you !" repeated Princess Helene, just as coldly.

He raised his eyes from his plate in surprise.

"Your Highness will scarcely be able to miss this sight ; our most beautiful woodland path leads past the ruins."

"I hope, Baron," said Princess Helene, thereby turning Lothar's gaze from his august mother-in-law's pointed nose,—"I hope you will accompany me on my rides ; Countess Moorsleben will be of the party occasionally."

"Your Highness has but to command," replied he, glancing at the pretty face of the Countess, who with difficulty suppressed a mocking smile at the "occasionally." At the Residence she had to ride every day or the little Princess would not go out.

Princess Thekla began to talk of a certain "milk cure" which she intended to try. She had suddenly become amazingly amiable : she joked with Lothar about his idyllic domesticity and called Beate time and again "my dear." Never had she eaten such delicious trout ; and when Lothar arose, a glass filled with sparkling champagne in his hand, to express his pleasure at the revered grandmother's visit, she graciously extended to him her thin hand for a kiss, and with emotion pressed her lace handkerchief to her eyes. Under the pretext of being fatigued, she rose before dessert, and the ladies retired to their rooms. Frau von Berg sat for a long time at Princess Thekla's bedside, and when she finally sought her room, it was with head erect; she added, on arriving there, a postscript to the letter begun that afternoon :

"Everything is in the best order ; the little one is burning with love and hatred. For whom the first flame burns we know, and the last flickers for Claudine.

"In a few days the trees in the forest will whisper a great piece of news. At the beginning of next week a large *fête* is to take place here ; it will be grand. Princess Helene talks of a dance in the garden under the lindens. *Nota bene.*—Combined with her ill-nature there is a certain kindness of heart, so we may expect some silly act and must be upon our guard !

"A. v. B."

She sealed the envelope and carried the letter downstairs ; one of the kitchen-maids took it in the semi-darkness of the subterranean cellar, and with a smile thrust a dollar in her pocket. Frau von Berg had to pay a high tax.

In the darkened sitting-room a woman's merry laughter rang out. When Beate entered, the form still sat in the arm-chair writing at her work-table by the last ray of daylight.

"Why, Joachim !" cried she, in her ringing voice, "would you ruin your eyes altogether ? "

He started ; he had entirely forgotten where he was.

"My God," said he, in affright, seizing his hat, "I have dallied too long with the old book ; pardon me, cousin, I will clear the field at once."

"Not now," said she, still laughing, "for Lothar will want to see you too ; your visit was of course for him ? " And she gently pushed him back in the chair and sought her brother.

He stood in his room at the window, staring out upon the road.

"Lothar!" she implored. "Come over! Joachim is still sitting there and has forgotten time and place in the ancient days of Spain—you know, the book belonging to grandfather, in the white leather binding."

"How came Joachim to be here?" asked Lothar, taking a cigar case and ash tray from the elegant smoking table.

"I found him here when I came from the Owl's Nest; and as I had all manner of things to do, as you can believe, I was prevented from entertaining him, but I could not send him home tired, and the book occurred to me. You see, he has been well entertained."

She looked at him with a smile, as he walked by her side through the lighted hall and turned into the corridor.

"Tell me, Beate," he asked, "did you write those words on the door after he had entered or before?"

"*Before*, of course!" she replied, innocently, and then she blushed. "I do not understand you!" she added, indignantly.

"Well, you know, sister," said he, with a trace of roguishness, which suited his aristocratic face admirably, "*No admittance* is generally written on doors which shut in something one wishes to keep entirely for oneself."

"Oh, you horrible man," panted Beate in confusion, hastily rubbing her hand over the words printed with chalk. Soon afterward all three sat in the sitting-room, over their wine, and Joachim, being reminded of many things by the book he had read, related his traveling experiences. He talked exceptionally well. "Like music," thought Beate, oblivious to all else; oblivious that the candles in the dining-room were burning needlessly; oblivious to the fact that she had not locked up the remainder of the food, and had forgotten to order the breakfast for the morrow. The bunch of keys in her belt did not jingle; not the slightest sound reminded her of her duties. At the windows the lindens rustled in the evening breeze and the perfume of new-mown hay penetrated the room.

It was late when Lothar led his cousin through the wood to the Owl's Nest. Upon his homeward way the Duchess' *coupé* drew near him. He knew who was within it; hurriedly he passed the vehicle; as he drew up at the door

of Neuhaus, a window above him was shut noisily, and in
the silent room overhead a passionate young face was
again buried in the cushions. Princess Helene had seen
him drive away in the direction of the Owl's Nest. God
be praised, he was now at home!

A change had taken place at the Owl's Nest ; Fräulein
Lindenmeyer had company.

First, there had been a voluminous correspondence, and
then on the morning following the day on which Claudine
rode out with the Duchess, Fräulein Lindenmeyer entered her room, her face flushed with excitement, an open
letter in her hand.

"Ah, Fräulein Claudine, dear Fräule', I have a great
favor to ask."

"Well, my dear, good Lindenmeyer, it is already
granted," Claudine had replied, as she steeped the tea for
Joachim's breakfast.

"You must tell me frankly, dear Fräulein, if you do
not like it, I will do all I can to prevent any inconvenience, but——"

"Out with it, Lindenmeyer," the beautiful girl had thus
encouraged the old housekeeper ; "I do not know what I
could refuse you, unless it was that you might leave the
Owl's Nest—and *that* I would not agree to."

"I leave here ? Oh, Fräulein, I would not think of
such a thing ! Oh, no, it is not that—I expect—I am to
have company, if you will allow it."

"Who is it, my dear Lindenmeyer?"

"The forester's wife's second daughter, Ida ; she needs
instruction and wants to learn fine needlework. So the
forester's wife has taken it into her head that she would
learn best from me. I will do it gladly, if you consent ;
she could use the little room back of mine if——"

The good old soul folded her hands over her letter,
and her eyes looked with anxious expectation at her young
mistress.

"That will be very pleasant for you," was the kind reply. "Have the girl come soon ; she can stay as long as she likes."

So the next day, as Claudine entered the kitchen to perform her housewifely duties, a small, round, girlish form stood by the crackling fire, handling the cups and the tea-kettle, as if she had never been anywhere else. A pair of roguish blue eyes glanced at Claudine over a *retroussée* nose, and the owner of those eyes made a rather awkward curtsey as the pretty, slender form crossed the threshold.

"Why, my dear child ! " said Claudine in surprise.

"Ah, dear Fräulein, let me do it ! " implored the girl. "I cannot sit in Aunt Doris' room all day and embroider ; I should die ; could I not do a little housework ? If you please, let me do it ! "

"I cannot, dear Ida—is not that your name ?—certainly not ; I should only contract bad habits."

"I should so gladly like to learn something," said the girl, casting down her roguish eyes.

Claudine smiled. "From me ? Well, you have come to a poor teacher—I am learning as yet myself."

"Dear Fräulein, I will tell you the truth—I know quite a little about housekeeping, but in many other things I am very ignorant ; I should like to obtain a position as maid in S——, and I thought I might learn here how to assist a lady at her toilette and so forth. Let me do the work here, which is very light, and give you my insignificant help in sewing and as lady's-maid."

The girl's eyes looked imploringly into Claudine's, while she felt weary and sad ; she made no reply, but hastened to Fräulein Lindenmeyer.

"Confess, Lindenmeyer," said she, forcing a gayety she did not feel, and addressing the old lady as she had in her younger days, "you invited company in order to take the burden of the housekeeping from my shoulders ?" As she spoke, her eyes filled with tears.

"Ah, darling," lamented the kind-hearted creature, "Ida has made a stupid beginning, and we planned it all so carefully ! Do not be angry ! I cannot bear to see you come downstairs in the morning so heavy-eyed and pale ! There is an old proverb which runs : *Beds of roses and fields can only thrive under one hand.* If you want to be fresh at court you must have freedom, or else your clear, white complexion will speedily be spoiled. Heine-mann says so too ; he was worried on your account. And, Fräulein Claudine, Ida will be benefited by it. She might obtain a position as maid to Countess Keller through her aunt, but she does not know enough. Indeed, it is so ! " assured the old lady.

So Claudine unexpectedly received an assistant, although she strove against it. With the entrance of the fresh, simple girl, the house was made cosily comfortable, and never was mistress more faithfully served, never was child more spoiled than Claudine and little Elizabeth. Heinemann beamed when he met the neat maid upon the stairs or heard her singing the old folk-songs in a low voice in the kitchen—that she might not disturb the Baron. Nor did little Elizabeth cry any more when Aunt Clau-dine drove away in the Duchess' pretty carriage, and Claudine did not sit at the table so anxiously, unable to enjoy a morsel of food.

"We are quite aristocratic ! " smiled Joachim, when Heinemann for the first time served the simple dishes and Claudine remained quietly seated ; " I am glad for your sake, sister."

Claudine had given up her journey. When she men-tioned her project to the Duchess, the latter burst into passionate sobs. "I cannot keep you, Claudine, go ! " So, terrified and touched at the same time, she had prom-ised to remain. Now the court carriage which bore her to Altenstein came earlier. The Duchess' fondness for the dignified, handsome girl increased daily, and Claudine was now quite composed ; she drove in the Duchess' carriage and sat in her boudoir, reading aloud or talking. Occasionally, of course, the Duke entered hastily and unannounced, to be greeted by a joyful exclamation on the part of his wife, while Claudine no longer feared meet-ing him. No ardent glances were cast upon her ; he did not whisper a syllable to her, she knew he would keep his word. She knew him through his mother : of how many a mad escapade had the old Duchess told her, of the care he had occasioned her, of the prayers she had uttered for this son before the *prie-dieu* in her bedroom beneath the Virgin's picture, over which hung a tiny lamp, prayers that he might not be ruined by the rashness of his youthful acts !

And the old lady had then added, it was only his buoy-
ant spirit, his heart was always noble; he could be in-
fluenced, if the proper words were found. And Claudine
thought she had found them. She had one of those noble
natures which do not rest until they have discovered the
good in the human soul; which seek and seek, and when
they have found the good, know no bounds in their forgiveness.

She silently pardoned the Duke the insult he had
offered her, when she saw how gallantly he struggled
with his passion; how he essayed to be more patient
with his wife; how he respected in her his wife's friend.
As such, she was shielded against love and hatred—that
was her belief. Claudine wrote to the Dowager Duchess;
they were grateful, touching words with which the lovely
girl expressed her pleasure at being able to call herself
the Duchess' preferred companion. "Oh, if your Highness knew," she wrote, "how happy I am in the love
and confidence of the most noble of hearts; I think only
of how I can repay the honor of being the friend of this
amiable Princess. Even that which your Highness occasionally found fault with is, on better acquaintance, no
longer a failing; Her Highness does not only show her
affection for her husband, her whole being is so permeated with this affection, that Her Highness would have
to dissemble, was she to hide the same."

Claudine was gayer than she had been for some time.
She impatiently awaited the carriage which was to bear
her to Altenstein. In the intelligent atmosphere which
floated about the invalid Duchess, she felt her own sorrow to be more insignificant. The Duchess had one day,
as timidly as a schoolgirl, put a couple of volumes in
Claudine's hand. They were charming little poems, composed by herself. First the merry verses of the betrothal
days, then the more deeply tender words of bliss of the
young wife, and, finally, the verses which she had written
at her sons' cradles. Perhaps the songs were a shade too
tender, too sentimental; but when Claudine glanced at
her who had composed them, she thought they *could* not
be otherwise than filled with exceeding happiness and sad
forebodings.

There were, too, among them several short stories,
peculiarly thought out. There was always a couple who

loved each other above all else—and who were separated
by death, by some chance, by an inevitable fatality—but
never by the guilt of either. Claudine was surprised at
the sorrowful terminations, but did not dare to speak of
them, for she feared lest she might render the Duchess
still more melancholy than she was inclined to be.

Eight beautiful, quiet days passed by. The Neuhausers
had not disturbed that peace, as the Duchess had at first
feared. Princess Helene had appeared in the Duchess'
apartments several times like a whirlwind, but gave all
plainly to understand that she was in the greatest haste
to return to her dead sister's sweet baby! Meanwhile
the old Princess lay upon a couch at Neuhaus with an
injured foot. Claudine saw Beate once only, and then,
curiously, when the latter had strolled over early in the
morning to the Owl's Nest, to obtain more information
as to a few of the customs of Princesses, and to leave a
quantity of excellent cake, bonbons and confections.
She spoke in favor of the new arrangement at the Owl's
Nest, with regard to Fraulein Lindenmeyer's company ;
but, on the whole, she was quiet and depressed, and at
Claudine's questions impatiently shrugged her shoulders
and said she desired nothing but to be four weeks older.
It was worse than she had imagined ; there was not a
corner of the entire house in which one could be safe
from the Princess, that will-o'-the-wisp, and Lothar replied to her complaints with simply a shrug of his
shoulders.

Claudine bent her head as if she expected a blow which
would destroy her last hope ; but Beate ceased and spoke
of something else—namely, that Berg grew daily more
intolerable ; she exercised a decidedly great influence
over the old Princess.

"It is a matter of indifference to me," she added.

On this especial day, a typical summer day, the Duchess
had ordered tea to be served in the park, on that spot
where the forest trees bordered the garden, where Joachim's wife had fallen asleep for eternity.

The Duchess' hammock swung under the old oaks, and
Claudine, in a thin, white dress, sat beside her in a comfortable bamboo chair reading. Before her upon the
Japanese table lay Frau von Katzenstein's knitting ; the
latter was standing on one side, preparing tea. In the

shade of a group of chestnuts, as far from the ladies as
the width of the graveled walk, the Duke was playing
ninepins with the two eldest princes, Captain von Riekle-
ben and Herr von Palmer; the laughter of the children
and the clatter of the falling pins could be heard, and the
Duchess' eyes turned in that direction with a blissful
expression.

"Stop, Claudine," said she. "The day is lovely, the
sun so bright, and this story so dismal. It seems so un-
natural to me to-day—what do you think will happen?
To those in the book, I mean."

"Your Highness, I fear, it will end horribly," said
the young lady, obediently laying the book upon the
table.

"He has already procured poison," added the Duchess.

"Yes," replied Claudine, "she will die."

"She?" exclaimed the Duchess, in surprise; "why,
dear Claudine, what a horrible idea! He wants to poison
himself because he feels he cannot live with her, nor can
he exist without the other."

"I do not know, your Highness," stammered the girl;
"from the tone of the story, I supposed——"

"Please give me the book!" cried the Duchess. She
opened it and read the end. "My God, Claudine, you
are right," said she then.

"Psychologically, nothing else is possible; if your
Highness has followed the description of this man's
character——"

"I was struck by nothing peculiar in it," interrupted
the Duchess. "No, Claudine—it is improbable. Thank
God, such fancies belong to the realm of madness. We
will not read any more of the book, the world is so delightful and I am so happy to-day."

She threw aside the silken coverlet which was spread
over her pale red foulard dress, and waved her hand toward the chestnut trees.

"See, Claudine, there comes the Duke; he seems to
be tired of playing.—My dear friend, I am too indolent
for our game of dominoes, but perhaps Fraulein von Gerold will take my place?—Please bring the table here,"
she commanded, turning in her hammock, resting her
head upon her hand and watching the Duke seat himself
opposite Claudine, divide the dominoes and pile his up.

Claudine's slender fingers suddenly began to tremble. She bent her head over the black and white dominoes, and a rosy blush mounted even to the roots of her luxuriant fair hair. Over there, on the other side of the lawn, something blue loomed up—fluttered nearer like a butter-fly, and then suddenly paused. And behind that "something blue."

"Ah, my child," chided the Duchess in a semi-whisper, "you seem absent, the Duke will win the game."

"Oh, this is an idyllic group ; just as if Watteau had arranged it ! I fear, Baron, we are intruding," cried the Princess, attired in a light blue linen, turning around with a half-mocking, half-vexed expression towards her mother, who was behind her, leaning on her son-in-law's arm, and followed by the gentleman and lady-in-waiting. And she saw that Lothar's face, as if cast in metal, did not stir a muscle.

Her Highness, the old Princess, held up her lorgnette and said, without changing her expression : "*En avant* my child ; you wanted to surprise Elise—therefore, an-nounce us—if you please ! "

Princess Helene advanced ; but she no longer fluttered, she walked slowly and her black eyes looked very dis-contented. She noisily closed her parasol as she ap-proached, and then paused with a pouting air. "Pardon me, your Highness, if I am disturbing you——"

The Duchess looked up and laughed. "Whence come you, madcap ? " She extended her hand. "Did you fly over the walls, or——? "

"I came in the Neuhaus carriage. Mamma, Baron Gerold, and the others are back there, and ask permission to be allowed to greet your Highness. "

She bowed gracefully to the Duke and kissed the Duchess' hand. Claudine, who stood beside the latter, Her Highness did not seem to see ; with comical eager-ness she began to wave her parasol, as if to give those approaching a signal that they were welcome.

The Duke advanced to meet the old Princess and led her to his wife : during the exchange of greetings, Lothar stood next Claudine, but in vain did she await a word from him, she received only a silent bow. The visitors seated themselves, and an animated conversation was carried on by the royal ladies. Princess Thekla begged to be excused for having been so remiss in inquiring after Her Highness' health; but she had met with an accident on the steps of the Neuhaus castle and for six days had had arnica compresses on her foot, and Princess Helene's visits, too, had been so fleeting, she could not be enticed from the nursery and the Neuhaus castle; she had indeed borrowed a linen apron from Fraulein Beate and had followed her into all the rooms, into the attic, into the cellar and store-room. As she spoke the old Princess shook her finger in a playful, menacing manner at her little daughter. "Yesterday I caught her in the kitchen preserving raspberries! Yes, hide your hands!"

The Duchess turned to Princess Thekla with a smile. "How is your little granddaughter?"

"Well, she is improving," replied the old lady, reluctantly, "but not enough by far. Good Berg has obeyed the orders of the doctor, whom the Baron called in, somewhat too strictly—no medicine, but cooling baths and fresh air from morning until night; the child is much too delicate for that. Now, as a preventive against colds, she takes aconite and is kept in the house until noon."

"My daughter walks a little, although still uncertainly," added the Baron calmly, "and as she is the normal size of a two-year-old child she climbs about by means of sofas and chairs."

"Not enough by far," repeated Princess Thekla, interrupting him."

"I am satisfied with that 'little,'" he replied.

Meanwhile Claudine had turned to Countess Moorsleben and addressed some insignificant remark to her. Her reply was made in a few words, while the young lady's merry brown eyes were turned in quite another direction.

In surprise Claudine lapsed into silence. The Princess, opposite her in the rocking-chair, had been staring fixedly at her for some time. Claudine turned her pretty blue eyes calmly and inquiringly upon those bold, black ones; then the dark, curly head was turned away and a contemptuous smile flitted about the rather too full lips.

"The young ladies must play a game of croquet," proposed the Duchess. "The gentlemen will gladly join them. My dear Claudine, accompany the Princess and Countess Moorsleben and give the order for the arches to be set up."

Claudine rose.

"Pardon, your Highness,—I am obliged!" said Princess Helene, "I am somewhat fatigued." She laid her head on the back of the rocking-chair and slowly rocked herself. Countess Moorsleben immediately resumed her seat when her mistress refused to play. Claudine did the same.

Ices were served, as well as tea and coffee in dainty Sèvres cups. The gentlemen now came from the playground and joined the company; Claudine suddenly found two gentlemen behind her chair; Herr von Palmer and Captain von Reikleben. She turned to the latter and was soon conversing with him; she knew his younger sister at school and inquired for her; he told her of her marriage and her happiness, which had exceeded all expectation; despite their limited means she was happy and contented.

"Oh, yes," agreed the young lady, "the tiniest home can be made delightful with a little contentment."

"You yourself are the most speaking example; the Owl's Nest is an idyl, a dream, where you rule as the fairy of peace," interpolated Palmer. "To be sure, the consciousness that it is only an episode certainly helps to complete the charm; it is easy to be contented if one sees a temple of happiness in the distance."

Claudine looked at him inquiringly.

He smiled confidently and helped himself to a crystal cup with ice from the table at his side.

"Rather obscure, Herr von Palmer; I do not understand you," said Claudine.

"Really not? Ah, my dear young lady, with your brilliance too? It must seem very homelike to you here," he continued, changing the subject; "it is to be hoped that the time is not far distant when you will again occupy the home of your fathers. Those constant drives from and to the Owl's Nest are tedious. I think pretty soon they will be more so, when the festivities are going on at Altenstein and Neuhaus."

"I am unfortunate to-day, Herr von Palmer; again I cannot clearly see the meaning of your words."

"Then take the words as prophetic, Fräulein von Gerold!" said a clear voice, and the Hereditary Prince, a handsome youth of twelve, with his mother's large, sentimental eyes, pushed his *tabouret* over to Claudine. Prophets always speak obscurely," he added.

"Bravo, your Highness!" cried Herr von Palmer, laughing.

"I hope Herr von Palmer has prophesied truly," continued the Hereditary Prince, looking with the boyish, bold admiration of his age at the lovely girl. "You could very well come and stay with mamma, Fräulein. She told papa only yesterday it would be fine if you had not always to drive away."

Herr von Palmer still smiled.

"I cannot do that unfortunately, your Highness; I have my duties at home," replied Claudine, with composure; "how gladly would I otherwise return to my beloved Altenstein!"

"It is a charming place," said the captain, in order to change the subject, "what a lovely garden!"

"It was grandpapa's hobby," remarked Claudine sadly.

"Did you not play 'Robbers and Princess' here with your brother and other children when you were young?" asked the Prince, without removing his eyes from the young lady's face.

"Down there,"—she nodded and pointed to the left,— "by the wall, where the gate is; it was used as a sally-port."

"Captain," cried Princess Helene aloud, "I should like to play a game of croquet now! Come, Isidore!"

The Countess and the Captain rose and hastened towards the lawn; Princess Helene still hesitated.

"Baron," said she then, turning to Lothar von Gerold, and her voice assumed an imploring accent, "will you not join us?"

He rose and looked at her, bowing his assent.

"Has your Highness included all the persons who are to participate in the game?" he then asked.

"Why? You see we are two to two."

"Not more than four? Ah, is that so! Your Highness!" he turned to the Hereditary Prince, "Princess Helene wishes to play croquet—I know how fond you are of the game."

"Her Highness' tiny foot tapped the turf impatiently.

"I am sorry," replied the Prince gravely, "but Fräulein von Gerold has just promised to point out to me the spot on which it would be best for my brother and me to build a fortress.   That is more interesting to me."

Baron Lothar smiled.   For a moment he paused and saw the young Prince offer Claudine his arm with amusing importance.

The Duchess glanced at the lovely girl leaning on the boy's arm with an astonished air.   "Why does not Fräulein von Gerold play ?" she asked the Baron.

"Her Highness, Princess Helene, has just chosen her partners herself," he replied.

"Pray, Baron," said the Duchess, pleasantly, but firmly, "go after your cousin and tell her, how sorry I am that they *forgot* to invite her, and bring her back with you if possible ; the Hereditary Prince's tutor, who is just coming, will take your place so long."

The Baron bowed and withdrew to excuse himself to the Princess and to relinquish his mallet to the tutor, an amiable man, but one who stood in awe of the ladies. Then he slowly and by a roundabout way took the road his cousin had taken.

The old Princess' nose during this episode turned suddenly sharp and white.

"Pardon, your Highness," said she, putting the dainty cup with a clatter upon the table.   "Helene surely had no intention of wounding; she means well, she loves your Highness devotedly.   Her honest heart runs away with her, and——"

"I do not see what honesty has to do with it, dearest aunt," replied the Duchess, her cheeks crimson with excitement.

Herr von Palmer looked at the Duke, who took not the slightest notice of the interchange of words.   His Highness toyed with his eyeglass, as he gravely looked after the white, supple form of the girl upon whose arm the young Prince so confidently hung, asking her all manner of questions.   She had some time since disappeared in a jessamine grove, when the Duke slowly turned his head and met Princess Thekla's eyes.   They looked more sparkling than usual, and upon her thin face lay a malicious expression.

"He is courting early," said the Duke carelessly, "the youth is all fire and flame ! "

"And he has good taste ! " said the Duchess, entering *into the jest merrily.*

"He inherits that from his father," said the old Princess' shrill voice, and the most affable, innocent smile in a moment took the place of the malicious expression while she drew herself up in her chair.

The Duke politely removed his hat and bowed.

"Yes, my dearest aunt, I always preferred seeing a pretty woman rather than an ugly one, and if you mean the Prince has that quality from me, you make me very happy : I thank you."

Herr von Palmer's sharply-cut face beamed with suppressed merriment. It would be delightful if Berg could hear it ! Princess Thekla nervously pulled at the lace on her pocket-handkerchief ; but the Duchess glanced beseechingly at her husband ; she knew his antipathy for Aunt Thekla. It dated from his youth, when that aunt, endowed with a talent for espionage, had ferreted out some of his mad escapades, to report them to the Dowager Duchess, of course not always truthfully. She did not now address another word to His Highness, but turned to the Duchess and overwhelmed her with truly exceptional attentions, which had a compassionate tone, such as is used in speaking to persons who innocently bear a great sorrow ; attentions which wound nervous, proud natures deeply.

The Duchess did not understand her, but she was annoyed by all her questions, advice, and propositions, and when at length Princess Thekla sighed, "If I only knew positively that your Highness would be benefited by this Altenstein ?" she grew impatient and asked to be taken indoors, as she felt fatigued.

This gave the signal for breaking up ; in a short while the square beneath the oaks was vacated, the gay balls lay neglected upon the path, and the two Princesses with their suite rolled along the road towards Neuhaus.

Claudine, with the young Prince, walked towards the end of the extensive park. She inwardly rejoiced at escaping from the range of Lothar's eyes, which wounded her. The little Princess' intentional slight had scarcely pained her ; it seemed to her so very childish that she did not take the trouble to think of it further ; she had often

received slights from that person ; they dated from balls
and other court festivities, when she—against her wish—
rather cast the Princess in the shade.   Why the Princess,
on this especial day, dared to show her aversion in such
an open manner, she did not understand.   Her little
Highness must have been very ill-humored ; or had she,
with the clear, penetrating spirit of love, divined Claudine's feelings for the man whom *she* desired to win?   But
no !   The Princess was so sure of the matter, so sure,
that she even borrowed Beate's kitchen-apron and played
at being housewife in her future home.   Lothar, too,
must have been sure of the fickle, coquettish little heart ;
or he would not scarcely have dared to remind her so
ironically of the rudeness of which she had been guilty.

Claudine suddenly frowned and bit her lips.   What did
it concern him if she was insulted?   He would surely not
have noticed it if she had not borne the name of Gerold.—
Constantly that absurd family pride !   She knew herself
how far things should go ; she knew how to defend herself ; she wanted no protection, no compassion, least of
all from him.

With her youthful escort she reached the most isolated
part of the park, where from her childhood bushes and
trees had grown, and were allowed to grow, as they
would.   It was a humid, mossy wilderness, through
which ran a small stream, on the margin of which the
bracken grew in luxuriant beauty.   Under the tiny bridge,
made of birch-boughs, the water rippled as oddly as when
she, a child, rambled about here.   There was the half-
ruined moss cottage, which at her play was used now as
a prison, now as a knight's castle ; how often had she sat
therein as an imprisoned chatelaine !   A melancholy feeling possessed her as she told the Prince of it and showed
him everything.   There, too, was the stone beneath
which lay Joachim's favorite dog, the little yellow beagle,
called Lola, which was so sensible that she never betrayed him when the children played hide-and-seek ; she
lay as still as a mouse beside her young master when the
others drew near.   Those were happy days ;—where were
they ?

"Where does that lead to ?" asked the Prince, pointing
to a narrow, low gate in the wall.

"To the village, your Highness," replied Claudine.

"The gate was used by the servants in former days when they went to church."

The Prince drew the lovely girl along the walls, overwhelming her with all manner of questions. Suddenly he perceived a bird in one of the high trees, and, forgetting his lady and his knightly duty, gave chase to the jay, which flitted through the boughs, as if to entice the boy, now appearing here, now disappearing there, always farther away.

Only after the lapse of some time did Claudine, who, deeply absorbed in her melancholy memories, had walked heedlessly along, become aware that she was alone. She drew a deep breath and passed her handkerchief over her eyes. What would she have? Nothing was different from what it had been! By a shake of the head and tears one cannot recall that which is lost; by weeping and longing one can gain nothing which is denied one by God's decree. "The time will come when the pain will be allayed;" she comforted herself thus, "it must come; it would not be possible to live with so burning a wound in one's heart!"

She paused; a couple of large tears trembled upon her lashes. Now, when she was alone, all the grief she experienced when in *his* presence burst forth; she thought just then that she could not bear to see him beside another, with smiling composure, as the acknowledged property of a superficial, capricious creature.

"Pardon, cousin," suddenly said his voice in her ear. She turned with sudden terror, and a sparkling drop fell upon her hand, which she hastily covered with the other, while the old haughty expression overspread her pretty features.

"I would not have ventured to disturb you," he continued, advancing a step nearer. "But Her Highness commissioned me to tell you how sorry she is to know that you were hurt."

"Her Highness is always kind," was the cold reply. "I am not hurt; one learns to overlook such things—and to judge them as they deserve."

"It seems you have learnt much of late," said he, bitterly, walking beside her. "I remember the time when you timidly avoided all glances, and I believe it was not so long since—in the halls of the Residence castle."

"Certainly!" she replied. "A faint heart is quickly strengthened when it feels that it must act for itself. I am, moreover, three-and-twenty years old, cousin, and have of late been rudely aroused from my life of girlish carelessness."

"There is something sublime in a proud woman's soul," he answered, sadly. "It is only a pity that this pride can so easily be wrecked by the first onslaught of life.—To me it is always something touching," he continued, "when I see how a woman, who does not know the world, places herself as heroine, with almost unparalleled courage, in an impossible position; one would like to close one's eyes, in order not to see the shipwreck, and yet is unable to do so; one would like to draw her back from the edge of the dizzy abyss, and one will only receive a cold, smiling rebuff for it."

"Perhaps, however, there is one, who, besides the necessary courage, possesses the necessary strength to remain at the post," said Claudine, trembling with excitement, walking more rapidly.

"Possibly!" he replied, shrugging his shoulders. "There are natures which look upon themselves as exceptions. 'See, I can dare this, unpunished!' They are the most speedily crushed."

"Do you think so?" she asked with composure.

"Well, there are, too, natures which think enough of themselves to choose that path which their conscience and duty call them to tread, without looking to the right or left, and without heeding the unasked counsel."

"Unasked?"

"Yes!" she exclaimed, and her lovely eyes gleamed with passionate agitation. "How is it, Baron Gerold, that you presume to address to me, as soon as we meet, your dark prophecies, your enigmatical sarcasm? Have we ever stood in such a position towards one another, that you should venture to presume so far?"

"Never!" he replied in a low voice.

"And we never shall," she continued bitterly. "I can, though, assure you, if it will be any comfort to you, that the name of 'Gerold' shall not suffer through me, for—and that is probably your only care—I know my duty."

He turned pale.

She hastened on; he remained somewhat behind her

and caught up with her again at the pretty little lodge in which Heinemann's only daughter lived with her husband. Claudine paused at the open window; there sat Heinemann's neat granddaughter behind the white curtain weeping bitterly. The mother, a pleasant-looking woman, approached her former young mistress, wiping her eyes with the corner of her apron.

"Her betrothed has broken with her to-day, Fräulein," she explained.

The girl pressed her hands to her eyes and drew back sobbing behind the curtain.

"Why has he done so?" asked Claudine compassionately, mastering her own agitation.

"She is to blame, Fräulein," began the woman sadly, bowing to the Baron, who was advancing: "the young master at the manor, where she was in service, paid her some attention, and William thought she was not true to him."

"That was wrong of William," said Claudine curtly.

"Ah, Fräulein," apologized the woman, "he cannot be blamed. I know she is good, I know my child; but such a young man—Lisette should have left the place, as I advised her; then it would not have happened. You see, Baron," she continued, turning to Herr von Gerold, and making him an awkward bow, "not a soul will believe her, it is the way of the world; and were she to tear out her hair, no one would believe that she had done nothing wrong. Many a time to-day have the words occurred to me which your grandmother—God rest her soul—wrote in my prayer-book on my confirmation. There it is," said she, turning to the window and taking from the sill a volume bound in black and gold, and handing it open to Claudine; "there it is, under the pastor's words."

Claudine took the book. There, under the words, "Blessed are the pure in heart"—written in a delicate hand—were to be seen the old Baroness' bold characters: "Be not only pure, but avoid *appearances* of impurity." The book trembled in Claudine's hand; she returned it without a word.

"Let him go, my child," now said Lothar, and his voice sounded strangely harsh; "he would be an unpleasant husband with his leaning towards jealousy and moral preaching."

The girl started up. "No, no! He was so kind and good; I cannot survive, if he does not return."

"One can survive a great deal, little one," said he gently, "one does not die so easily from blighted hopes."

Claudine nodded gravely to the girl; the pallor of excitement still overspread her face.

" Farewell, Lisbeth," said she, "and do not grieve for one who does not trust you."

"Ah, gracious Fräulein, do not say that!" cried the girl, hurrying from the window.

Claudine turned and walked on, Lothar by her side. Her grandmother's words blazed before her eyes and cast a peculiar light upon her own position. What if people were already whispering about her? What if her words were credited? What if any one believed that she had already forgotten her honor? She suddenly turned to him and looked at him with anxious, inquiring eyes.

He walked calmly beside her. No, no, no! How could she be so mad?

"The square is deserted," said he, pointing ahead, "they seem to be in the castle."

Indeed there was no one under the oaks but a lackey, who was clearing away the things, and who said that Their Highnesses had driven to Neuhaus, and that Her Highness awaited Fräulein von Gerold in her room. The carriage would return from Neuhaus.

She turned towards the castle; the evening sun gilded the summits of the trees and caused the innumerable windows in the sandstone walls, which were gray with age, to gleam. A rosy shimmer colored the atmosphere; from the village came the chime of the vesper bells.

"Farewell," said Lothar, pausing, "I must look for His Highness to bid him good-bye. You know these paths of course, and the services of a guide can be dispensed with."

He bowed low; she thought, ironically low.

Proudly she bent her head. She knew that the bond of relationship which had united them superficially in the isolation of a country life was forcibly sundered when she rejected "unasked counsel." Had she been too severe?—For a moment her foot hesitated; then she walked with redoubled haste up the shady path which led to the principal allées.

At a bend the Duke suddenly appeared. He removed his hat, and holding it in his hand, walked beside her. He talked of the park and pointed to a group of fine copper-beeches, which stood out well against the green background of larches.

"Where did you leave the Baron, Fräulein?" he next asked.

"My cousin has just left me," she replied; "if I am not mistaken, he was going in search of your Highness, to bid you good-bye."

"Ah! Well, he will know where to find me. This time I have designs upon him; I will keep him this evening; he shall play a game of billiards with me; my capricious little cousin must be punished." He smiled as he spoke, and glanced keenly at Claudine. "I hope you were not wounded by that childish whim?" he asked, as they entered the avenue leading to the castle.

"No, your Highness!" replied Claudine, looking towards the castle sadly. At the steps two gentlemen stood conversing; at that moment one of them turned.

"By Jove, Captain," said he softly, "look—it is just like Louis XIV. paying court to Lavallière."

The person addressed made no reply, but he glanced with surprise at the couple approaching with such apparent unconcern.

Above, at the Duchess' window, a white handkerchief fluttered, and the Duchess' thin face was to be seen wreathed in smiles.

With a low bow the gentlemen allowed the Duke and Fräulein von Gerold to pass. The Duchess' beautiful friend looked strange; a hard expression lurked about the usually so gentle lips. Arrived at the castle, she ascended the stairs as slowly and languidly as if she were carrying a heavy load upon her shoulders. "Now all is over," said she once more, entering the ante-room of the Duchess' apartments.

"Claudine," cried the latter, who had been impatiently awaiting her favorite at the window, and who flung her arm about the lovely maiden's neck, "you stayed so long! When you were gone I grew so uneasy; I longed to follow you, I really cannot exist without you. Do you hear, Claudine?"

She drew the silent girl beside her upon the small couch,

in the shade of the red curtains, and gazed into her sorrowful, blue eyes.

"Dear heart, you were wounded, the child was ill-
mannered and shall be punished. It is the story of the
gosling, which, by the side of the swan, could only attract
attention by screeching. Claudine," added the Duchess,
in a whisper, "I have found out what you are and what
the others are." She pressed the girl's cold hand. "I
love you so dearly, Claudine," she whispered, "I should
so much like to call you by your name when we are alone!
Do you agree to it?"

"Your Highness! I pray you!" she stammered.

"Not *your Highness*, Claudine! Do you think I will
call you '*Claudine*,' if you call me *your Highness?* I am
to be addressed as *Elizabeth* and you as *Claudine*. Ah,
please, please!—I have never had a single soul in my life
with whom I could have such intercourse. Grant me the
pure, beautiful consciousness that you are my friend and
no inferior. Please, Claudine, say *yes!*"

"Your Highness is trying to atone for the trifling insult
by too much kindness," said the girl, with agitation. "I
cannot?—I dare not accept it."

Suddenly she rose and pressed her hands to her temples,
as if to consider what she should do.

"I thought you more sensible, Claudine," said the
Duchess, "than to be disconcerted by so simple a thing!
The familiar form of address is the abstract of all confidence, all love! And because I chance to be a Duchess,
am I to forego it? You must not think that, and you do
not think so. Come hither, Claudine, and give me a
sister's kiss!"

Claudine kneeled before the affectionate woman; she
longed to cry: "Cease, cease! It would be better for
you and for me, were I to go away, as far from you as
my feet can carry me!" But beneath the glance of those
feverish eyes which gazed so imploringly and affectionately into hers, she could not utter the words. Then a
kiss sealed her lips. The next moment she felt something
cold on her arm; a narrow, golden circlet in the form of
a horse-shoe, the nails represented by sapphires and brilliants, glittered there.

"Will your Highness . . . will you . . ." she corrected

tearfully, "never regret this choice?" And her grave, pale face was upturned inquiringly to her friend.

"I have a keen sense of divining human worth, and I know, Claudine, I have given my heart to no one unworthy of it."

Princess Helene returned to Neuhaus exceptionally ill-humored. During the drive she had sat in one corner of the landau in silence, and Princess Thekla in the other, just as silent.

Countess Moorsleben, who was seated in the carriage, could only suppress a smile with difficulty, so much did the two faces look alike in moments of vexation.

In the upper apartments of the Neuhaus castle the storm broke upon the head of Frau von Berg, who was summoned to the young Princess' room. The girl overwhelmed the evidently highly-insulted woman with the wildest reproaches, just as if she were to blame that four hundred years before an old Gerold was inspired with the idea of building a strong castle in that neighborhood, which castle had gradually been merged into that insufferable Altenstein. It was a horrible place, a desert; it was as clear as day that no sane person would ever have made such a purchase if certain "intentions" had not actuated him.

It was unparalleled, that one should have to accept a rebuke publicly from Her Highness on account of such—such a—— In her rage she could find no suitable word. It was a fine thing that *she*, Princess Helene, should have to ask pardon of Her Highness' maid-of-honor!

"Oh!" said the handsome woman who with bowed head allowed the storm to break over her, "To ask pardon? Your Highness did nothing, surely?"

"I simply did not see her, for I cannot bear her," declared the Princess.

Frau von Berg's eyes gleamed.

"Surely, your Highness, that was bad," said she softly. "Her Highness is truly bewitched by this friend; one might almost believe pretty Claudine brewed love-potions in her old Owl's Nest. How unpleasant the scene must have been to the Baron!"

10

"Unpleasant!" burst forth the Princess. "Do you think so, Alice? He was not slow in leaving the croquet-ground, to bring his cousin back at the Duchess' command, appeased."

After these words the Princess rose from her chair, covered with gray and blue cretonne, and ran to the window. Frau von Berg saw her clinch her fists and tap the floor nervously with her foot ; she saw that it was almost impossible for her to maintain her composure.

"What should he have done, your Highness?" asked Frau von Berg. "But, indeed, it is not impossible ; who understands the hearts of men?" And she smiled behind the Princess' back.

Suddenly she turned as if stung by a viper ; she saw the smile still hovering about the mouth of her confidante ; the next moment something flew past the artistically-dressed head and fell upon the floor beside the stove. It was only the Princess' soft, blue silk work-bag which contained Her Highness' embroidery, which never became more than a beginning ; but the fact remained : it had been hurled at Frau von Berg's head.

The handsome woman raised her handkerchief to her eyes and began to sob.

"Do not cry!" commanded the Princess. "You know it maddens me, if—I know you too well ; you are malicious, Alice."

"Indeed, I am not, your Highness!" assured the woman. "I was thinking of—one smiles sometimes out of pity."

"I do not need your pity!"

"Who says it was meant for your Highness? I pity the Duchess! Her Highness seems to me like a lamb, which has invited the wolf as a guest. Her Highness worships this Claudine, and—your Highness, it is tragically comical to see a person feeding his bitterest enemy with sugar-plums."

The Princess made no reply. She now sat behind the cretonne curtain on the broad window-sill, swinging her feet, while her burning eyes stared at the road on the other side of the park, a bit of which could be seen.

"How can *I* help it, if people are blind?" said she, finally. "I thought your Highness loved the Duchess?"

"Yes, she is kind and has always favored me. But mamma says she is eccentric, and that she has shown plainly enough to-day. I cannot help her."

The clock upon the rococo chest, the antique one, with brass locks and handles, struck seven. The little Princess remarked it impatiently.

"So late?" said she. "The Baron has forgotten that we were to choose the place in the garden this evening for the dance."

"Perhaps Her Highness asked him to remain," suggested Frau von Berg. "Fräulein von Gerold sings every night, and the Baron, your Highness knows, is passionately fond of music."

"But the Duchess knows he has guests!" exclaimed the Princess, with sparkling eyes, looking menacingly at her tormentor.

"If Her Highness commands?" said the latter, softly apologetic.

"Commands? Do we live in the Middle Ages? Then, indeed, my cousin might even *command* that he marry her favorite?"

Frau von Berg innocently entered this somewhat forcible jest. "Who knows, your Highness; were it to be that favorite's ardent desire?"

That was too much for Princess Helene. She ran up to Frau von Berg and seized her angrily by the shoulder; her thin face was pale.

"Alice," said she, "you are wicked! I feel that you are! You pain me to the quick; what you say is horrible, but—it is not impossible. Alice, I shall no longer have a peaceful hour; I wish I were dead like my sister! She was at least happy *once.*"

"Your Highness is jesting!"

"No, I am not—for God's sake, do not think so! I should be beside myself were she away from these mountains! Why did she not go to Switzerland with the Dowager Duchess? Why does she remain here?"

"Yes, why?" repeated Frau von Berg, kissing the Princess' hand.

"Poor child!" she then sighed.

"Ah, Alice, do you know of no means? Tell me one! I can bear this doubt no longer!" whispered the passionate maiden.

"I, your Highness ? What can I do ? If chance does not help to open Her Highness eyes——"

"Chance?" repeated the Princess bitterly.

"What else? Her Highness has not one soul who is kindly disposed enough to do such a friendly service for her."

"A fine *friendly service!*" replied the Princess scornfully, "say rather, a barbarous act; for this I know, as surely as that I am standing before you, Alice, that the discovery of this affair would break Elizabeth's heart."

"Would your Highness prefer to see the noblest, the best of creatures systematically deceived? I must confess, our views of 'friendship' differ widely," replied Frau von Berg reproachfully.

"You probably never loved any one dearly, Alice. So dearly that you would rather die than lose him? No, you have not; do not tell me so. Where others have a heart, you have an empty space! Do not look at me so; through me the Duchess shall not learn it, Alice; moreover, I never maintain anything that I do not positively know, and here such proofs are lacking at present."

Frau von Berg smiled and stroked the Princess' hair; a tear glittered in her eye.

"How could such a pure, childlike heart believe in such guilt?" she asked softly. "It would not even understand the proofs."

The Princess shook off her hand. "Pray, do not act as if you had your pockets filled with them," said she, irritated at the contact.

"I have not my pockets filled with them, it is true, but *one* proof would be sufficient, your Highness."

The girl's face blushed crimson with shame. "It is not true!" she stammered. "No woman would be so dishonorable as to simulate friendship where she practices treason. It is horrible, Alice."

"Oh, your Highness, you do not know life!"

The Princess suddenly put her hands to her brow and ran into her bedroom, slamming the door behind her slight form. Frau von Berg was left alone in the pretty but simple room; she looked at the door and a smile again flitted over her face. Then she drew a note-book from her pocket and took out a letter. "Here it is," she murmured, glancing lovingly at it. Its power had already been felt. Within her boudoir sat Her Highness, Princess Thekla, penning to Her Highness, the Dowager Duchess, a letter full of virtuous indignation.

In the adjoining chamber passionate sobs could be heard. Frau von Berg left the room and soon returned with fresh water and raspberry-juice. Without any hesitation she entered the Princess' bedroom.

"Your Highness must compose yourself," she implored tenderly, mixing the cooling drink.

She kneeled before the weeping girl, who sat upon the divan at the foot of the bed, and looked at her as if imploring pardon.

"These inflamed eyelids must disappear," she went on; "if I am not mistaken, the Baron just drove into the court. Upon the table in there are the cuts for the fancy-dress ball and a large number of beautiful samples from Monsieur Ulmont."

The Princess rose, allowed Frau von Berg to arrange her hair and to bathe her eyes. "Do I look very bad?" she asked.

"No, no; as bewitching as ever!" was the answer.

Below, the dinner-bell rang. A few minutes later, the Princess descended, as if she wished to lose not a minute of the delightful hour; her eyes beamed, her lips smiled. At the open doors of the dining-room, in which the candles burned upon the gleaming table, stood Beate in the rustling gray and black striped taffeta dress which she now wore regularly at dinner. "My brother begs that your Highness will excuse his absence; Her Highness requested his presence; the carriage has just returned empty," said she, bowing slightly, and speaking in the tone which at times sounded so harsh.

The gayety upon the Princess' face vanished; she sat silently by Beate's side; the old Princess excused herself on the plea of a sudden headache. Countess Moorsleben with difficulty suppressed a yawn; the chamberlain conversed in low tones with Frau von Berg; otherwise not a sound was audible but the slight clatter of the plates, or Beate's voice, which rang out as loudly and clearly as always. Once she addressed the Princess, who looked at her, but made no reply, and who, before dessert was brought in, rose, beckoned the Countess to remain where she was, and like a spoiled child ran into the garden.

When, in the course of a couple of hours, she returned to her room, her hair was wet with dew and her eyelids swollen. But the eyes beneath them did not see what was before them—they saw a cosy room, and at the piano a beautiful girl, around whose fair head the rays of light wove an aureole, and one was listening to the sweet, soft tones which involuntarily won his heart. It was distracting!

"Bid Frau von Berg come to me," said she to the chambermaid. "I want no light!"

In a few moments Frau von Berg's train rustled over the threshold of the dark room, and the Princess' small, trembling hand groped for hers.

"Give me the proof, Alice!" whispered an unsteady voice.

"Here it is," replied Frau von Berg, tranquilly, laying the fatal letter in the Princess' right hand. "I do not believe it is worth the trouble. Throw the note away, your Highness, when you have read it."

"Very well, Alice, thank you. You may go."

The Princess went into her bedroom, and by the light of the pink lamp which depended from the ceiling, read the letter. "In spite of that, a friend! Poor Liesel!" she murmured.

She made a gesture as if to tear the note, and paused again. A hot flush suffused her cheeks, she breathed with difficulty. The atmosphere of the room was sultry, and through the open window streamed the sweet, intoxicating perfume of blooming lindens, as intoxicating as the longing for happiness and bliss which filled the girl's heart. She longed for happiness at any price, even at the greatest! With trembling fingers she folded the note as small as possible and put it in a golden medallion, which she wore around her neck. A picture was in it, the head of a man; she once took it secretly from her sister when she was a bride—Lothar's bride. It was her greatest secret.

"Only in case of necessity!" she murmured again, putting the medallion in its hiding-place.

———

In surprise Fräulein Lindenmeyer shook her head with its red-beribboned cap. It was remarkable what had

become of the once so deserted Paulinenthal ! In the
woodland paths were to be seen light costumes, and
merry voices rang out ; it seemed as if the entire city had
chosen this spot for their summer excursions. A number
of fine carriages had just driven past, and not an egg was
to be had in Xleben. Everything went to Brotterode, the
resort half-an-hour distant from the Owl's Nest, which, as
the forester's wife said, strangers overran this year.
Every little cottage was disposed of, and the proprietor of
the "Trout" was so pompous. He had the families of
two Counts on the first floor, and in the rear of the house
lived a Frau von Steinbrunn with two daughters ; all had
their carriages, and there was constant driving to Altenstein and Neuhaus.

Yes, the entire court circle had followed the ducal party,
as a tail made of paper follows the kite. This summer the
mountains at home were considered incomparably beautiful by the *élite* of the Residence ; it was totally different
from Switzerland, or the Tyrol, from Ostend or Nor-
derney. Those who had already gone returned by that
way. In the primitive dining-room of the tavern at Brotterode, where the painted walls were ornamented by pictures of the Duke and Duchess, in truly shocking colors,
where they sat upon deal chairs at small tables, ate dry
roast-beef and dried plums as compote, and drank doubt-
ful red wine, a lively mood prevailed, notwithstanding.
They had the prospect of picnics in the woods, of croquet
and lawn tennis in the Altenstein Park. The Duchess
was said even to have spoken of a *bal champetre*, of a
fancy-dress ball in the moonlight under the oaks of the
castle garden.

This summer promised on all sides to be quite unusually gay ; above all else, it was interesting to watch the
romantic friendship of Her Highness for lovely Claudine ;
veritably wonderful things had already been heard.
"They are said to be very intimate," related Countess X.
——"The other day they were seen dressed just alike,"
said Frau von Steinbrunn.

"Pardon ! that is not so. The Duchess wore red
ribbons, Claudine von Gerold blue," said a young officer
in civilian's dress, who was spending his furlough here instead of at Wiesbaden.

"The Duchess is said to have overwhelmed her with

ornaments and valuables ; they are together all day, reading, chatting, and driving ; probably they compose poetry
together too. Princess Helene told Isidore von Moorsleben that they called each other Elizabeth and Claudine,"
cried Countess Pansewitz.

"Impossible ! Incredible ! "

"The Gerolds are particularly fortunate ! "

"What does His Highness say to it?" suddenly asked
the bold voice of a young diplomat.

His Excellency, with a white head and a venerable air,
at the other end of the table cleared his throat audibly
and shook his head in disapprobation.

They all looked at one another with smiles and expres-
sive glances, drank their wine in silence, and passed
around the compote dishes once more; His Excellency's
wife, after a pause, began to talk of the weather. A
couple of Countesses, with glances at their daughters,
took up the new theme eagerly, and wondered if one
would venture to mount the high watch-tower, one of the
favorite points of view in the country !—And when the
meal was concluded, the elder ladies assembled and
whispered and shrugged their shoulders, or held their
handkerchiefs to their mouths and smiled behind them.

Up to that time, they had not succeeded in convincing
themselves with their own eyes, for, until then, the ladies
and gentlemen, anxious as to the health of the Duchess,
had been forced to be content with inscribing their names
in the book which lay in a room on the first floor of the
Altenstein castle. Still they heard a great deal ; they
surmised, they combined. All were anticipating the
coming Thursday ; for that the royal visitors would appear at Baron Gerold's *fête* was certain ; they expected to
hear some great news on that day, news of no less importance than the announcement of a long-expected betrothal.

Yes, it would be interesting ! And during all this sur-
mising, during all the expectations, those at Neuhaus and
Altenstein lived on apparently undisturbed.

Princess Helene sat in the Neuhaus garden, and by her
side stood little Leonie's elegant perambulator. Her
Highness still played the affectionate aunt in the stormy

manner in which she did everything that entered her head. She dragged the child everywhere with her; she tried with indefatigable patience to teach her niece the word "papa," while the shy, black, childish eyes looked at her in astonishment, the defiant little mouth remained closed. She did not know that even the youngest child can read the features, and the impatience and passion which sparkled in the Princess' glance made the poor little being fearful. Usually in a short while she began to cry.

Then she was carried about, soothed, kissed, and overwhelmed with unheard-of caressing words, so that Beate, in her room, wrung her hands and listened anxiously to hear if no one would come to the child's aid. But who should? Lothar sat as if buried alive in his chamber, whither he was in the habit of retiring after meals; Princess Thekla generally lay upon her couch, yawned, or wrote letters; and Frau von Berg—well, she supported Princess Helene in her extravagances; the large, overbearing person bowed almost to the dust before her youthful mistress.

The old nurse, who came up in affright, was made use of to somewhat soothe the sweet pet, and, when she had partly succeeded, to return her to her royal aunt until she began to scream again. Beate, who, hitherto, had never known what nerves meant, for the first time experienced a peculiar tingling at her finger-ends; she felt a roaring in her eyes, she said; she once surprised herself on the verge of tears. That was when Lothar apathetically declared before the *fête* that it was a matter of indifference to him how she arranged it. There she was, she, who in all her life had never attended to anything of the sort, left to attend to concert programs, the arrangement of dances and cotillions. She felt inclined to tell the truth to him who paced his darkened, cold room so silently and thoughtfully.

"You are the master of the house, and if you invite guests, you must have the necessary patience to undertake a host's duties."

But, before she had opened her lips, he turned, and she saw a pale face with an expression so anxious that she was startled; of late she had not found time to look at him.

"For God's sake, Lothar," said she, approaching him, "you are ill!"

"No, no!"

"Then you have some trouble!"

"Trouble such as a man has who puts his entire fortune, his hope, his future, on a frail bark and sees it driven from the safe harbor into storms and waves; who stands there without being able to do anything, and who knows that to sink is equivalent to misery and despair," said he softly.

"But, Lothar!" exclaimed Beate horrified. She was not accustomed to hearing him speak in such riddles, and with such a bitter accent. Almost beseechingly she asked: "Confide in me, Lothar; explain yourself more clearly--you terrify me!"

"Oh, nothing—nothing, Beate; do not heed my words," came involuntarily from his lips. "I shall conquer it—when Neuhaus is again peaceful and still. Beate, be indulgent with me."

But his sister did not desist. "Lothar," she began resolutely, although her heart ached, "I believe you men are in some things dull of comprehension; I think, this time, you need only to put out your hand."

"No, my sensible little sister, not this time," he replied. "Over my open hand another is victoriously extended; when I perceived that, I withdrew mine silently, clinched it so, and now do not ask any more questions; cease, Beate."

"You are the same silly youth you always were," she murmured, turning away. "Why, she follows you like your Diana there;" she pointed to the dog which with intelligent eyes followed every movement of his master.

She then went into the hall, and with a clouded brow saw Princess Helene in a light morning dress, followed by the Countess, come down the broad stairs to disappear in the garden. The Princess' black eyes were fixed sharply upon the heavy oak door which led to Lothar's apartments, and, in Beate's anxious heart, indignation was aroused. Surely that was what he meant! No one could show him more plainly that he was beloved; according to her opinion it was much too plain! To her passionate eyes, that fluttering, nervous manner was unspeakably disagreeable; God alone knew what was passing in her brain ; the cow-pen and stable were as little secure from her invasion as the nursery or the mausoleum at the end of the park, the key of which she had lately asked for, in order to place wreaths upon Lothar's parents' tombs, a thing which Lothar himself had neglected to do.

Beate shook her head and ascended the stairs to the attic where the boxes and chests stood. There she seated herself and yielded to her inclination to weep. Was it happiness he longed for in fear and despair? That high-born, passionate creature !—Had his first marriage been happy ? Why was Lothar so ambitious ?—She thought of his future by Helene's side ; of the deserted house of his fathers, in which *she* would remain alone, guarding and protecting it as now. He would go out with her into the gay life of the capital, would travel as he had with his first wife, and then he would come for a few days alone ! What should the high-born wife do there ? Her presence now only meant encouragement ; her feigned interest in the housekeeping of the manor was only a proof that she, too, would gladly condescend, as her sister had once done.

And when he came, brother and sister would look into each other's eyes to find that they had aged ; the one in the sultry, oppressive, court atmosphere, the other in solitude and yearning for her own happiness.

She was herself startled at the sobbing sound which escaped her involuntarily; she clinched her teeth, and with tearful eyes opened the chest which stood nearest her, and hastily drew forth rugs and gay draperies. They were costly stuffs ; she wished to have the hall decorated with them. Joachim had collected them upon his travels, those Smyrna textures and Turkish materials, and at the auction she had bought them with her own means. Whilst she examined the colors of the wonderful weave, the tears rolled down her face.

What ailed her ? She did not recognize herself so !— Energetically she wiped away the tears and forced herself to think of cotillion bouquets and favors, innumerable china plates and cups, of a hairdresser, of ices, almond-milk, and God knows what not, and finally of the absurd idea of the little Princess of converting the simple coffee-party into a fancy dress ball.

She hastened down the stairs again, gave orders, **sent**

out messengers, talked with gardeners and maids, and
in the midst of the confusion came the refusal from Claudine and Joachim.   They had scarcely reckoned upon
the latter; but Claudine? Beate hastily sought her
brother.   She found him in the garden; he stood beside
Princess Helene and the Countess upon the improvised
ball-room floor that was built under the lindens.   The
carpenters were just through, and a couple of gardeners
were decorating the roughly-hewn boards with evergreen,
and were drawing festoons from pillar to pillar.

"Lothar," she began, "Claudine has sent her regrets;
will you not go over yourself and ask her to come?"

At that moment he looked still paler.

"No!" he replied, shortly.

Princess Helene's eyes gleamed; she had noticed his
pallor.

"Then I will drive over, if you will allow me," said
Beate.

"You will have to direct your steps to Altenstein.
You will certainly not find her at the Owl's Nest."

"I shall find her this evening," replied Beate.   "I
shall not return without her consent."

"You seem to be unlucky, Baron," said the Princess,
with a strange gleam in her eyes, "as mamma told me;
the Duke, too, will probably refuse to grace the *fête* with
his presence.   Her Highness, who has just written relative
to a slight question of toilette, informed mamma of it sorrowfully."

A vein on the Baron's brow swelled; otherwise not a
muscle of his face quivered; he eagerly watched the gardeners, who were fastening red and white flags upon the
posts.   "It looks well," said he, calmly; "does not your
Highness think so, too?"

Her Highness nodded.

"Why not the colors of our house as well?" she asked,
with charming amiability.   "The yellow and blue alter-
nating with red and white?"

"I do not like the combination," replied he.   "They
are striking contrasts."

Beate, who was on the point of retiring, turned away
in affright.   But the Princess smiled, she may have con-
strued those words differently from Beate.

On the afternoon of this day, Claudine stood beside her brother's writing-desk, bidding him adieu.

"Have my regrets been sent?" he asked.

She nodded. "Yours and mine. Farewell, Joachim!"

"Yours?" he asked in astonishment.

"Yes! I do not care for such *fêtes;* do not be angry, Joachim!"

"Angry? I simply do not understand you; you will grieve Beate deeply."

A slightly mischievous expression flitted over his sister's beautiful face.

"Oh, I think I shall again conciliate her. Joachim, let me remain here; you have no idea how I anticipate this day, the afternoon under the oak, the evening with you."

He extended his hand to her. "As you like, Claudine. You know whatever you do is right to me."

Claudine descended the stairs, gave a farewell kiss to the child, who was making doll's clothes under Ida's guidance, and looked into Fräulein Lindenmeyer's room. She was sleeping in her easy-chair; softly Claudine closed the door and slipped through the hall out into the garden, at the gate of which stood the ducal carriage. In the course of half an hour she sat beneath the oaks of the Altenstein garden and read aloud to the Duchess from Joachim's work, "Spring Days in Spain." The story of his love was skillfully interwoven in the wonderful description of the country.

"Claudine,"—thus the Duchess interrupted the reader, —"your little sister-in-law must have been very charming. Describe her to me!"

The girl fixed her blue eyes upon the royal lady. "She somewhat resembled you, Elizabeth," said she.

"Oh, you flatterer!" threatened the Duchess; "but you have inspired me with an idea—forgive me, that the interesting reading gives rise to a question of toilette. How would it be, Claudine,—if I were to take a fan and a mantilla and come to Neuhaus as a Spaniard? It is a good idea, I think. And you, Dina?"

"I—I have sent my regrets, Elizabeth."

The Duchess looked disappointed. "What a pity!" said she, slowly and thoughtfully. "The Duke too has declined."

Claudine's pale face turned paler. Her friend's eyes were fixed inquiringly upon hers.

"Are you warm?"

"But why is His Highness not going?" asked Claudine, evasively.

"He has given me no reason," was the reply.

"Elizabeth," said the lovely girl hastily, "if you bid me, I will retract my refusal; I can easily do so with Beate."

"I do not 'bid' you, but I should be pleased," said the Duchess, with a smile.

"Then excuse me an hour earlier, I would like to inform Beate myself of my changed resolution."

"Certainly! Although it will be hard for me to spare you. But tell me, why did you not want to go to Neuhaus? I cannot believe, Claudine, that you took Princess Helene's caprice so seriously that you would make your kinsmen suffer by it."

As she spoke the Duchess took her friend's hand and looked into her blue eyes.

But the long fair lashes were not raised, and upon her cheeks burned a brilliant blush.

"No, no!" she cried. "It is not that. I had promised Joachim a quiet evening; I thought you would not miss me in the glamor and excitement of the *fête.*"

"I never feel more lonely than when in the midst of a throng," replied the Duchess softly, holding firmly in hers Claudine's hand, which she attempted to withdraw.

"I will go with you, Elizabeth."

"Willingly? I will not release you until you say so."

"Yes," said she, with hesitation, laying her cheek against the Duchess. "Yes!" she repeated, "because I love you dearly."

The Duchess kissed her. "I love you too, Dina! Since the time of my betrothal I have not felt this blissful sensation. And this is one advantage: in friendship one does not as easily experience disappointment as in love, it inspires a calmer happiness!"

Claudine looked keenly at the Duchess.

"Yes, yes, love, marriages bring many things with them, dear child," smiled the latter; "little annoyances, little disappointments. Only think, Claudine, with what confidence the eighteen-year-old girl advances to the altar ! But, my child, I am the happiest of women, for *he* loves me. To know oneself to be loved, to confide in the love and fidelity of one's husband, in that lies a wife's bliss—and to lose that confidence would be for me synonymous with death."

While the book lay forgotten upon the maiden's knee she talked softly of her first meeting with her beloved, of the tender affection which she cherished for him at once, of her surprise on being informed that he had sued for her hand. How she had clasped her hands and asked with quivering lips : "Me? He wants me?" She told how, during their brief engagement, she had written to him daily, how with a feeling of happiness, with unequaled pride, after the wedding she had stepped upon the balcony of her father's castle, to show her handsome courtly husband to the thousands who thronged the great square below ; and how then they had both driven in the spring night to the quiet little castle in the neighborhood of the Residence, where they were to spend the early days of their honeymoon.

On alighting, her train had caught in the carriage, and she had, so to speak, fallen at his feet ; they had both laughed, and, because her foot pained her, he had carried her up the stairs in his arms, through the deserted corridors in which the lamps burned dimly, to their rooms ; and arrived there they seated themselves at the open window and listened to the nightingales in the park, and saw the lights of the castle reflected in the pond, and the warm air was laden with the perfume of violets.

The Duchess' eyes sparkled at the memory of that happiness, and when the Duke's tall form in faultless summer attire turned the nearest grove, a wonderful light flitted across her delicate, emaciated face.

Advancing, he bowed, but was evidently not very gay.

"Am I disturbing the ladies ? " he asked. "Doubtlessly their toilettes are being discussed ? Absurd idea, a fancy dress ball ! "

"Yes, indeed ! " cried the Duchess. "Claudine, where will you get a toilette on such short notice ? "

"I have a whole chest filled with grandmamma's elegant materials," she replied. "I think I can surely find something among them."

"The gentlemen's dress suits will look very odd by the

side of gypsies and ladies with wigs," scoffed the Duke. "Of course, one of Helene's whims, that is clear."

"Why do *you* not go, Adalbert? Do I Why do you refuse Gerold his favor? You formerly humored him in every way," implored the Duchess.

He shrugged his shoulders. "It cannot be arranged," said he curtly, changing the subject at once.

"Then, Claudine, we shall have to be satisfied with each other, I as a Spaniard—and you?"

"In one of the unbecoming costumes of the Empire, your Highness; short waist, narrow skirts and——"

"Pardon! the costume is not unbecoming," interrupted the Duke, "on the contrary. But it requires a perfect form and a certain grace. I can call to mind the charming picture of Queen Louise, of my own grandmother, Duchess Sidonie, in the gallery of our castle." He kissed his finger-tips. "That style was charming."

Claudine was silent. The Duke said a few more words, then he withdrew and Claudine resumed her reading.

It was almost nine o'clock and not yet night, when she drove to Neuhaus. Herr von Palmer was standing at his window behind the curtains and heard the carriage roll out of the castle court. He twirled his long, carefully dyed mustache with his waxen fingers, which gleamed in the darkness. He knew the arrow lay in the string, the bow was bent; only one impulse was needed for a poor human heart to be pierced—"to be rendered powerless," as Herr von Palmer called it. It was necessary, it was indeed high time; this friendship was gaining ground; the Duchess now treated him miserably, more miserably than ever; he knew the reason why. Were the arrow to strike *her* too—it would serve her right. "What Berg says is absurd, that the little Princess is afraid for Her Highness;" such natures are tough.

"A superb idea to choose the little Princess, who was beside herself with jealousy, to be the one to press the trigger; superb, superb," said he, with admiration, pacing the room. "Only a woman's brain could devise that. There will be a gigantic explosion, beautiful Claudine! The rooms of the castle at the Residence will not see you

again. Inoffensive forever! Lothar does not think about
her, the overbearing fool, with his royal marriages ; how
Berg can think so is enigmatical to me. But the Duke
may think of her as much as he likes. If Her Highness'
suspicions are aroused, there will be no expedient for the
lovers : they must part! Who shall afterward find favor
in His Highness' eyes will depend on me. Berg is still
handsome enough, and old love does not rust. She still
loves him, and would enter into my plans with the greatest readiness."

An endless line of brilliant plans opened before the
man's eyes ; at their head the seductive title of "Court
Marshal" beckoned to him. His old, palsied Excellency,
Von Elbenstein, who at the same time performed the
functions of Lord Great Master of the House, and whose
duties he, Palmer, had performed for months, could not
possibly live much longer. His Highness had, too, already spoken words of encouragement. Of course, he
knew there would be envy among the court *chargés* if he,
the foreigner, whom His Highness had picked up on the
street, so to speak, in Cairo, were to receive this position.
He smiled again, and whistled several measures of the
Fatinitza March.

"It will not be long, my good people ; I shall yet enjoy
my life, as long as I can enjoy it." As he spoke, Paris
and a charming little *hôtel* in the Champs Elysées rose before his eyes. Then farewell to a Prince's service ! But
Alice ? Perhaps she would live there ; perhaps. *Nous
verrons !*

He took his hat and went to the table, where the captain was just brewing a peach punch, for the first luscious
fruit from the ducal hothouses had arrived.

Claudine stopped the carriage at the entrance to the
Neuhaus linden avenue. She wanted to enter the house
and Beate's room unperceived. Avoiding the hall, she
entered the back door unseen, flitted noiselessly through
the corridor, and knocked softly at the sitting-room door.
Steps came through the room and the door was opened.
"It is I, Beate," she whispered. "Shall I disturb you ?
Just one moment!"

11

"It is really you!" cried her cousin, drawing the girl into the still dark room and towards a chair.

"No, no," objected Claudine. "I only wanted to tell you that I will come the day after to-morrow, if you will let me."

Beate laughed heartily and kissed her.

"Well," she called out into the darkness, "who was right, Lothar? My trip was not even necessary."

Claudine started; a form at the window rose. Her cheeks burned.

"Her Highness insisted," she stammered.

"It is exceedingly kind of Her Highness," said Baron von Gerold, in a voice strangely husky. "His Highness has just done me the honor to withdraw *his* regrets."

Claudine grasped the back of the chair; she trembled, but said not a word. What an unpleasant coincidence !

"But, do sit down," urged Beate. "We no longer see or hear anything of each other. I have, of course, little leisure, but, as you are here, help me to arrange the seats at table; I do not know all these people who are invited and have accepted."

"Excuse me, Beate; I have a headache, and the carriage is awaiting me without," said Claudine, evasively, turning to go. "Let them choose for themselves," she added, as if aware of the discourteous act she committed in refusing Beate this trifling favor.

"Of course," agreed Lothar, "Fate will hear devout prayers and bring *the* lot ! Permit me to escort you to your carriage ?"

Beate really pouted somewhat; she remained in the room. Lothar, by the side of the agitated girl, walked through the lighted hall into the garden. Neither spoke.

The windows of the castle on the first floor were all illuminated; Princess Helene liked light, a great deal of light. She had risen from the table early, in order to try on costumes. The light which shone through the windows extended to the shadow cast by the trees. The linden blooms diffused an intoxicating perfume. It was a warm summer evening. The moon was hidden behind dark clouds.

They walked along hastily. Before them flitted a shadow; a second followed. Lothar did not notice it, but Claudine involuntarily paused.

"Do you see anything?" she asked, anxiously.

"No!" he replied.

"Ah—it was only my imagination," she apologized.

She advanced to the carriage, bowed her small head with a cold "Good-night," and entered it.

The sound of the wheels died away in the silent garden. The man, who had looked after the vehicle, now walked slowly along the footpath outside the park walks, towards the woods, as if he wished to gain his composure in the solitary paths.

"Alice," passionately whispered Princess Helene, emerging from behind the tree-trunk, "Alice, he drove away with her!"

"Your Highness, that was but an obligatory courtesy."

"Oh, but I *can* not bear it, Alice! What was she doing here? What did she want? Alice, speak!"

The Princess' agitated whisper became audible conversation.

"But, my God, your Highness," began the handsome woman, as if in her painful surprise she could find no words, "what shall I say? I myself am amazed!"

The Princess proceeded hurriedly to the park gate; there stood an old sandstone bench, behind which she kneeled in the darkness and waited—waited with throbbing pulses for his return. Frau von Berg's voice rang out in vain through the dark, sultry garden. She finally went upstairs and smiled at her reflection in the large pierglass, while she wound about her abundant hair the coquettish scarf which she, as an Italian, was to wear several days later. The Princess did not return for hours, when she entered with pallid cheeks and tear-swollen eyes. She did not sleep much that night.

The *fête* at Neuhaus was at its height. The warm, breezeless summer evening made it even possible for the delicate Duchess to remain in the open air. The red curtains of the tent which stood under the lindens, not far from the dancing platform, were opened wide; she reclined there in a comfortable chair, surrounded by a number of ladies and gentlemen. The wonderful light, produced by the twilight, moonlight, and hundreds of

colored lanterns, caused her thin face, beneath the black
lace mantilla fastened with pins set with brilliants, to
appear paler than usual, and her eyes still larger and more
glowing.   She wore a crimson satin petticoat with the lace
flounce and the black gold-embroidered bodice of the Andalusian.   A white bear skin was spread at her feet ; upon
her tiny, black satin shoes glittered buckles of brilliants.
She looked beautiful, she knew it ; the Duke's glance had
betrayed it to her, and the betrayal caused her to become
radiant with delight.

Princess Thekla, attired in gray *moiré*, sat behind her.
Before them stretched a most charming panorama, beneath
the boughs of the old lindens whose emerald leaves shimmered in the light.   Youth and beauty were there ; gleaming gems, dazzling shoulders, brilliant colors, and strange
effects of light.   These groups of fantastic forms, as though
arising from fairy realms, were caressed by the soothing
fragrance of the linden blossoms, intoxicated by the electri-
fying tones of a Strauss waltz.

"A *fête* like those in Goethe's time at Tiefurt," said the
Duchess.

"Especially when one sees the lovely Gerold ; pray,
your Highness, look at that form, it is truly classical !
Wonderful ! "

The speaker, a small, aristocratic man, whose thin face
bespoke genuine delight, stood behind Her Highness'
chair, his eyes fixed upon Claudine.

"Oh, yes, my dear Count," replied the Duchess, looking at her favorite with beaming eyes ; "she is, as always,
the belle of the evening."

"Your Highness is too modest," said the Princess Thekla,
casting a truly annihilating glance in the direction indicated.

Claudine stood upon the lawn, without the garland
wreathed dancing-platform.   The old gentleman had not
exaggerated ; never had her peculiar beauty been set off to
such advantage as it was on this evening in her great-
grandmother's gown.   She wore her magnificent hair at .
the back of her head in an antique knot ; a few stray locks
curled on her neck and upon her brow ; a small diadem, in
the center of which one star of brilliants sparkled, crowned
her lovely head.   The low waist displayed perfectly-
formed arms and shoulders, lightly veiled by a silken scarf.
A short, narrow skirt of a white, transparent silken texture,

ornamented on the hem with broad silver embroidery, dis-
closed to view tiny pink shoes with pink bows. This
costume was made with a pale pink train of heavy silk,
bordered with wide silver embroidery. A pink sash,
with silver interwoven, terminating at the side in fluttering
ends, was fastened around her waist ; a bouquet of roses
ornamented her breast. All the bewitching beauty and
grace of this girl was displayed to the full by the old gown
which her great-grandmother had once worn, when she,
likewise maid-of-honor at X——, had been present with her
mistress at a *fête* at Weimar, at one of those unconstrained,
intellectual redoubts, which Karl August and Duchess
Amalie so loved, and which an immortal soul has glo-
rified.

Yes, memorable souvenirs were attached to this dress !
The train had swept the floor by Goethe's side, at the time
when he still paid tribute to beauty. He had spoken with
admiration of the young Baroness' eyes, and during her
entire lifetime that had been the worthy woman's pride.
In her diary was still to be read : *Young Goethe, the Duke's
friend, jested with every pretty face, and paid me a compli-
ment about my eyes.* From the folds of this gown still
arose a delicate scent of lavender, the perfume of the intellectual, active, brilliant past.

It had surely completely intoxicated His Highness ; he
had stood for fifteen minutes before the lovely girl, who,
the heavy folds of her train in her hand, as if ready for
flight, looked past him with restless eyes, seeking an
opportunity to escape. A respectful circle had been formed
around her and the Duke, in order to give His Highness
at any price an opportunity to chat with beautiful Fräulein
von Gerold. Yet, while all were apparently self-engrossed,
and chatted, jested, questioned, all eyes were covertly fixed
upon the incomparable, charming creature who was so
openly selected for ducal devotion and favor.

Princess Helene who, gowned as a Greek, had entered
a quadrille with His Highness' adjutant, saw this with
secret delight : she turned her dark head so energetically,
that all the gold coins on her blue velvet cap jingled and
sparkled. She must see how the Baron judged that *tête-à-
tête* in public. He had, a moment before, been leaning
against a tree-trunk, a glass of iced champagne in his hand,
with which he had touched several glasses which had

been upraised to him. He now had disappeared. Quickly she turned towards the side on which Claudine stood, and her lips were compressed—then the Baron advanced to the couple.

"Pardon, your Highness, Her Highness the Duchess wishes to speak to Fräulein von Gerold. Allow me, cousin?"

The Duke hastily passed his hand over his beard; he was just in the midst of a dissertation on costumes and head-dresses and seemed loth to interrupt it.

Claudine bowed low and laid the tips of her fingers on Lothar's arm, he leading her slowly towards the Duchess' tent.

"Go to Her Highness for a moment," said he calmly, "otherwise it might attract attention. Afterward——"

She paused and looked into his unmoved face. "I believe Her Highness desires to speak to me?"

"No," he replied, with composure; "I simply saw that you were upon nettles, and that a hundred eyes were upon you. Moreover," he added, "as I have to see you here this evening, I should prefer to admire you in the vicinity of your friend. I think, you in your fair beauty by the side of the Andalusian would be the most attractive feature of the evening. Grant us that pleasure!"

She drew her hand from his arm. The sense of relief with which she had obeyed his request gave place to indignation; but she could not reply, for she was in the Duchess' presence.

"Claudine," said the latter, extending her hand to her favorite, "are you not dancing? I should like to see you in this quadrille. I believe the fourth couple is lacking in that set. Herr von Gerold, if you please!"

She could not refuse; mechanically she took his arm. A place had hastily been made for the host and his partner. Claudine stood opposite Princess Helene and the Captain; Lothar was silent; they were a remarkably quiet couple, although the handsomest of all.

The Princess' light blue satin skirt brushed hers in the figures; a trembling, icy hand occasionally touched hers. She scarcely noticed it. Once only did she look in the Princess' face and read therein deadly contempt. The black eyes stared malevolently into hers. She felt ill-at-ease; she raised her eyes inquiringly to the Captain, he returned her glance with one of eloquent rebuke. Proudly she threw back her head, and scarcely was the final curtsey made and had Lothar offered her his arm, than she asked : "Where is Beate ? "

"She is probably in the castle," he replied.

She thanked him, and hastily took the road leading thither. On account of the Duchess' condition, the table was set for a few chosen ones in the large hall ; the folding doors were open and afforded a fine view of the lighted garden ; the table was almost embedded in the orangery.

The walls were effectively draped with Joachim's tapestry, mixed with arms and standards ; the steps, too, of the beautiful old staircase were covered with costly materials. Prosaic Beate had produced a real masterpiece of decorative art.

She stood at the table, and repeated her instructions to half a dozen lackies, and Claudine was forced to smile when she saw how obedient the people were to the abrupt peasant girl, which plain costume the severe mistress had that day donned. She gayly clapped her hands, as she saw Claudine.

"Indeed, my dearest child," she cried, "you are charming to-day in your old-fashioned gown. And how well your great-grandmother's finery is preserved ! Not even the silver is tarnished ! "

She patted her cousin's cheek, kissed her, and, pointing to the table which gleamed and glittered, she asked :

"Is that right, Claudine ? The fireworks can be best seen from her Highness' seat. You are a little lower down ; these twelve covers are for the Princesses and their knights. The others must find places at the small tables in the garden or in the hall, as chance throws them together ; there stands the basket with the lots. I have followed your advice."

"Please, Beate, excuse me from the ducal table," exclaimed Claudine, imploringly. "I prefer sitting somewhere else."

"So that Her Highness may be vexed with me all evening ! No, my dear, it cannot be ; make the best of it. Who will be your neighbor, I do not know. But excuse me, I must go to the housekeeper once more."

"Beate ! " cried Claudine, trying to catch the white sleeves of the peasant ; but the latter had disappeared

behind the drapery which on this day shut off the hall
from the corridor. She was alone ; and with hesitation
advancing again to the door, she stood upon the platform and looked into the garden. She would have liked,
at that moment, to have walked in her thin shoes along
the stony woodland paths to her peaceful, retired home.
Over there could be heard the tones of the waltz ; she felt
so bitter. She knew she was innocent, yet the oppressive
sensation did not leave her. She knew that the Duke had
agreed to be present principally because the passing
through of the Grand Duke von Z., whom he had intended
to meet at the nearest station, was postponed. Nevertheless, she had read upon all faces so peculiar an expression, devout, curious, crafty.

All had been in such haste to retire when His Highness
drew near, and *he* had taken her from the Duke's vicinity
with a remark as rude, as ungallant as possible.

She compressed her lips ; the bitter smile died away
and was followed by the old, severe, proud expression.

She suddenly raised her head. A peculiar sound, which
rose shrilly above the low music caused her to listen ; she
could not tell whether it came from the hall or from without. It sounded like the cry of a frightened beast. But
now—no, it was a child's voice—anxious, piercing, it
resounded from above. The next moment Claudine
rushed up the stairs, hastened through the broad, upper
corridor, and stepped to the open door through which
came the cries.

The pink light of the hanging lamp lighted the room
but faintly. At first Claudine saw nothing but the little
one's large, soft rug covered with a confusion of dolls and
other toys, and the empty bed, the curtains of which
were thrown back. The room seemed deserted ; the
weeping had ceased, there was no sound. Claudine's
eyes roved about the room, she advanced a step nearer,
then in affright she paused. There—in the open window,
not on the inner window-sill, no, upon the stone parapet
without cowered the child ! Her long nightgown was
wound about her tiny legs ; fear had suddenly possessed
her ; she sat there, her back to the depths, staring with
tearful eyes at the unexpected apparition of the strange
lady. The slightest movement and the child would fall.

Breathlessly the young girl stood still for a moment,

her dress scarcely rustled; rapidly thoughts coursed through her brain. Would the child be frightened, if she advanced?

"Merciful Father, help me!" she murmured. Suddenly across her set face flitted a smile; she hastily took off her bracelet and turned it round and round temptingly, while she took a step forward—another and another. Now she seized the long gown; a faint cry escaped her— the tiny form fell backwards, but with her other hand she grasped it firmly, and the next moment she was kneeling upon the carpet, the frightened child in her lap; her trembling knees refused to do their duty, half-swooning, her head rested against the posts of the console-table, while her large blue eyes looked fixedly from her livid face. Someone as terrified, as pale, as trembling, kneeled beside her; two warm lips were pressed upon her hands and upon the child's cheek.

"Lothar!" she whispered, trying to rise.

He took the child from her lap, carried her to her bed, and then approached her, who now stood erect, seeking to pass him. "Claudine!" he cried, in an unsteady voice, his form barring the way.

"It was almost too late," said she, attempting to smile, while her still pallid face was almost distorted by the effort.

He took her hand and led her to the bed.

The child sat up and laughed; he raised her and held the little one's face to the girl's pale cheek.

"Thank her!" said he, in a voice which quivered with emotion. "Your father cannot."

Claudine saw the hands which held the child tremble. She kissed Leonie.

"I was very angry with myself to think that I had accepted your invitation, cousin," said she coldly—"I can now forgive myself."

An embarrassing pause ensued. The child, with a cry of delight, reached for the star on the golden hair; Claudine had to bend her head to loosen the tiny fingers; it took quite a while. Without could be heard the hissing sound of a rocket, the signal for supper to begin. Music, laughter, voices, reached them more distinctly, and a red glow entered the windows.

She had stepped to the mirror to arrange her disordered

locks. She did not see the passionate, sorrowful glance which followed her from the dark eyes, as she had not seen a few moments before, standing in the open doorway, as if wafted thither, a dainty form in a pale blue silk dress, which form disappeared at once, as if something repulsive was to be seen in the dimly-lighted room, while in reality there was presented the most charming *genre* scene, worthy of a Meissonnier—a slender maiden by the side of the Baron, who held his smiling child in his arms.

"I will see that the nurse comes," said Claudine, as she turned to leave the room ; "otherwise the little venturesome creature might escape from her bed a second time."

At that moment, however, there entered not the careless nurse, but Frau von Berg.

"You will be kind enough, Frau von Berg, to remain beside Leonie's bed, until the nurse, whom, by the way, you seem to have trained excellently, is at her post. I should not like to have the child run the risk again of falling out of the window, as she very nearly did just now." He uttered the words calmly, almost sarcastically.

Claudine hastily stepped into the corridor ; she could not see the surprised look upon the face of the handsome Italian, who, upon a few despairing words whispered by Princess Helene, relative to the scene witnessed by her, decided once more to look into the nursery by virtue of her office. Claudine was at the end of the passage when Lothar caught up with her. Side by side they ascended the stairs which led to the hall.

All the persons in the hall and without were involuntarily filled with admiration at the sight of the beautiful feminine form in the old-fashioned gown which appeared upon the richly-decorated staircase.

"Magnificent! Charming!" murmured the Duke, his eyes growing somewhat sad. The Duchess waved her bouquet of pomegranates.

"Claudine," said she, as the girl stood before her, "we have decided to draw lots with the rest, why should not the Duke and I trust to chance to-day too? Our amiable hostess has had to cast our names in hastily."

And as Countess Moorsleben in a flower-besprigged, rococo costume with a coquettish curtsey presented Her Highness with the silver dish which contained the gilt-edged cards with the names of the gentlemen, the Duchess' delicate hand was boldly thrust in and took out one of the small rolls. Princess Thekla refused. The hand of Princess Helene, who stood a step behind Her Highness, trembled as she took the card. It seemed as if the Countess was on the point of passing Claudine by, but the Duchess with a smile touched the shoulder of the young lady with her bouquet; she was compelled to pause.

"Dearest Claudine," said the royal lady, "your fate invites you," and she who was thus addressed now took one of the cards.

"Do not read it yet !" said the Duchess, who was very much excited by the incident. Her dark eyes gleamed; she leaned lighly on Claudine's arm. "See, Dina," said she softly, "with what curious faces the cavaliers watch the ladies ! Indeed if Adalbert is not casting a comically fearful glance at my good Katzenstein. How odd she looks as Frau von Goethe ! "

The powdered head of the pretty maid-of-honor was to be seen here and there among the throng; finally she held aloft the empty silver basket, and at the same moment the orchestra began the overture to the "Midsummer Night's Dream."

The ladies were to lead to the table the gentlemen assigned to them by lot; so Princess Helene had decreed. With the soft tones of music were mingled the rattling of the papers; loud laughter, exclamations were heard.

Her Highness' eyes sparkled. She had found upon her card the name of a bashful young lieutenant.

"Well, Claudine ?" she asked, as she glanced at her friend's slip of paper. "Oh !" she cried—"His Highness."

Claudine turned pale; the paper in her hand trembled.

"A peculiar coincidence !" whispered a low voice behind her.

The Duchess turned slowly and examined Princess Helene from head to foot coldly. The innocent joy suddenly vanished from her eyes. Silently she slipped her arm through Claudine's and drew the girl forward through the crowd, which respectfully made way.

"Here, my friend," said she to the Duke, who was still standing beside Palmer, "is the neighbor at table whom

a kind fate has provided for you.   Herr von Palmer, please
bring me Lieutenant von Waldhaus ; he has been assigned
to me."

Herr von Palmer hastened away.   The royal lady stood
beside His Highness and Claudine, her smiling face hidden in the pomegranate bouquet.   At length, glowing and
breathless, a fair, tall Hussar came up and bowed low before Her Highness.

In a few seconds the people were seated at the tables ;
a broad, glittering stream of youth, beauty and magnificence went from the hall, where the Duchess, under a
crimson canopy, presided at the table with her young
cavalier, to the garden.   They sat upon the carpeted
steps in the silvery moonlight, under the lindens in the
rosy shimmer of the lanterns, listening to the low music
which floated through the soft summer night.

The Duke, with Claudine, turned toward the garden
and pointed to the shade of the lindens.

"It is sultry here in the hall," said he.

Upon the steps he paused and looked into the girl's indescribably beautiful face, which was contracted with
pain.

"For God's sake, Fräulein," said he, in terror and compassionately, "what do you think?   I am neither a rob-
ber nor a beggar, and—you have my word.   Do not
grudge me this innocent pleasure ! "

Mechanically she descended the steps with him to one
of the small tables under the lindens which was set for
four.   Her long pink train still lay upon the grass in the
gleaming moonlight, betraying her presence ; she herself
stood in the shadow, behind her chair, erect.

"Eh ! " exclaimed the Duke, suddenly, "Gerold, there
is still room here ! "

The Baron, with his lady, the young, naïve wife of the
Landrath von N——, ascended the steps ; he was restless.
He hastened to the Duke's table at such a pace that the
pretty woman by his side, in green gauze trimmed with
pearls, and with water-lilies in her hair, could scarcely
follow him.   "Your Highness called me," said he.

He drew a deep breath as he held his lady's chair while
she seated herself, and he beckoned to the servant carrying a dish with food.

The little Princess had fallen by lot to Herr von Palmer.

She sat in the hall at Her Highness' table, as did Princess Thekla. From her place the Duchess could see the table at which her husband supped ; the forms of the four persons were as if bathed in a Rembrandt-like light and shade. She raised her champagne glass and drank to the Duke. Baron Lothar rose once, advanced to the stairs, and toasted Their Highnesses. The Duke drank to the ladies.

Princess Helene's eyes were fixed with a veritably demoniacal expression upon the table below in the garden. They seemed very gay there ; the Duke's sonorous laughter rang clearly in her ears. Occasionally she turned her pale face with the sparkling eyes toward the Duchess, and observed with secret satisfaction how she constantly directed glances thither ; they seemed to contain a dread question, although her lips smiled, although she seemed gayer than she had been for some time. At that table, too, the mood was gay. Frau von Katzenstein, who had a young man for her escort, was charming in her dry humor. At dessert, when the bonbons vied with the rockets outside, Princess Helene seated herself beside the Duchess. She had asked Herr von Palmer to change places with her, to which request he gladly acceded. Her Highness had virtually ignored him. All of her remarks were addressed to her young cavalier. At first the little Princess was silent. Notwithstanding her mad jealousy, her heart throbbed violently at the thought of what she was about to do. Contrary to all etiquette, she emptied her champagne glass several times. Herr von Palmer had it filled each time unobserved.

In her mad, passionate excitement her brain worked. She looked down again. A large Bengal light just flashed forth and showed her the hated one beside *him* distinctly ; they were not speaking, no, but his face was turned towards her, as if he wished to drink in to the full the sight of the lovely girl in the white flood of light. Her rebellious blood, heated by wine, mounted to her brain.

"Your Highness," she whispered, without consideration, leaning towards her, who was just taking up fan and bouquet. "Your Highness ! Elizabeth, for God's sake, you are too confiding ! "

Had the Duchess not heard her words ? She rose slowly and with dignity. The signal to rise was given, chairs were pushed back, and without, among the green trees, blazed the monogram, A. E., with the ducal coronet. All hastened back to the garden, to dance.

"Princess Helene!" said the Duchess to her cavalier, when, a few moments later, she entered the tent adjoining the ballroom. She had on her light cloak and looked chilly. She did not seat herself; the order for the carriage had been given. The Duke still stood under the lindens, chatting with Claudine.

Princess Helene hastily advanced; upon her flushed face lay a sort of desperate defiance.

"Explain yourself more plainly, cousin," said the Duchess to her, aloud, motioning Frau von Katzenstein to retire. There was no one else in the small, rosy-lighted tent, before the open curtains of which the guests passed to and fro in the moonlight.

"Your Highness!" cried the passionate girl, violently, "I cannot bear to see you deceived thus!"

"*Who* is deceiving me?"

Once more all the kindness in the girl's nature gained the upper hand. She looked at the woman struggling for breath; she knew what her next words meant for that life.

"No one! No one!" she cried. "Let me go, Elizabeth—send me away!"

"Who is deceiving me?" again asked the Duchess, firmly, although with an effort.

The Princess clasped her tiny hands, and her eyes were turned upon Claudine, who was still detained by the Duke. The Duchess' eyes followed hers; a startling pallor overspread her face.

"I do not understand you," said she, coldly.

The Princess' heart beat wildly against the box in which she kept the Duke's letter.

"Your Highness does not *want* to understand," she whispered. "Your Highness *wishes* to close your eyes!" She raised her clasped hands and pressed them to her blue silk waist; at that moment she saw again the scene in the darkened room at the child's bedside. "Claudine von Gerold!" she cried.

She did not finish. The Duchess' form reeled. With a slight cry of terror, the Princess supported her, but only for a moment; the Duchess was again mistress of herself.

"It seems as if the sultry, oppressive night begets

fever," said she, with a smile about her pale lips. "Go
to bed, cousin, and drink cool lemonade—you are delirious!—Call Fräulein von Gerold, dear Katzenstein," she
said, turning to the lady-in-waiting, who had hastened
up, and from under her little lace cap looked anxiously
into the Duchess' ghastly face.

When the lovely girl approached she said, pleasantly,
and so loudly that those standing around her could hear
her, as she employed the familiar form of speech:

"Take me to the carriage, Dina, and do not forget that
to-morrow you will sit beside a sickbed. I fear this
beautiful *fête* has been too much for my strength."

She leaned heavily upon Claudine's arm, and, accompanied by the Duke, Baron Lothar, and the suite, and
bowing on all sides, she walked toward the steps where
the carriage waited. As she did so, she overlooked
Princess Helene's low bow. When Claudine returned, by
the side of Lothar, she carried the Duchess' bunch of
pomegranates in her hand.

She remained a few moments among all those who suddenly seemed to have eyes no longer for her; but she
did not observe it; she longed for rest. "Good-night,
Beate, I am going home."

"How strange the Duchess was on bidding you farewell!" said Beate, as she walked with Claudine through
a side-path to the carriage. "She gazed at you as if she
longed to look into the depths of your soul, and yet as if
she had to apologize to you for something. There is
something childish about this woman! How charming
was the manner in which at the last she handed you the
bouquet from the carriage and said, 'My dear Claudine,'
as if she could not do enough for you."

"We love each other dearly," replied Claudine simply.

Princess Helene danced far into the night.—In mad delirium, thought Frau von Berg, who had returned, after
pouring the vials of her wrath copiously upon the nurse's
head. The little Princess' black eyes glistened with tears
amid her laughter, and her hand was clinched as she held
her ivory fan. Suddenly she felt as if she could no longer
bear the inward unrest, the anguish of heart; she flung
herself in the shadow of a bower upon a seat and pressed
her glowing cheek against the cool iron. Frau von Berg
stood before her with a gloomy air.

"My God," said she, "if any one were to see your Highness thus!"

"Is the Baron coming?" asked the weeping Princess, hastily drying her eyes.

Berg smiled.

"Oh, no; he is talking with Landrath von Besser about fire insurance."

"Did you see, Alice? Claudine von Gerold was favored by the Duchess with her bouquet on leaving; that was"—here the Princess laughed—"the result of my well-meant warning."

Frau von Berg still smiled.

"Excuse me, your Highness, the Duchess could do nothing else! Upon a mere 'on dit' such a character does not drop a friend. I thought you knew Her Highness better. You yourself insisted so upon 'proofs'!"

The Princess put both hands to her ears as if she did not wish to hear any more.

"Proofs!" repeated Frau von Berg once more. "Proofs, your Highness!"

Directly after her return the Duchess at once retired to her bedroom to rest. How easy it is to say "to rest," how natural it sounds, and how coyly sleep flies from the anxious heart!

She sipped her refreshing raspberry juice, and, her arms under her head, lay in her quiet room. Occasionally she coughed and her cheeks began to glow.

The exciting *fête* had been too much for her, she should have remained in the sick-room, where she belonged—but it was so hard to be so young and yet so frail! Would it ever be better?

She put her hand to her left side, she felt a peculiar, dull ache there. Strange, what could it be? Was it physical? Was it her heart?—Like paralyzing, icy fear it crept through her veins and dulled her thoughts.

"Impossible!" she whispered. She suddenly knew whence the dull ache came. Impossible! She sat up in bed and looked about her as if to assure herself that she was still awake, that no nightmare was tormenting her. There lay the brilliants which the maid had taken out of her hair, upon the silken cover of the toilet table. She had dismissed the servant so hastily, that she could not put things away ; she felt an urgent desire to be alone. Usually, too, she enjoyed a chat with her good Katzenstein ; but on this day the amiable old lady was dismissed in the corridor.

There hung over the red silk arm of the chair the lace mantilla ; by her side lay one of the roses which Claudine had worn on her bosom, and which she had asked for because she liked the perfume. How beautiful the girl had looked !

The Duchess seized the hand-glass in its ivory frame and looked into it. Two sunken eyes, a thin, sallow face, were reflected in it by the faint pink light. She let the glass fall upon the coverlet and lay back, tormenting fear upon her features. "Merciful Father !" she whispered. She took the picture of the Duke from the table beside her bed, gazed at the handsome, proud face, and then pressed it passionately to her lips.

Oh, *she* knew best, how much one could love that man !

With the picture pressed to her breast beneath her clasped hands, she lay still, gazing into space. Claudine's attractive form, as she had seen it a few hours before her, rose before her eyes ; she saw her beside the Duke at the table, at the dance under the lindens—the girl had so often changed color. How embarrassed she always was when His Highness entered the room ! She sang so unwillingly, when *he* was present ! She was at times so deeply depressed, then again so gay !

" Poor Claudine ! A fine friend she who is thinking of you, who first drew you forcibly hither in order then to doubt you ! "

No, she did not doubt. Absurd gossip ! The little Princess was at times almost incomprehensible !

" Poor Claudine ! "

The Duchess smiled, and yet suddenly cold drops of perspiration stood upon her brow, and through the buzzing of the turbulent blood in her ears rang the clear merciless sound of a bell, the Princess' voice.—" Your Highness does not *want* to see, your Highness does not *want* to understand ! " so decided, so horribly distinct ! " Our Father " escaped her lips, and her hot hands pressed the picture tighter to her restless, throbbing heart. Her lips murmured the Lord's Prayer. "Amen! Death rather than such an experience—let me die,—good God, let me die!"

She reviewed her whole wedded life. She herself had prodigally ornamented the altar of her happiness with roses; was she ignorant of the lamentable fact that otherwise it would have remained unornamented,—that she had been the *sole* one to pay it tribute? How came she to do so? No, she had not fancied that happiness, she really possessed it! He was always so kind, so gallant, so considerate, and especially so now that she was ill!

"Kind! considerate! Is that all love can give?"

She moaned; it seemed to her suddenly as if a veil had been torn from her eyes,—a veil which allowed her to look into an unbounded gulf of despair.

But never had he ever given her cause for jealousy, that vulgar passion which, Princess Thekla said, a Princess should never possess.

"I do not know that passion," she had then responded. "I have, thank God, had no occasion for it." At this moment, however, the reigning Duchess, the Royal Princess, felt that she too had fallen a victim to that passion, in such a terrible degree that she likewise lay upon the rack without hope of rescue. Again she looked in the glass, then she put her hands to her eyes. Had she been blind? What could she be to him—she, the invalid on the brink of the grave? Nothing, nothing but a burden. Not that, oh, not that!

Could they not wait until she was dead? How much longer would it last? "Ah, pity, mercy, only so long! Mercy!"

She sank back in a fainting condition, unable to move, and yet feeling that she was awake, that it was horrible reality, that her fate had flung aside its smiling mask in order to show its true face—such a disconsolate, despairing face.

She did not know how long she lay there. She had not the strength to collect herself. She saw a fair head resting upon *his* breast, as hers had once done; and she lay in her coffin and could not move, although she tried. The cold perspiration trickled down her brow; with a mighty effort she at length started up and pulled the bell-rope in wild despair. In affright, the maid rushed in.

"Open the windows!" moaned the Duchess, sitting up in bed, "I am suffocating!"

The maid hastened to the window, and pulled back the curtains, when the first glowing rays of the morning sun penetrated the room and fell upon the young woman lying anxious, feverish and agitated upon her bed.

She looked out as if inquiringly into that wonderful, beautiful world, over the summits of the trees of the park trembling in the morning wind to the bluish green fir-wooded mountains. She inhaled the pure, fresh air, she heard the twittering of the birds in the branches, and she burst into tears—tears of shame at her despair, her mistrust.

For some time she lay there sobbing, and finally she fell asleep. When she awoke, Claudine was at her bedside.

She was arranging a bunch of roses which she had begged from Heinemann's bushes, and was so busily engaged with them that she did not notice how the Duchess' eyes were resting upon her. When she raised her eyes, a happy expression passed over her anxious face.

"Ah!" cried she, kneeling by the couch with her roses. "How you have startled me, Elizabeth! What ails you? Early this morning Frau von Katzenstein sent for me. Did the *fête* yesterday make you ill?"

The Duchess' head was supported by her hand, and she gazed fixedly into the pretty face in which anguish and sorrow spoke so plainly. Then she caressingly stroked the perfumed blonde hair. "I am already better," said she softly; "how kind of you to come." During the entire afternoon she remained silent, but she followed Claudine constantly with her eyes. Towards noon she wanted to rise, but she staggered like one intoxicated and was forced to return to bed.

"Stay with me, Claudine," she implored.

"Yes, Elizabeth."

The invalid opened her weary, sunken eyes, and as if surprised at the hasty consent, she asked:

"Can you leave home without anxiety?"

"Do not speak of it, Elizabeth. Were I needed, I should come nevertheless. I will write a few words to Joachim and have him send me a few necessaries. Do not make yourself uneasy!"

"Tell me something," said the Duchess, towards evening. The entire day she had lain almost motionless with closed eyes.

"Gladly, Elizabeth ; but what?"

"Something of your life."

"Ah, there is little to tell. I think, Elizabeth, you know it all."

"All?"

"Yes, my dear Elizabeth!"

"Have you never loved, Dina?"

A glowing blush suffused the girl's cheeks ; slowly she bent her head.

"Do not, Elizabeth," she besought in a low voice, "ask me any more—I——"

"Can you not tell it to me?" asked the Duchess softly. "Give me your confidence, Dina—give it to me—you know all of my secrets."

At that moment the maid announced the Duke, the lovely girl rose, and with a bow passed by the Duke into the adjoining room.

"Claudine! Claudine!" cried the invalid, and, as she hastily returned, the Duchess pointed to a seat by her couch. "Remain here!" she said, in a tone of command. It was the first time she had spoken thus to her. Obediently Claudine seated herself. She heard how sympathetically the Duke conversed with his sick wife, how he expressed the hope that on the morrow she would be able to participate in the garden party, that surely mamma would be there too.

"I will try to be well," she replied.

"That is excellent, Liesel! You will try," laughed the Duke. "If all invalids thought so, there would be fewer patients. The will has really some effect on convalescence. Ask the doctor."

"I know it, I know it," said she hastily.

"The doctor maintains you are to-day only psychically ill," said the Duke ; "I do not see how it could be so! I think, you simply took cold, my child. You must certainly be more cautious ; night-air is not good for you. In the winter you shall surely go to Cannes."

"In the winter!" thought she bitterly, while aloud she said with a defiance foreign to her: "But I will not be careful!"

His Highness looked in amazement at the usually sub-

missive creature. "You are indeed ill," he replied, with
a sharpness called forth by unreasonable perverseness.
And turning to Claudine, he said, changing the subject:
"Your cousin indeed prepared a delightful *fête* yesterday;
what tasteful arrangement, what original toilettes!
Yours, for example, Fräulein, simply grand! Was it not,
Elizabeth?"

"I cannot stand the sound of voices, Adalbert; please
go," said the sick woman, with nervously quivering lips.
And when he, with an impatient gesture, was about to retire, she extended him her hand, while her eyes filled
with tears. "Forgive me!" Then she seized Claudine's
hand, and holding it in her feverish right hand, she lay
back and closed her eyes.

He was gone.

The sky in the mean time was overcast with heavy,
dark clouds; the air was sultry and oppressive. In the
dim light, the Duchess' face looked like that of a corpse.
She lay there motionless, and Claudine sat beside her
for hours. She felt strangely ill at ease.

The news of the Duchess' illness was soon spread
abroad.

"She looked so remarkably pale towards the last," said
Princess Thekla, as they sat at supper in the Neuhaus
dining-room.

"My cousin was sent for early this morning," said
Beate, in whom not a trace of weariness was to be seen,
although she had not gone to bed at all, that all the
traces of the festivities might be put away under her
supervision. Every silver fork was again in its place,
every cup, every piece of furniture, nothing remained of
the fairyland of the previous night, not even was anything of it to be seen in the people themselves. "She
has just written me," continued Beate, "that she is nursing the Duchess, and has removed to Altenstein
altogether."

"Quite a touching friendship!" exclaimed the old
Princess, who was in a very ill humor; for that morning,
while she still slumbered sweetly, Baron Lothar dismissed

the nurse, bag and baggage; and Frau von Berg brought
a note to her bedside, interrupting a blissful dream.   It
contained the dismissal from her position as governess
"of my daughter," in all formality, to be sure very
politely made, but the fact remained, although in a courteous manner the Baron at the close invited the lady to
partake of his hospitality as long as she liked.

She donned a dressing-gown, and, contrary to all etiquette, rushed into Princess Helene's sleeping-apartment.
Her Highness looked miserable, with dark circles under
her eyes, as if she had wept more than she had slept during the night.

"What does it amount to?" was the impatient consolation given.   "Come to mamma, Alice; I will speak
with her.   Countess Moorsleben is going to her parents
soon."

"Mamma" at once bade her beloved Alice come to her.
It was, indeed, unheard of to dismiss a "lady" as if she
were a menial; a lady whom *she* had chosen herself.
She did not dare, however, to raise any objections; the
curt reason given by the Baron was all too cogent : one
must be *pro forma* vexed with her, who had almost caused
the death of her beloved grandchild.   Moreover, he had
not spoken, and, unfortunately, one could not "command" him to a marriage as to a waltz.

Frau von Berg was not satisfied with the arrangement;
she sat, as pale as an innocent, injured angel, in her
room, outwardly composed, inwardly "beside herself"
with anger.   The nursery was at once changed, close to
Beate's old comfortable bedroom, near by the broad, airy
court, where the horses, cows and poultry were to be
seen,—the same view which had delighted the child's
father and aunt.   And the same faithful person who had
formerly cared for them, now bore the child upon her
arm, a neat woman of about fifty, with the kindliest eyes
in the world under her black, peasant's cap.   Lothar had
early that morning fetched her in person from the cottage
at the end of the village.

"What touching friendship!" Princess Thekla had
cried ; but Beate did not notice the sarcasm, and Lothar
did not want to notice it.   He looked dreamily out into
the dark night.

"The Duchess is frequently indisposed, as we all know,

mamma," said Princess Helene, her eyes constantly on Lothar.

"Of course! Perhaps she has been annoyed by something," said the old Princess, significantly. "Then, too, this sultriness is suffocating; I should never have believed that it could be so warm in the mountains; I think continually of the cool, billowy North Sea. Herr von Pankewirtz," she turned to the chamberlain, "have you had word from Ostend, if we can have the rooms at the *Hôtel de l'Océan ?*"

Beate looked in surprise at her brother. The enormous trunks, which the august Princesses had brought to Neuhaus, led their host and hostess to conclude they intended making a longer stay.

Herr von Pankewitz made an apologetic gesture. "Your Highness, the proprietor telegraphs that unfortunately my order came too late ; but he thinks, some other hotel——"

"You will, I hope, accompany us, dear Lothar." Princess Thekla interrupted the affable old man thus, and turned with an unusually amiable air to Baron Gerold. "The remembrance of our beloved dead will likewise attract you to the spot where you spent together the brief weeks of your engagement."

Lothar bowed with striking gallantry. "Pardon, your Highness—I do not like to see places a second time with which such sorrowful memories are connected ; one is so easily disposed to accord to the past too great a right, while it is a man's place to gain, by every means in his power, outward and inward composure, in order to be satisfied with the present,—with his duty. But aside from that, I have of late noticed that my presence in Neuhaus is more than necessary ; it would, too, be beneficial to my estate in Saxony, were the master's eye to rest upon it. Only now," he continued, as he attentively handed Princess Helene the *compote* dish, "only since I have been forced to live so long in southern climates, only now do I love my home truly, this tiny spot upon which I grew to manhood ; I should really not like to go away from it for another moment."

The Princess cast a despairing glance through the window ; occasioned, perhaps, as much by the threatening appearance of the sky as by her son-in-law's stubbornness. "A wife, a mother, of course looks differently at the memory of one who has departed this life," said she coldly, "less heroically. Pardon, Baron!"

"Your Highness," he replied with warmth, "it would be bad were it to be otherwise! Women have a right to outward signs of mourning as well as to those of joy; it is they who scatter flowers at the merry *fête*, it is they who decorate the grave. What a shimmer would life lack were they more heroic!"

Princess Helene blushed scarlet. How came her mother to think of going away—now? The fork in her hand trembled, she was forced to lay it down. Countess Moorsleben cried: "Are you ill, your Highness?"

"Indeed—I am—suddenly dizzy," stammered the Princess. "Excuse me, if I——"

She rose, and, her handkerchief pressed to her eyes, with a slight bow, she passed out, motioning the Countess to remain behind. She flew up the stairs and into Frau von Berg's room.

"Alice!" cried she, beside herself, "mamma talks of going away! It is terrible—all is lost!"

Frau von Berg, who, in a light-blue morning dress, trimmed with cream-colored lace, walked up and down the room, occasionally, with half closed eyes, holding to her nose her English smelling salts, each time moaning slightly, paused and for a moment forgot her *rôle* of invalid.

"Gerold has refused to accompany mamma," continued the Princess with agitation, pulling her handkerchief, the delicate Valenciennes of which she tore. "He suddenly raves of his woods, like a veritable peasant's son whom one advises to emigrate to America. What shall I do at Ostend? especially when I know that you are not here, Alice? I cannot bear it," she asseverated, flinging herself upon the sofa, "I will leap from the train on the way, I will throw myself into the sea, I——"

The Princess' white face gleamed almost unrecognizably in the darkness which had speedily fallen upon the motionless form of the woman standing there.

"Ah, my God, all is lost!" cried she, as the latter maintained silence. "I will go, and she will remain!" And she began to weep passionately, again burying her head in the cushions. "I feel it, Alice, I feel it! He! loves her; he loved her before," she sobbed.

Frau von Berg smiled. She had no longer reason to spare any one; she hated all these people since her defeat of that day, and experienced something like the blissful sensation with which an anarchist thinks by means of a small dynamite cartridge to blow the innocent and the guilty into the air.

"Princess, no unnecessary tears," said she coldly. "You must now act. Before all things, I think the Duchess should be shown that your Highness did not speak in delirium last night. Everything else would then be arranged."

In spirit Frau von Berg already saw the whole clique fly in the air; for her part, too, the childish, irresolute creature before her!

"But I cannot tell her, I cannot!" murmured the Princess. "I once saw them shoot a doe, and she looked at me just that way yesterday; I cannot! I did not sleep the whole night on that account."

Frau von Berg shrugged her shoulders. "Your Highness must then go to Ostend; the idyll here will develop without being disturbed."

The wind-storm, which raved without, cast sand and leaves against the windows, and furiously blew the linden-boughs; then came the first vivid flash of lightning and played upon the mocking, distorted face of the handsome woman, who leaned against the window and looked out at the storm.

"I will write to her," now said the Princess; "she would not receive me." And after a pause, during which a thunder-clap caused the house to shake: "I owe it to her—yes, yes, I owe it to her; you are right, Alice. Come to my room, I am afraid."

Frau von Berg lighted a wax-candle on the writing-table, and accompanied the Princess across the corridor to her room. Upon the full, white face lay a trace of infinite satisfaction. "At length!" thought she, in secret clinching her fist. If one spark of kindness had been in her, the previous evening had extinguished it. How haughtily she had passed her by, when Baron Gerold had rebuked her—Frau von Berg, *née* Cometzky; she, whose ancestors were as old at least as hers; they were descended directly

from the Sobieskis. Her eyes gleamed ; the Duke had
yesterday spoken to her for the first time in quite a while,
and she had boldly ventured to remind him of past days
when, as a young Prince, he was blindly in love with her ;
and old love——

"What do you think, Alice?" the Princess interrupted
the bold flight of these thoughts. "How shall I write?"

The graceful Princess seated herself at the rococo writing desk, before her a crested sheet of paper ; as yet there
was nothing on it but : *Dear Elizabeth!*

"Something like this, your Highness :—that anxiety—
for Her Highness' happiness induced you to confirm the
hint thrown out yesterday ; your Highness could not be
responsible for it to your conscience, and so forth, and here
is the proof——"

The Princess turned her head and wrote. Without the
storm raged, and, when a thunder-clap shook the house,
the girl's hand paused. Occasionally the Princess passed
her hand anxiously over her brow ; then the pen again
flew over the paper, and finally the girl handed the paper
to the woman standing motionless in the center of the
room.

The latter drew nearer the small taper and read. "As
usual, *con passione*," said she. "Touching! And now his
Highness' note, your Highness," and her eyes glittered
like those of a cat eager for prey.

The Princess drew the chain from under her white,
embroidered dress : with hesitation she took the letter
from the medallion and then closed her hand over it.
One last struggle took place in her heart. Frau von Berg
leaned against the wall, beside the table, and played with
the tassel on her gown. "Moreover," said she slowly,
without looking up, "she looked superb yesterday, did
Claudine. These fair women with the limpid blue eyes
have a peculiar charm." However, she noticed that
the Princess addressed the envelope with trembling
fingers.

At that moment the Countess appeared to summon her
young mistress to her mother's presence. The old Princess had one of the nervous attacks and was in a condition in which she broke things, tore materials, and rushed
about uttering oaths. On this day she raged as did the
weather without. The Princess returned to her room in

half an hour with tear-swollen eyes; she had with mute defiance accepted the whole flood of reproaches. But she was surely not to blame that her mother could no longer breathe the oppressive air, and that the Dowager Duchess had so coldly answered Her Highness' letter. Why did she write to that severe lady with the faultless manners, the lady who had always shown great affection for Claudine? The paper still flickered upon the writing-table; the pen, hastily thrown aside, lay beside the writing materials, but the tiny hand was raised to her brow—the letter? Where was the letter?

A vague fear possessed her; she rushed through the corridor to Frau von Berg's room.

"Alice!" she cried in the darkness, "the letter! Where is the letter? I would like to read it once more!"

No answer.

"Alice!" cried she violently, stamping her foot.

All was still.

Heedless of her tear-stained eyes, she descended the stairs; through the half-opened door of the hall came wonderfully refreshing air; it had ceased raining. Without upon the flag-stones a form flitted to and fro.

"Alice!" cried the Princess for the third time hurrying out. "The letter? Where is the letter?"

"Your Highness, I promptly disposed of it."

A half-stifled cry escaped the agitated Princess' lips. "Who ordered you to send the letter?" she stammered eagerly, seizing the lady's shoulder.

"Well, your Highness," replied the latter, not in the least disconcerted, "I had just an opportunity."

But the Princess was not calmed. "And where shall I say I obtained this horrible billet?"

"You found it!" replied Berg.

"I never lie!" exclaimed the Princess, and her dainty form seemed to become taller. "I shall say I got it from you, as true as there is a God above, and I shall be speaking the truth, Alice!"

"As your Highness may think,—then I found the letter," replied she. "I gave it to the groom, whom the Baron sent to Fräulein von Gerold at Altenstein; he was to deliver it to Frau von Katzenstein; I wrote a few words to the effect that she should hand the enclosed billet to Her Highness to-morrow morning."

The Princess had become quiet ; she grasped the brass door-knocker, which shimmered in the moonlight, and which was surmounted by the star-adorned stag. She could no longer think clearly, she felt unutterably miserable. Frau von Berg knew quite well that it was a letter from Beate which the groom took away with him ; but why should she say it ? In that way the fire would be fanned.

The Princess turned back to the hall, and there she stood still. Fear, unspeakable horror, stole over her.

Beate was just coming out of Lothar's room, her basket of keys on her arm. "Princess!" cried she in affright, "how you look!"

She was recalled to her senses. She hastened upstairs to her room, and then she ran her hands through her hair and lay through the night dressed upon her bed, half unconscious, dreading the dawn of day.

When the storm came up the Duchess sent for her children ; the youngest clung closely to her, who, supported by pillows, sat up in bed ; the Hereditary Prince stood bravely at the window and looked out into the night ; while Claudine had the second Prince upon her knee. Beside the Hereditary Prince stood the Duke, listening to the pattering of the hail and watching the masses of water which the storm flung against the panes ; the Duchess talked to the baby ; in the adjoining room were Frau von Katzenstein, the Princess' governess and the maid.

When the thunder grew more distant and the rain fell less heavily, the royal children were sent to their room. The Hereditary Prince for a moment gazed in Claudine's face.

"Were you afraid?" he asked.

She pleasantly shook her pretty head.

"I like that," said the slender youth. "Mamma is always afraid."

The mother drew her child to her.

"You like Fräulein von Gerold altogether?" she asked, with a sad smile.

"Yes, mamma," replied the boy; "were I a man, I should marry her."

No one laughed at these childish words; the Duke at the window did not stir, and Claudine was embarrassed. The Duchess nodded. "Sleep well, dear, dear children, God bless you."

When the sound of the tiny feet had died away, she said softly: "I am very tired, Adalbert!"

The Duke likewise withdrew. He kissed his wife's brow before leaving the room. "I hope you will be better to-morrow!" he said.

"I promise you I will!" she replied, cheerfully.

Claudine wanted to share the night-watch with Frau von Katzenstein. She went into the room assigned her, the one in which she had slept when a child, and put on a more comfortable, warmer dress. Then she returned and seated herself by the bedside, quiet and patient.

The Duchess lay there with closed eyes. The small clock ticked softly; the image of the Madonna gleamed faintly; the girl's eyes lingered upon that sweet face and then wandered to the pale one of the invalid. Then her head sank back in the cushions, she closed her eyes and fell into a reverie.

She was tired from the preceding night; a languid dreaminess possessed her; she saw herself with his child upon her arm, and felt his kiss of gratitude upon her hand, and she smiled in her sleep. Then she started up and sat there waking, while horror stole over her. She looked into the Duchess' eyes, which were fastened upon her with a peculiar keen expression so strangely fixed!

"Elizabeth," she asked, with a slight shudder, "can you not sleep?"

"No!" was the curt reply.

"Shall I read aloud to you?"

"No, I thank you!"

"Do you want to talk? Shall I arrange your pillows?"

"Give me your hand, Claudine; was I trying to-day?"

"Ah, Elizabeth, you are never that!" cried the girl, kneeling beside her.

"Yes, yes, I feel it. But then—my heart is sick and you must forgive me."

"Tell me, Elizabeth, has anything grieved you?"

"No, I have only been thinking of death, Claudine."

"Do not think of *that!*"

"You know, Claudine, there is no remedy for love and death. I believe I would not fear death, I have more dread of living on."

"You are surely ill, Elizabeth."

"Yes, and I am so weary. You must sleep too ; it is better I should be alone ; if you please, go ! The maid is awake in the next room ; go ! I am obliged to look at you if you sit here."

Claudine bent sadly over the feverish hand and retired. Towards midnight she crept in her night-gown to the sick-room, and listened behind the red silk curtain to hear if the Duchess was asleep. All was still ; but, as by the motion the folds were gently stirred, the large dark eyes of the sufferer were turned slowly with the same fixed question-ing expression as formerly upon her.

"What do you want?" she asked.

Claudine stepped forth. "I was anxious about you," said she. "Pardon me."

"Tell me," said the Duchess, completely unnerved, "why you did not wish at first to go to Neuhaus yester-day ?"

Claudine was surprised. She drew nearer. "Why I did not want to go to Neuhaus?" she repeated, with a blush. Then she was silent. It was impossible for her to say : "Because I love Lothar, and because he insults me wherever he sees me,—because he mistrusts me, be-cause——"

The Duchess turned abruptly. "Cease, cease ! I re-quire no answer. Go, go !"

Helplessly the girl turned towards the door.

"Claudine ! Claudine !" resounded behind her, in a heart-rending, anxious voice. The invalid was sitting up in bed with outstretched arms ; fearfully her imploring eyes were fixed on hers.

She came back, seated herself upon the bed and took the frail, trembling form in her arms.

"Elizabeth," said she tenderly, "let me remain with you !"

"Pardon me, ah, pardon !" sobbed the Duchess, kiss-ing the girl, her dress, her long, fair hair, which fell loosely upon her neck, and her eyes.

"Tell me," she whispered,—"tell me aloud that you love me!"

"I love you very dearly, Elizabeth," said Claudine, drying the large drops which trickled down the sick woman's face, as a mother does her child. "You do not indeed know how much, Elizabeth."

Exhausted the Duchess fell back. "Thank you—I am so tired!"

Claudine sat there awhile; then, when she thought the child was asleep, she gently withdrew her hand from that of her friend and left the room on tip-toe. A strange feeling of horror went with her. What ailed the Duchess? That stare, that coldness, that passionate tenderness, what did they betoken?

"She is ill!" said she to herself.

She stood in front of the glass to arrange her loosened hair—a suspicion stole over her; the hand which held the tortoise-shell pin dropped. She proudly shook back the golden wealth of hair. Neither she nor the Duchess was small enough to believe gossip. One of those prophetic, incomprehensible combinations of thought suddenly caused the remembrance of the vanished billet to occur to her. At that moment her heart palpitated violently. Then she smiled—who could tell in what woodland nook it moldered in the rain and dew?

She took the tiny prayer-book from which her mother had read aloud to her every evening, and opened it:

"Protect me, Lord, from slander and defend me from mine enemies! Let no harm come to me and mine and no plague approach our dwelling," she read, and her thoughts reverted to the peaceful house from the tower-room of which her brother's student lamp shone out into the wood. And from these they turned to the bed of the motherless child at Neuhaus.

"Guard us, dear Lord, as you guarded us yesterday!" she whispered, again glancing at the book. "Have mercy upon the sick, who sleeplessly toss upon their beds, languishing for relief—" she read on—"and all nigh unto death, to whom this night shall be the last."

The book fell from her hands, fear possessed her, the terrified face of the Duchess suddenly stared at her. She buried her head in the pillows—how came she to such a terrible thing?

Only after a long interval did she rise and wrap herself in the covers. The lamp she left burning on the table; she did not care to remain in the dark.

The next morning was so bright, so clear, so delightfully fresh. The sun sparkled in a million dew-drops on the broad lawn of the Altenstein park, where a number of workmen were making preparations for a *fête*; how merry and gay everything appeared! They had erected a staff with a gayly-colored bird upon it, set up a merry-go-round, whose horses wore crimson equipments, a Punch-and-Judy show and a red-and-white striped tent, from the top of which floated a number of crimson flags and streamers. In the shadow of the trees was a platform for the musicians and a board floor for dancing, all for the little folks.

On this day the Hereditary Prince was to celebrate his birthday, and this was the surprise given him by his father's mother, besides the beautiful pony which was secretly led into the stall the night before, and which stood there at the manger, although he could scarcely reach it.

The Dowager Duchess was expected about noon according to the dispatch which had arrived early that morning. At two o'clock the family dinner was to be served, and for the afternoon a number of invitations, principally to children, had been sent out. Even little Elizabeth from the Owl's Nest, and Leonie, Baroness Gerold, were invited by great solemn cards.

The Duchess' indisposition, added to the inclement weather of the day before, had aroused considerable doubt. Would the *fête* be able to take place? But, thank God, the dreaded postponement had not been announced. Her Highness was better, and the weather perfect. They could look forward to the interesting afternoon as to a continuation of the previous one. It had been simply divine at Neuhaus, "as piquant as a chapter by Daudet," said Her Excellency Plassen to Countess Lilienstein, as they took their morning stroll in the forest, and then they whispered mysteriously, and Her Excellency cast down her eyes.

"If she is only shrewd enough, he will marry her; the result is assured," said the lady finally.

"Do not fear, my dear Countess, the Gerolds all understand their advantages. The Baron too will get the second Princess—he is, to be sure, very coy——"

"Slyness, dearest Plassen."

"Ah! They are already like intimate relations; the Duke calls him 'cousin' occasionally."

"He may be—doubly related!" And she laughed at her wit.

"Does the Duchess really suspect nothing?" asked one of the gentlemen in the bowling-alley of the "Trout," where they were taking their morning dram. "Or does she purposely overlook it?"

"Possibly, she is a sensible woman," said Baron Elbenstein, holding a ball in his hand.

"Why not altogether?" corrected stout Major Baumberg; "the poor woman sees what concerns her husband through a golden glass—she has no suspicion—she defies the Duke."

"Just for that reason—she would not grudge him his happiness!"

"Deucedly handsome woman, the Gerold!"

"Charming!"

"Above all others!"

"And coquettish!"

"And sly, sly! What a fine stroke of diplomacy; she runs from the position of maid-of-honor to this wilderness just at the moment when the paternal manor is sold by auction. . . Famous, is it not?. . And he nibbled!" said a melancholy attaché.

His Excellency with the venerable white head raised his bristly brows. "Her Highness is a sensitive woman," said he, in his chronically husky voice. "Gentlemen, I beg of you!" He was not heard.

"We are posted on the subject!" cried one who had just made a good shot.

Yet once more His Excellency interceded for the girl so severely condemned and sought to prove that it was unfounded calumny; but in the midst of his speech, his husky voice gave out; he coughed several times, mopped his heated face, angrily drank his beer and left the scandal-mongers.

"Incredible! Incredible!" he murmured to himself. And when he met a couple of young ladies, who as they chatted passed him by, he watched the pretty forms closely.

13

" I'll wager, they too are whispering scandal ; greenhorns,
who as yet have no opinion. Ah, I wish that——" But
His Excellency could not prevent the whispering with his
most emphatic oaths. Softly, softly they whispered on.
Like the summer wind the tree-tops rustled, it passed
from ear to ear; even the servants put their heads together, and it had spread farther and farther ; the swallows
twittered it in the nest of the village mountains, and one
neighbor told it to the other. And in one of the poorest
little cottages sat an old peasant woman, writing with
childish enthusiasm to the gracious Fräulein von Gerold,
asking her to tell the Duke he should free her son from
the military, if *she* did so, it would surely help her.

In the castle all was astir early. The neat kitchen-
maid, who, at the sound of the electric bell, entered Claudine's room, brought several letters with her.

" Do they know how Her Highness is ? " asked Claudine.

"Oh, very well ! Her Highness slept well, and will at
eleven o'clock receive the Hereditary Prince in the red
drawing-room."

"Thank God ! "

Claudine sent the girl to the maid, and through her asked
for further orders. When she had made her toilet, she
broke the seals of the letters ; one was from Beate, who
promised her to care for little Elizabeth and to fetch the
child to the *fête*.

"I am coming to the court ball with two nieces," she
wrote. " How venerable that sounds—and how comical
it is in reality. God grant that Her Highness may be
better when you receive these lines. Lothar is already invited to the table with Their Highnesses. I wish, Claudine,
that if he wants to marry a Princess, he would settle the
matter. This long delay is foreign to him, he is usually
such a resolute man. Perhaps now, when the old Princess wishes to go away? Ah, Claudine, I thought my
sister-in-law would be a different person once. Until we
meet again ! "

With sorrowful eyes Claudine laid the letter aside and
mechanically opened the second. What a large, awkward
hand, and what an idea! Claudine smiled ; she should
ask the Duke to release the son of a poor widow from
military duty ? Suddenly she turned deathly pale. My
God, what did it mean? How came the old peasant

woman to her? This was a letter such as the Duchess was in the habit of receiving.

She proudly threw back her lovely head. Absurd! Such people have strange fancies. She concluded to show the letter to the Duchess : she would be amused.

A heavy load lay upon her breast; the absurd letter pierced her heart like a fine needle.

Why was she not called to Her Highness?

Some one knocked, and the kindly face of Frau von Katzenstein looked in. "May I?" she asked, and soon after she stood before Claudine. "Her Highness awoke so merry," she related. "She wanted to arrange the birthday table herself. She breakfasted in bed, and forbade us to awaken you, dearest Claudine, that you might get your rest. The maid received orders to lay out for dinner a red silk dress with cream lace, and now——"

"Is Her Highness worse?" asked Claudine breathlessly, taking a step towards the door.

"Stay, dearest child, I must tell you more ; the Duchess got some letters this morning, and suddenly—I had cut open the envelopes—I heard a peculiar sound, like a deep sigh ; when I entered from my room the Duchess lay among the pillows with closed eyes. I worked over her, and finally Her Highness said, with a strangely heavy tongue : 'Go out, Katzenstein, I want to be alone.' I went reluctantly, and when in my anxiety I tried to enter, the Duchess had locked herself in—something she has never done before. His Highness has sent twice, requesting admission, the Hereditary Prince is impatient, the orchestra is in the garden awaiting the order to begin, and as yet there is no sound in the Duchess' room."

"My God, she has not received bad news from her sister?"

The elder lady shrugged her shoulders. "Who knows?"

"Come, dear Frau von Katzenstein! Her Highness acted strangely yesterday, and was very much excited."

The lovely girl with the anxious face stood at the small tapestry-hung door leading into the Duchess' bedroom, and listened. Not a sound to be heard.

"Elizabeth !" cried she, softly and fearfully.

Within the cry was heard. Before her bed kneeled the Duchess, who raised her head. Her fixed eyes turned in that direction, but her lips were more firmly compressed.

In her hand she held a small, torn note.—The doubt, the fear was past. With certainty, composure returned to her, a terrible, fixed composure, and with it pride, the pride of a Princess, all-powerful and strong. No one must suspect how poor she was.

Only this brief respite, only this one hour, to soothe, to quiet her mortally wounded heart. Would that be grudged her?

"Elizabeth!" again rang out; "for God's sake, I am dying of dread!"

Suddenly the Duchess rose. She took a step towards the door, her hands pressed in despair to her temples. Then she opened it.

"What do you want?" she asked, coldly.

Claudine entered and gazed into two fixed, glowing eyes, upon a form haughtily erect.

"Elizabeth," she asked, gently, "what ails you? Are you ill?"

"No!—Call the maid!"

"Do not fight so against it, Elizabeth; lie down. You look so feverish; you are suffering," stammered Claudine, noticing the terrible change. The mask had fallen from the smiling face.

"Call the maid and bring me a light!"

Claudine did as she was bidden.

The Duchess held a paper to the flames. She let it fall to the earth only when the fire played about her thin, transparent fingers, and then she trampled upon it.

"So!" said she, as she laid her hand upon her breast and drew a deep breath. A quiver flitted across her face, as if she felt severe physical pain.

She suffered herself to be dressed, but she chose a dark costume. Her face, with the two burning spots under her eyes, looked remarkably sallow in the dark heliotrope dress. She allowed her maid to do everything, but, when she fastened a yellow rose in her hair, the Duchess impatiently plucked out the flower and threw it upon the ground.

"Roses!" said she, with an indescribable emphasis. As if in deep thought, she then stood in front of the mirror, Claudine somewhat behind her with an anxious expression.

At length the Duchess began to laugh. "Do you know

the proverb," she asked, "'To understand all, is to pardon all'?"

And without awaiting a reply, she turned to the maid : "Tell His Highness I am ready."

She beckoned to Claudine, and with her passed through the boudoir to the red *salon.* The luxurious room was filled with the perfume of flowers. The presents were arranged upon a side-table—toys, books, a magnificent little gun. In the center of the table, in a richly-carved frame, was a photograph of the Duchess. She took the picture in her trembling hand, and gazed at it as if it were something strange, something she had never seen.

"It was exactly like you," said Frau von Katzenstein. "Your Highness looks so bright, so happy in it."

"It is a poor photograph," replied the Duchess, harshly. "Take it away ; it is untrue, it is not I."

As she left the room Frau von Katzenstein cast a despairing glance at Claudine.

At that moment a lackey opened the door, and the Hereditary Prince entered, followed by the Duke, who bore the youngest Prince upon his arm, and led the second by the hand. With a cry of joy the boy was about to rush to his mother, but his step faltered, and the Duke, too, paused and glanced at the form which stood so strangely rigid at the table, in the dark, nun-like dress. She looked in her husband's eyes as if she longed to look into the very depths of his soul. The music began below ; through the open window rang out solemnly, "Praise the Lord, the mighty King of Hosts."

For an instant it seemed as if she could not maintain her composure ; she tottered, and buried her face in the Hereditary Prince's hair.

"Mamma, congratulate me !" besought the boy, impatiently ; only after the kiss upon his mother's hand could he see his gifts.

"God bless you !" she whispered, seating herself in the chair which the Duke rolled up for her.

Claudine had retired when the latter entered. She was obliged to do so ; it was a solemn family celebration, and no one had asked her to remain. She stood by the window in the adjoining room. The cries of the royal children were mingled with the strains of the gay march which arose from below.

"What, for God's sake, ailed the Duchess?" she wondered, anxiously.

"Grandmamma! Grandmamma!" rang out joyously. A glad tremor of surprise passed over the girl. Her beloved, revered mistress, her kind friend, had come. She could scarcely restrain herself; she would have liked to have flown to her to kiss her hand. Now the kindly voice could be heard; but did it not show a trace of sadness to-day?

"My dear child, my sweet Elizabeth, how are you to-day?"

For a long time there was silence. Then the voice said, with a sad ring:

"Altenstein does not seem to have benefited you; I shall take you to Bavaria with me."

The music without drowned the sound of further conversation.

Claudine was upon nettles. Would not Her Highness inquire for her? She knew she was with the Duchess; she had written to her herself. To be sure, she had received no answer; it struck her as peculiar. The inexplicable anxiety of that morning again possessed her.

In the other room all was still. The Dowager Duchess must have retired to rest after the long drive. The children had returned to their apartments. They heard only the steps of the Duke, who impatiently paced up and down the room.

"Claudine!" cried the Duchess.

She would learn to bear seeing the two together. And when Claudine appeared she looked from her to the Duke. How excellently they were schooled! His Highness barely glanced at the beautiful girl.

They must have practiced well! Ah, no, they had an easy dupe in her, the confiding, credulous simpleton! For an instant burning jealousy possessed her; a longing to destroy at *one* blow the woman now standing beside her.

"Pass His Highness that glass of wine," said she. "He has forgotten that I handed it to him."

Claudine did as she was bidden.

In the mean time the Duchess rose and left the room. She feared she would not be able to suppress the hysterical laughter which threatened to choke her.

"What ails the Duchess?" asked the Duke with a frown, as he drank his wine.

"I do not know, your Highness!" replied Claudine.

"Go to her!" said he curtly.

"Her Highness is in her bedroom and does not wish to be disturbed; she would like to see Fräulein von Gerold in an hour in the green salon," said the maid, who entered at that moment.

Claudine went out by another door and sought her room.

The curtains were drawn in the Duchess' bedroom and she lay upon her couch in the semi-darkness. She knew Claudine was alone with him. Now he would kiss her hand, draw her to him, and say:

"Bear with her caprices, my darling; she is ill, bear with her for *my* sake!"

And in the eyes of both the hope of a brighter future would gleam, for—when below, in the vault of the castle chapel, a new coffin——

She did not shudder at this thought, she merely smiled; it is well that one knows there must be an end!

Ah, how much concealed, bitter suffering had been laid to rest with those who slept below in the sarcophagi! It is so comforting that there is "oblivion" and sleep.— Alas, this waking, called life, may last a long time!

She felt something like the sense of reproach which possesses a sensitive person when he knows that the patience of others is tried too long, and who, however, cannot help it. Therefore this oppression, it was so difficult to breathe.

If it were not for the children!

Well, they would scarcely miss the sickly, suffering mother, and—they were boys. How fortunate that was! Poor little Princess, she was to be pitied! Ah, and the world? Did it know of it? Did it smile at and whisper about the betrayed wife who made a friend of her husband's favorite?—She moaned; the pressure upon her chest increased.

Again she rose, her hands clasped over her breast, and roved about the room. Nothing was left for her but to be proud and forbearing. Were the day only past! Were it but night, that she might be alone to weep!

Below in the court she heard the rumble of wheels;

upon the corridor could be heard the steps of busy servants ; the guests repaired to the salon in front of the old
Gerold banquet hall, which was in the middle building,
which connected both wings of the castle. Claudine,
too, who sat in a fauteuil in her room, heard it. At every
foot-fall she turned her head, and when it died away, a
flush suffused her face. Why did not the Dowager
Duchess summon her ? Why, at least, did not Fräulein
von Böhlen, her successor, come to greet her ? It was
the custom for the ladies to call upon each other. And
the pale, languid-looking young lady with the light, reddish hair and the innumerable freckles had knocked half
an hour before at Frau von Katzenstein's door.

In front of her upon the table lay a watch. At a quar-
ter of three she would have to go over to the green drawing-room, where the Duchess awaited her, to escort her
to the guests. She had changed her dress ; she wore a
short summer gown which the Duchess had given her a
few days before, pale blue foulard trimmed with white
lace and silver ornaments in the form of Edelweiss
blossoms, as brooch and hair-pins. The fan of blue
ostrich plumes lay beside her long yellow gloves. With
hesitation she took up the gloves and stroked them ; it
was time to go.

In the corridor Claudine met Fräulein von Böhlen,
who, apparently, was on her way to her mistress' room.
The ladies had met at the court festivities ; Fräulein von
Böhlen had too often been at the Dowager Duchess' soirées.
Her father, once the deceased Duke's chamberlain, had
made himself obnoxious to his successors by all manner
of intrigues, and had been forced to retire to private life
under circumstances in no way glorious. The old Princess supported the family, which thought it was deeply
wronged. Her kindly-disposed heart forgot and forgave
the unpleasantness which had been caused, by calling
the daughter to fill Claudine's place.

Fräulein von Böhlen's reddish gold head seemed to be
held back by some kind of instrument : she appeared
unable to bend it in greeting. Claudine, who, in her
genial manner, had extended her hand, suddenly stood
alone. The young lady's somewhat rumpled, cream-colored train had rustled past her and disappeared behind
the folding-doors at the end of the corridor.

Calmly Claudine turned and entered the tiny ante-room of the Duchess' apartments. Frau von Katzenstein's face wore such a comical expression, so kindly, so compassionate, and so embarrassed.

"Her Highness has given no sign of life," she stammered, then she was still—the Duchess had appeared upon the threshold. Her first glance was at her friend ; Claudine had never looked lovelier than in that light, girlish costume. The Duchess bowed her head and walked through the room to the door opposite ; within could be heard the lowered voice of the Duke and the cold one of Princess Thekla.

The Duchess paused. "Give me your arm, Claudine," said she then almost hoarsely, and side by side they passed under the red portières which the lackeys pushed back, followed by Frau von Katzenstein. In the salon, in which were about twenty persons, silence for the moment reigned.

Was that the Duchess ?

A small, dainty form half-hidden behind the fan-leaf palm grasped the crimson velvet curtains as if seeking support ; her trembling knees almost refused their service in the low, graceful curtsey. Princess Helene advanced a few steps at a sign from her mother ; but her dark head was bent in vain, her cousin did not kiss her.

None resumed their seats. All stood around chatting. Baron Gerold's eyes were fixed upon Claudine ; the Duchess' arm still rested within that of the girl. Their eyes were fixed upon the middle door, and now a flush of pleasure passed over her beautiful face—the Dowager Duchess entered.

Upon the kindly, furrowed face, beneath the silvery white hair, to-day lay an expression of unusual severity. But Claudine saw it not. Leaning on the girl's arm, the Duchess approached her mother-in-law and bent over her hand, while Claudine bowed low. The young girl's eyes looked with joyful expectation in the royal Duchess' face.

"Ah, Fräulein von Gerold, I am surprised to see you here ; did you not tell me your brother could not do without you ? "

The old lady's hands were crossed one upon the other ; at these words she turned to Frau von Katzenstein, as if Claudine were not present.

Proudly Claudine drew back, and for one single instant her eyes met those of her cousin. Silence again reigned; only the Dowager Duchess' pleasant voice could be heard addressing her "dear" Katzenstein.

Claudine did not look about her; a paralyzing horror stole over her; nor did she know how her feet bore her to the Duchess. She wanted to speak, but at that moment the doors were opened, the Hereditary Prince, who that day had the honor of escorting his grandmother to the table, solemnly advanced to the old lady with his small person, and the next instant Her Highness' silver gray train rustled over the carpet.

"Will your Highness permit me to retire?" stammered Claudine, turning to the Duchess, "my head aches violently——"

For a moment the unhappy woman's heart yearned with compassion for the girl whose pallid features betrayed a terrible agitation of mind.

"No," she replied in a whisper, for His Highness was just approaching. "I myself am ill and must make an effort—do you do the same."

Claudine (with the others) walked down the corridor and by Lothar's side entered the reception room behind their Highnesses, who greeted their guests. The Hereditary Prince received congratulations, and the doors of the dining-room were flung open. Claudine's seat was opposite Lothar. She had no clear idea of how the dinner passed over; she, to be sure, answered her neighbor's questions; she ate, she drank, but as if in a dream, automatically; Princess Helene, by Baron Lothar's side, spoke remarkably quickly and then sat silently by; occasionally her sparkling black eyes were turned upon Claudine, as she toyed with a dessert spoon. And when Claudine's strangely-absent glance met hers, she turned red and relapsed into her forced gayety. How it came about—who can tell? it hovered in the air, it sparkled in the champagne glasses, it spoke in looks and manner without words, each one at the glittering board knew it; something had happened in the royal apartments; the Dowager Duchess had come to mediate. That ideal friendship was at an end; lovely Claudine von Gerold sat there for the last time.

All those apparently gay people felt dejected like those

who longed for the bursting of the storm and yet feared it. His Highness seemed remarkably impatient ; no wonder—the Duchess, quite contrary to her custom, looked flushed ; she frequently passed her handkerchief over her brow and drank iced water.

At length the Duchess rose; the meal was ended and coffee was served in the adjoining drawing-room.

"Her Highness has retired and wishes to speak with you," whispered Frau von Katzenstein to Claudine.

The girl flew up the stairs and along the corridor. She only wanted certainty—and what had she done ? Yet she was haunted by a horrible suspicion. The Duchess sat upon her couch ; her head resting against the back.

"I want to ask you," she began, with a distorted face, —then she cried out : "My God—I—Claudine !" And a stream of blood gushed from her mouth.

The young girl caught her in her arms ; she did not tremble, she uttered no sound, while the maid rushed away to summon help. The Duchess' head lay on her breast, she was unconscious.

The next moment the Doctor, the Duke, and the Dowager Duchess appeared. The Duchess was carried to her bed ; the feverish excitement began, as is common in such cases. Claudine, with her terrified face, with her blood-stained dress, stood by, unheeded; although she frequently extended her hand to help, no one noticed it, no one seemed even to see it.

"Has anything occurred to disturb Her Highness ?" asked the doctor.

The Duke pointed to Claudine. "Fräulein von Gerold, you were with her last, do you know——"

"I have no idea," she replied.

At that moment the Dowager Duchess' severe and hostile eyes rested upon the girl. She sustained their glance ; she did not bow her head guiltily. "I know nothing," she repeated once more.

Below the concert began again. The Duke hurriedly left the sick-room to forbid the continuance of the concert—and he stood face to face with Princess Helene. She was breathless from running, she had been in the garden when she heard the terrible news. Her fearful eyes spoke more plainly than words.

"Your Highness," said the doctor who had followed

the Duke, "it would be well for your Highness to telegraph to Professor Thalheim ; Her Highness is very weak."

The Duke looked at him in surprise ; he turned pale.

"She will not die! For God's sake say, no!" whispered Princess Helene. "Not that!"

And horror-stricken, she drew back when Claudine stepped out with her blood-stained dress.

Claudine found Beate in her room.

"Heavenly Father, how terrible!" cried the brave girl ; "depend upon it, dear, our *fête* is to blame for it."

"Ah, no;" said the girl softly, as she took off her clothes.

"Do not worry so, Claudine ; you look so miserable! Below," continued Beate, "all have dispersed. I sent the nurse with Leonie and Elizabeth into the park. In front there are still a few groups who wish to know all about it. The Princes are in their room, the Hereditary Prince is weeping pitifully. Who would have thought it?"

"Will you be kind enough to take me in your carriage?" asked Claudine.

Beate, who was putting on her hat at the mirror, turned hastily. "You do not want to go now, Claudine? You cannot——"

"But I can, I shall——"

"Her Highness desires to speak to Fräulein von Gerold," said the maid at the door.

"Now, you see, Claudine, you cannot go," said Beate, with undisguised satisfaction, tying the pale yellow ribbons on her bonnet.

In the sick-room all was quiet and dark ; every one had been dismissed ; only in the ante-room the Duke paced the floor. Claudine took the seat which a motion of the Duchess' hand signed to her at the foot of the bed ; in a faint whisper she implored her to remain, as she *had* something of importance to say to her.

Below in the Hereditary Princes' room sat Princess Helene upon the floor beside the boy ; she was not in tears, but her hands were clasped as if she were praying or as if she were asking pardon of some one. Princess Thekla was in the Dowager Duchess' apartments. The old lady, very much agitated, was seated in one of the low easy-chairs which still bore the Gerold arms ; she scarcely heard what Her Highness said in a low voice ; she was horrified to find "Liesel" in such a condition.

"Yes, such emotion," sighed the Princess, "is scarcely comprehensible : this gentle Claudine is a schemer."

"My dear cousin," replied the Duchess, "it is well known that the man always is to blame for the greater part of the guilt in such cases—do not let us forget that, please ! "

"But why is she tolerated here?" continued the Princess, goaded on by this reply, her sallow skin assuming a darker shade.

"Will you kindly bear in mind that His Highness alone commands here, my dear?"

"Certainly—pardon—but it is strange when one thinks——"

"Yes ; but there are cases in which it is better not to think," was the answer given, accompanied by a sigh.

"Baron Gerold asks the favor of consulting with Her Highness upon a matter of importance," announced Fräulein von Böhlen.

The Dowager Duchess agreed at once. The next moment Lothar was in the room. Princess Thekla smiled affably upon him, and rose. "A private audience? Will your Highness permit me ? "

"Your Highness' presence will in no way prevent me from laying my request at Her Highness' feet ; so much the less so, as your Highness surely takes a certain interest in the new matter in hand."

The old Princess cast a keen glance at him from beneath her lace cap. "Speak, Gerold," said she.

Fräulein von Böhlen, who slowly retired, knew from the indifferent manner of her usually so obliging mistress, that her thoughts were reluctantly turned from the Duchess' sickbed. The young lady bowed with the compassionate, melancholy air which for some time she had worn ; in fact, from the day when she had seen her mistress reading a letter, with tearful eyes. And yet, inwardly, she rejoiced. The secret fear that Claudine would one day return to her old post, and that she would be obliged to resume her former distasteful, homelike life, no longer tormented her ; for never would the severe Dowager Duchess desire to have near her she, who, with a bold hand, had shaken the most sacred bonds, the peace of her family. She smiled, for she was now alone, and her thoughts flew to the future as she, standing at the window, looked out upon the sunny garden. What cared she for the grief and sorrow of others? She felt only one thing; she would never hear the complaints about every penny at home, she would not have to pass with a careless, haughty air the shops where long bills were standing, and from which duns came weekly; she would not need to clean her gloves with benzine; she would not hear the servant complain to her mother that she was starved. She now stood secure in the agreeable position of a maid-of-honor, and Claudine von Gerold, the "charming, never-to-be-forgotten Claudine," whose hand was as soft "as a lady's," was out of the question! What did the supercilious creature desire more? She had found a powerful protector! Fräulein von Böhlen suddenly blushed—she would gladly have changed places with Claudine Gerold—In the Dowager Duchess' room all was still. Only occasionally could be heard the Baron's voice, then the shrill, clear laughter of Princess Thekla, and the next moment the slender form of Her Highness, clad in a lilac-colored silk dress, stood before the startled lady-in-waiting.

"Princess Helene! Find the Princess!" she gasped with difficulty, and the sticks of her ivory fan clattered against one another as if fever shook the hand that held it.

Fräulein von Böhlen vanished; breathlessly the Princess came up.

"We are going to Neuhaus! Where is the Countess?" were the words which greeted her.

"For God's sake, mamma, what has happened?"

Princess Helene knew so well the mood which was mirrored in the old Princess' face.

"Come!" was the reply.

"No, mamma—dearest mamma, let me remain here. —I could not stay at Neuhaus comfortably!" implored the Princess.

"Who says you need? We take the express for Berlin to-night. Come!".

"No, I cannot!" came from the pallid lips. "Do not force me; I should run away from you on the way—I cannot leave her."

Rage overcame the old lady; she seized the dainty arm with her bony fingers. "*En avant!* We have nothing more to do here!" she hissed. But her daughter disen-

gaged herself. "I shall do my duty !" she cried, beside
herself, and fled from the room. When the old lady followed her, it was as if the air had absorbed the white
form, the corridor was so quiet and deserted.

Princess Thekla with Countess Moorsleben drove to
Neuhaus alone. Before them rolled the carriage containing Beate and the children. Her little granddaughter's
jubilant cries rang in her ears.

With a pale face the Countess stood before Frau von
Berg, who had hastened up. The young girl was furious
at the treatment she had received from Her Highness on
the drive.

"Oh, I should like to go to mamma at once !" cried
she. " How am I to blame that Her Highness has had a
hemorrhage ? "

Frau von Berg still smiled, but she had suddenly paled.
"A hemorrhage ? " she asked.

"Yes, and a very severe one. They have telegraphed
to H——."

"And Princess Helene ? "

"She would not come with us ; she acts as if she would
like to lie at the door of the sick-room."

"And where is the Baron ? "

"With Her Highness, the Dowager Duchess ; at least
he was there, when we drove off. Böhlen said he asked
for an interview with her."

"And Fräulein von Gerold ? "

The pretty Countess shrugged her shoulders. "In
every one's mouth," she replied. "I am sorry for her.
They say the Duchess has found out her husband's infi-
delity ; His Highness looks as if he would like to set the
world on fire."

"My God, this scandal had to be discovered once,"
said Frau von Berg, shrugging her shoulders. "But
where is she now ? . . . Is she sitting in the tower of the
Owl's Nest, looking expectantly towards Altenstein—or—
has the proud Claudine flung herself into the castle
pond ? "

Countess Moorsleben gazed upon the face which so illy
concealed its satisfaction ; savage joy gleamed in the
black eyes. It was not joy at the conviction of the
wrong-doer, for Frau von Berg, indeed, had little reason
to count herself among the righteous.

"Madame," said the pretty Countess, maliciously, "I have been wondering all morning who was the originator of the saying: 'He who lives in a glass house, should not throw stones'?"

"I asked you, Countess, where Fräulein von Gerold remained after the *eclatante* proof of disfavor?" emphasized the lady, crimson with rage.

"I do not understand you, dear Frau von Berg," replied the Countess, as gently as possible. "You know more than I do. Disfavor? *Eclatante* ?—Fräulein von Gerold is sitting at Her Highness' bedside."

Frau von Berg gasped for breath and rustled into Her Highness' room, from which had just come a peremptory summons.

The Duchess was asleep ; the silence of death reigned in the large mansion.

Baron Gerold sat in Captain von Rinkleben's room ; he had asked the jovial officer's permission to remain there; he desired to await the news of Her Highness' condition. He lighted the Havana offered him, but he did not smoke with very much enjoyment ; he took up a book, but he could not read. His face was careworn, and tormenting anxiety caused him to wander aimlessly to and fro.

Herr von Palmer's door was bolted ; he was in a very bad humor. A fine day that had been, truly ! When he had entered His Highness' study that morning, to consult him about the necessary changes to be made in the castle at the Residence, the Duke met him with an air of surprise and an open letter in his hand. It was a confidential letter from Prince Leopold, his cousin, asking how it came that the Court Marshal had for almost three years made the firm of C. Schmidt of R. on the Rhine no payment. The head of the firm asked the Prince to inquire into it, as upon direct inquiries only other orders had been received, while no heed was taken of the account. Even in the last letter they had been told that if any more claims were sent the custom would be altogether withdrawn.

Herr von Palmer smiled and said there was some misunderstanding, but His Highness bade him see to and settle the matter as speedily as possible.

It was very unpleasant, very! As if such a pack of tradespeople did not *have* to lend at least so long—until Herr von Palmer would be in a position in a few years calmly to go away! It was some consolation to have Berg for a supporter. How finely had she brought about the "Impossibility" on the Prince's birthday! The old Duchess had dropped Claudine—that was excellent! His Highness would not have the courage to enact this pastorale any farther under his mother's watchful eye.

The last rays of the setting sun glinted through the broad high window in the Duchess' bedroom.

"Claudine!" whispered a faint voice.

The girl, who had been lost in deep meditation, rose and kneeled by the sufferer's bed. "How do you feel, Elizabeth?" she asked.

"Oh, I am better; I feel that the end is approaching."

"Elizabeth, do not speak so!"

"Is there any one here who could hear us?" asked the Duchess.

"No, Elizabeth, His Highness has gone down to the little Princes, the maid is in the adjoining room; Frau von Katzenstein is with the Dowager Duchess, and the nurse is asleep over her prayer-book."

The invalid lay quite still, watching the glowing sunbeam upon the picture of the Madonna, which almost imperceptibly rose higher and higher, finally sparkled upon the carved foliage of the gilt frame and then disappeared.

"Why had you no confidence in me?" she asked suddenly in a sad voice. "Why did you not tell me all frankly?"

"Elizabeth—I had nothing to conceal from you."

"Do not lie, Claudine!" cried the Duchess solemnly; "One should not lie to a dying woman!"

Claudine proudly raised her head. "I have *never* lied to you, Elizabeth."

A bitter smile flitted over the pale, emaciated face of the sufferer.

"You deceived me with every glance!" said she, horribly clear and cold, "for you love my husband."

A veritable shriek interrupted, and Claudine's head fell heavily upon the red silk cover of the sick-bed. What she had feared, what she felt for a certainty—the lips of the woman whom she loved so dearly, so truly, now told her.

14

"I do not reproach you, Claudine,—I only want you to promise me that after my death——"

"Merciful God!" moaned the girl, rising wildly. "Who has aroused within you this horrible suspicion?"

"Suspicion? You might ask: who opened your eyes to the horrible truth? And he—loves you—he loves you!" whispered the Duchess. "Ah God, it is but natural."

"No! no!" exclaimed Claudine, beside herself, wringing her hands.

"Be silent," implored the sick woman wearily, "or else let us talk calmly; I have so much still to say."

Claudine rose, her head was dizzy. What should she do to prove that she was innocent?

A hectic flush again burned upon the Duchess' cheeks, she breathed with such difficulty.

"Elizabeth, only *this* once believe me, trust me," implored the girl.

The invalid suddenly sat up.

"Can you *swear*," she asked calmly, "can you swear that there never was any question of love between you and the Duke? Swear it, swear it by the memory of your mother, and if you can do *that* at my death-bed, I will believe that my eyes have not seen aright."

Claudine stood there, transfixed with horror. Her lips moved as if to speak, but no sound issued from them; she simply bowed her head. The Duchess sank back among the pillows. "You have not the courage for *that!*" she murmured.

"Elizabeth," cried Claudine now, "believe me! Believe me. My God, what shall I do that you may believe me! I repeat to you, you are mistaken!"

"Be still!" said the Duchess with a contemptuous smile.

His Highness entered. "How are you, Liesel?" he asked affectionately, and bending over her he tried to push the damp hair from her brow.

"Do not touch me!" she cried, and her eyes grew large with anguish. "It will soon be over," she then murmured.

In despair Claudine leaned against the door; the Duke approached her and asked softly and anxiously: "Is her Highness delirious?"

Claudine, whose breast threatened to burst, suppressed

with her handkerchief the sobbing cry which was about to escape her, and tottered into the adjoining room.

He followed anxiously. "What has happened?"

The invalid's eyes were fixed upon the door through which the couple had disappeared. The whole terrible, forcibly suppressed agony overpowered her and confused her thoughts. She lay there with clinched fists and glowing eyes. What, she would not even confess to the dying woman? And she had meant so well—she intended mentioning in her will that they should marry. That should be their punishment for her ruined happiness. And *she! she!* what a depth of wickedness must that creature keep pent up within her, she who had called upon heaven to witness her innocence!

A wild, suffocating anguish lay upon her aching breast.

Her husband re-entered the room; he advanced to the foot of the bed and looked at her keenly. Claudine, who had forcibly controlled herself, held a glass in her hand.

"Drink, Elizabeth," she implored, bending over, and slipping her arm under the Duchess' head. "Drink, you are so warm—it is the medicine which always helps you."

Motionless the Duchess lay there with tightly compressed lips. Her large eyes hung with a peculiar stare upon the girl's pale face, and then roved over to her husband. The glass in Claudine's hand began to tremble. "Oh, please drink!" she besought in a faint voice.

A shrill outcry and the glass was dashed from Claudine's hand.

"Poison!" screamed the Duchess, sitting up in bed with the expression of a madwoman, her hands outstretched in despair. "Poison! Help! Am I not going fast enough for you?"

Then she fell back exhausted and a stream of blood flooded her white gown and the bed.

Claudine, who had fallen upon her knees, sprang up; she, too, looked like one distracted. With superhuman strength she collected herself, hastened to the bed, helped raise the sick woman and rested her against the Duke's breast, while his pale face expressed deep agitation.

"Liesel," he murmured, "why, Liesel, great God!" She lay like a corpse, with closed eyes.

The room was speedily filled with people. With a grave air the old physician stood before the patient; he

looked at his watch, counted the feeble pulse, and
shook his head. "At nine o'clock he may be here, your
Highness," he whispered to the weeping Dowager
Duchess, "but—until then—composure—do not show
any anxiety. It is best that your Highness remain near
by. I will stay in the next room."

"Claudine!" murmured the Duchess. "Claudine!"

The Dowager Duchess looked about for the former favorite; she had disappeared. In her anxiety the old lady
went out into the corridor and asked the way to Fräulein
von Gerold's room. But the door was locked, and within
no one was astir.

Claudine had given way on reaching her own room;
she had not one clear thought.—It had come to that!
The world looked upon her as degraded, as the Duke's
favorite—his own wife was dying with that impression!

Oh, the absurd foolhardiness of her mad pride! If she
could call down the stars from heaven as witnesses of her
purity, no one would believe her; no one, neither the dying nor the living, nor the one who reviled while he
warned her! God alone knew that she was pure; but
God no longer wrought miracles! Lost! Lost!—She
had become the disgrace of her family; the whole land
would point to her: See, see, that is she for whose sake
our poor Princess broke her heart! Who should rescue
her? The Duke?—He could not enter the lists for her;
they would all pretend to believe him, and would laugh
behind his back.—Merciful God! what had she done to
the people that they should hate her so bitterly?

If she could but die! By that means she would not
remove the stigma, but she would be dead! She would
feel nothing more! She thought and thought; the little
pond in the park—said a voice within her. It is so quiet
and so cool there—so cool! They would perhaps find
her there, and people would say: She had still a sense of
honor; she could not live with guilt in her heart! One
alone might say, as he stepped up to her coffin: "My
sister, my pure, proud darling—I believe in you!"

At Neuhaus, a small, dark maiden would rest her head
upon the handsome man's shoulder, and a sweet voice
would say: "What care I, Lothar, that one of your
family heaped disgrace upon the name of Gerold? Forget it; I love you nevertheless!"

Several loud knocks at the door, caused her to start up.

"Fräulein von Gerold," cried out the shrill voice of Fräulein von Böhlen, "the Dowager Duchess awaits you!"

Mechanically she went out, heedless of the fact that her hair was hanging down her back, and the golden strands fell over her brow ; heedless of the fact that she was in her loose house dress. Like one demented she entered the room in which no lamp had been lighted, upon whose bright carpet the moonlight fell in two broad, shimmering streaks.

"Claudine !" came softly from the window.

She advanced and bowed.

"Sit down, Claudine."

But she did not stir ; she stood there as if paralyzed. "Is the Duchess dying ?" she asked, hoarsely.

"That lies in God's hands, Claudine."

"Oh, through me, through me !" murmured the girl.

The Duchess did not reply. "I have a question to ask you," began the old lady at length, "it is a strange one at this hour, Claudine, when the angel of death stands at the door of the house ; but he for whom I am to ask it has imposed it upon me as a sacred duty, to be fulfilled immediately. Baron Gerold requests you, Claudine, to replace his orphaned child's mother and his wife."

"Your Highness !" exclaimed Claudine. She retreated a step and leaned heavily against the edge of the mantel-piece. "Thank you," said she then, "I ask no sacrifice of him."

"Very well !" replied the old Princess severely. "You had it in your power to silence, at one blow, all malicious tongues ; you had it in your power to prolong an ebbing life for a short time, that it might take wing in peace."

"Your Highness !" moaned Claudine.

"My poor, unhappy daughter !" sighed the Princess.

"Your Highness, my life for the Duchess," she implored, "but not *this* humiliation !"

"Your life ? That is easily said, Claudine——"

"Ah, could I but prove it !" she cried, advancing with clasped hands to the Princess' chair. She stood in the full light of the moon, which showed the dimmed eyes, the despairing image of the girl.

The Duchess was startled. "Claudine! Why, Claudine!" said she kindly.

"Does your Highness really believe that I am dishonorable?" she asked. The words sounded so strangely quiet, so dejected.

"No, my child, for *such* an one Baron Gerold would not desire for his wife!"

She drew back. "For that reason only?" she stammered.

"It was very difficult for me to believe the rumor," continued the Duchess. "But, child, I know life; I know my hot-blooded son; I know his power over the hearts of women—and you, who fled from him, were suddenly thrown daily with him! Child, child, I believe that you are only the Duchess' friend; but you were venturesome to play so lightly with your reputation, you did not know how to avoid *appearances,* and therefore—take the hand extended to you," added the Duchess, persuasively. "No one will dare, not even the boldest scandalmonger, to maintain that Lothar von Gerold has taken to his heart a wife who is not as pure as the snow. And he, my son —his eyes would never again seek her who was another's."

"I have lost my self-possession altogether, your Highness," said Claudine.

"You must compose yourself, my child, he is waiting below, torn between doubt and hope."

"Your Highness," besought Claudine, "he does not love me. It is a sacrifice which he offers to the honor of our name. I *cannot* accept it; have mercy on me, your Highness!"

"Then do you, too, make a sacrifice!" cried the Princess, irritated by the opposition. "Is your honor not worth a sacrifice? Is *she* not worth it, who is struggling with death, over there?"

"Your Highness!" whispered Claudine, and an idea flitted across her poor, weary brain. "I will—I will speak with Baron Gerold."

The Duchess pitied the despairing maiden. She poured out a glass of water and brought it to her. "First, compose yourself, then he may come," said she gently, leading the trembling girl to a seat.

"The Doctor!" said Fräulein von Böhlen entering. The doctor followed closely behind her.

"Your Highness will pardon my intrusion," he began hastily, "but I consider it my duty to inform your Highness that the august patient is in imminent danger. Her Highness is completely exhausted by the loss of blood, almost to death. Professor Thalheim proposes transfusion ; I am not averse to it,—every means should be tried. His Highness desires to furnish the necessary blood, but —as it is no trifling operation—it might have serious results which imperil life, such as blood-poisoning and so forth—so we must refuse His Highness, as, too, the law emphatically forbids——"

He hesitated. Claudine sprang from her chair and extended her hand. "Doctor, I beg to be the one who——"

"You?" asked the old gentleman, looking in astonishment upon the girl's pale face, the agitated features of which expressed a deep yearning. "Really, Fräulein von Gerold! Well, then, come, but quickly! We have no time to lose. But wait, Fräulein, I must impress upon you that we have to open an artery."

"Ah, dear Doctor!" said Claudine in a low voice, and with a shrug of her shoulders, which signified: "If it is nothing but that!" And she hastily preceded him, in her anxiety lest some one else might come before her, forgetful of etiquette.

The old Princess had scarcely comprehended the words. Transfusion? Was it transfusion? When she entered the Duchess' ante-room, the doctors were already busy with the invalid : in front of Claudine stood a deaconess who was putting back the sleeve of her white cashmere gown. The Dowager laid her hand upon her son's shoulder ; he had just come from the Duchess' bedside into the small room in which stood Frau von Katzenstein and the maid with anxious faces.

"Adalbert," she asked softly, "Adalbert, what is this? The doctor said they would have to open one of her arteries to let her blood into Liesel's veins?"

He nodded absently ; he did not turn his eyes from the sorrowful, smiling face of the girl.

"For God's sake, Adalbert," continued the Princess, "shall we allow Fräulein von Gerold to do this? It seems to be dangerous!"

He now looked at her in surprise. "This requires more courage than to fling, from a secure ambush, the dart

which mortally wounds a poor woman, or which drags
into the mire a guiltless girl's reputation. I cannot prevent her from making this sacrifice," he added, shrugging
his shoulders. "*I* least of all ; otherwise they might say
I was more anxious for her life than for that of my wife."

A deaconess now drew the curtain, and Claudine's lovely
white form was to be seen for a moment in the middle of
the room. She stood like a sacrificial priestess of mercy.
" From arm to arm, colleague," said the Professor's voice,
"it is safer."

But the Duke no longer saw nor heard—he had left the
room. In terrible agitation he paced the Duchess' salon,
the same in which he had spoken to Claudine of his love.
At that moment he would have given years of his life to
have blotted out that hour. Poor girl, poor woman !
He had not wanted *that!* He had aimed at happiness
with the desire of a man who is accustomed to victory.
He had felt a genuine liking for his mother's pretty maid-
of-honor ; she repulsed him, and he allowed himself to be
repulsed ; for the first time he yielded to a woman of character, and his mistake became a fatality. Who, in
heaven's name, had slandered Claudine to the Duchess ?

Upon the mantelpiece burned one single light, just as
on that miserable, memorable evening.

The cold dew of agony stood on His Highness' brow.
"Only so much time," said he half aloud, " in which to
explain all to her, that she may not die in the belief that
I am guilty."

There is something grand, holy, in the love of a wife.
She had deified him, notwithstanding all his errors, notwithstanding all his coldness, all his indifference. He saw
her eyes fixed upon him with the old, tender light from
which he had so often impatiently turned his. He heard her
soft voice as she said, in the adopted dialect of the country :
"Eh, my Adalbert?" She had lived on so contentedly,
grateful for the crumbs of love he had thrown to her, so
blissful at one affectionate word, so modest in her require-
ments. How trifling seemed to him at that hour her insignificant faults, her weaknesses which once had seemed
so insufferable to him !

He stood by the window, and recalled the same day
eleven years before. Then, too, there had been fears for
her life ; he saw himself at her bedside, at the cradle of

his first-born—she lay so pale, her eyes alone beamed; notwithstanding her weakness, she had smiled so proudly. Then he had only uttered formal words of thanks; his whole interest was centered in the child, the heir—*she* had but fulfilled her duty. Suddenly he leaned his head against the panes and covertly wiped his eyes. Would they not soon inform him how things were going over there?

The entire castle seemed under a peculiar bann; in the corridor the lamps burned dimly, and lackies stood about with anxious faces; below, in the gentlemen's room, sat the courtiers, but they only talked in whispers. In the children's rooms the governess and nurse looked sadly at each other, and in the kitchen the servants whispered and told dismal stories. The old superintendent of the linens had seen the white lady distinctly in the moonlight on the stairs in the left wing; she had walked so slowly, step after step, so heavily and bent, as the phantom was in the habit of walking when a death was about to occur, the old woman related, and the eyes of the listeners opened wide with horror.

All knew that one last attempt was to be made to save the sufferer; Fräulein von Gerold's name was in all mouths.

Frau von Berg sat in Herr von Palmer's room; she had been sent by the "august mamma" to fetch the Princess. So she had taken advantage of the opportunity to bid her friend "good-evening," to ask about the state of affairs, and to announce the wonderful news, that in the presence of Princess Thekla, the Baron had proposed for the hand of his cousin through the Dowager Duchess.

The handsome woman was completely upset by it.

"If I only had the Princess safely in the carriage!" she lamented, pacing the floor, while Herr von Palmer rocked nervously. "Who can tell what folly she may perpetrate?"

Yes, where was the Princess?

The old linen-keeper had seen the white lady; it was the little Princess; and that she walked with so heavy a step and with bowed form was owing to the anguish caused her by the intelligence that Her Highness was at the point of death, and that Fräulein von Gerold too was in danger. She had gathered that from the incoherent words of the old maid, whom she had seen at the linen-keeper's, when she returned from the garden whither fear had driven her ; far, far, away where nothing could be seen of the castle into which such misfortune had entered through *her*.

When, with tottering steps, she entered one of the Duchess' apartments, the Duke stood at the window, and when he turned in the dim light, she saw upon the usually so cold, handsome, impassive face, deep agitation, and in his eyes traces of tears. That was more than she could stand !

In an incoherent, confused manner she accused herself and confessed all, kneeling before him, his hand in hers. He did not interrupt her by a word ; he simply asked, when she paused exhausted :

"The letter, Helene ? How, in God's name, did you obtain the one letter I ever wrote to Claudine and which evidently has been falsely interpreted by the Duchess ? "

"Your Highness implored that Claudine should remain your wife's friend *notwithstanding*."

"Notwithstanding the fact that I had insulted Fräulein von Gerold—certainly ! "

"Cousin, cousin, punish me ! " cried the Princess, beside herself. " Tell me what I can do to make amends."

He shrugged his shoulders. "How did you get the letter ? "

"Frau von Berg——" stammered the Princess, falling at his feet. The Duke raised and led her to the nearest chair. He had no word for her ; he turned abruptly and left the room.

———

The operation was over; the Duchess had more color and her pulse beat more strongly. Claudine's healthy life's blood seemed to have lent her new strength ; it was almost miraculous. She lay softly slumbering, while through the open window came the perfumed breath of the summer night and deep silence reigned in the room. Motionlessly the deaconess sat in the shadow of the draperies, and only the soft, regular breathing of the sufferer was to be heard.

Claudine was in her room with a bandaged arm. She felt exhausted ; but it was not alone owing to the loss of blood, the whole strain throughout the day was making itself felt. Her feet would scarcely bear her, and yet, with a persistency bordering on obstinacy, she refused to lie down. She had still to speak with Baron Gerold, she said, and then she desired to drive home immediately.

The old Duchess, who had gratefully followed her from Her Highness' bedside, besought, like an anxious mother, that she would defer the conversation for that day ; she must take care of herself after the operation ; but Claudine adhered to her resolution.

"I do nothing by halves ! " she said with exceptional composure and grave eyes.

The Professor who was called in, was almost severe.

"Very well," said the man, famed for his categorical manner, "let the interview take place, but the drive must be given up. And now drink a glass of wine." He held the glass to her lips with an air which would admit of no resistance ; she took a swallow. But when she heard steps upon the corridor, she turned towards the old Princess :

"Will your Highness permit me to speak with my cousin *alone* ? "

Her Highness retired sadly and with a shake of her head ; Frau von Katzenstein and the Professor followed her.

"Good luck to you, Baron," said the Professor, in passing by, "say yes to everything, and be it ever so strange."

He entered almost impatiently. He had been wandering restlessly about the park, when the lackey had found him, without a suspicion of what had in the mean time transpired at the castle. His startled eyes fell upon the sling in which Claudine wore her arm, upon the loose morning dress, upon the disordered hair, and the pallid, horror-stricken face of the lovely girl.

"What has happened here ? " his eyes asked, but not a word escaped his lips ; he pointed mutely to the bandage on her arm.

"A trifle," she replied, pointing to a chair, "nothing but a small wound made by the instrument of the doctor who needed some blood for the Duchess. Now to business, Baron."

"And you say that as if it were nothing ? " he cried, beside himself. "Do you know it might be equivalent to death ? "

"You forget that an authority performed the operation and—if——"

"Of course you have no one in the world who would be grieved by your loss; no one whom you needed to ask beforehand : 'May I do it? Have I the right to risk my health, possibly my life?'"

"Yes," she answered—"I have one—Joachim—but there was no time."

"Joachim!" he repeated with the same bitterness. "I, who had just asked for your life for myself, for my child, I was not worthy of a thought!"

He spoke in à low, grieved tone. Suddenly she grew dizzy and sank exhausted in the chair beside which she had been standing.

"I wanted to talk with you about it," she began again looking past him. "I promised the Dowager Duchess it should not last long. You are very magnanimous, cousin, I do not indeed know how to thank you ; I can of course only do so by refusing your magnanimity—and——"

He stood there motionlessly and looked at her.

"And that would be," she continued, "to reject a means which might prolong the life of a sufferer—so says the Dowager Duchess. I cannot do so; forgive me! But I will make you a proposition ; to be betrothed does not mean marriage. If the Duchess recovers then—we will break off—if she should die, we of course will do the same ; it is but a means of calming her ; it is a little forcible, I know, but an engagement is only a promise, and, to be sure, all promises are not kept. God knows, how often it happens that two people separate before marriage ; it is no disgrace—I—I——"

She had spoken quicker and quicker ; now the fair head leaned faintly and with closed eyes, against the cushions. He drew nearer ; his face twitched strangely.

"I," she began again, "I shall not leave here ; but you, Lothar, are free ; after the announcement of our betrothal, which announcement, unfortunately, must be made, you will easily find an excuse for going to some distant corner of the world, until——" she suddenly raised herself—"I do not say this for myself, indeed I do not! What matters it about me? My clear conscience is sufficient for me—but the poor woman over there—do—you understand, Lothar?"

"So we are to enact a comedy?" he asked.

"Not for long! Not for long!" she murmured, raising her pretty, but heavy eyes to his face, as if imploring pardon.

Suddenly he seized her right hand with a violent, passionate movement.

"Let it be so," said he, "but you are ill, and, above all, before the comedy begins——"

"Let it begin at once," she implored; "go to the Dowager Duchess, and tell her that I have given you my consent. In the mean time I shall prepare to drive home; I am so tired, so very tired."

"I will go," said he calmly, "and you will lie down, you will *not* drive home."

"I will!" cried she angrily, changing color; "do not forget that this is only a comedy, that you as well as I, notwithstanding, can follow our own wills!"

He restrained himself and left the room. "Say yes!" the doctor had advised—only—yes! Claudine stared after him as if in a dream; she felt her strength ebbing more and more, she felt so weak and humiliated! She would have preferred to have torn the bandage from her arm, and to have allowed her life to flow away with her blood; involuntarily her fingers touched the sling. Suddenly before her eyes swam a fiery sea of blood, and it seemed as if her chair was beginning to reel. She wanted to grasp the chair, but, instead, clutched at the air. "Halt!" she murmured; but everything around her swam, her head sank back, and she felt as if she were being raised, then all was a blank. The deaconess, who entered at the Duchess' orders to look after the agitated girl, found her unconscious. With the noiseless care of her calling, she fetched help and laid the swooning girl upon the couch, where she speedily revived.

"It is nothing but exhaustion, Baron," said the doctor, whom Lothar summoned from the smoking-room, where the two physicians were sitting with the courtiers, "nothing more. Leave the patient undisturbed; to-morrow she will be well and strong, with such youth and strength! You may drive to Neuhaus, comfortably, dear Baron!"

Herr von Gerold himself instructed the maid, and bade her call the deaconess if she noticed anything unusual in the Fräulein's condition; then he asked Frau von Katzenstein, too, to watch the sick girl. The old lady was about

to go into Claudine's room to bring him news of her ; he
waited in the hall.   He heard Claudine talking within—to
whom ?   He could distinctly understand every word ;
Frau von Katzenstein had not closed the door tightly.

"Forgive me !" rang out Princess Helene's voice ; it
did not sound imploring, but rather, commanding.

Lothar frowned ; he had difficulty in restraining himself from entering at once.

Frau von Katzenstein discreetly returned.   "Her Highness is with Fräulein von Gerold," she whispered.

"The Duke bade me beg your pardon, Fräulein von
Gerold," he again heard within.   "I therefore ask your
pardon.   Do you hear ? "

Beside himself, the Baron crossed the threshold of the
dimly-lighted room.   A flood of crimson suffused the
girl's white face resting against the cushions of the couch,
when she saw him.

"Oh, my God," she stammered, and made an evasive
gesture with her right hand.   A violent palpitation of the
heart deprived her of the power of speech.

It did not surprise her that he had entered there ; she
thought of nothing except that a crushing blow would
fall upon the defiant, little creature who had so haughtily
approached her to "apologize" at the Duke's command.

The Princess had not perceived him ; she stood there
like the embodiment of defiance, her contrition turned
into indignation at the sight of her hated rival.   "You
will not ? " she asked.   "I have not long to wait, I must
go to Neuhaus ; mamma has sent Frau von Berg after
me ; but I shall not drive with her, I do not want to.   I
shall ask Baron Gerold for his carriage.   So, for the third
time—I ask your pardon, Fräulein von Gerold ! "

"Princess, I do not know why forgiveness is asked—
but I grant it with all my heart," replied Claudine, with
quivering lips.

"Your Highness, this is a new way of asking forgiveness of a deeply-injured person," now said Lothar's agitated voice.

The Princess turned as if shocked by electricity.   Claudine's eyes looked at him imploringly—she held her
breath—oh, she knew from personal experience how terribly the certainty of having lost one's beloved, acted
upon one.

"It requires the perfect kindness and self-forgetfulness of my betrothed to accord your Highness the so-strangely asked pardon."

It was spoken. A silence of death reigned in the room; Claudine again saw the crimson flood before her eyes. How? Could a man treat so mercilessly the woman he loved, for whom he had sued for weeks? Was it an act of despair, because he was *forced* to give her up?

She extended her hand. "Princess," said she faintly, as if *she* would beg forgiveness.

But the dainty white form did not reel, as Claudine had feared; she proudly threw back her dark head with its wealth of short curls. "My congratulations," she said curtly. In the forced voice, only, did Claudine recognize the terrible emotion of the girl whose ardent love had just received its death-blow.

The Princess ignored the hand offered her, and haughtily bent her head. "Escort me, Baron!" said she, in a tone of command, preceding him.

In spite of her resistance, Lothar seized Claudine's extended hand and pressed his lips upon it. Claudine withdrew the member hastily and impatiently.

"Wherefore?" she asked, turning away her head. "It is unnecessary according to the terms of our agreement."

They were gone. Claudine rang and accepted her maid's aid in disrobing, after which the lights were extinguished. Frau von Katzenstein cautiously stole through the darkened room toward the bed—there was no sound behind the curtains, the patient probably was sleeping the sleep of exhaustion. But when Frau von Katzenstein looked more closely, she saw the girl sitting up in bed.

"Why, Claudine, are you not asleep yet?" whispered the kindly old lady anxiously, pressing a kiss upon the pretty face. "I have just heard of your betrothal," she added with emotion; "God bless your heart's union, my dearest Gerold!" With those words she left the room.

Claudine pressed her hand wildly to her brow. "Heart's union," she repeated bitterly. "What terrible irony!"

She grieved and moaned until far past midnight, until her thoughts grew confused. The most trying day of her life was over; how much torture and suffering were yet to follow!

Early the next morning Claudine was awakened from a heavy sleep by a messenger from the Dowager Duchess who sent her a fine bouquet of flowers and a diamond ring.

It pained her to think of the preceding day, and only with an effort could she rise.

The Duchess' maid appeared when she was dressed, and summoned her to the sick-room.

With faltering steps she crossed the threshold of the same ; the room was flooded with sunlight ; at his wife's bed stood the Duke with the little Princes ; the two youngest held roses in their hands, the eldest something that sparkled and glittered.

The Duke advanced to her and kissed her hand. " Accept mine and my sons' deepest gratitude for your noble sacrifice," said he, leading her to the bed. " See for yourself, Fräulein, what a miracle it has wrought ! "

The Duchess extended her hands while the Hereditary Prince clung joyfully to her. " I always knew," said he, " you had courage, Fräulein von Gerold, and we, my brother and I, give you this because you have made mamma well again."

He held towards her a costly jewel and the others silently offered their flowers to her.

"Claudine," whispered the Duchess.

According to her custom she kneeled beside the bed, but her cheek was not laid confidingly as formerly against her friend's ; she waited like one of the painted suppliants in the castle chapel, with downcast eyes and an impenetrable air. " Oh ! why these thanks ! I did nothing ! " said she.

Unseen by her, the Duchess signed her husband to withdraw ; softly he went out, the two eldest princes followed him ; only the baby remained seated upon the bed, playing with some roses.

"Thanks, Claudine, a thousand thanks ! and, too, accept my sincerest congratulations on your betrothal ; I just heard of it from mamma. It surprised me, Claudine ; why did you never tell me that you loved him ? "

Claudine made no reply at first, then her silence terrified

her. If she enacted her *rôle* so badly, the whole comedy
would be in vain ! Here, above all, she must be
brave !

"It was difficult for me to speak of it," she stammered,
"I did not know if he returned my love."

The Duchess pressed her hand.

"Claudine," she murmured, "you know—I am sorry
for the Duke, for he loves you !"

"No, your Highness !" cried the girl. "He does not
love me !"

"But, Claudine," assured the sick woman, "see, I have
a letter from him in my hands to you."

Claudine started up. "A letter? I never received but
one from His Highness, and that——"

"Pst !" whispered the Duchess. "Quite right ! I did
not understand it yesterday, but to-day Adalbert explained
its meaning to me himself. He has told me all; it was
not easy for him. I know all, Claudine, and I pity him
because you are now lost to him."

"Elizabeth !" stammered the girl, whose utterance was
choked by compassion. "It was an error of His Highness, and what human being——"

"Yes, an error ! Oh, I understand, I can understand it ;
but in here it has grown so desolate, so lonely, Claudine."

For a moment she laid her hand upon her breast and
then caressingly stroked Claudine's arm, which hung in
the sling.

"Elizabeth," said the latter, "you have always been so
charitable, you have always judged the deeds of others so
leniently—will you be a severe judge here ?"

The Duchess shook her head. "No, I have pardoned
him. The short span of time still left me shall be pleasantly spent. Ah, Claudine, for the first time since I have
been his wife, did he talk with me this morning as I have
always hoped, waking and dreaming, he would ; frankly
and freely, kindly and gently. It has come too late, yes,
yes,—but it is sweet, so sweet, and therefore I have forgiven him. There is still a remnant," she lowered her
voice, "a remnant of silly vanity in me. Do you know,
I always wanted to please him and did not consider that
I was so miserable, so sickly a creature. So I took the
mirror and looked in it ; at first it hurt me a little, but
then——"

She paused, and her eyes filled with tears, while she forced a smile.

Claudine could not help it, a couple of large tears rolled down her cheeks.

"I am so sorry for him," said the Duchess, once more ; "I will be kind, patient, and loving towards him. And she for whom I am sorry, too," she added, "is Helene. —She loves your betrothed ! "

"Yes ! " breathed the girl.

"Oh, you beautiful woman ! to whom all hearts are drawn, favored by God," said the invalid. "How can it seem to be loved thus?" The words sounded so sorrowful, so hopeless.

Claudine rose and turned to the window ; she dared not show her emotion.

"I will not detain you longer, Claudine," continued the Duchess, "you have so many, many duties to-day. You must appear before mamma as a bride and before your little child as a mother, and you and he will have so much to talk over. Go, Claudine, go, and God's blessing go with you ! "

She smiled ; the tiny prince had joyously taken the lace cap from her dark hair and put his open mouth to her pallid lips. She turned away her head hastily. "My darling," Claudine heard her murmur, "mamma cannot kiss you, mamma is ill."

The agitated girl could scarcely kiss the transparent hand with composure and leave the room calmly. She sank into a chair on reaching her apartment, and buried her tearful eyes in her hands. In surprise the maid looked at her. Was that a bride ?—A rich, happy bride, who sat there so pale and gloomy ?—The maid stooped and picked up an *etui* which had fallen unheeded from her mistress' lap ; in falling it had opened, and the contents, a magnificent necklace of brilliants, sparkled brightly before the amazed eyes of the servant. Claudine did not notice it ; she felt only one thing ; she could not bear the dissembling which was now to begin. Absently she changed her dress. As the one she wore the day before had been spoiled and she had no other, she was obliged to put on a black lace dress which she sought to enliven with a few roses. But they, as colorless as her face, made the dark toilette no gayer, while the white sling contrasted strongly with the black gown. So she went, on Lothar's arm, to the old Duchess' apartments, where both remained to *déjeuner*, to which they were invited by His Highness, and where they received the courtiers' congratulations.

Early in the afternoon Lothar drove with her in his carriage to Neuhaus. The servants of the manor were assembled upon the *perron* and welcomed the young couple with ringing cheers. Beate stood on the threshold with outstretched arms, in her right hand a bunch of roses, by her side old Dorte in whose arms was the little one in a white dress. Down Beate's broad, smiling face trickled bright tears of joy.

"Dina, darling child," cried she, drawing the girl to her, "who would have thought it!" And she took the child from her nurse: "There, worm, you have a mother, and what a mother!" she rejoiced.

Lothar put an end to the loud rejoicings with a glance at silent Claudine.

"She cannot hold Leonie, Beate," said he, giving the child back to the nurse, immediately thereafter to conduct his betrothed into the nearest room, in order to free her from the glances of the people. "You must not annoy Claudine to-day with questions; see that we have some refreshments, little sister, and then you will drive to Brotterode with us."

"But, Lothar, there is to be a grand concert to-day at the Casino——"

"Just for that reason, dear Beate."

His sister, with a shake of her head, went out to give her orders, and as she made a hasty toilette she muttered, quite contrary to her custom:

"I believe affianced people prefer to sit in some isolated arbor, and those who by nature do not incline to such nonsense drive on the first day of their betrothal into the midst of the scandalmongers!"

But to-day she could not understand everything; her thoughts were still confused from the events of the forenoon, when the august ladies took their noisy departure; nor during the night had she closed her eyes. When, late the evening before, Lothar had driven home alone with the Princess, her head stood still with fright for a moment; it is true she merely glanced at her brother's face, but she knew at once that he was betrothed.

There was such a peculiar brightness upon it. And the Princess ran up the stairs so hastily.

"She will now inform her mamma of her good fortune," she had thought to herself. And, to be sure, Lothar called her to his room, and when she entered, he was leaning on his gun-cupboard, his favorite position when he had anything important to say.

"Listen, Beate," said he, anticipating her, "I am engaged."

She pressed his hand and kissed him heartily on the mouth.

"I congratulate you, Lothar."

"Are you not pleased, Beate?"

"Lothar," she said, "one always thinks when a brother marries, one will gain a sister, but—" and she smiled good-naturedly—"you cannot possibly imagine your Beate as a Princess' sister? We would be like a good domestic fowl and a golden pheasant—eh? But that is of no moment, if you are happy."

"I have the prospect of being so. And if a swan will not suit the domestic fowl better than a golden pheasant, I hope the two will agree, out of common decency. I am betrothed to Claudine, my clever sister!"

"To Claudine! Well, her cleverness might truly be scoffed at, if things were managed so secretly! God be praised!" she said, when she had in a measure recovered from her surprise, and she playfully seized her brother by the sleeve: "Sit down and tell me all about it."

He told her all he could—of the operation, of the Duchess' danger, of Claudine's courage, and ready sacrifice—all, but not that which she wanted to know. She was, however, discreet; she asked nothing further. His nature was reserved, and would, for nothing in the world, have allowed another to get a glimpse of his heart: that was a Gerold family trait, a peculiarity.

During the recital, Beate brought forth her newest hat which she had obtained for the *fête* of the day before, and thought, as she put it on, of the departure that morning, and of the terrible scene in the nursery. After her bath, little Leonie lay asleep in her bed. Her Highness, Princess Thekla, appeared, ready to set out; behind her, Frau von Berg, and asked nothing more nor less than—the child! Thereupon old Dorte stood with outstretched arms before the bed and explained in her low-German dialect: the master would have to tell her himself first, that the child was to go away with her grandmother! Then their Highnesses at that moment forgot themselves so far as to try to push aside the old peasant ; but so rough a woman stands as firmly in her place as the gigantic firs in the forest without.

"May God forgive me," said she, energetically evading the aristocratic hands, "that I should fail in respect to one who belongs to our most august ducal house! But He will forgive me; I am doing my duty ; I will allow nothing to be stolen from my master."

"Silly thing," chid Frau von Berg, "who wants to steal? Her Highness is the child's grandmother."

"My master must tell me himself," was the stolid reply.

"Your master is not at home ; come, be reasonable !"

But that argument was of no avail ; Dorte had her arms akimbo and remained at her post. Suddenly she succeeded in pulling the old-fashioned bell-rope ; many an impatient summons had been rung therefrom, but none such as rang out to-day.

The nursery bell was familiar to the entire household ; in that room the old master and mistress had lain ill and died—it was no wonder that every one thought some accident had happened, and that Lothar, who had just returned from his morning ride in the fields, hastily preceded the rest down the corridor ; Beate behind him, the servants rushing from all sides.

He dismissed the latter, and the door of the nursery was locked behind him and Beate.

"What is taking place here?" was his first question.

He seemed not to trust his eyes when he saw Her Highness, who had excused herself from breakfast on the plea of headache, and who now stood here with heightened color, saying, in a commanding voice: "I desire to take my granddaughter with me, and this person——"

"Ah! Your Highness thought I was so engrossed with my happiness that I should forget the hour of your departure? Or rather, your Highness did not wish to await my return home and intended to go by an earlier train? Therefore the carriage at the door. And your Highness wishes to take your grandchild with you—" his voice sounded like the roll of distant thunder—" without first obtaining my permission ? With what right, may I ask ? "

" She is my daughter's child ! "

" And *mine!* The father's claim surely supersedes that of the grandmother, your Highness ! "

"Only for a few months, Gerold," said the Princess, who, by this time, realized that in her anger she had committed an act of folly.

" Not for an hour ! " cried he with emphasis, and a striking pallor overspread his face. " I wish to shield the child from the poisonous miasma which blows without, and which seeks out the purest blossoms in order to destroy them ; I wish to guard her against learning contempt of mankind so early. My daughter shall be reared, as was the custom formerly in the home of my ancestors, simply, naturally, and—to think simply ; and here it shall be done, here at Neuhaus, your Highness, under my special supervision and that of my future wife ! " Swiftly he pushed aside the hangings of the tiny bed in which the little one lay with widely open eyes. " Would your Highness like to say ' good-bye ' ? " he added coldly.

The Princess for a moment stepped to the cradle, touching the child's forehead with her lips, and then, without another word, rustled through the corridor to the hall, where Princess Helene, with the maid-of-honor and gentleman-in-waiting, awaited her mother.

The old Princess entered the carriage with the most suave smile upon her lips ; Beate, who bowed low, received, however, merely a condescending nod for her hospitality of weeks : Lothar sat opposite them. When the horses started, from two dark eyes a long, lingering glance was cast at the old house, a glance so impregnated with sorrowful regret, that Beate's heart swelled with pity notwithstanding her feeling of relief. Poor, defiant little Princess!

Beate surprised herself standing before the mirror, tying her ribbons. She sighed deeply. Thank God, peace again reigned in the house ! Upstairs the bracing forest air wafted the last breath of the penetrating patchouli from Frau von Berg's room, and the housemaid had long since cleared away the remnants of a costly crystal vase which the old Princess, in a paroxysm of rage, had flung against the stove. In the boughs of the linden a piece of light blue ribbon fluttered, ribbon which the wind had wafted hither from Princess Helene's toilette table, and upon the lawn furniture and mattresses were airing ! To-morrow everything would be as it once had been—God be praised !

" Pardon me," said she, in a clear voice,. when, a few minutes later she entered the sitting-room, where Claudine sat upon the estrade and looked out of the window, while Lothar thoughtfully stood before his father's picture, the distance of a whole room from his betrothed. " Pardon me, I am rather late ; has coffee been served ? Very well, I see it has ; I am ready for our drive ! "

She was somewhat surprised ; she had expected to see the couple side by side, affectionate and loving. Instead, Lothar now approached his bride formally and offered her his arm as if at a court ball. " A drive in the open air will do you good, Claudine ! "

Beate began to be really vexed at such ceremony.

" Please, Lothar," replied Claudine, " give orders to stop at the Owl's Nest after the drive ; I long for rest—I still feel very much fatigued."

" Yes, of course ! We must pay, too, Joachim a be-trothal visit," was the reply.

It was a very quiet drive. When the carriage rolled down the hill towards the valley, from which the red roofs of the little bathing resort shimmered, Claudine leaned back with a sigh. That too ! She had suspected that he wanted to exhibit her as rehabilitated.

As they turned into the *allée* the strains of a waltz came from the Casino. Upon the square in the center of which rose a music-hall, stood numerous tables with red and white covers. The entire Casino audience sat chatting at one enormous board which the elegant head-waiter guarded with an Argus eye that no unworthy person might seat himself there. With that object he was in the habit, three hours before the commencement of the concert, of laying down a few primitive looking notices upon which were to be read " Engaged ! " and to turn over the chairs. If only two of the company came and if certain ones could not obtain a seat, he still shrugged his shoulders : " I am sorry, sirs, these seats are taken."

But to-day none of the seats were vacant, and the con-versation, more animated than it had been for some time, turned upon the affair at Altenstein. The story of the Dowager Duchess' dislike to her *ci-devant* favorite was upon all lips, naturally exaggerated, and made worse. According to one version, the Dowager was said to have asked Claudine to leave the castle immediately ; another told of a withdrawn pension ; a third maintained that the lovely Gerold had known how to bring it about that she might still appear at table, and emphasized the fact that the Duke was the only ruler.

"Oh, incredible ! And what besides ! In addition the Duchess' hemorrhage !—Poor woman, poor woman ! Of course brought on by grief and excitement ! "

To be sure one could not blame the Duke for the adventure, since Claudine was so frivolous. They shrugged their shoulders and smiled at the poor, deceived wife who thought she had a friend in her.

"Oh, shameful ! " complained an older Baroness ; well, that suited the Gerold precisely ; how did it leak out ?"

"How does Baron Gerold take the matter ! He turned as pale as a corpse when the Dowager ignored Claudine."

A veritable confusion of tongues was heard at these words ; but suddenly all was still ; some one had said : "There is the Neuhaus carriage ! "

Right ! And very near by !

They had sufficient presence of mind to appear as if they had been talking of something totally different. The ladies turned to one another and waved their fans ominously, but the eyes of old and young alike at the table were turned in the direction in which the vehicle was approaching. The fine horses pranced along to the strains of a waltz ; coachman and footman upon the box gleamed in faultless blue and yellow liveries, and inside ?——

Suddenly at the long table all hats were simultaneously raised ; the gentlemen rose, the ladies bowed and nodded pleasantly.

What, Claudine von Gerold—her arm in a sling, by the side of the Baron !—Slowly, very slowly, the carriage passed the preferred table, then it drew up at the door of the Casino. Two gentlemen of the party rushed breathlessly forward, a young Hussar and the doleful *attaché*. The Lieutenant wished to inquire for the Duchess, his highborn partner at dinner at the Neuhaus *fête*, and as he "of course supposed that Fräulein von Gerold knew best," and so forth. The *attaché* had other reasons ; he came at the whispered request of Her Excellency : "One must know what this means."

"The Duchess is better," replied Claudine, pleasantly.

"But you, Fräulein, seem to have been injured ?" remarked the *attaché*, twirling his moustache.

"A trifling, insignificant wound, Herr von Sanders," interpolated Lothar. "I think my betrothed will soon again have the use of her arm—Oh, pardon ! I forgot to say that you have before you a newly-pledged pair of lovers—we plighted our troth last night. It is a surprise, is it not, sirs? Ah, Claudine, there comes the water, I hope it is fresh and cool."

He shook hands with the gentlemen, and congratulations and words of thanks were exchanged. Meanwhile Claudine drank the water and returned the glass.

"Drive on !" now commanded Lothar, taking off his hat and bowing low and gravely to those at the table ; in a few minutes the rapidly revolving wheels had reached the isolated, woodland path, the final chords of the waltz still vibrated through the air filled with the scent of the firs.

Then at the table in front of the Casino all tongues were suddenly silenced just as the noisy tones of the horn concluded the piece of music. Only by degrees did they gain their composure. Oh ! how differently that sounded !

"Well," said his venerable Excellency with dignity, "I said at once there was nothing in all that talk !"

"Ah, heavens, there is so much gossip !" sighed the sympathetic Baroness. "Who finally found it out ?"

"Antonie von Böhlen wrote it to me to-day," said one of the pretty Countesses von Pansewitz, "but I was not to speak of it."

"Tell it any way !" exclaimed the Countess Dowager, irritated by the reticence.

"Claudine Gerold allowed her artery to be opened because the Duchess was bleeding to death, and so her blood was let into the Duchess' veins," said the Countess. "Antonie writes that had it not been for that, the Duchess would have died. Oh, God ! it is terrible, I could not have done it."

"Heavens, how terrible !" cried the ladies together.

"How courageous ! It was madness !" said the little officer with sparkling eyes.

"Zounds! one might fall in love with her for that!"
exclaimed His Excellency, and received in return a reprov-
ing glance from his wife.

"She looked remarkably pretty just now," murmured
the doleful man more dolefully than usual. "Zounds,
why have I not two estates? Enviable Gerold!"

"He has sent in his resignation," said the Hussar,
"he is to attend to his property himself!"

"What else do you know, Lola?" the Countess thus
encouraged her daughter.

"Oh, she received so many brilliants," eagerly related
the Countess, "and the old Duchess nursed her like a
daughter and kissed and petted her."

"Ah, charming!"

"When will they be married?"

"They will surely unite at the Residence."

And so forth. In their innermost hearts all grudged
Claudine her happiness, but dared not by so much as a
word to attack the reputation of Baron Gerold's betrothed.
There was now a different rustling in the woods, and the
ladies concluded unanimously to send the young fiancée
a fine basket of flowers as a token of their gratitude for
the rescue of their beloved Duchess.

In the mean time the betrothed arrived at the Owl's Nest.

Gardens and buildings basked peacefully in the light of
the setting sun, and the broken rose-windows of the ruined
convent shimmered in a rosy light. Claudine's lovely
face was suddenly overspread by painful anxiety; the old
arched doorway was wreathed with garlands of asparagus
and roses!

"Lothar," she murmured, lightly touching his arm as
she alighted, "I beg of you—return home with Beate; I
would like to prepare Joachim first. I will send you word
when I can see you; I cannot play the comedy *here*, it
is out of my power."

He apparently struggled with indecision, but one glance
at the half-despairing blue eyes caused him to yield; she
must, indeed, still feel indisposed. He made no reply, but
simply turned and bade Beate keep her seat. He accompanied her as far as the door, where little Elizabeth joyfully ran to meet her and kissed her resisting hand.

"At what time would you like the carriage to drive to
Altenstein this evening?" he asked. "Of course you
will permit me to escort you thither?"

She turned in the doorway and nodded farewell to Beate ; in her agitation she had completely forgotten the kind-hearted woman. But the latter was unaware of it, she was looking up at the tower window.

"I thank you, Lothar," said Claudine, now softly but firmly, "I shall not return to Altenstein ! I shall remain here. I will inform the Duchess of my decision. You do not believe it ? " she continued smiling faintly. "I assure you, I have not the strength for this game. Did I not try to do my duty faithfully to-day ? Have pity on me ! "

She gravely bowed her head and entered the house. Fräulein Lindenmeyer came to meet her. In her joyous haste the old lady almost fell over the threshold of her room ; she had her cap with the red ribbons on and extended both arms.

"Ah, gracious Fräulein, what a piece of good fortune! " she exclaimed, weeping for joy. "We know it, we know it ! From whom, do you think ? Old Heinemann's granddaughter was here ; she brought the news fresh— why did not your betrothed come with you ? "

Claudine had to allow herself to be embraced and kissed, had to shake hands with Heinemann, who hastened up, and to accept Ida's congratulations. Confused, she at length ascended the stairs. How difficult it all was !

Joachim looked up from his book when she entered ; he needed but a few minutes in order to return to the real world. Then he sprang up, approached her, and raised her head. "My brave little sister—betrothed? Look at me, my darling," he implored.

But she did not lift her lashes from which large drops fell. "Ah, Joachim, Joachim ! " she sobbed softly.

He stroked her silken hair.

"Do not weep," he said gravely, "tell me, rather, what have they been doing to you out there ? "

Then the storm of grief burst forth, unbounded, uncontrollable. She did not spare herself, she hid nothing of the humiliation which had mercilessly fallen upon her, against which her pride powerlessly rebelled. "And, Joachim," she sobbed violently, "the worst is that I love him, have loved him as only a girl can love, for years ! On the day when he stood at the altar by the side of Princess Katharina, I thought I could not live any longer ;

and now Fate, with mocking derision, casts the longed-for happiness in my lap and says:—'There—but gently! It is only gilding which clings to it, it is not genuine. There is what you have prayed and wept for for years!' Believe me, he has taken me, as he took the silver at the auction, at any price because he would rather die than allow the name of Gerold to bear a blemish; he has taken me—for the sake of the family honor, for nothing else—nothing."

She ceased, for she was exhausted, but her bitter, passionate sobs continued.

Joachim did not reply; his hand still rested upon her fair head. At length he said gently: "What if he loved you, nevertheless?"

She suddenly started up.

"Oh, my God!" cried she, and upon her tear-stained face was an expression of compassion for her brother's credulity.

"No, you dear, innocent man, he does *not* love me!"

"But, if he should! He was never one of those who could conceal their feelings. You know he would always rather have bitten off his tongue than have uttered an untruthful word. He was always so, Claudine."

"Yes, thank God," cried she, angrily, and drawing up her form, "he did not venture upon that too! Do you think Lothar would have sued for me with pretenses of love? Oh, no, he is not untruthful. And when I proposed the comedy to him, it did not occur to him to assure me that it would grieve him were we to part later. No, he is honorable—horribly honorable!" She suddenly collected herself. "Poor fellow," said she softly, taking her brother's hand, "I am disturbing your work with my bad news. Bear with me, Joachim; I shall grow calmer, I will be your little housekeeper, your faithful companion, again. Oh, had I never gone away! By degrees I shall conquer all, all, Joachim!"

She kissed his brow and went into her room, the door of which she bolted behind her.

Like fresh, cool spring water did the peace of her own little home work upon her mind. She went from one piece of furniture to another, as if she must greet each one, and finally paused before her grandmother's picture.

"You were such a sensible old lady," she whispered,

"a id what a simple grandchild you reared ! She atones for the reason won too late with her life's happiness ! "

She wearily laid aside her lace dress, donned a plain, gray house-dress, seated herself in the old arm-chair at the window, and looked out into the dusky night.

Meanwhile, below in the sitting-room, little Elizabeth crept sadly to the finely-spread table ; it looked so pretty with the bowl of roses in the center, the artistically-drawn serviettes which had cost Fräulein Lindenmeyer so much pains, and the chairs with their rose garlands for the betrothed. Even the cake baked by Ida herself ! The child had put a new blue dress on her doll. Where did they all stay so long?

She ran down into Fräulein Lindenmeyer's room. "When is the wedding?" she asked impatiently. She thought the festal preparations meant the wedding.

"Ah, my pet," sighed the old lady, looking at Ida with a shake of her head, "who knows," she added with Schiller, "what slumbers in the past ! " It surely sounded different from the words which the kind soul had intended addressing to the couple : "Denn wo das Strenge mit dem Zarten—" What a couple, who on the first betrothal day did not remain together ! Or was it a new fashion? In her time it was different ; they did not want to part at all, but sat side by side, and gazed in each other's eyes. She sighed.

"Clear the table, Ida," she murmured, "the wasps will come into the room after the cake ; it will only get stale. Oh, our fragrant garlands ! That is the fate of the beautiful on earth ! Ida, Ida, I feel very strange ! "

"Elizabeth would like some cake," said the child, tripping out of the room behind the girl.

Heinemann sat upon a bench at the door, whistling a melancholy air ; as Ida cleared the table, she sang the words ; strangely sad they sounded in the garden through the open window.

> " Saszen einst zwei Turteltauben,
> Saszen beide auf einem Ast.
> Wenn sich zwei Verliebte scheiden,
> Denn verwelket Laub and Gras—"

They had both no idea how deeply the words cut Fräulein Lindenmeyer. The old lady leaned out of the window.

"Be quiet," she implored, half aloud; "that is no song to sing when one is just betrothed; it sounds like the croaking of frogs."

Claudine, too, had heard the song. "If they part," she added, "at least they would have been united once. But we!"

The first snow in the mountains! Up there it falls early; in the plains Saint Martin's summer perhaps still reigns, while up there the snow lies white and gleaming upon the firs. Then within the houses it is cosy; the large stoves do their duty, and the windows are bordered with green moss that the cold wind can find no crevice through which to creep. It is especially cosy in the evenings when the lamp swings above the table and its light falls upon the gleaming tea-service.

It was never so cosily warm, so comfortable, in all the mountain district, as it was in the sitting-room of the Neuhaus castle. It was only a pity that the spinning-wheel no longer stood upon the estrade; it was so well-suited to those four walls. Without, the snow flew and the wind howled; within, the lamp burned upon the antique writing-table.

Beate was writing.

"These are household matters, Lothar; now to matters of the heart! I was just at the Owl's Nest and found Claudine in the sitting-room; she was teaching little Elizabeth. I should so dearly like to write you something especially pleasant, but it is always the same. She never speaks of you, and if I broach the subject, I receive no answer, at least none that satisfies me. She shows only interest in *one* thing, and that is the Duchess' health. She lives like a nun and is very pale; her one diversion is long walks for hours and alone. Joachim, the egotist, does not seem to notice it, or does not want to; but I told him the truth to-day. He brought another bulky manuscript for Claudine to copy; I took it from her and said: 'If you will allow me, I will see to this; you are giving the poor girl too much work.' You know she has dismissed Ida, and does everything alone: cooks, sews, and irons, and not badly either! Then, besides her domestic duties she is to slave like a penny-a-liner

and completely ruin her eyes. As if they had not suffered
enough from weeping ! God knows she is scarcely ever
seen without strangely inflamed eyelids, although to my
repeated question : 'Have you been crying ? ' she always
replies : 'I ? Why should I cry ? '

"Joachim looked at me in amazement ; I am certain he
feels terribly that I should look into the secret depths of a
poet's soul. He did not dare to oppose me ; nor would
it have availed him aught, for he is one of those whom one
can render submissive by means of energy ; that alone
impresses him !

"But pardon, I am writing so much about Joachim, and
you want to hear about Claudine. You asked me if she
wears the engagement-ring. It will certainly grieve you,
but I cannot tell an untruth, Lothar—the golden circlet is
not upon her hand. I asked her about it, but she grew
embarrassed and did not reply. She has a severe expression about her mouth ; it pains me to look at her. You
should have courted her differently ; but of course as
matters were——

"Sometimes I think perhaps she did like the Duke—
No, no, Lothar, I will not worry you, I am so stupid in
such things ; I do not know what there is between you,
and I do not wish to force myself into your secret. God
grant that this cloud may ·pass over ! But one thing I
know, if it does not soon, you will both be very miserable.
At times it comes over me, and I should then like to go
and ask : What sort of a defiance is this ? One here, the
other there. Do you love each other, or do you not ?
But you have forbidden it, so we must go on thus !

"I always take Leonie to the Owl's Nest, but *she* acts
as if she did not see the child, who is so healthy and
lovable now. Joachim says with her dark hair and eyes,
she is like a 'Spanish Baby.' I once, however, watched
Claudine covertly ; she then hugged and kissed the child ;
but when I entered, she was the same as she always is !

"Frau von Katzenstein recently wrote Claudine that
Princess Helene was with the Duchess at Cannes ; she
is said to be self-sacrificing, and to wait upon the invalid
with indefatigable patience ; the Duchess, too, praises
her in her letters to Claudine. Her Highness writes
almost daily, and Claudine replies promptly ; but the
correspondence seems to afford her no pleasure. She

looks at times thoroughly vexed when the postman brings
a scented letter with the ducal crown. The royal lady
asks in every letter : 'When is your marriage to take
place, Claudine? Why do you write nothing of your
betrothal, of your happiness?' Occasionally an orange
blossom lies among the leaves. What Claudine's answer
is, I do not know, but I suspect from the question being
repeated so often, that she makes none.

"What a long letter this is! And I want to write more
to-day ; I am beginning to copy Joachim's manuscript, I
have looked it over. It is the second volume of his Spanish
'Reminiscences.'

"What else do you wish to know, Lothar? ask me ; I
will tell you frankly. Do not remain too long in your
lonely castle in Saxony. God grant that the Duchess may
continue to improve ! The poor woman is said to be so
restless, to long for her German home and for her children.
Yesterday she sent Claudine some roses ; one of the far-
traveled blossoms stands before me in a glass, and looks
out in surprise at the snow which is flying in the evening
shadows. What a quiet storm ! I enclose you a lock of
our little one's hair.

"Princess Thekla has Frau von Berg with her, do you
know? And do you know the Duke did not take Herr
von Palmer with him to Cannes? It is remarkable, he
could never formerly do without him."

She addressed the letter and was about to go to the
nursery—it was the hour when the child ate her evening
meal, which conscientious Beate never failed to taste,—
when Heinemann was announced.

"Well," she asked, when the old man entered in a pilot
coat and high boots, his fur cap in his hand, "what has
happened?"

"God be praised, nothing ! But we have received a
telegram. Our Fräulein must go away with the night-train.
She would like to borrow a sleigh from Fräulein von Gerold
in which to drive to the station."

With composure Beate ordered the horses to be har-
nessed, and with her own hand poured out a glass of
liqueur for the old man.

"I will drive with you," said she, "and you can sit
behind."

"Yes, Fräulein requested that you would ; I had forgotten it," murmured the man.

Scarcely fifteen minutes later Beate drove out into the snowy forest. What could have happened?

The Owl's Nest stood out darkly from amid the snow-covered firs, while its lighted windows shimmered brightly in the darkness. Fräulein Lindenmeyer met Beate in the hall ; she looked solemn, and her eyes were filled with tears. Her hands were clasped and she whispered, to terrified Beate : "The Duchess is dying !"

Beate flew up the stairs to Claudine's room. The latter was hastily packing a trunk ; she turned a sorrowful face towards her.

"For Heaven's sake, Claudine," cried Beate, "are you going to Cannes?"

"Oh, no," replied Claudine, "only to the Residence ; the Duchess wants to die at home."

She put her hands to her face and wept.

"They are going to bring her back? Ah, God! My dear Claudine, do not weep ; dear Claudine, you must have known that this apparent recovery was but temporary."

"There is the dispatch from Frau von Katzenstein, Beate ; the Duchess expects to find me at the Residence. They arrive to-morrow morning ; the dispatch is from Marseilles. I wanted to ask you, Beate, to occasionally look after the little one," continued Claudine. "Joachim is so busy with his work, and Fräulein Lindenmeyer is very forgetful. I thought of writing to Ida, but Lindenmeyer told me she had a position."

"What do you talk so much about it for?" asked Beate, apparently angry, helping her cousin with her cloak. "It is understood ; wrap up good and warm, and——"

"But leave the child at the Owl's Nest," Claudine interrupted ; "Joachim is accustomed to having Elizabeth come up to his room at dusk, to sit upon his knee and listen to his stories."

"Certainly," replied Beate. "But what I wanted to say, Claudine "— she hesitated—"was—do not forget your engagement ring," she added softly.

Claudine turned with a startled look. "Oh, yes, you are right," said she sadly, taking the ring from a box.

Fräulein Lindenmeyer stood weeping beside Beate in the hall, while Claudine bade Joachim good-bye.

"Oh Lord, so young to die!" sobbed the old lady,

16

who, in her grief, could find no suitable quotation. "To leave husband and children, and so far away ! God grant that she reach home alive ! "

"God grant it ! " repeated Claudine, as if unconsciously, as she drove into the snowy night with Beate who would hear of nothing else but that she see Claudine into the railway coach ; she cared almost like a mother for her brother's intended bride. And when the train disappeared, she drove home with serious thoughts. The sleigh-bells jingled with a peculiarly solemn sound in the woods which were so quiet ; she thought of the express train, rushing through the country, bringing with it the sick Duchess. It must be very serious for them to undertake the journey ; it could only be because she wanted to die at home. And she thought of Claudine's tears. What a meeting between the two ! When the Duchess left Altenstein for Cannes, she had fainted. Now the last parting had come. Claudine, too, thought of her friend, as she rode alone. Such a journey is terrible ! "So soon ! " rang in her heart. Yes, they all knew it was but a short respite which was granted the poor life, and yet it came too quickly ! To the girl the future looked dark, darker than the night without.

She had only a short distance to ride, and at Wehrburg would have to wait two hours ; the winter arrangements were inconvenient. There gleamed the lights of Wehrburg. The train slackened its speed, and finally stopped. She alighted and walked along the platform to the waiting room ; she did not raise her veil as she entered, and quietly seated herself in a corner.

Not far from her, conversing in whispers sat a gentleman and lady, the latter, likewise, rendered unrecognizable by a thick, gauze veil ; only the movement of the head, seemed familiar to Claudine. Up to that time she had simply seen the gentleman's short, gray hair. He wore a costly fur coat ; his hat lay beside him. He was looking through a guide-book, and when he turned the page a large brilliant glittered upon his finger. It is unpleasant to wait on a winter night in a poorly warmed and lighted waiting-room. Involuntarily one examines one's companions in misery and wonders : what are their plans, whither are they going, what tie unites them ? Are they husband and wife? Are they father and daughter?

Claudine, in her sadness, gazed too at the only human beings who, besides the sleepy porter, shared the room with her. The lady spoke softly and eagerly; her head was close to that of the man, who fidgeted uneasily in his chair.

"Nonsense!" Claudine now heard him say in French, "I have explained a thousand times, I shall go to Frankfurt and then return."

"I do not believe you," whispered the lady violently; "I adhere to what I have said—if you deceive me, you know how I will be revenged."

"Well, that would be no benefit to you, my dear!"

"This shall not be," said she in a louder voice than she intended, and her small hand, clinched into a fist, struck the table. Soothingly the man laid his right hand upon it and looked anxiously around.

Claudine's veil was thick; it completely hid her features and her astonished eyes. That was indeed Herr von Palmer—and of course—Frau von Berg only could hiss that way when she was provoked. That was her luxuriant hair, her full figure. What in the world——

"I beg of you," said he, now caressingly, "what could I do without you there, *m'amie?* Be reasonable and grant my request!"

Just then a train rushed into the station, the windows rattled. The bell rang and the porter called out in a singing tone: "Train for Frankfurt-on-the-Main!"

Hastily Herr von Palmer rose. "Stay here!" said he violently.

"I shall not be prevented from escorting you to the coach," she replied derisively; "who knows how long I shall be deprived of your presence."

He made no reply, but rushed out, followed by the lady. Claudine involuntarily rose and approached the window; she saw Palmer hurriedly enter a first-class coach. The lady stood there, wrapped in her furs. Then the train started and she returned to the waiting-room. For a moment she stared at veiled Claudine; then she put back her own veil and ordered tea and the newspapers.

Right: the silk veil had concealed the painted face of the enemy.

Herr von Palmer was probably going to meet the ducal party, but what cause had the lady for anxiety? Beate was probably correct; they seemed very intimate, and the passionate woman was jealous.

At length *her* train came. Claudine waited to see which coach Frau von Berg would take; there were only two first-class in the train. One Frau von Berg entered; so she approached the other, which the guard opened for her at once. For a moment she hesitated, there sat a gentleman—should she travel second-class?

"Is the non-smoking compartment of the second-class empty?" she asked.

"No, madame, there are five men and a woman in it, and a family with children in the ladies' *coupé.*"

So she entered the first-class compartment, and took her seat at the window. The gentleman in the corner was asleep; nothing was to be seen of him but his cap, his furs, and a dark red rug. Well, the ride would not last longer than two hours. She laid her fair head with the dark fur cap upon the cushions, she was so tired; but her sad, disquieting thoughts would not allow her to sleep. The Duchess would die, then she would have lost a faithful friend and—have won her freedom; as soon as the last spark was extinguished, on the day of the funeral, she would lay her engagement ring in Lothar's hand and breathe freely. Her bosom heaved, the thought of that breath pained her. Ah, the life that would follow! So colorless, so monotonous, the life of a poor, patrician maiden, who by degrees would become a monosyllabic old maid. The life of a recluse!—And if Joachim were to marry again! If, to all the joylessness, was united the consciousness of being superfluous? If, some day, Beate were to go from the Paulinenthal with a husband? Ah, no, Joachim would remain, *must* remain with her. How would he find the leisure in which to woo, in his retirement, in his busy life? Joachim and his child were left to her; it was sinful cowardice to think thus. She had still so much more than some others!

She sat upright and looked at the frost on the window panes. Then she started in affright. Amid the rolling and the rumbling of the train, which had just drawn up short before a station, she did not hear the gentleman in the coach rise and cross over to her. Only when she felt something brush against her cloak, did she look up—before her sat Lothar.

" Is it really you ? " was the delighted inquiry. "Recognized in spite of the veil. But what am I saying? There is no other golden hair like this. And you are going to the Residence, too?" An expression of pleased surprise flitted over his face. Involuntarily his right hand moved as if to grasp an extended hand ; he had removed his fur cap ; he now put it on again as if to hide his embarrassment.

Claudine sat there like a statue. She had regained her composure with remarkable rapidity.

" Yes," she replied curtly, overlooking the hand ; she held both of hers in her muff, as though she wished to hold them fast. "Chamberlain von Schotbach telegraphed me that the ducal party will arrive to-morrow, and I started out at once."

" But, tell me, how are they all in the Paulinenthal ? " he asked.

" Well," she answered.

"And my little one ? "

" She is well—I think."

" You *think* ? " he said with bitter emphasis.

For a while both were silent. The train stopped ; without, the snow crackled under the tramp of the men's heavy feet ; a coach door was closed ; the bell rang and the carriage rolled on.

" Claudine," he began with hesitation, " I wrote to you the day before yesterday. The letter will reach the Owl's Nest this morning."

She bowed her head without looking at him.

"I was in a terrible mood," he continued ; "imagine how I lived in the old, sparsely-furnished castle, two hours from the nearest town, completely snowed in. Picture me a having just returned from the chase, drenched, sitting beside a smoky fireplace which gives out scarcely any warmth ; the snowstorm raging at every window, and I so alone, so terribly alone, in the deserted building ! In addition I had visions, at times : I could see the Neuhaus sitting-room, my child playing there ; I could hear her merry voice, and indeed almost smell the baked apples which at this season of the year are never lacking in the pipes of the stoves." He paused a moment. " And I would think : My God, why do you sit here with such gloomy thoughts ? In such a moment, I rose, fetched my portfolio and wrote at once to ask you if——"

She interrupted him violently.

"Wherefore ask? I cannot force you to keep your promise. I did not even really require you to go to Schloss Stein. You have always known how to find your way to Berlin, Vienna, Paris or some other city still farther distant."

He let her finish speaking.

"I wanted to ask you in my letter," said he calmly, "if the comedy could not end, Claudine? It is sinful——"

She started up. Was he in earnest?

"You tell me that now?" she cried indignantly. "Now when the end is so near? The poor woman will probably live but four-and-twenty hours more! Are you in such haste to obtain your freedom?"

"You are very bitter, Claudine," he replied impatiently, and yet there was a trace of pity in his voice. "But you are right; in the face of the sad day which we are nearing, one should not mention these things;—meanwhile——"

"No, no! Do not speak of it!" she assented with a deep-drawn breath.

"Meanwhile I can do nothing else," he continued inexorably. "The latest is that Her Highness has turned direct to me." He took out his pocketbook and handed her a note; "it is better you should read it yourself."

Claudine made an evasive gesture.

"It is written by the Duchess," he emphasized; "the poor woman is embittering her last days with sorrow. If you will permit, cousin, I will read it aloud to you."

And scarcely glancing at the girl's pale face, he began :

" MY DEAR BARON :

"These lines are penned to you after a long inward struggle, by a dying woman, who implores you to help her as much as possible in an unusually delicate matter.

"Tell me the truth about a question the indiscretion of which you will pardon for I shall soon be among the dead. Do you love your cousin? If it was only an act of magnanimity to ask her hand, then, Baron, give the poor girl back her freedom, and be convinced that thereby you will assure the future of two persons who are dearer to me than all else.

" ELIZABETH."

Claudine's blue eyes stared in despair at the tiny scrap

of paper. Merciful Father, what could that be? Did the
Duchess still labor under the old terrible delusion that her
husband loved her or she him? Or had Princess Helene
confided in her, and the Duchess wanted to mediate between Lothar and her?

"And you?" came at length from her lips.

"I am on the way to take Her Highness an answer,
Claudine. You yourself know, I hope, that it was unnecessary for the Duchess to require the truth. I have
always acted openly all my life; only once did I practice
deceit, because, from a sense of delicacy, I had not the
courage to speak, because I believed that I had to redeem
a given pledge and should it be at the cost of my life's
happiness! Let us leave that, it is past. Never since
then has any consideration kept me from acting uprightly.
I shall briefly explain to Her Highness, that——"

A slight cry interrupted him; imploringly Claudine extended her hand to him and her eyes gazed anxiously in
his.

"Be silent, I am not the Duchess!" she stammered.

He paused in the face of that despairing gesture. The
girl sprang up and fled to the other side of the *coupé*. At
that moment lanterns flitted past the window, the train ran
slower, in the dim morning light the Baron recognized
the station of the Residence; above the town towered the
old, gray, ducal fortress. Claudine alighted before he
could come up to aid her. A royal lackey and a court
carriage awaited her. As she hastily entered it, Lothar
stood at the door. In the cold, gray light his face looked
very different from what it had before; it seemed to
Claudine as if he had aged years in a few months.

"I pray you, cousin, fix the hour for an interview," he
asked with courteous firmness.

"To-morrow," she replied.

"Not until to-morrow?"

"Yes!" said she curtly.

He stepped back with a bow, a few minutes later seated
himself in a hotel carriage and drove in the lumbering
omnibus through the South gate, through which the ducal
carriage containing Claudine had just driven hastily.

"How," thought he, rendered anxious by her strange
behavior, "if the Duchess were right, if she really loved
the Duke? If she really were indifferent to me?"

He had always flattered himself that he understood women; he had thought he knew Claudine thoroughly—to-day for the first time, he felt serious doubts of it.

Meantime she had driven up the steep Schlossberg and alighted at the door of the wing occupied by the Dowager Duchess. The rising sun bathed the snowy gabled roofs, the towers and the walls in a crimson glow, and at the same moment upon the main tower of the city which lay below in the gray dawn the ducal banner was unfurled, a signal that the mistress was returning home; yes—returning home to die.

In the second story Claudine found a couple of cosy rooms at her disposal, and in the course of the forenoon, was summoned to the Dowager's presence. The kindly woman's eyes were swollen from weeping; she sat in the pleasant corner-window, gazing over the roofs of her city, far into the snowy land. Oh, how often had Claudine sat with her in the cosy room, with the stiff, costly furniture of the first Empire, and the many, many pictures on the walls: and had with her mistress enjoyed the fine view. At the present hour neither had eyes for those beauties. They looked out upon the road along which the invalid was to be borne thither.

The Duchess had had another hemorrhage in Cannes; she wanted only one thing,—to see her children and to arrange several things before her death. The little Princes remained at home; they must not disturb their mother; the doctor had wished it, although she objected. "Doctor, I shall die of longing!"

The old Princess shook her gray head slowly, as she related all this. "It is hard—it is especially hard for Adalbert; they understood one another perfectly. They were upon the safest road to become a happy pair. He writes so affectionately of her, and now," she sighed, "God alone knows what has yet to be gone through!"

Their Highnesses had forbidden any reception, but the Dowager Duchess wanted to drive to the station, nevertheless, and gave orders that Claudine should accompany her. Towards two o'clock they drove down the Schlossberg; a dull November sky lowered over the city, and large snowflakes fell. Notwithstanding the inclement weather, hundreds of people stood in the street which led to the station.

The Duchess' landau drew up at the door of the royal waiting-room ; the police tried to keep back the throng which pressed silently forward. All stood quietly in a wide circle around the equipages. Several gentlemen were upon the *perron ;* the express which was to bring the ducal family was already signaled. At length the carriages rushed into the station. Suddenly all was animation. The Duke was the first to alight ; he kissed his venerable mother's hand ; then he, himself, lifted his suffering wife from the coach. All eyes were fixed upon her pale, thin face, whose large eyes sought the Hereditary Prince. She embraced the Dowager Duchess and kissed her child with a sad smile. "Here I am again," she whispered faintly. She could scarcely walk the few steps to the waiting-room ; the Hereditary Prince and the Duke supported her ; pleasantly but languidly she returned the greetings. Princess Helene and her maid-of-honor, Frau Katzenstein and the gentlemen of the suite all hastened up in confusion.

When she saw Claudine, her face twitched ; she waved her hand and pointed to the carriage.

The lovely maiden hurried over. "Your Highness," she stammered with emotion, bending over the Duchess' hand.

"Come, Dina !" whispered the latter, "drive with me ; and you, my darling," she turned to the Hereditary Prince, "Adalbert will drive with mamma." And when she was lifted into the carriage, she said, as they drove through the throng so respectfully silent : "Bow, my child, bow pleasantly ; the people all know how ill I am."

She, too, made an effort to lean forward and feebly waved her white handkerchief.

"The last time ! The last time !" she murmured. Then she seized the girl's hand. "How good that you are here !" Above at the door she dismissed her friend. "When I have rested, I will call you, Dina."

Claudine sought her quiet room and looked down into the wintry castle courtyard, which had suddenly lost the appearance of loneliness. Equipages drove to and fro, the guards drew up, and the large baggage wagons came slowly up the mountain. Below the bells of the Marienkirche rang, perhaps for a wedding ; here and there lights gleamed, notwithstanding the early afternoon hour, and it snowed, snowed continually. Hours passed. Claudine's

tea was served in her room. Seated in an arm-chair, she
watched the flickering, blue flame under the machine and
thought of Lothar and how he had described his loneliness and longing in the deserted castle in Saxony. Ah,
yes, it was difficult—very difficult—to be alone with tormenting thoughts, with terrible uncertainty! She was
almost angry with herself; ah God! she knew it only too
surely!

Princess Helene looked well; her face wore another, a
more becoming expression. The passionate, restless look
had vanished—she had hope, well-founded hope.

What did the Duchess want with her? Ah, it was clear!
After she had received Lothar's answer she would say to
her: "Claudine, be magnanimous, give him back his
word! He feels bound."

She knew, of course, that he would never break the engagement. He was thrown upon her magnanimity.
Ardent, passionate defiance possessed her. And if I do
not now want to? If I would rather be miserable by his
side than miserable without him? Who can prevent me?
She shook her head. Oh never! No!

The old-fashioned clock upon the console struck nine.
To-day surely the Duchess was fatigued; there was no
more hope of seeing her. She suddenly felt chilly in the
dark room; the light under the kettle had long since gone
out; in the grate only a faint red light glowed. She
began to wander about; she would wait until ten o'clock,
then she would retire. Perhaps she could sleep. But at
ten o'clock the maid came and bade her come downstairs.

She walked along the corridor and down various stair-
cases, until she reached the well-heated and lighted hall,
until she reached Her Highness' apartments. She had
rarely been there; at the festivities which took place at
the castle, she had always only accompanied the Dowager
Duchess to the state rooms and had sought to avoid the
little evening gatherings in Her Highness' salon. But to-
day she again felt the peculiar charm of these fine rooms.
Everywhere that rich red upon walk, carpets, and hangings, everywhere the subdued light of lamps with crimson
shades, everywhere groups of exotic plants, and everywhere magnificent, brilliant paintings in wide, gleaming,
gold frames.

Oppressive! "As feverish as the spirit which dwells

within these walls," had once said His Highness, who, accustomed to the pure forest air, felt as if he would suffocate in the heavy, perfume-laden atmosphere. A feverish longing to beautify poor reality ; the yearning for life and happiness spoke from the surroundings which resembled a fairy palace.

The Duchess lay in her bedroom, in the low bed with its heavy red hangings, whose folds a gilded eagle, above in the ceiling, held in his claws. Here, too, was a reddish light, which tinted the pallid face with a deceiving pink.

"It is late, Dina," said the sick woman in a low voice, "but I can sleep scarcely at all, and I cannot be alone ; I am afraid. I have therefore had the curtains of the bed so arranged that I cannot see the door. Moreover, I am possessed by an inexplicable fear that something terrible might cross the threshold, our household phantom, the white lady who will come to announce to me something I already know : that I must die. Do not laugh, Dina ; I used to like to lie in the dark. Tell me, Claudine, tell me all. I fear I shall not hear your voice much longer ! How are things with you, Dina ? Speak !"

Claudine felt impelled to rush from the luxurious chamber, with its gilded ceiling and the oppressive Mayflower perfume which came from the conservatory. "I am all right, Elizabeth ; I am only sad because you are ill," said she, seating herself at the bedside.

"Claudine," began the dying woman, "I have still so much to write and to arrange, and when my father and sister are once here—they will soon arrive—and when fear, that suffocating fear, possesses me again, it will be too late. Help me with it a little."

"Elizabeth, you will excite yourself needlessly."

"No, ah, no ; I pray you, Dina !" She turned her emaciated face and looked at the girl with her large, glowing eyes, as if she wished to see into her friend's heart. "You are a strange bride, Claudine," she began in a whisper, after a pause, "and your betrothal is strange, too. He there, you here. Claudine, confess, it was a noble sacrifice on your part, when you gave away your hand on that dreadful day. Speak, Claudine, you do not love him ?"

With veritable fear, her eyes hung upon the girl's pale face.

"Elizabeth," was her reply, as she crossed her hands over her breast; "I love Lothar; I loved him when I did not even realize what love was; when still a child I loved him!"

The Duchess was silent, but she breathed quickly.

"Do you not believe me, Elizabeth?" asked Claudine, softly.

"Yes, I believe you, Dina; but does *he* love you? Say, does *he* love you?" whispered the Duchess.

She lowered her lashes. "I do not know," she stammered.

"If you knew he did not love you, would you nevertheless become his wife?"

"No, Elizabeth!"

"Would you be able to decide to give your hand to another who loves you unspeakably?"

The lovely maiden sat by, as motionless as a statue.

"Claudine, do you know why I came home?" asked the Duchess, with passionate excitement. "To save a longed-for happiness, with the last remnant of my strength for him, who is the dearest to me in this world. When I went to Cannes," she continued, "my absurd weakness, my vain, wounded heart still struggled with better feelings. Claudine, the Duke loves you,—he never loved me. He loves you with all the fervor and honesty of which his noble heart is capable. I have, during the years of our married life, learned to read every feature of his face. —He loves you, Dina! He will never forget you. Do not sit there so silently; for God's sake, answer!"

"You are mistaken!" cried Claudine anxiously, extending her hand evasively toward the Duchess; "you are mistaken; His Highness does not love me, it is a mere fancy on your part! You must not worry about such things; you should not have come home for that reason."

"Oh, do you think, Dina, that one can cast off love as one would a dress?" asked the Duchess, bitterly. "That one can set about it as if one were going to take a walk? From this day forth there will be no more love-period! The heart is not constructed thus!"

Claudine was silent. "I shall never marry," said she then, softly and firmly, "if our hearts are not mutually inclined, never ! Pardon, Elizabeth, I can make you no illusive promises. Dispose of everything ! Of my life, if it must be, but do not ask that ! "

The Duchess looked past Claudine with tearful eyes. For a while all was still in the room.

" Poor man ! I planned all so wisely for you," said she to herself in a low voice. " It is not to be ! " Then, somewhat louder : " What confusion—you love Lothar, and he—poor little Princess ! "

" Elizabeth ! " cried Claudine, and her pallid lips quivered, " I will not stand in the way of his happiness— what opinion have you of me ? Never, never ! Do me a favor," she continued hastily, " give him his freedom back in my name—I know you will speak with him on this point."

" To-morrow," said the Duchess.

" Then give him this ! " She drew the engagement ring from her finger. " Here is the Princess' happiness ; take it and—let me go my own way, alone, far from all that reminds me of him ! "

She sprang up and went over to the door.

" Claudine," besought the Duchess in her faint voice, her fragile fingers clasping the ring, " Dina, do not leave me thus ! Which of us is the poorer ? Help me, rather, that there may be some blessing from all this."

Claudine came back. " What shall I do ? " she asked with resignation.

The Duchess asked for water. Then she bade Claudine bring a certain casket to her ; she opened it and handed the girl a piece of paper.

" It is a note of the little souvenirs which I wish to have distributed after my death. Keep it—it is a copy, the Duke has the original."

" You should not excite yourself thus, Elizabeth."

" Oh, I shall be calmer when all is arranged, Dina. Read it aloud once more, to see if I have not omitted anything. No one shall say : 'She forgot me ! ' "

In a trembling voice Claudine read. Occasionally a flood of tears caused the writing to become indistinct ; all was so delicately arranged, each bequest showed such deep, tender feeling.

" To my dear Claudine, I bequeath the Brussels lace veil which I wore as a bride——"

A brilliant flush suffused the girl's grieved face—she knew what the Duchess meant.

"Take it back, take it back!" she sobbed, kneeling by the bed.

"Oh, how terrible! How terrible!" said the Duchess. "You and he—unhappy. You, my two beloveds!"

Claudine kissed the Duchess' hot hands and hurried out of the room, grief raging violently within her. In the conservatory, under the magnolias and palms, she wept; the splashing of the fountain at her feet soothed her wild despair; in a few moments she was so far composed, that she could quietly say "Good-night." When she looked through the silken hangings, towards the bed, the sufferer lay there, apparently asleep, a sorrowful expression about her mouth.

In the ante-room, Claudine met the old physician; he greeted her gravely.

"Is the end really so near?" asked the agitated girl.

He extended his hand sympathetically. "As long as there is life, Fräulein, there is hope. But according to human estimation, Her Highness' life will go out like a candle, she will fall asleep from exhaustion."

Claudine involuntarily pointed to her arm. "Doctor?"

"Ah, Fräulein," said the doctor with emotion, "that is no longer of any avail. All is over here!" He pointed to his breast. "I must go to the Duke to take him the report of Her Highness' condition;" he spoke softly as he went along the corridor beside the young lady. "His Highness too has just had a very disagreeable shock. Do you know about it? Palmer has disappeared, leaving dire confusion behind him."

"He went to Frankfurt last night," said Claudine in surprise; "I thought he was going to meet the ducal party; I saw him at the station at Wehrburg."

"The rogue," muttered the old gentleman, "has for some hours been on the other side of the border. To meet the ducal party! who told that fable, Fräulein?"

"I heard him speaking of it to Frau von Berg;" Claudine suddenly paused; the whole affair was clear to her.

"They are well matched," laughed the doctor; "I will tell His Highness of it. We will receive word to-morrow probably, that Her Grace, too, has disappeared. One should not be malicious, still I am pleased on account of

the old Princess ; she protected Berg in a remarkable
way. Good-night, Fräulein."

And so it was. The next morning they learned at the
castle that Frau von Berg had suddenly vanished. She
left no "confusion" behind her, but a package of letters
directed to the Duchess, and a letter to His Highness.
But the angel who kept guard on the threshold of the sick-
chamber in the form of Frau von Katzenstein, immediately
divined that the contents of the package was not suitable
for Her Highness' perusal, and she therefore promptly
delivered them up to the Duke. The old lady arrived just
at the moment when His Highness, the veins upon his
brow swollen with anger, was going through a heap of
papers ; the chief of the police likewise was in the room.

The Duke thought Frau von Katzenstein was bringing
him news of Her Highness. Instead, the lady gravely
offered him a package of letters tied with a blue ribbon,
the uppermost of which was unmistakably in His Highness' handwriting and bore the address of Frau von Berg.

The Duke turned pale.

"And that was to be given to Her Highness ?" he asked,
looking with dismay at the proofs of a gay bachelorhood,
of the time when he had supped with Herr and Frau von
Berg, and had played *baccarat* in the handsome woman's
dainty blue drawing-room. That woman, who should
not have breathed the same atmosphere with the woman
whose life was numbered by days, to whom those days
had been made days of torture by an infamous act—
that woman still dared to venture to disturb the peace of
the death-bed.

"Thank you, madame," said the Duke with emotion.
And he took the letters and threw them in the grate, and
the other papers soon followed. Involuntarily he wiped
his fingers afterward on his cambric handkerchief. "Let
the rogue go, Herr von Schmidt," said he then, contemptuously, bowing in token of dismissal to the chief of police.

When the latter had withdrawn, the Duke paced the
floor in agitation. One of the letters, a short note, lay un-
burned before the grate ; the Duke noticed it and picked it
up. It was in Herr von Palmer's well-known handwriting.

"Last night," it ran, "I handed the lovely Claudine
a note from the Duke ; I stole it from her, when I helped
her into the coach. Herewith I enclose the valuable

scrap of paper to be done with as your talent prompts. My treasure will know how to fire the mine so skillfully that both of the clever ladies so kindly disposed towards us, will fly up in the air——"

"So, Palmer had a hand in that too!" He smiled bitterly, as he recalled the passionate, dark-eyed, little creature into whose hand was thrust the quick-match. The mine had exploded, the first victim lay there, and—the culprits had escaped.

The sly person had at least been guarded, had understood how to deceive with smiling diplomacy such as had never been practiced at any court. There were no tradesmen who had not bills against him ; and none of them had received a penny for a year. The Duke's officials had a task to learn of all the people in whose debt he was. In the ducal tax-office people pressed with accounts after Palmer's flight was discovered. The Duke laughed angrily when he learned the details.

The Dowager Duchess, very particular in money matters, was indignant that she had to pay for a landau the second time, and only with difficulty bore the thought that in the same carriage she had driven calmly past the house of the manufacturer who had so frequently sent Palmer dunning letters.

The entire Residence was up in arms, and wished the fugitive in jail and on the gallows ; but such sly birds generally escape.

Claudine learned all this through the maid ; it scarcely aroused her interest. She thought only of what the days would bring her, of the decision of her fate. The Duchess' condition was no worse ; she had slept several hours, but had not yet asked for her friend.

Claudine stood at the window and looked out at the gray November sky. It still snowed ; the world lay before her, so gloomy, so dead, and depressed her grieved heart still more. Suddenly a deep flush flitted over her face. A carriage rolled into the court and drew up at the door of the wing occupied by the Duchess. As her room was situated in the middle building in which were the state rooms, she could distinctly see who alighted from the carriage and entered the castle. It was *he ;* Lothar's tall form had just disappeared behind the gleaming panes of the inner door. He came to bring Her Highness his reply,

She had to seek support, so great was her emotion; what meant the absurd ray of hope in her tortured soul? Every word she had heard him utter since they had met again for the first time in the Neuhaus garden, since the day on which she had gone thither to inform Beate of the discovery of the wax, had been as cutting, as sharp, as steel. He had shown his mistrust and contempt wherever he could; he did not love her, no, no! Once had her heart pulsated absently with bliss,—that was in the dark summer night, when he rode up to gaze at her window—one moment, one single sweet moment. But annihilation followed in its wake; it was a military custom: he was reconnoitering to see if all was in order—the family honor as well!

She turned from the window and went to the table upon which still stood the breakfast. She seized the decanter filled with sherry, and poured out half a glass; as a rule she did not like sherry, but she felt so weak at that moment! A tap at the door caused her to put down the glass before she had emptied it. "Come in!" she said in so faint a voice that the person without could not possibly have heard the words. Notwithstanding Frau von Katzenstein opened the door, and with a kindly but grave expression crossed the threshold. In her hand she held a small basket covered with white tissue paper.

"My dear Gerold," said she affectionately, "Her Highness just commissioned me to hand you this." She stood the basket on a side-table and drew nearer Claudine. "The Duchess would like to see you in half an hour," she added, pressing the girl's hand. "Excuse me for not staying, but I cannot leave our patient long."

"How is she?" Claudine's quivering lips managed to articulate.

"She does not complain to-day; she says her chest feels lighter and easier," replied the old lady, who was still breathless from climbing the stairs.

"Oh, you have put yourself to trouble," said Claudine absently; but Frau von Katzenstein had already passed through the door.

Claudine scarcely gave the basket a thought. In half an hour she was to know if he had taken her ring—they would surely tell her the truth!

17

She began to wander about restlessly, although her feet would scarcely bear her. Then she stepped to the window; the guard had cried, "Out!" The Duke was just driving across the court in the hunting-sleigh; he was seeking to escape anger and care. She too felt the desire to run out into the park to cool her heated brow in the snow-laden air, to walk until she was tired, to find sleep and oblivion. Mechanically she paused before the basket which the Duchess had sent her, probably a gift from her travels—the Duchess never failed to give pleasure.

She raised the paper a little; in a few minutes she would have to go down to thank her; she must know for what. In the basket, lined with light blue silk, upon costly lace, lay a sprig of myrtle—and that sprig was drawn through her engagement-ring.

The pale, panting girl was upon the stairs; she hastened through the corridors, and only on reaching the Duchess' ante-room did she feel that her feet would no longer carry her. There stood the doctor whispering with Frau von Katzenstein. The old lady pointed to one of the adjoining rooms and laid her finger on her lips.

"Her Highness is sleeping," said she softly.

As if in a dream Claudine advanced to the Duchess' so-called *study ;* it was a small room, paneled half way with fine wood; antique, gilded leather hangings covered the walls; bookcases and a writing-desk of dark oak, heavy curtains and thick carpets and the busts of Goethe, Shakespeare and Byron formed the furnishings. It was almost dark there on that gloomy day. Through one of the doors whose portière was partly drawn back, one could look into the conservatory, and there stood, in the full light of day, which streamed in through the glass doors, Lothar; he had his back towards her and was examining with evident interest a bunch of yellow roses.

Involuntarily Claudine drew back into the shadow of the high bookcases. She could not see him; she did not want to, she could not meet him now. With violent heart-throbs she leaned back in her protecting corner; she did not want the ring, which seemed to her a gift of pity; she knew he returned it, because he did not wish to break his word—and *she*—dared not, she could not keep hers. Suddenly she looked about her to see if she could not escape, for she heard Princess Thekla's harsh voice.

"Well, Baron," she said, "at last we see you again?
Do you know I am very angry with you? You have
been here since yesterday and have not shown yourself
at the red castle!"

"It was wrong of me, surely, your Highness! But I
found so many things to do here, and besides—one does
not pay visits on one's wedding-day."

"Wedding-day?" repeated the old lady with a shrill
laugh. "I think your jests are very ill-timed—the Duchess
is sick unto death! Really, Lothar, you are at times
very strange; do you know that Her Highness might die
to-day?"

"Ah, your Highness thinks I am making an inappro-
priate jest? Nothing is further from my thought. I myself was surprised at the news; but the Duchess wishes
our bonds to be united to-day—of course, if my bride will
consent."

"My congratulations, Baron!—Why should not your
bride consent?" she asked mockingly. "She consented
so quickly to the engagement, and, as a matter of course,
marriage follows. It is, however, an odd caprice of Her
Highness."

"Odd? Is it so odd, that before she dies Her Highness wishes to steer the happiness of two beings, so to
speak, into a safe harbor, out of the reach of all the intrigues and artifices to which they are exposed as long as
they are not united? I confess, I do not think it so odd;
I gratefully accept this 'odd caprice'."

"You were not formerly so submissive, Gerold; since
when have you been so weak? You knew how to defy
my consent when I refused you my daughter's hand.
Since when do you acknowledge the right of the stronger
—or rather the right of the more powerful, or——"

"I fear no honest enemy," he replied slowly, and his
words had an annihilating keenness. "Your Highness
knows undoubtedly from the fable, that the lion is always
magnanimous; I do not fear him as an enemy, I fear the
reptiles which creep about unperceived and spatter the
innocent with their venom. I cannot protect her who is
to become my wife, from malicious slander before she is
really my wife, for I am fighting with an unequal weapon.
Notwithstanding my court life, intrigue is to me unknown
ground; they might just as well require me to read flu-

ently and to translate old Assyrian characters. And, your
Highness, I should never learn it, even from the most
prominent example."

But the Princess did not seem to understand. "Or,"
she repeated, continuing her speech, "are you anxious to
be sure of your bride's fidelity, when you know it to be
safe behind the bolt of the marriage-vow?"

"Your Highness is right in part," he answered politely.
"But I am not anxious as to the fidelity and firmness of
my bride; I am anxious because I do not yet know if my
bride has forgiven me for placing myself in her way with
the persistency of anxiety, to force her to say 'yes.'"

The old Princess laughed curtly. "One might almost
fear, *cher baron*, that in case your bride does not pardon,
you will take your life, or else do something terrible."

"Take my life? No! For I have a child to whom my
life belongs; but I should be a miserable man, your Highness, for I love my bride."

Claudine stepped forth; she took a few steps towards
the door, then she paused. She saw the Princess in the
black silk, fur-lined mantle; she saw the fan-leaf palm
waving over her velvet hat, and how the yellow, emaciated
face was colored by the flush of angry surprise. She had
to hold fast to the carved lion's head of the bookcase, for
the voice of the old Princess said with indescribable contempt:

"That you love the lady, Baron, is no guarantee to
me of the qualities of her who is to become my grandchild's step-mother."

"Your Highness," said he sharply, "probably wishes
to hear from me once more, that I preserve the entire
right of guiding Leonie's training. In what way will it
be done? I assume the responsibility cheerfully! She
who will be the child's mother is in my eyes the noblest,
the best, the most unselfish being on earth! Never have
her thoughts strayed from the path which honor and
propriety point out to a woman, never, I know. In her
love for her sick friend, my bride may have forgotten that
thousands of spiteful, envious tongues were busy turning
and twisting her actions; in my heart she stands still
higher yet. To play the honorable in the eyes of the
world, is very easy, your Highness; but alone, supported
by the courage of a clear conscience, to defy the world,

which would destroy us—to remain firm in that which one knows to be right, and yet to know that one is misjudged, —to remain firm, while under all circumstances one performs the duty which one accepted from a sense of honor, and were it only the much-doubted duty of friendship, for that is necessary ; purity of soul and a strong character, qualities which up to this time I have vainly——"

"Lothar !" exclaimed Claudine. The glass cupola swam before her eyes ; it seemed as if the floor upon which she stood was undulating. Then she felt two strong arms around her, and "Claudine" resounded in her ear.

" Do not be so hard," she whispered, "do not be so hard ! The thought that others are angry is so unpleasant when happiness dawns upon us so abundantly."

They were alone. She now looked at him with her blue eyes swimming in tears. "Not a word," said she, laying her tiny hand upon his lips, "not a word, Lothar —it is not the time now to be happy. I know enough, and—death sits over there."

" But you will not oppose the dying woman's wish ? " he implored humbly.

" I shall not."

"And we will drive home to our peaceful Neuhaus, Claudine ? "

"No," she said firmly, "oh, no ! I will not leave her, who has suffered so cruelly on my account, as long as she lives. I am no longer afraid, for I now know that you and I belong to each other forever, that you will trust me and believe me, in me, always, steadfastly. And you —you can travel in the meantime ; once more I give you permission ; and when you return, when my heart can again rejoice, when I feel I have the right to be happy— then I will come to you."

In the Duchess' apartments toward evening a marriage was solemnized. All in the castle knew of it, from the linen-keeper in her neat mansard to the scullery-boy, who, below stairs, was preparing himself for his future career. They knew that immediately after the ceremony the young husband left, and that Frau Claudine von Gerold took her place at the Duchess' sick-bed.

Her Highness was very weak. She had been present
at the marriage ; she had, with trembling hands, put the
bridal veil upon the girl's lovely fair head. Her Highness,
the Dowager Duchess, and Frau von Katzenstein were the
other witnesses. In the presence of those present the
young pair bade each other farewell.

And now at the foot of the bed beside Claudine sat a tiny,
dainty maiden, and both had tear-stained eyes. The
Duchess had swooned after the ceremony, and the doctor
had repaired to the Duke to prepare him for the inevitable.

The end was near.

Without, the snow clouds had broken, and the stars
glittered upon the wintry earth. In the Princes' room
the lamp-light shone upon their fair heads ; the children
suspected nothing. That night every one else was awake.
The lights in the castle shimmered upon the snowy landscape, and below, in the houses of the town, they prayed
for the Duchess, who was always kind and charitable,
who lay upon her deathbed.

In the ante-room the Duke paced to and fro ; occasionally he cast a glance into his wife's sleeping apartment.
Then he heard a soft voice :

"Adalbert, has Claudine gone?" The young wife at
these words moved noiselessly to the side of the bed.
"You are still here?" asked the dying woman.

"Let me remain with you, Elizabeth," besought Claudine. "Gerold has various matters to attend to before I
can go to Neuhaus."

The Duchess smiled feebly.

"You do not know how to lie, Claudine ; I know why
you have remained ! Poor child, what a sad marriage !
—Call Adalbert !" she then added : "Is Helene there?"

The Princess came. Claudine and she stood side by
side.

"Shake hands," besought the Duchess.

Princess Helene seized Claudine's hand. "Forgive
me !" said she, weeping softly.

"And now call Adalbert !" commanded the sufferer.

He came, seated himself on the edge of her bed, and she
silently pressed his hands as he eagerly asked her pardon.

"If I could live to comfort you, my poor friend !" she
murmured. "It is so difficult to have to deny ourselves,

I know. But—they love each other, and you—you will be so lonely, so lonely ! Ah, if it were in my power, how happy you should be ! "

"Do not speak so," said he. "I shall only be unhappy, my Liesel, if you leave me ! "

"Say, 'my Liesel' once again," she asked, looking up at him, and her glazing eyes gleamed for a second with the old, tender light of love.

"My Liesel ! " he murmured in broken accents.

She pressed his hand.

"Now go, Adalbert, I would like to sleep. I am so weary ! Kiss the children for me ; go ! " she urged.

And she slept.

The young wife sat watching faithfully at her post. Only once her eyes grew heavy ; the drowsiness lasted scarcely a moment, for she collected herself with a shudder. The Duchess lay there so strangely still, a smile upon her lips, her hands folded.

Claudine took one of her hands, "Elizabeth ! " said she anxiously and aloud.

She no longer heard.

The Princess, too, advanced and sank sobbing by the bed.

Then the Duke, the doctor, and the maid-of-honor came.

It was still, so unnaturally still in the bright, luxurious room. All left, but the Duke and Claudine. She sat at the bedside, and through the open window of the adjoining room came the deep tones of the church-bells which, on that cold, dark, winter morning announced to the land that its Princess slept the sleep of eternity.

The two who had been the dearest to her on earth, watched beside the dead.

The liver-wort bloomed in the garden of the Owl's Nest, and yellow, blue, and white crocuses peeped forth from the black spring earth. Old Heinemann was working at his rose-bushes, took from them their winter coverings and tied them to freshly painted, green sticks. Since noon the sun had been shining warmly upon the old grave-stones, and the young leaves stretched themselves ; they longed for light and air.

The old man was doubly diligent to-day : he had asked a holiday for the morrow ; he wanted to go to Altenstein to his granddaughter's wedding, she was to marry her old sweetheart.

Fräulein Lindenmeyer's pleasant face smiled behind the glistening window-panes ; occasionally she turned her head towards the room, to talk ; there stood plump little Ida, sprinkling the clothes. Ida was there again at the request of young Frau von Gerold, because the latter was going to move to Neuhaus. When? No one knew. The Baron was still away on his travels, and his wife wore deep mourning for the Duchess.

It was remarkable what restlessness the lady's tiny feet developed that day. She had wandered about the entire house with her jingling bunch of keys, had looked into all the cupboards and chests, had inspected the master's closet and the child's wardrobe ; she had counted up the expense books and the household fund. She now shook her head at herself and her unrest ; she did not understand herself ; she had neither the necessary self-possession to write, nor could she make up her mind to practice her hour, which she usually enjoyed so thoroughly. At length she decided it would be best to take a walk. As she had not seen Beate and Leonie for several days, she concluded to stroll over there ; perhaps Beate knew more about Lothar's plans ; she had received news from him last from Milan.

They had not corresponded ; the young wife did not wish it.

"We can relate everything verbally," she had implored. "It is so much nicer ; I will hear, through Beate, if you are well and where you are."

She put on her cloak, twisted her lace scarf about her head, and went up to bid Joachim "Adieu."

"Where are you going?" he asked.

"To Beate's, Joachim."

He rose and gazed at her tenderly. "How soon will the time come when you will go away forever?" said he.

"At the thought that I shall one day leave you, I seem to myself faithless."

"Oh, my darling, you do not know how happy I am to know that *you* are happy!" He accompanied her to the garden gate. "Are you going alone?"

"I am not afraid, Joachim." She gently pushed him back and walked quietly away. The sun was setting behind the trees; the clouds were flying rapidly over the sky; but the wind which wafted them was warm and soft; it blew the scarf back from Claudine's white brow and bent the budding branches; it played through the tender grass by the roadside and whispered of coming beauty, of blossom-time, and of glorious sunlight. With rapid steps she walked on, as lightly as if she had had wings. She looked now at the ripples of the stream, which flowed on at her side taking the last sun from the mountains, now up at the clouds, and smiles and gravity passed in changing lights over her face. She felt so odd, and once she said half-aloud: "What if he were there?"

At the entrance to the Neuhaus park she paused; in the linden allée the wind rustled through the branches, and the castle lay there so silent and dark. For a moment maidenly shyness paralyzed her feet; with palpitating heart and a bright blush she leaned against the sandstone posts and did not dare to put her foot in the garden. Again she thought: "If he were here?" No one had seen her, that was well! She suddenly determined to turn back.

Then fearfully, she stepped aside; along the avenue came a horseman at a rapid pace. In spite of the twilight she recognized him. She knew whither he was riding—and an unutterable sense of bliss possessed her. But he must not see her. Then she uttered a slight exclamation; the hunting dog, which leaped wildly about the horse, had recognized her and rushed up to her. At the same moment the horse stood still; its rider flung himself from the saddle and embraced the young lady.

"At last!" said he. "And you are here—thank you!" She could not reply, but simply wept. As they slowly approached the house, she finally managed to say: "I felt that you were here. When did you come, Lothar?"

"Fifteen minutes ago, my dearest."

"Where were you going?" she asked, and a roguish smile which suited her serious face remarkably well, hovered about her mouth.

"To you, Claudine," replied he simply.

She smiled up at him blissfully. "And now you shall

know, Lothar, I have always loved you. God be thanked for turning your heart to me."

"For turning it to you?" he asked with emotion. "I have loved you since the day on which I so unexpectedly met you in the Dowager Duchess' apartments. Do you remember, you sang Mozart's 'Violet'?"

"And afterwards: 'Will you give me your heart?' Do I remember it? But, Lothar, if you loved me then——"

"Do not ask me, Claudine," he said evasively, "such sad, dark days, years have elapsed since then, years in which I have suffered more than I can tell."

She was silent, she looked at the clouds again and hung more heavily upon his arm. On her other side was the dog, behind them came the horse whose bridle hung over his arm.

"Only one thing," she whispered with hesitation, looking in his agitated face imploringly. "Lothar, if you loved me, why did you wound me with cutting words whenever you could, why did you humiliate me so, even in my own eyes, so that I almost despaired?"

He looked at her with a smile. "Oh, little simpleton, because I was driven to it by anguish and jealousy, because my heart was sore with longing for you and because I saw what must come. I knew the world and its wickedness, and knew that you would be crushed to earth if calumny, if baseness fell upon you ; because you, defiant child, rendered it difficult for me to watch over you ; finally because you *would* not understand me.— Cease, Claudine !—Those times are past. I have you and can be your guide in all paths from this hour forth. Thank God !"

The horse with lowered head went alone to the stables ; both ascended the stairs. Baron Gerold opened the door.

"Enter your house, Claudine," said he, with emotion ; "it, not the world without, shall be our home—if you will it so !"

She smiled through her tears. "If I will it so ? Do you not trust me yet? I want nothing more in the wide world."

Three years have passed. In Joachim von Gerold's study sits Frau Beate in the twilight on a winter evening, chatting with her husband.

"Where is Elizabeth?" he asked.

"Why, dearest, you grow more and more absent! Where should she be? At Neuhaus, of course. She cannot live without her Aunt Claudine; she begged so long that I sent her down with Heinemann. It is so beautiful in the Neuhaus nursery and there is nothing as sweet as Claudine's baby. But she will soon be home."

"Have you read the paper to-day?" she then asked.

"No? Well you have missed a great deal. Listen, Joachim, I will tell you: first, it says that the rumor of the betrothal of our Duke with Princess Helene gains ground. I think it very suitable, Joachim, for there is much that is good in the little girl, notwithstanding her caprices. She nursed the Duchess so assiduously at Cannes, and since that time she has truly overwhelmed Claudine with friendliness; she would like to make amends. I am convinced it will be no love-match, for I suspect she has not yet forgotten Lothar; but she is marrying the Duke because she thinks she is fulfilling a duty."

"I hope so, for His Highness' sake," said Joachim calmly, "life without a pair of kindly eyes and a soft, womanly hand is very cheerless." He took Beate's right hand and kissed it.

Frau Beate laughed; it was fresh, silvery laughter not the harsh, short laughter which had once irritated him and which she had forgotten. He cannot understand how he could ever have called her "barbarous" with that kind heart. He confessed to her once, and she laughed heartily and said: "I felt fitted for nothing but housekeeping, and you looked down upon me from your heights,—I loved you then, you and your poems, I then thirsted for all the grand thoughts which beautify common life. But no one would believe me. So I became a genuine, domineering housewife, too strict and particular."

For a while she gazed dreamily before her.

"Thank God, that is over. But now, listen," she continued with her news. "It says too, Joachim, that Lothar has bought back Altenstein. The sharp-witted reporter says: 'Probably Baron Gerold wishes some day to give

the old family seat to his second son, born a few months
since : we hear that Baron Joachim von Gerold will for
the present live in the castle which once belonged to
him. How clever people are ! We will look after ourselves, Joachim ;—you will not get me out of the Owl's
Nest, I have been too happy here."

"Yes, yes !" said he hastily, "We will stay here,
Beate. We have plenty of room since it has been
added to ; and it is so quiet and peaceful. It is to be
hoped the Neuhausers do not think of asking it of us."

"Oh, pshaw, Joachim ! They think of nothing but
themselves," smiled Beate. "But they are not to blame,
we are no better.—Do you know, darling, to-day is the
anniversary of our engagement ?" she asked. "See, how
you forget everything ! Yes, to-day it is two years since
we sat at Elizabeth's bed and knew that the child was
saved—it slept the sleep of convalescence. And we spoke
in whispers of death, the life of the soul and immortality.
You read to me the poem you had composed on the death
of your wife, and complained of how lonely you were
now that Claudine was gone, too, and how the child was
left alone—and——"

"And then I asked you, Beate——"

"And I said 'yes.' "

"And then we talked of who could have bought back
my library for me."

"Of course !" she laughed. "I had always a dangerous compassion for the dreamiest, the most unpractical,
the most helpless creature in God's wide world." She
kissed him and took her basket of keys. "I must go to
see old Lindenmeyer," she excused her going thus : "she
asked for me, and she sits so patiently in her arm-chair
and knits stockings for Claudine's children. She must
have a supply of them."

As she went down, the door flew open, and a child, a
girl, crosses the threshold, holding Heinemann's hand, the
next moment to drop it and to fly towards the stately
woman with a cry of joy. She paused in the hall and
caught the child in her arms with a merry laugh.

"Dear !" said she, with maternal pride, taking the rosy,
little face between her two hands. "Was it nice at
Aunt Claudine's, little daughter mine? What did you
play ? Was Uncle Lothar at home ?"

"Yes! But uncle was cross, and so was Aunt Claudine," said the child, looking anxiously at Heinemann.

The old man had taken off his cap upon which sparkled the first snow crystals of winter, and turned it over and over.

"Were they not, Heinemann?" asked the child.

The old man's eyes gleamed mischievously.

"They quarreled horribly," he confirmed gravely, winking at Frau Beate, "and before me. When I came in to put on Elizabeth's cloak, because the sleigh was at the door, the master said: 'Put on the dress, Claudine, I gave you a short while since, and drive to the Residence with me to His Highness' wedding. I should really like to see if I can still be jealous,' he said."

"And then," interrupted the child, "Aunt Claudine grew sad and said: 'As you like, Lothar.'"

"Of course," nodded the old man with a grin. "And then it began.—'No, as you like!' cried the Baron.—'No, as you say, Lothar,'—'No, please, you are right, Dina, what shall we do there, we will remain at home.'—'But if I should like to go, Lothar?' 'I know that, Dina; we will stay here.' So they quarreled, madame, for fifteen minutes. Finally——"

"Well?" interrupted Beate with a smile, "who gained the victory?"

"Madame, the one who always triumphs when a married couple dispute," replied the old man roguishly. "The Baroness, of course. She sent her love to Madame, and on our Duke's wedding-day, she and the Baron will come over to enjoy a cup of tea with you and talk over old times."

THE END.

Trieste

Trieste Publishing has a massive catalogue of classic book titles. Our aim is to provide readers with the highest quality reproductions of fiction and non-fiction literature that has stood the test of time. The many thousands of books in our collection have been sourced from libraries and private collections around the world.

The titles that Trieste Publishing has chosen to be part of the collection have been scanned to simulate the original. Our readers see the books the same way that their first readers did decades or a hundred or more years ago. Books from that period are often spoiled by imperfections that did not exist in the original. Imperfections could be in the form of blurred text, photographs, or missing pages. It is highly unlikely that this would occur with one of our books. Our extensive quality control ensures that the readers of Trieste Publishing's books will be delighted with their purchase. Our staff has thoroughly reviewed every page of all the books in the collection, repairing, or if necessary, rejecting titles that are not of the highest quality. This process ensures that the reader of one of Trieste Publishing's titles receives a volume that faithfully reproduces the original, and to the maximum degree possible, gives them the experience of owning the original work.

We pride ourselves on not only creating a pathway to an extensive reservoir of books of the finest quality, but also providing value to every one of our readers. Generally, Trieste books are purchased singly - on demand, however they may also be purchased in bulk. Readers interested in bulk purchases are invited to contact us directly to enquire about our tailored bulk rates. Email: customerservice@triestepublishing.com

You May Also Like

ISBN: 9780649635177
Paperback: 220 pages
Dimensions: 6.14 x 0.46 x 9.21 inches
Language: eng

Life's Pleasure Garden; Or, the Conditions of a Happy Life

W. Haig Miller

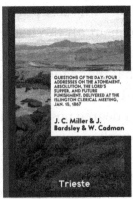

ISBN: 9780649685547
Paperback: 142 pages
Dimensions: 6.14 x 0.30 x 9.21 inches
Language: eng

Questions of the Day: Four Addresses on the Atonement, Absolution, the Lord's Supper, and Future Punishment. Delivered at the Islington Clerical Meeting, Jan. 15, 1867

J. C. Miller & J. Bardsley & W. Cadman

www.triestepublishing.com

You May Also Like

ISBN: 9780649587384
Paperback: 240 pages
Dimensions: 6.14 x 0.50 x 9.21 inches
Language: eng

The Riverside Library for Young People.
Number 13: Four-Handed Folk, With Illustrations

Olive Thorne Miller

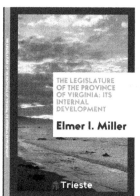

ISBN: 9780649546138
Paperback: 192 pages
Dimensions: 6.14 x 0.41 x 9.21 inches
Language: eng

The Legislature of the Province of Virginia: Its Internal Development

Elmer I. Miller

www.triestepublishing.com

You May Also Like

1807-1907 The One Hundredth Anniversary of the incorporation of the Town of Arlington Massachusetts

Various

ISBN: 9780649420544
Paperback: 108 pages
Dimensions: 6.14 x 0.22 x 9.21 inches
Language: eng

Biennial report of the Board of State Harbor Commissioners, for the two fiscal years commencing July 1, 1890, and ending June 30, 1892

Various

ISBN: 9780649194292
Paperback: 44 pages
Dimensions: 6.14 x 0.09 x 9.21 inches
Language: eng

www.triestepublishing.com